Evaporating Genres

Gary K. Wolfe

EVAPORATING Genres

ESSAYS ON FANTASTIC LITERATURE

Wesleyan University Press
Middletown, Connecticut

Published by Wesleyan University Press,
Middletown, CT 06459
www.wesleyan.edu/wespress

Library of Congress Cataloging-in-Publication Data
Wolfe, Gary K., 1946–
Evaporating genres : essays on fantastic literature / Gary K. Wolfe.
p. cm.
Includes bibliographical references and index.
ISBN 978-0-8195-6936-3 (cloth : alk. paper) —
ISBN 978-0-8195-6937-0 (pbk. : alk. paper)
1. Fantasy fiction—History and criticism. 2. Science fiction—
History and criticism. 3. Horror tales—History and criticism. I. Title.
PN3435.W65 2011
809.3 876—dc22   2009026962

Contents

Preface

This book consists of a series of eleven essays on fantastic literature that for the most part initially were conceived and written, over a period of decades, without benefit of an overarching thesis or argument. My original intention was simply to gather some of the scores of essays that I had published in a wide variety of venues—some now long out of print, some incomplete or truncated even in their original published form—and to re-examine these ideas in light of my current thinking and more recent developments in these genres. But in revisiting this material, a few things quickly became obvious: For one thing, I realized I would have to be pretty selective to keep the volume down to a reasonable size, and for another, that didn't turn out to be as much of a problem as I thought it would be. Many of those earlier pieces deserve to remain well-buried, as some reveal the pretentiousness and methodological trendiness of an ambitious younger scholar and others focus on such a narrow range of texts that they might be of interest only to a few specialists. By the time I had narrowed the list to a couple dozen pieces—still more than I needed—a pattern had begun to emerge, reflected both in the title of this book and in its longest essay. There *was* a kind of overarching argument regarding the chronic instabilities of the fantastic genres, and while this argument is constructed most explicitly in the three opening essays, parts of it were evident in germinal form even in those earlier thematic pieces, which at first might seem to point in a contrary direction by tracing apparently stable tropes such as the artifact, the post-apocalyptic world, and the frontier. Such tropes, as these essays show (and as I've tried to make clearer in afterwords to some of them), may have been persistent and recurrent, but they were anything but stable, and the manner in which writers have employed them evolved as the genres themselves evolved.

The book's title dates back to an observation that struck me with some force when, in 1994, I was reviewing for *Locus* magazine Ellen Datlow and Terri

Windling's annual anthology *The Year's Best Fantasy and Horror*. Here's what I wrote then: "Fantasy is evaporating. I don't mean that it's disappearing altogether—quite the opposite—but that it's growing more diffuse, leaching out into the air around it, imparting a strange smell to the literary atmosphere, probably even getting into our clothes." Something of a joke, to be sure, but one drawn from years of reading annual "year's best" anthologies, from a variety of editors, in the fields of fantasy, science fiction, and horror: The borders *were* growing more diffuse, not only among genres themselves but between the whole notion of genre fiction and literary fiction. If anything, this pattern accelerated markedly after I wrote that 1994 review, not only in the year's best anthologies I continued to read, but in the variety of fiction I encountered in my monthly review column in *Locus* magazine. A few years later, when Joan Gordon and Veronica Hollinger invited me to contribute to a collection of critical essays that they were editing on postmodern culture and science fiction, it was an idea that seemed to demand developing at greater length. That essay, "Evaporating Genre," originally was written in 2001 (at less than half the length of the rewritten and updated version here), and the patterns it sought to describe have continued to evolve rapidly in the years since. Those years have seen considerable discussion—in academic papers, at scholarly and literary conferences, in writers' own musings on their work—about the blurring of boundaries between genres, between genre and literary fiction, between traditional and postmodern forms, even between fiction and allied narrative forms such as graphic novels, movies, video, hypertexts, gaming, memoirs, and various forms of performance art.

This has been especially evident in the genres of fantastic literature—science fiction, fantasy, and horror—which have given rise to a whole gaggle of terms and movements to describe this weakening of boundaries, some of which are mentioned in the essay "Twenty-First-Century Stories." The essays I ended up including touched upon these issues, or upon writers particularly relevant to these issues—even though many of the essays in their original form predated the current debates. For this reason, I've considerably revised and updated all of the material here, and appended afterwords to three of the essays—"The Encounter with Fantasy," "The Artifact as Icon in Science Fiction," and "The Remaking of Zero." In both the internal revisions and the afterwords, my goal was to bring into the argument some much more current examples; when such examples seemed to buttress the structure of the original essay, I incorporated them internally; when the purpose was merely to show how a particular theme had evolved in recent years, I added an afterword. The broad question of what is happening to genre fiction, and the related question of what this might imply about how we read and talk about genre fiction, provided a template for organizing all the essays into what I hope will achieve a semblance of coherence.

* * *

The first section of essays, on genres, explores various aspects of fantastic genre literature and how we read it, and the first three chapters in particular concern different aspects of genre instability, of that blurring of boundaries. "Malebolge, or the Ordnance of Genre" (written not for a scholarly publication but for the literary journal *Conjunctions*) offers a general historical perspective on how, over the course of nearly two centuries, we "unlearned" how to read the fantastic as serious literature—including how the mechanisms of genre reinforced that disdain—and how a group of modern writers have set about reclaiming it. Several of the contemporary authors mentioned here were featured in that special issue of *Conjunctions*, edited by Peter Straub, which since its appearance in 2002 has become something of a touchstone among anthologies that seek to loosen genre boundaries. "Evaporating Genres"—which, revised and expanded to nearly twice the length of the version that appeared in 2002, is really the seminal essay for this book—also begins with an historical approach, examining in more detail how contemporary genres such as science fiction developed their specific market identities, then moving on to explore the various strategies that writers of science fiction, fantasy, or horror have employed to subvert or transform the genre expectations that largely derived from those market identities. "Tales of Stasis and Chaos," by burrowing even further into the specific histories of genres in terms of their content, looks at genre instability from yet another viewpoint, the tension between static and dynamic world-models, arguing that the latter tend to displace the former as genres evolve and grow more complex over time.

"The Encounter with Fantasy" is the first essay to examine a particular genre in more depth, returning to the question of how we read the fantastic and fantasy in particular, and focusing on the experience of the individual reader when confronting a text that depicts manifestly impossible events and beings. What keeps us engaged with such a text beyond the introduction of various marvels and the simple exigencies of plot? How do we know when a fantasy is a fantasy? Here again, we interrogate the boundaries of literary fantasy, seeking to locate it in contrast to the personal psychological fantasies of the schizophrenic on the one hand, and broad cultural myths and folktales on the other.

The final three essays in this section shift the focus to science fiction, and specifically to themes: the alien artifact ("The Artifact as Icon in Science Fiction"), the end of the world ("The Remaking of Zero"), and the space frontier ("Frontiers in Space"). While at first these explorations might seem at odds with my overarching argument regarding the instability of genres—after all, these are old reliable tropes to which science fiction has returned over a period of many decades—they actually reveal in retrospect that the seeds of such instability were already evident in the tropes themselves. The artifact may serve as a convenient icon for opening up science fiction's sense of wonder, but it can serve a similar purpose in detective or fantasy fiction, or even historical fiction: As a narrative device, it's as much a borrowing from these related genres as it is a science-fictional invention. The post-apocalyptic worlds discussed in "The Remaking of Zero" may come about through science-fictional means such as nuclear war or environmental catastrophe, but the worlds themselves relate to various traditions of millenarian thought and characteristically lead to moral confrontations not unlike those we see in religious allegories or fantasy narratives such as Stephen King's *The Stand*. The frontier would seem to be an inevitable science fiction theme, but it's equally characteristic of a broad swath of American literature, and its deployment in science fiction historically has taken the form of an ongoing negotiation with related genres as diverse as the Western and the utopian tale. All three of these essays suggest that even the most clearly genre-based science fiction has engaged in dialogues not only with other genres and modes of narrative, but also with contempory cultural anxieties and dreams.

The essays in Part II, on writers, focus largely on the careers of those authors who have worked to reconfigure materials not only from the fantastic genres, but from a variety of modernist and postmodernist literary devices and even from personal experience. In other words, these might be read as case histories of particular authors whose work illustrates the arguments developed in the earlier essays on genre. "The Lives of Fantasists," written for a special issue of the British journal *Vector* on writers' lives, explores how a few contemporary fantastic writers, unlike earlier counterparts who often regarded genre as a kind of craft largely divorced from lived experience, have chosen to use genre materials as a lens through which to focus the sorts of very personal observations and experiences that are more often associated with "mainstream" literature.

These are authors who for the most part celebrate the notion of genre instability, and who represent a kind of paradigm shift from an earlier model of genre as a box in which one works toward a more liberating model of genres as toolboxes, from which one takes what one needs for a given story. "Peter Straub and the New Horror" explores in more depth how one of these authors has drawn freely not only on personal material, but on various postmodern narrative techniques and the conventions of multiple genres, to redefine the possibilities of the genre he has been associated with most closely: horror. "Twenty-First-Century Stories" continues this exploration by examining the work of a group of mostly younger writers—Kelly Link, Jeffrey Ford, Elizabeth Hand, Theodora Goss, and M. Rickert—for whom any sort of specific genre identity is a slippery proposition at best, though they are all clearly writers of the fantastic. Here we engage most directly with recent discussions of "slipstream," "interstitial art," "fabulism," and other terms sometimes applied to the general movement toward weakening genre boundaries and subverting genre expectations. I say "we" because both of these essays were written with Amelia Beamer, a fiction writer as well as a critic, and both are based on ideas worked out in papers that we co-presented at the International Conference on the Fantastic in the Arts in 2007 and 2008, respectively.

The final essay, "Pilgrims of the Fall," is in a sense intended to provide a context for the entire rest of the book, by examining the earlier history of science fiction and fantasy criticism and scholarship, and suggesting that even here there is evidence of a kind of weakening of boundaries among the various communities that have contributed to the critical discourse on the fantastic. Curious parallels have always existed between fantastic genre literature and the criticism associated with it: both historically have been marginalized by the "mainstream" of their relative worlds, both formed communities in relative isolation from that mainstream, both have displayed a certain sensitivity to the summative pronouncements of "outsiders," both have struggled to gradually gain a degree of acceptance, both have done so in part by looking outward and negiotiating with parallel modes of discourse. Once, science fiction writers talked largely to each other; once, science fiction critics talked largely to each other. That is less the case today. The criticism of fantastic literature is far less insular than it once was, and in its own way this represents a kind of genre instability within the world of critical discourse—which I regard as a thoroughly salutary development. This final essay concludes with a consideration of the career of a key figure in this emergent and eclectic discourse, the critic and encyclopedist John Clute. Its odd title is borrowed from Clute's description of the critical act as a "surgery of the fall," combined with a kind of punning reference to the Pilgrim Award annually presented by the Science Fiction Research Association to distinguished critics and scholars. Even in a book of literary essays we're allowed to have puns, and whenever we're allowed to have puns, we're allowed to have bad ones.

Acknowledgments

When all their roots are traced, the essays here represent more than three decades of thinking and writing about fantastic literature and genre fiction, but the thinking wasn't all mine. I owe a considerable debt to all the editors of journals and critical collections (listed below) who commissioned and/or accepted some of these pieces in their earlier forms, as well as to my colleagues in the International Association for the Fantastic in the Arts, where many of these ideas developed in poolside or dinner conversations (a few even made it into formal paper presentations). I particularly want to thank those friends and colleagues who, after years of conversations and debates, may recognize some of their own ideas reflected in fragmentary and distorted form here, and who on more than one occasion helped talked through knotty problems, while challenging weak ideas and stimulating better ones, and sometimes (but not always) commenting on all or part of the manuscript: John Clute, Peter Straub, Charles Brown, Joan Gordon, Veronica Hollinger, Brian Aldiss, William Senior, Graham Sleight, Roger Schlobin, Russell Letson, David Hartwell, Cheryl Morgan, Joe Haldeman, Niall Harrison, Rob Latham, Brian Attebery, and many others, some of whom (such as Algis Budrys and Thomas D. Clareson) are no longer with us. Farah Mendlesohn, who suggested assembling these essays in the first place, read the manuscript and made a number of excellent suggestions and corrections. I also owe a particular debt to Amelia Beamer, who not only was my co-author on two of these pieces, but who carefully and insightfully edited most of the others, keeping a sharp eye out for opacity, jargon, and general blathering, and suggesting many useful lines of inquiry and revision. Neither she nor anyone other than myself bear any responsibility for what howlers remain.

I am also grateful to Roosevelt University's Research and Professional Improvement Committee for providing the research leave that afforded the time necessary to assemble and rework these essays, and to Dean John Cicero and Professor D. Bradford Hunt for arranging for my administrative duties to be covered during this period as well.

An earlier version of the chapter "Evaporating Genres" appeared as "Evaporating Genre: Strategies of Dissolution in the Postmodern Fantastic," in *Edging into the Future: Science Fiction and Contemporary Cultural Transformation*, ed. Joan Gordon and Veronica Hollinger (Philadelphia: Pennsylvania State University Press, 2002), 11–29. The current essay is nearly twice the length of the version that appeared there.

"Malebolge, or the Ordnance of Genre" appeared in slightly different form in *Conjunctions* 39 (Fall 2002): 405–19, ed. Peter Straub and Bradford Morrow.

A preliminary version of "Tales of Stasis and Chaos" was delivered as the guest scholar address at the International Conference for the Fantastic in the Arts in 1998 under the title "Stasis and Chaos: Some Dynamics of Popular Genres" and subsequently published in *The Journal of the Fantastic in the Arts* 10, no. 1 (1998), 4–16.

"The Encounter with Fantasy" appeared in *The Aesthetics of Fantasy Literature and Art*, ed. Roger Schlobin (Notre Dame, Ind.: University of Notre Dame Press, 1982), 1–15, and later in *Fantastic Literature: A Critical Reader*, ed. David Sandner (Westport, Conn.: Praeger, 2004), 222–35. It has been revised somewhat for this volume.

"The Artifact as Icon in Science Fiction" originally appeared in *The Journal of the Fantastic in the Arts* 1, no. 1 (1988), 51–69, and has been revised for this volume, with an afterword added.

"The Remaking of Zero" appeared in *The End of the World*, ed. Eric S. Rabkin, Martin H. Greenberg, and Joseph Olander (Carbondale: Southern Illinois University Press, 1982), 1–19, and has been revised here, with an afterword added.

"Frontiers in Space" appeared in *The Frontier Experience and the American Dream*, ed. David Mogen, Mark Busby, and Paul Bryant (College Station: Texas A&M University Press, 1989), 248–63, and has been revised for this volume, with an afterword added.

"The Lives of Fantasists" appeared in somewhat different form as "Framing the Unframeable" in *Vector* 249 (2006), 4–7.

"Peter Straub and the New Horror" was presented in abbreviated form as a paper at the 28th International Conference on the Fantastic in the Arts in Fort Lauderdale, Florida, on March 16, 2007, and, in slightly different form, as "Peter

Straub and Transcendental Horror" in *The Journal of the Fantastic in the Arts* 18, no. 2 (2007): 217–31.

A very abbreviated version of "Twenty-First-Century Stories" was presented at the 29th International Conference on the Fantastic in the Arts in Orlando, Florida, in March 2008. The full essay, in slightly different form, appeared in *Foundation: The International Review of Science Fiction* 103 (2009), 16–37.

A much shorter version of "Pilgrims of the Fall" (the portion focusing on John Clute) appeared as "Surgeries of the Fall" in *Polder: A Festschrift for John Clute and Judith Clute*, ed. Farah Mendlesohn (Baltimore: Old Earth Books, 2006), 182–91, and was translated as "Zergliederungen des Sturzes," in *Kunst Welten: Phantastische Kunst und Literatur*, ed. Hannes Riffel and Berit Neumann (Leipzig: Freundeskreis Science Fiction Leipzig, 2006), 36–45.

PART I

genres

In the seven essays that follow, and for the most part through-out this book, "genre" is used largely as a term of convenience. From the pure perspective of literary theory, persuasive argu-ments can be made that none of the major fields discussed here—science fiction, fantasy, horror—are true genres in any taxonomic sense, and thus that the whole notion of genres evaporating, destabilizing, or negotiating with one another is a chimerical argument. After all, there have long been science fiction stories that are also horror stories, horror stories that are also fantasies, fantasies that are also historical fictions, and so on. Perhaps each of these is really no more than a mode of storytelling, or a set of specialized narrative tools, or a collection of writerly techniques. Certainly the long and apparently fruit-less quest to arrive at a simple and universally accepted theoreti-cal definition of science fiction would seem to support such a view, as would the oversimplified discussions of fantasy in terms of the "impossible" or horror in terms of its reader affect.

But the ways in which literature is written, published, dis-tributed, read—and even reviewed—do not always or easily yield to the pure perspectives of literary theory. Clearly there are writ-ers who identify themselves with science fiction, fantasy, and horror, just as there are authors who flee from the mere sugges-tion of such labels. Clearly there are publishers who find benefits in such labels, and bookstores that shelve books according to such labels, and readers who seek their reading of choice on such shelves, and who sometimes attend fan conventions clearly labeled "science fiction," "fantasy," and "horror." Each field has its own canons, its own awards, its own fan organizations, its own zines and websites and podcasts and even to some degree its own artists. Moving a little closer to the realm of theory, each also has characteristic narrative conventions, iconography, rhetoric, and language. Each has a core of prepared and knowledgeable readers familiar with these conventions, along with a less defined cadre of occasional readers—often those who once read more regularly and still check in once in a while—and a still more diffuse group of what we might call culture-bound readers—those who normally might not read in such a genre at all until prodded by the *zeitgeist* or by Oprah. Such readers might come to Philip K. Dick by way of the movies, to Stephen King by way of the bestseller list, or to Cormac McCarthy's *The Road* by way of Oprah's book club, but few would identify themselves as even desultory readers of the fantastic genres. They are generally not much interested in what the genre as a whole has to say, but they may be willing to dip into it if led there by a favored writer.

As with the genres themselves, genre readers may be mutable and unstable groups, and not merely in terms of target markets or subsets of fandom. Nearly all these readerships, though, think they know what they're pointing to when they point to it; they possess a functional sense of genre as something more than a sales category but perhaps less than an art form distinct from the general arts of fiction; for the most part, they seldom pause to consider it as a complex of literary tropes, cultural markers, and reading protocols. That functional, largely commonsense approach to genre is what governs my use of the term here.

one

Malebolge, or the Ordnance of Genre

Not all popular genres are meant to blow up. We pretty much expect from mysteries today something of the same thrill that readers expected a century ago; tempestuous romances only seem to get more tempestuous; and the Western long ago quietly faded away into elegiac ghost towns waiting for Cormac McCarthy or Larry McMurtry to show up with more ammo. But the fantastic genres of horror, science fiction, and fantasy have been unstable literary isotopes virtually since their evolution into identifiable narrative modes— or at least into identifiable market categories—a process that began a century or more ago and is still going. Although at times they have seemed in such bondage to formula and convention that they were in danger of fossilization, these genres are in fact wired more like those ticking, blinking time bombs in the final moments of bad suspense movies that must be disarmed by cutting either the red wire or the green wire: Make the wrong choice (which the hero never does) and the movie probably would get a better ending—or at least a less formulaic one—as its fundamental assumptions are shot to hell and what had seemed one thing is now another. (Never mind, for the moment, that bad movies never actually end this way. We are discussing fiction here, and one of the curses visited upon genre fiction is that it is too often and too easily confused with the film genres of the same names.)

A good deal of cavalier wire-cutting is going on these days among writers using the resources of what were once fairly clearly delineated genres, and for the most part this is a salutary and exhilarating development, bringing with it a sense of breached ramparts and undiscovered terrain. What had seemed to be one thing is becoming another. But in order to understand fully the implications of this shift, this new superposition of fictional states, we have to understand a bit about how the bomb got in the basement in the first place, and what its components are. An important key to this understanding, I would argue, involves revisiting not only what is written under the various rubrics of science fiction, fantasy, and horror, but what is *read*, and how it is read, and how certain selective vacancies of sensibility have distorted our capacity to receive the fantastic as a viable mode of literary exploration. In particular, what I hope to do here is trace, in broad outline, an account of how we *unlearned* to read fantastic stories over nearly two centuries, what became of such stories as a result, and how the fantastic has begun to re-emerge in varying ways in recent decades from the back alleys to which it had been consigned, bringing with it distinctive modes of apprehension and style.

This brief history might as well begin with a real-life anecdote. Toward the end of my graduate studies at the University of Chicago, a number of students who had participated in a Theory of Fiction seminar launched into a rambling coffeehouse debate that lasted most of the academic year, turning on the question of what formally constituted a novel. After a raft of theoretical models had been considered and ultimately rejected, after principles of exclusion had been refined and multiplied in what we might now recognize as a fractal pattern of growth, several members of the group—perhaps even the entire group, I don't remember—arrived at a consensus: The formal novel, they decided, the *properly* formal novel, meaning one that satisfied all the rules of exclusion, consisted of a set that included *Middlemarch* and excluded everything else. Whatever simple delights might have been offered by earlier narratives, these were invariably contaminated by the viruses of romance, Gothicism, sensation, satire, social documentarianism, allegory, and even myth. At their best, they only represented the forward slope of this peak experience, this *überroman,* while subsequent efforts represented only refinements of style, form, and structure, if not outright abandonment of the ideal in the guise of Modernism and all that came after. At that time, I counted myself as much an admirer of *Middlemarch* as anyone in the room, but at the same time I knew that I had derived substantial degrees of pleasure and discovery from stories that not only demonstrated no effort whatsoever to look like *Middlemarch,* but that seemed to be part of another, more distant mountain range altogether. I also was aware that Eliot herself had written such a story in "The Lifted Veil" (1859), one of the more compelling psychic fantasy tales to emerge from Victorian literature.

More than thirty years later, I received an e-mail message from the daughter of a close friend, who had enrolled in another literary theory seminar, this one at Oberlin College. The text that had come up for discussion was Stephen King's *'Salem's Lot,* and the immediate cause of the message was a discussion during which one of her classmates had dismissed the novel as "meaningless pleasure" and the rest had more or less agreed that the book's genre origins, along with its manifest intent to entertain, all but precluded any further discussion of it in aesthetic terms. In what amounted to a kind of discovery brief, my friend's daughter e-mailed a number of writers and critics familiar with genre fiction (including King himself) to seek refutations of this argument—or at least to expose the subtext of passionately held but unexamined assumptions which, as is often the case in undergraduate English courses, had passed for literary debate in her class. Had it been possible, through some time-warp, for these Oberlin students to get together with my own University of Chicago classmates from three decades earlier, they might well have voted *'Salem's Lot* a good candidate for the Anti-*Middlemarch*, a work so steeped in sensation and story that it more closely echoed the primitive thrills of a lesser age than the psychological subtleties of high Victorian domestic realism. (It's not, to my mind, one of King's most compelling works, but that's beside our immediate point.)

To the best of my knowledge, none of the participants in my *Middlemarch* discussion, most of whom later became professors of English, ever published a version of their argument (although the Oberlin student, Emma Straub, did publish the responses to her survey in an online magazine called *The Spook*), but they didn't need to: The fundamental assumptions that powered this debate had been laid out more than a century earlier, among Victorian critics and essayists who sought evidence that literature, like technology and industry, could be measured according to the forward thrust of evolutionary progress.[1] "A scientific, and somewhat skeptical age," wrote an anonymous essayist in the *Westminster Review* in January 1853, "has no longer the power of believing in the marvels which delighted our ruder ancestors," just as it might prosecute a necromancer for "obtaining money under false pretenses" or a showman for "exhibiting a giant at a fair." (Some scholars have suggested, on the basis of internal evidence, that the essay may have been the work of George Eliot, who was assistant editor of the magazine at the time.[2]) "Falsehood is so easy, truth so difficult," added Eliot under her own pen name in *Adam Bede* (1859, the same year as "The Lifted Veil"). "The pencil is conscious of a delightful facility in drawing a griffin—the longer the claws, and the larger the wings, the better; but that marvelous facility which we mistook for genius is apt to forsake us when we want to draw a real unexaggerated lion" (223). Both Emma Straub, who had grown up in a house frequented by genre writers of every stripe, and myself, who had spent many years enjoying science fiction, fantasy, and horror fiction, had found ourselves deposited, Oz-like, in the realm of the unexaggerated lion. It's a familiar case to many, and as Emma's case illustrates, it's far from closed.

At first blush, comments such as Eliot's might simply seem to be fanfares for the rise of domestic realism as a dominant aesthetic for the Victorian novel, or the literary equivalent of Herbert Butterfield's Whig fallacy of history, but the groundwork being laid here also helped set the terms of discourse concerning fantastic literature in all its forms for the next century and a half. Prior to the rise of this characteristically Victorian aesthetic, the fantastic had gained sufficient prominence in Romantic era criticism and art as to constitute virtually an alternate mode of seeing. In 1741, Johann Jakob Bodmer, a German philologist and translator, claimed of the imagination that it "not only places the real before our eyes in a vivid image and makes distant things present, but also, with a power more potent than that of magic, it draws that which does not exist out of the state of potentiality, gives it a semblance of reality and makes us see, hear and feel these new creations."[3] More than a century and a half later, when Joseph Conrad invoked similar terms while articulating his artistic goal in his famous preface to *The Nigger of the Narcissus*—"to make you hear, to make you feel—it is, before all, to make you *see*"—he was referring not to "new creations" of the imagination but to the representation of the simple efforts of a laborer in a nearby field. What had happened? How had the skills of evocation become so circumscribed?

Between 1798 and 1800 in Germany, the brothers A. W. and Friedrich Schlegel devoted a good deal of space in their journal *Das Athenaeum* to debates over the rules of fairy tales and other forms of fantastic literature, a debate eventually joined by such then-prominent fantasists as Novalis, E. T. A. Hoffmann, and Ludwig Tieck (whose three-volume 1844 collection *Phantasus* is given a frame story in which characters also debate the aesthetics of *Märchen*); one recurring tenet of these debates was that the fantastic might well demand a separate mode of understanding from more clearly representational forms of narrative, as well as from homilies and allegories (which instantly subvert their own fantastic elements by reminding us, for example, that a talking fox is not a talking fox, but a lesson). William Blake, in "A Vision of the Last Judgment," set imagination or "visionary fancy" apart from the cruder modes of fable or allegory—a distinction that would remain crucial in discussions of fantasy for decades to come—and, most famously, Samuel Taylor Coleridge offered his argument, in the early chapters of *Biographia Literaria*, that "fancy and imagination were two distinct and widely different faculties." Fancy, for Coleridge, was "no other than a mode of Memory emancipated from the order of time and space"—much as Blake disdained fable and allegory as "daughters of Memory"—whereas imagination was "the living Power and prime Agent of all human Perception."

Within decades, such notions had come to be regarded largely as peculiar artifacts of Romanticism, even though versions of them continued to be argued by novelists and critics such as George MacDonald, G. K. Chesterton, E. M. Forster, and eventually, of course, by more nearly contemporary and contemporary writers such as J. R. R. Tolkien, C. S. Lewis, and Ursula K. Le Guin.[4] For the most part, however—as these examples attest—the articulation of the fantastic as a mode of storytelling became the province of the storytellers themselves rather than of the critics. The critics, for the most part, were elsewhere. By the end of the century, the notion of fantastic or dream-like narratives as remnants of a more primitive consciousness even gained something of the patina of scientific authority, as Freud's description of what he called "primary process" thinking (in *The Interpretation of Dreams*, 1900) made it clear that this was something of far more importance to small children and savages than to rational adults, who wisely banished it to the unconscious and went about their business guided by the logic and causality of secondary process thinking. (It wasn't really until the 1960s, under the influence of Pinchas Noy and others, that analytic theory began to recognize "primary process" as an important component of the sense of selfhood.[5])

Ironically, this devaluation, or at least devalorization, of the fantastic began at a time when the outlines of the modern popular genres of the fantastic were first being laid down in a series of seminal works: The Gothic novel and the stories of Poe provided a rough template for what would become horror fiction; Mary Shelley's *Frankenstein* (also derived largely from the Gothic, but with the crucial distinction that her protagonist rejected supernaturalism and alchemy in favor of experimental science) established many of the preconditions of science fiction; the extended fairy-tale narratives of the German Romantics and their English imitators (which included Thackeray and Ruskin as well as MacDonald) first articulated the portaled alternate realities that became a key element of modern fantasy. Each of these works spawned substantial numbers of imitators during the next century; genre literary historians have now pretty firmly established lengthy bibliographies of scientific romances before H. G. Wells, of supernatural horror tales before Bram Stoker and H. P. Lovecraft, of large-scale visionary fantasies before J. R. R. Tolkien. Many of these works are even worth reading today, and some are absolutely startling. Few, however, have survived outside the narrow interests of collectors and genre historians.

Despite the temptation for champions of the fantastic to seek conspiracies of suppression—suggesting that residual Puritanism led Victorian readers to view the unfettered imagination with something akin to panic, for example, or that fantastic tales implied a kind of mutability of history and reality that the dogma of realism could not subsume—the fact is that the protocols for reading the fantastic were not so much suppressed as diverted: into children's literature, into historical novels, into false medieval narratives, into the literature of sensation, sometimes even into the substrata of the tale being told (this is more or less what happens to Gothic supernaturalism in the novels of the Brontës). The once-estimable Lord Bulwer-Lytton may have written science fiction (*The Coming Race*, 1871) or weirdly cockeyed spiritualist fantasy (*A Strange Story*, 1862), but his most famous end-of-the-world tale remains *The Last Days of Pompeii* (1834), in which the apocalyptic vision is mitigated by the comforting conceit that the world being destroyed isn't ours, and that the events described with such obvious relish aren't going to happen to us, but already happened to someone else, someone not English. Victorian apocalypses offered something of the same lascivious *frisson* as those popular marble sculptures of nubile girls in chains, such as Hiram Powers's *The Greek Slave*—the rationale may have been historical representation, but at the level of pure voyeuristic sensation, the intent was unmistakable: I only read *Playboy* for the stonework. George Mac-Donald may have written two of the seminal adult fantasy novels in English, *Phantastes* (1858) and *Lilith* (1895), but the wider popularity of his children's fairy tales such as "The Golden Key" (1867) and *At the Back of the North Wind* (1871) permitted many readers to regard these fairly radical nonconformist visions as little more than aberrant offshoots of his career as a children's writer (although he did write a number of realistic provincial Scottish novels as well). Lest we suspect that this particular strategy of marginalization was peculiar to the Victorians, we might take a look at Edmund Wilson's famous 1956 *Nation* review of Tolkien's *The Lord of the Rings*, which he easily dismissed as "a children's book that has somehow got out of hand, since, instead of directing it at the 'juvenile' market, the author has indulged himself in developing the fantasy for its own sake" (313). The notion of "fantasy for its own sake" as a kind of aberrant indulgence is a succinct expression of what had happened to the reading of the fantastic over the preceding century.

The act of reading fantastic literature became marginalized not only ideo-logically, by virtue of its content, but commercially, by virtue of its venues of publication. The two are not unrelated: Each of the emergent genres of the fantastic (fantasy, horror, science fiction) included tropes and images that were highly sensational, and therefore highly degradable. Despite the wishful think-ing of many science fiction historians, Mary Shelley's *Frankenstein*, with its Gothic trappings, didn't immediately give rise to intellectual works of science fiction about the possibilities of science or the nature of artificial life, but rather to a series of often lurid stage adaptations (two separate productions were already onstage when she returned to England in 1823) that continued through-out the nineteenth century and segued into the movies throughout the twen-tieth. The Gothic novel itself seemed to split into two streams: On the one hand, the brooding, atmospheric tales of the Brontës and their successors, some of which eventually earned canonical status; on the other, such penny dreadfuls or "bloods" as *Varney the Vampire* by (probably) John Malcolm Rymer, which ran endlessly and almost plotlessly for some 109 weekly installments between 1847 and 1849, and which may still represent some sort of low point in the history of horror fiction, which has more than its share of low points. (To be sure, there was a middle ground, characterized by the classic English ghost story and by such writers as Wilkie Collins and Joseph Sheridan Le Fanu, though Collins now is remembered principally as a precursor of the mystery novel and Le Fanu as a writer of popular romances.) And fantasy, as we've already seen, tended to remain associated with children's books, although Arthurian and other pseudo-medieval fictions remained popular throughout the century, emerging as full-fledged fantasy narratives in the prose work of William Morris by late in the century.

In America, the question of commercial marginalization of the fantastic genres eventually would express itself even more dramatically, with the rise of the pulp magazines and the attendant culture of pulp. The sensibilities of the Gothic novel had quickly found a home in the American wilderness in the work of Charles Brockden Brown, Nathaniel Hawthorne, and Edgar Allan Poe, al-though for the most part these writers shied away from overt supernaturalism, and certain works by Poe and Hawthorne even are cited frequently as precur-sors of science fiction (Poe's "Mellonta Tauta," for example, or Hawthorne's "Rappacini's Daughter"). But science fiction as something resembling a genre in the modern sense became much more visible in the pages of the dime novels—a particularly delicious and often-imitated example was Edward Ellis's

1868 *The Steam Man of the Prairie*, featuring a steam-operated robot in the Wild West—and eventually in the pages of the cheaply made magazines published by Frank Munsey and others (some date the beginning of the "pulp era" to 1896, when Munsey transformed a former boys' weekly paper into an all-adventure-fiction magazine called *The Argosy*). By the 1920s, the outlines of what would become the familiar pop genres of horror and science fiction were being sketched out in two important pulps: the former in *Weird Tales*, founded in 1923, and the latter in *Amazing Stories*, founded in 1926. *Weird Tales* published a fair amount of fantasy of the "sword-and-sorcery" variety (most notably Robert E. Howard's "Conan the Barbarian" stories in the 1930s), but it wasn't until 1939 that a fairly serious—though short-lived—attempt was made to create a modern fantasy pulp tradition with the publication of *Unknown*, intended as a fantasy companion to editor John W. Campbell Jr.'s successful science fiction magazine *Astounding*.

From a purely literary standpoint, the pulp tradition didn't do anyone much good. All we have to do is look at the adjectives in the titles of these pulps to figure out what was going wrong: *Weird*, *Amazing*, *Astounding*, and dozens more: *Wonder Stories*, *Marvel Tales*, *Terror Tales*, *Horror Stories*, *Eerie Mysteries*, *Fantastic Adventures*, *Startling Stories*, *Strange Stories*, *Astonishing Stories*, *Bizarre*, *Stirring Science Stories*, *Thrilling Stories*, (and later *Thrilling Wonder Stories*), *Gripping Terror*, *Imaginative Tales*, *Rocket Stories*, *Planet Stories*, and on and on, an endless parade of gerundives and adjectives that seemed to promise their readers passivity: These are not stories that you have to read, these are stories that will *do things to you*, that will leap off the page unmediated by any readerly acts of decoding, grab you by the suspenders, and pummel you into submission. Your task is not to understand—to see, feel, or hear—it is merely to be horrified, astounded, amazed, astonished, terrified, stirred, gripped, and thrilled. Don't ask what's behind the curtain: We're exhibiting a giant at a fair here. It shouldn't be surprising that the famously lurid cover art for these pulps (which has become a fetish in itself among collectors) shares certain principles of color, composition, and draftsmanship with the art of sideshow posters and traveling circuses.

More important than their appearance, though, was the manner in which the pulp magazines turned their stories into perishable goods, complete with sell-by dates. The history of literary ephemera dates back centuries, of course, but even in the dime novels and the Salisbury Square bloods, the stories *were* the products; one presumably picked up the next installment of *Varney the*

Vampire because it *was Varney the Vampire*, because the text was roughly co-equal with the text-product being sold. But readers of *Weird Tales*, even though they would quickly develop favorite writers, picked up the next copy because it was *Weird Tales*, trusting the editors to fill the magazine with stories that fulfilled some often unarticulated template of what the magazine represented. In the science fiction field, at least, this led to enormous power devolving on the editors, who essentially took over the debate as to what the field was or ought to be. Even today, the Hugo Awards presented at the annual world convention of science fiction fans are named after the field's first famous editor, Hugo Gernsback, who founded *Amazing Stories* in 1926, and readers often refer to the genre's "golden age"—the period that introduced such now-revered authors as Isaac Asimov and Robert Heinlein—as "the Campbell era," after John W. Campbell, Jr., who began editing *Astounding Stories* (which he quickly renamed *Astounding Science Fiction*) in 1937. The authors, on the other hand, sometimes were reduced to writing stories on demand to satisfy an idea of the editors, or in more demeaning cases to writing stories that would exactly fill a hole in the next month's issue or that would somehow make sense of a prepurchased cover illustration. This is a tradition that would continue for years after the pulps had been replaced by the only slightly less garish digest-sized magazines of the 1950s. And few if any writers for these magazines had any reason to believe that their stories would survive beyond the few weeks that the magazines containing them remained on the stands. What passed for literary debate about the nature of the fantastic was by now purely proletarian: In the letter columns of the magazines, a farmer from Kansas might have an equal platform with the writers and editors themselves, and might even have an edge, since he (or she) was holding next month's quarter.

For most serious readers, the fiction in the pulps was all but invisible, at best a guilty pleasure, at worst an assault on the moral order. But at the same time, amid all the lurid tales of hungry elder gods looking for a snack and galaxy-busting backyard scientists, a kind of outsider aesthetic was being forged, just as it had been forged among the Victorian children's fantasists or the inheritors of the Gothic tradition. This aesthetic didn't really begin to be articulated until some of these ephemeral tales began to be collected in books. H. P. Lovecraft, for example, died in 1937 after building a considerable following as well as a circle of imitators in the pulps, but it wasn't until two years later that two of these imitators, August Derleth and Donald Wandrei, founded a publishing firm called Arkham House with the express intent of preserving Lovecraft's work, which they had been unable to sell to mainstream publishers. Even before that, an early horror anthology titled *Creeps by Night* had been assembled by no less a luminary than Dashiell Hammett in 1931, and Lovecraft himself had been reprinted (along with such other *Weird Tales* regulars as Robert E. Howard and Clark Ashton Smith) in a British anthology series, originally titled *Not at Night*, edited by Christine Campbell Thomson between 1925 and 1937. In 1943 came the first science fiction anthology to be labeled as such, Donald A. Wollheim's *The Pocket Book of Science Fiction*. By the end of the 1940s, however, larger and more comprehensive anthologies began to appear. Science fiction saw Raymond J. Healy and J. Francis McComas's *Adventures in Time and Space* (1946), while horror fiction saw Herbert A. Wise and Phyllis M. Fraser's *Great Tales of Terror and the Supernatural* (1944); both eventually gained lasting influence by remaining in print for years as part of Random House's Modern Library. The indefatigable anthologist Groff Conklin mined both genres in a series of some forty-one anthologies over a twenty-two-year period, until his death in 1968. Genre fantasy, having never quite established a firm foothold in the pulps, didn't fare as well, although such occasional titles appeared as *The Saturday Evening Post Fantasy Stories*, edited by literary agent Barthold Fles in 1951, and a collection of tales from the short-lived *Unknown Worlds* in 1948.

The major significance of these anthologies was to provide a distillation of pulp and other stories that then began circulating among new generations of readers. But at the same time, evident in many of them was a sense that these fields had become "ghettoized," isolated from the literary mainstream, and a concomitant sense that the anthologists were about the business of establishing a kind of de facto canon, as well as a de facto literary history. Some of these anthologies literally hungered for respect: Hammett's collection of horror tales, for example, included Faulkner's "A Rose for Emily," while *Beyond Time and Space*, a 1950 anthology by August Derleth (the same one who had set about resurrecting Lovecraft) tried mightily to establish a pedigree by including excerpts from Plato, Rabelais, Swift, and Bacon. Judith Merril, who edited the most popular "year's best" anthologies of science fiction and fantasy in the 1950s, found ways to include selections by Eugene Ionesco, Robert Nathan, John Steinbeck, and even Walt Kelly and Garson Kanin in her generous definitions of these genres. This search for a usable past and respectable relatives continued well into the 1970s when genre fantasy, now established as a viable market segment, began to seek its own roots: the Ballantine Adult Fantasy series, with titles originally chosen by Betty Ballantine and later edited by Lin Carter from 1969 through 1974, reprinted works by William Morris, James Branch Cabell, and George Meredith together with classic genre and pulp writers; surely one of the irreproducible moments of the lingering 1960s was discovering the mass-market reprint of Book I of Ariosto's *Orlando Furioso* at the local newsstand in January of 1973, dressed up as a fantasy novel.

In the end, though, the renascence of the fantastic would not come about because of its search for illustrious relations, its efforts to carve makeshift canons from pulp fiction, or even the befuddled gaze of academia, which eventually produced a sizeable body of postmodernist theorizing, three or four academic journals devoted to science and fantasy fiction, and college courses in which *'Salem's Lot* could be assigned alongside works by Lovecraft, Tolkien, Heinlein, Le Guin, or (the most recent favorite among science fiction academics) Philip K. Dick. Instead, the signal development of the last few decades has been the emergence of a generation of writers—although "generation" is a misnomer, since these writers range in age from their twenties to their seventies—whose ambitions lay in what we might call recombinant genre fiction: stories that effectively deconstruct and reconstitute genre materials and techniques together with materials and techniques from an eclectic variety of literary traditions, even including the traditions of domestic realism. This eclecticism became most famously visible in the science fiction field in the 1960s with the "New Wave" associated with Britain's *New Worlds* magazine, which showcased experimental work by such authors as J. G. Ballard, Brian W. Aldiss, and M. John Harrison—each of whom, in their later careers, moved comfortably between mainstream fiction, genre work, and more indefinable literary fabulation. Science fiction since has been visited by a number of other such movements—the cyberpunks of the 1980s in the wake of William Gibson's *Neuromancer*, the "new humanists" who reacted to the cyberpunks, the "literary hard science fiction" ("hard science fiction" being an older term for stories that adhere rigorously to limitations imposed by physical science) of such authors as Greg Bear, Joe Haldeman, and Gregory Benford. Today, M. John Harrison is one of the touchstones of literary science fiction in England, just as Gene Wolfe is a touchstone in the United States; both authors, significantly, began their careers as genre writers in genre magazines, and Wolfe is still known mostly within the science fiction community for his complex, ornate, and infinitely subtle novels of distant futures.

Horror and fantasy, perhaps less politically organized than science fiction, have been less susceptible to manifestoes and movements, but they are not without their schools, from the "Lovecraft circle" of the 1930s to the "splatter-punks" of the 1990s—whose fiction was pretty much what the label suggests—or the current Goths, who seem to regard horror as a dress code as much or more than as a body of fiction; the fiction is often a mechanism for validating the attitude. Fantasy, at least of the broadly commercial variety, has been so dominated by the quest structure of Tolkien's *Lord of the Rings* that it barely leaves room for movements (although there have been a few, such as the "urban fantasy" associated initially with writers like Charles de Lint and later with the paranormal romance); some popular current fantasy series have long since left the simple quest-trilogy structure behind, and generate not so much sequels as metastases. But these fields as well have given rise to touchstone authors whose works seem to demand a reinvention of the ways in which we read genre. Peter Straub's 1979 novel *Ghost Story* may seem to offer a veritable motif index of supernatural tropes, but in fact is a serious and ambitious interrogation of the notion of the ghost story in all its forms, told in a complexly structured narrative that belies the notion that such tropes can support only linear tales of single-minded revelation. Angela Carter, in *The Bloody Chamber and Other Stories* (1979), revealed that the fairy-tale redaction—itself virtually a subgenre of modern fantasy—could unpack deep and troubling conflicts of culture and gender, while her novels freely manipulated time and space using techniques drawn from surrealism, magic realism, and science fiction. John Crowley, who began his career clearly identified as a science fiction writer, virtually exploded the possibilities of several familiar fantasy tropes in his iconically titled 1981 novel *Little Big*, in which the title refers not only to the notion of an ever-expanding inner world within the framework of the outer, but to the structuring of the novel itself; and in the *Aegypt* sequence of novels (1994–2007), which expands the notion to reveal a complex secret history of the world. Elizabeth Hand (who like Crowley began by writing science fiction), in novels such as *Waking the Moon* (1994) and *Black Light* (1999), has found ways of bringing the familiar tropes of ancient warring supernatural forces and the resurrection of a goddess into the domestic arenas of the college novel or the arts novel, without sacrificing the characterological demands of either. None of these writers, I would argue, can be read fully without an appreciation of their use of genre materials—of the valorization of Story that remains at the center of the fantastic genres even in their most demeaned forms—but none can be read fully with *only* an appreciation of those genre materials, either.

But matters grow yet more complex, in the work of these writers and others, as the borders of genre themselves begin to dissolve, along with the borders between genre fiction and literary fiction. Jonathan Carroll's first novel, *The Land of Laughs* (1980), was read by some as a horror novel, with its strange small Missouri town haunted—and perhaps formed—by the imagination of a writer who once lived there, but subsequent novels have made such easy readings all but impossible, as he combines ghosts, time travel, supernatural agents, aliens, and even such hard science concepts as cold fusion into narratives that at times seem cavalierly unconcerned with what genre they might be traveling through at the moment. Jonathan Lethem's first novel, *Gun, with Occasional Music* (1994) uses the form of the hard-boiled detective tale, but is set in a postliterate, drug-dazed, twenty-first-century dystopia filled with talking animals that function much like cartoon characters; his later novels have moved increasingly further from traditional genre structures, but have never quite abandoned the skillful structural use of genre iconography. China Miéville's second and third novels, *Perdido Street Station* (2001) and *The Scar* (2002) are set in a densely grotesque fantasy world—his New Crobuzon is one of the great urban environments of modern fantasy—but a world whose inhabitants and technology are a chaotic mix of science fiction, horror, and alchemy. Patrick O'Leary's 1997 novel *The Gift* seems a fairly conventional fantasy, until we find mention of spacecraft and personality matrices; while his 2001 novel *The Impossible Bird* is a posthumous fantasy of brotherly love in which the fantasy premise is rationalized by an appeal to alien conspiracies and information-laden hummingbirds. Even Stephen King, in what may turn out to become the most ambitious work of his career, combines classic quest fantasy motifs with apocalyptic science fiction, Western motifs, and his more familiar trademark horror effects in his "Dark Tower" sequence (1970–2004).

At the same time that genre materials begin flowing freely into one another, we begin to see evidence of an even more peculiar development: the non-genre genre story. By this I don't mean those attempts at using genre material by writers from "outside," such as the occasional ill-conceived science fiction novel by P. D. James, John Updike, or Paul Theroux, but rather those stories so closely informed by genre-based structures and sensibilities that they may convey the *feel* of a particular genre, and may open up to genre readings in a way different from how they open up to conventional readings, even though they lack traditional genre markers. Examples of this in—or near—the horror genre include Peter Straub's 1988 novel *Koko*, which shares with genre horror a concern for portraying extreme experience as almost mystically transformative, but lacks the direct supernatural elements that had once been regarded as a defining element of the genre. (Despite this, and perhaps as a sign of the changing times, the novel won a World Fantasy Award for best novel, and one of its competing nominees was the equally unsupernatural *The Silence of the Lambs*, by Thomas Harris.) By a similar token, novels such as Bruce Sterling's *Zeitgeist* (2000) and Neal Stephenson's *Cryptonomicon* (1999) bear all the hallmarks of good near-future science fiction—the world slightly estranged from our own by new developments in technology and exaggerated social trends, the elements of absurdist social satire, the sense of history as malleable—but in fact neither novel is even set in the future nor makes much use of the surface machinery of science fiction. The Stephenson concerns cryptography and early computer theory at Bletchley Park during World War II, combined with a contemporary tale of data espionage; Sterling's novel is about a cynically manufactured multicultural pop group designed to maximize the profit potential of the pre-millennium *zeitgeist*, and to be disbanded at the turn of the century. Both novels, however, are rife with the science fictional habits of treating speculative thought as though it were heroic action, and of manipulating ideas as though they were characters.

So now we have a situation in which novels containing no material fantasy at all are nominated for and receive fantasy awards; in which novels with little or no science fiction content gain huge followings among science fiction readers who recognize in them something of their own; in which growing numbers of writers view the materials forged in genre as resources rather than as constraints; in which the edges of the genres themselves bleed into one another; in which authors gleefully and knowingly cut the wrong wire. There is perhaps a certain danger in this, in drawing so freely on material that was once condemned to exile, in assembling story-machines that demand a wider repertoire of sensibilities on the part of readers, and it may not be an exaggeration to describe these writers as courageous. Genre writers still complain of the "ghetto" in which they see themselves forced to toil, but an only slightly more overbaked metaphor might be hell itself, and even a particular region of hell. In Dante's *Inferno*, it's curious to note how many of the sinners gathered together in the eighth circle, the *Malebolge* or ditches of evil, seem to be guilty of crimes of genre: the fortune-tellers and diviners, who pretend to see the future; the alchemists, who claimed their art could transform base materials into something wonderful; the sowers of discord; the evil counselors who sinned by glibness of tongue; the panderers and seducers; and, in the central pit, the giant Nimrod, the builder of the Tower of Babel. For the myriad of distinctive voices that make up the post-genre fantastic, the voices heard after the explosion, the risk yet arises of that baleful gaze from the moral poet, still suspecting the crime of fantasy for its own sake no matter how elegant the tale. Dante may never have read a word of Tolkien or Lovecraft or Heinlein, but he was pretty certain he knew a shell game when he saw one, and the imagination has never entirely escaped the shadow of his suspicions.

two

Evaporating Genres

Genre Coalescence

For the first several years of their history, the major publishers of American mass-market paperback books numbered each new title sequentially, providing what is now a fascinating chronicle of popular reading habits during the 1940s, as well as a valuable resource for tracing the prehistory of what we now regard as the major market genres of popular fiction. In May 1943, Donald A. Wollheim's anthology *The Pocket Book of Science-Fiction* appeared as Pocket Book #214, following close upon the heels of #212 (Raymond Chandler's *Farewell, My Lovely*) and #213 (*The Pocket Book of True Crime Stories*), and tucked into a wildly eclectic list of titles that included not only Shakespeare's *Five Great Tragedies* (#3) and Dale Carnegie's *How to Win Friends and Influence People* (#68) but also a more specialized list targeted at specific audiences. These latter volumes, which characteristically followed the proprietary title formula "The Pocket Book of ——," began with broadly generic topics such as *The Pocket Book of Verse* (#62) or *The Pocket Book of Short Stories* (#91), but soon began to include such extraliterary oddities as *The Pocket Book of Boners* (#110)—mostly a collection of humorous schoolboy mistakes—*The Pocket Book of Vegetable Gardening* (#148), *The Pocket Book of Crossword Puzzles* (#210), and *The Pocket Book of Home Canning* (#217).

This is the context in which the first American mass-market science fiction anthology, and probably the first American commercial book to use the term "science-fiction," appeared. It seems clear that publisher Robert F. de Graff and the editors of Pocket Books—which began its mass-market publishing program in May of 1939 with a fantasy novel, James Hilton's *Lost Horizon* (following a 1938 test market edition of Pearl Buck's *The Good Earth*)—were, by the mid-1940s, still tentatively groping toward defining a variety of specialized readerships. Some of these readerships, like mysteries and Westerns, had crystallized long since as popular genres; nearly a quarter of the first one hundred Pocket Books published were classified as "mystery and detective stories" and given a separate list in the pages of promotional material that appeared in the back of each Pocket Book. Science fiction, on the other hand, was relegated to those specialty topics, like vegetable gardening and home canning, which presumably could be covered adequately in a one-shot publication. (Bantam Books, another mass-market paperback publisher that came to prominence in the 1940s, proved even more tentative in dealing with the field when it tried to market its first science fiction anthology, Judith Merril's *A Shot in the Dark* [1950], as "a different kind of mystery thrill," not mentioning science fiction at all in the book's front-cover copy, but including in the back pages a mail-order offer for several specialty-press hardcovers, presumably as a kind of market test.) Prior to the advent of Ballantine Books in 1952, according to paperback historian Kenneth C. Davis, science fiction "barely existed in book form at all. It was viewed by publishers as a sort of fringe genre that they knew or cared little about."[1] While this may have been true of paperbacks, the claim is more problematical in terms of the major hardcover fiction publishers. By 1949, Wollheim himself could publish an article in the *New York Times* heralding "a specialized class of novel called generically 'science-fiction.'"

Doubleday, for instance, announces that they are readying a title to head off their new science-fiction classification. Frederick Fell, Inc., announces a half-dozen such titles, an anthology and several novels, in a special science-fiction series with a colophon all its own. Other companies have slipped science-fiction into their line with less fanfare but no less prescience. Many book stores, among which are counted Scribner's and Brentano's, have pushed clear corners of their detective novel counters to make way for a host of strangely titled and fantastically jacketed volumes.[2]

The year after this article appeared, according to the *New York Times*, nearly fifty identified science fiction titles were published in the United States, with that number increasing again in 1951.[3]

As of the mid- to late 1940s, science fiction had yet to emerge as anything like an identifiable genre in terms of the rapidly expanding paperback book market—the market that would largely supplant cheap magazines within the next two decades as the principal medium of popular fiction. Yet, as the contents of Wollheim's anthology clearly demonstrates, science fiction had developed not only a clear identity, but a fiercely loyal readership in the pulp magazines that flourished in the two decades immediately preceding the rise of the paperback. Pulp fiction—which shares with paperback fiction the odd distinc-

tion of being a narrative tradition so marginalized that it is commonly identified by the technologies of its manufacture rather than its textual content—had
begun in general-interest adventure fiction magazines around the turn of the
century, and by the 1930s had developed special-interest microgenres or niche
markets to a degree never seen before or since, with magazines devoted to
everything from varsity football fiction and World War I aviation stories to tales
of "Oriental menace." Fantastic narratives were no stranger to these magazines,
and one of the more enduring, *Weird Tales*, debuted in 1923 and would play a
significant role in the development of the horror genre.

Science fiction, which famously entered this specialized pulp magazine market with Hugo Gernsback's *Amazing Stories* in 1926, was one of the more
successful of these new pop genres, with something like thirty-five different
magazine titles having been introduced by 1943, the year *The Pocket Book of
Science-Fiction* appeared. Why, then, would such an apparently successful genre
in the pulp magazines—as well as their immediate successors, the digest-sized
fiction magazines that came to dominate the 1950s short genre fiction market—
fail for over a decade to gain purchase in the burgeoning field of paperback
books, with its apparently similar patterns of readership? Literary elitism alone
hardly seems sufficient to account for this; despite the widely held belief among
science fiction readers and writers that it has long been the most unfairly
maligned of popular genres, an examination of early *New York Times* articles
and reviews about science fiction reveals that it was not generally treated with
out-of-hand contempt, and most of the reviewers assigned to the genre (Villiers
Gerson, Basil Davenport, eventually Anthony Boucher) were reasonably sympathetic, even if their reviews did eventually coalesce into a recurring column
called "Spacemen's Realm." Furthermore, it seems fairly clear from a perusal of
the early lists of Pocket, Bantam, Avon, and other paperback publishers that
marketability was a far more important concern than respectability, and it
seems likely that had a sufficient number of novel-length science fiction texts
been available and visible, the paperback houses would not have hesitated to try
to sell them, as they would come to do very successfully in the following decade.

Texts and Text-Products

But what does it mean for a text to be both available and visible? In the simplest
terms, an available text is simply one that exists as a potential candidate for

book publication or for paperback reprint. Visibility is a different problem, and one that raises crucial questions of genre identity: Even though a substantial number of reasonably contemporary novel-length science fiction narratives may have been published in America by the 1940s, they tended to be defined either as oddball mainstream thrillers (such as William M. Sloane's *To Walk the Night* [1937] and *The Edge of Running Water* [1939]) or as longish pulp stories or serials, with little crossover between the two. While both detective stories and Westerns flourished alongside science fiction in the pulps, each also had developed as a distinct tradition of popular novels—Mary Roberts Rinehart, Agatha Christie, Rex Stout, Dashiell Hammett, and Raymond Chandler are among those to appears on Pocket Books' list of mystery stories, while Max Brand and Zane Grey were among the somewhat smaller number of Western writers to appear. Nearly all of these writers had developed followings in the hardcover market as well prior to their entry into the paperback world, and many hardcover publishers had clearly defined lines of mystery and Western fiction. Equally important, Westerns and mysteries had quickly gained foothold as important genres in the newer mass media of film and radio, arenas in which science fiction would fail to succeed as a market segment until the 1950s.

While scores of novels that we can now readily identify as science fiction had appeared throughout the nineteenth and early twentieth centuries, including the scientific romances of H. G. Wells and the adventure tales of Jules Verne, the science fiction novel persistently failed to cohere as a genre in the manner of mysteries and Westerns.[4] Interestingly enough, the allied fantastic genres of horror and fantasy seemed to follow a similar pattern: While Gothic novels and several varieties of subgothic vampire stories retained popularity throughout the nineteenth century, a canon of popular horror stories failed to emerge clearly until well into the twentieth, and fantasy—although arguably the oldest narrative tradition of all—did not descend (or ascend) into genredom until about the same time. *Lost Horizon* may indeed have been Pocket Book #1, but neither its publisher nor its readers apparently saw it as an expression of an ongoing literary tradition connected with other nonrealistic texts: Its popularity, as both novel and film, seemed to derive neither from its origins in utopian discourse or its modality of lost-world fantasy, but rather from its appeal as simple romantic adventure, literally escapist fare for a world plagued by economic depression and the threat of war.

The fantastic genres as a set then—some would say the supergenre of the fantastic—remained locked into the original mode of their publication in the pulp magazines; in order for the texts to gain definition as an ongoing narrative project rather than as the contents of ephemeral periodicals, they needed to be, in effect, liberated: The texts had to be decontextualized from the text-products, which in this case were the pulp magazines.[5] For this reason alone, the appearance of the Wollheim anthology in 1943 marks a crucial moment in the history of science fiction developing a genre identity—although this decontextualizing process would not really gain momentum until the series of large hardcover anthologies that began to appear in the late 1940s and early 1950s from such editors as Groff Conklin (*The Best of Science Fiction*, 1946; *A Treasury of Science Fiction*, 1948; *The Big Book of Science Fiction*, 1950), Raymond Healy and Francis McComas (*Adventures in Time and Space*, 1946), and John W. Campbell, Jr. (*The Astounding Science Fiction Anthology*, 1952). These and other anthologies from the postwar period not only vitally preserved stories that had for the most part been consigned to ephemeral publications, but, by finding their way into public libraries, permitted the genre to begin to coalesce as something more than the object of momentary passions of pulp readers.[6] Science fiction now had a more or less permanent set of reference texts from which to derive its characteristic ideologies.

By the mid-1950s, science fiction clearly had arrived as something more than a set of text-products: In magazines, in paperback, hardcover, and specialty press books, even in film and television, science fiction had become a widely recognized and readily identifiable genre. And almost as soon as it arrived, it began to disassemble itself. Even by the late 1950s and early 1960s, only nominal relationships existed among the various media products marketed or perceived as science fiction: novels by authors as diverse as Kurt Vonnegut and E. C. Tubb, films as different as *The Day the Earth Stood Still* and *Them!*, TV programs as various as *Tom Corbett, Space Cadet* and *The Twilight Zone*, comic books featuring unlikely superheroes and noble mutants. Unlike mysteries or Westerns, each of which tended to appeal in the same ways to the same audiences, science fiction already had begun to experience a radical balkanization of its reader- and viewerships. Even the leading magazines of the 1950s developed distinctly different identities, reflected in both their readerships and their contributors—*Astounding* for more traditional "hard" science fiction, *Galaxy* for satire and social commentary, *The Magazine of Fantasy and Science Fiction* for literary quality and an early form of genre cross-pollination (originally titled *The Magazine of Fantasy*, it added "science fiction" to the title with its second issue). Similarly—although not to such a dramatic degree—the horror genre eventually would grow to encompass everything from Shirley Jackson and Thomas Tryon to Clive Barker and Stephen King, and fantasy everything from Robert E. Howard to J. R. R. Tolkien. The fantastic genres may have gained market individuation, but in a more formal narrative sense the genre markers themselves remained radically unstable.

Narrative Formulas and Emergent Ideologies

Because of the uncertainty of these genre markers, the fantastic genres contain within themselves the seeds of their own dissolution, a nascent set of postmodern rhetorical modes that, over a period of several decades, would begin to supplant not only the notion of genre itself, but the very foundations of the modernist barricades that had long been thought to insulate literary culture from the vernacular fiction of the pulps and other forms of noncanonical expression. Other popular genres that grew to prominence in the early twentieth century gained their followings largely through the development of characteristic tropes and conventional narrative formulas. In his landmark 1976 study of such stories, John G. Cawelti identified formulas for crime novels, the classical detective story, the hardboiled detective story, the Western, and even the "best-selling social melodrama" (Irving Wallace, Harold Robbins, etc.). Significantly, Cawelti's study included virtually no discussion of the three major fantastic genres that interest us here, and in fact it would be difficult for any critical approach based largely on narrative formula to accommodate the genres of the fantastic, which are more readily described as collective worldviews rather than patterns of repetitive action. In terms of the narrative geographies staked out by each of these genres, one might almost invoke analogs of the "matters" first identified by the medieval French poet Jean Bodel: the matter of science fiction is the geography of reason; of horror, the geography of anxiety; of fantasy, the geography of desire.

This is not to deny that each of these genres developed its own share of characteristic and clichéd narrative formulas—only to say that such formulas were never sufficient to be the defining characteristic of the genre. While we can readily recite a litany of familiar tropes from the pulp era—alien invasions, time travel, science gone awry, space exploration, galactic war, mutants as monsters or victims—by the early 1940s, *Astounding* was regularly publishing tales that could not be subsumed easily by such formulas, that drew on more complex and subtle explorations of history, economics, psychology, even labor relations. (By the standards of the pulp era, one of the most popular series in *Astounding*, Isaac Asimov's "Foundation" stories, was virtually without plotted action at all.) Science fiction, once it emerged from the cocoon of the space operas that dominated the early pulp era, began to explore its potential as a genre based as much in ideology as in story, eventually transforming itself into a dialogue and a dialectic about change that almost inevitably would lead to a blurring of its identity, as its favorite concerns and obsessions grew more congruent with the concerns and obsessions of the society at large, and with the capacity of rational action to address those concerns and obsessions. Horror, perversely naming itself not after narrative structures or settings or even ideas, but rather after its putative emotional effect on its audience, emerged from the shadow of the Gothic to discover that its key dynamic was not a particular story pattern, but an unanchored anxiety, which also came into eventual congruence with broader cultural issues. Fantasy—the oldest genre of all, but one whose principal pulp identity had been confined largely to sword and sorcery tales or lighthearted whimsy—did not really develop a clear market identity in America until fairly late in the paperback revolution (following the enormously successful paperback editions of Tolkien's *Lord of the Rings* trilogy), but quickly moved to catch up with its sister genres in the process of dissolving its own borders, as its authors began to discover that the Tolkien quest formula was but one expression of the genre's potential, and not a totalizing definition of it.

By the late stages of the pulp era (a decade or so later in terms of fantasy), the writers and readers of these genres had developed easily recognizable protocols and even consensus literary histories, all based in a kind of populist canon developed through common reading and in some cases through that proto-internet of conventions, hectographed or mimeographed fanzines, and magazine letter columns collectively known as fandom. The contents of these informal canons were often fascinating; while the texts included were not always popular or even widely available, they came to represent emergent ideologies that defined the genre in terms of both its market and its texts. Each genre's readers came to identify a central ideological lynchpin—Robert A. Heinlein in the case of science fiction, Howard Phillips Lovecraft in the case of horror, J. R. R.Tolkien in the case of fantasy—and to a great extent the dialectic of the relevant genre seemed to define itself in recapitulation of, or reaction against, the world-views of these central figures.[7] And in each field, the dialectic seemed to offer two possible routes for later writers: expansion of discourse to the edges of genre and beyond, or collapsing of the discourse into an increasingly crabbed and narrow set of self-referential texts. Both kinds of results tend to promote the dissolution of the original genre—the one by integration with other fiction, the other by implosion—and both are abundantly in evidence in each genre today.

The Construction and Deconstruction of Horror

In the field of horror, for example, the defining emblematic figure to emerge from the pulp era was H. P. Lovecraft, who shared with Agatha Christie and Dashiell Hammett the distinction of having been wittily skewered at some length by the *New Yorker's* high priest of modernism, Edmund Wilson. Lovecraft's turn came posthumously, in a November 1945 column that almost willfully avoided addressing the question of what might appeal to certain readers in Lovecraft's overripe prose, ersatz mythology, and paranoid misanthropy; as far as Wilson was concerned, such flawed texts could be enjoyed only by flawed readers, and the modernist community need feel no obligation to acknowledge further the existence of such populist aberrations. "The only real horror in most of these fictions," he wrote, "is the horror of bad taste and bad art."[8] By the time Lovecraft was brought to Wilson's attention, he already had begun to emerge as the coalescent figure in American horror fiction, thanks largely to Arkham House, the publishing house (founded by August Derleth and Donald Wandrei) that began assembling and reprinting his works in 1939, and continued in what amounted to a program of cult canonization over the next several decades. Partly because of his direct influence—members of the "Lovecraft circle" during his lifetime included such influential later writers as Robert Bloch and Henry Kuttner—and partly because of the availability of the Arkham House books, Lovecraft provided the standard against which later American horror writers would either measure themselves or rebel, or both.

Lovecraft's emergence from genre cult figure into the broader arena of the postwar fascination with literatures of alienation may be due largely to the work of another Wilson, Colin (unrelated, of course, to Edmund). Lionized originally for his widely popular 1956 study of alienation in modern literature, *The Outsider*, the determinedly eccentric Wilson devoted the first part of the opening chapter of his 1962 study *The Strength to Dream: Literature and the Imagination* to examining Lovecraft's radically alienated, antimaterialist fantasies. By placing Lovecraft even remotely in the context of such canonical writers as Yeats, Wilde, and Strindberg (the other authors covered in that first chapter), Wilson anticipated the eventual breakdown of modernist barriers that would permit Lovecraft to emerge as a cultural figure of some interest outside the narrow genre of his original reputation, and which in turn, over decades, would contribute to the gradual evaporation of horror as a narrative tradition isolated from the mainstream of cultural discourse. (Wilson also discussed a number of science fiction writers in *The Strength to Dream*, and devoted a substantial portion of a chapter to J. R. R. Tolkien—surely one of the earliest discussions of that author's fantasy in the context of broader literary culture.) A few years later, in novels such as *The Mind Parasites* (1967) and *The Philosopher's Stone* (1969), Wilson would appropriate and subvert the Lovecraft mythos in a manner that implicitly argued against the notion of horror as merely an isolated pulp genre.

For a good portion of the postwar period, the Lovecraftian aesthetic—remote, haunted villages, strange half-human families, forbidden books, and most of all ancient elder gods waiting to reclaim the world—dictated many of the terms by which horror fiction would be practiced in its relatively limited literary arena, with authors such as Fritz Leiber, Robert Bloch, Ray Bradbury, and Richard Matheson striving to introduce a more contemporary, urban ethos, while Lovecraft's more direct heirs, from August Derleth to Brian Lumley and Ramsey Campbell expanded upon Lovecraft's cosmic occultism in stories and novels that, in the beginning at least, were often little more than direct pastiches. But in 1967, the terms of horror fiction began to change radically. This was the year that Ira Levin's *Rosemary's Baby*, with its contemporary urban setting, its exploitation of the anxieties of pregnancy, and its eschewing of invented gods in favor of the oldest villain of them all, the devil, became a phenomenal bestseller and, in 1968, a highly successful film by Roman Polanski. A skilled storyteller who achieved his effects with a journalistic efficiency that contrasted dramatically with Lovecraft's florid style, Levin recast the horror story as a paranoid suspense thriller—an emerging genre that owed as much to the detective and espionage story as to the traditions of the supernatural tale. Almost with one stroke, the post-Lovecraft dialogues that had defined the rather small and insular horror genre seemed swept away, and just as the genre began to attain massive popularity, its boundaries already were beginning to dissolve. In 1971, the equally successful *The Exorcist* by William Peter Blatty also featured a very traditional Christian devil as its antagonist, combining horror fiction first with aspects of the medical thriller (as batteries of doctors and psychiatrists find themselves unable to address what's wrong with the possessed girl), and then with the didactic theological romance. The story also helped to break new ground in its depiction of graphic, visceral episodes of violence and obscenity.

By the later 1970s, of course, the terms of horror fiction were being dictated by an entirely new force, Stephen King, whose first novel, *Carrie*, appeared in 1974 and whose first major bestseller *'Salem's Lot*, appeared the following year. King was well aware of the Lovecraft tradition and the manner in which later writers responded to it, as evidenced by his informed 1981 nonfiction study of horror, *Danse Macabre*, and several of his first few novels seem deliberate redactions of classic horror themes—the vampire tale in *'Salem's Lot* (1975), "The Monkey's Paw" (a classic W. W. Jacobs tale from 1902) in *Pet Sematary* (1983), the haunted castle in *The Shining* (1977). But King also was interested, almost from the beginning, in dissolving the traditional boundaries of the horror story and merging it with other genres. The psychic powers that are featured in *Carrie* (1974) and *Firestarter* (1980) are more characteristic of 1940s science fiction than of most supernatural fiction, and science fictional devices are key aspects of both *It* (1986) and *The Tommyknockers* (1987). With the novellas in *Different Seasons* (1982) and novels like *Misery* (1987), King began to explore ways of moving the modalities of horror narrative outside the genre of supernatural horror altogether—a move that was accelerated by his colleague and sometime collaborator Peter Straub. Their famous 1984 collaboration *The Talisman*—the bestselling work of fiction for that year, according to *Publishers Weekly*—surprised many horror readers by borrowing its basic structure from the fantasy quest romance and scattering throughout the narrative allusions to writers from Mark Twain and L. Frank Baum to J. R. R. Tolkien and even John Gardner. Described by Straub's admirer and critic Bill Sheehan as "an eccentric hybrid of a book that is frequently vital and moving, and occasionally attenuated and overlong," the novel may well have confused critics and reviewers with its implicit refusal to abide by the largely self-referential traditions of horror fiction, and its consequent assertion that the membranes separating the fantastic genres from each other, and from external literary traditions, are highly permeable.[9] This genre-mixing trend was even more evident in the authors' 2001 sequel *Black House*, which added a serial-murderer mystery plot to the horror and fantasy aspects of the narrative.

Straub himself had been bombing the borders between mainstream and genre fiction since his earliest successes back in the 1970s. His first major bestseller, the 1979 *Ghost Story*, with its studied allusions to Hawthorne, James, and Stephen Crane, its leapfrogging chronology, and its multiple viewpoints, was an effort, he told Stephen King, to do "something which would be *very* literary, and at the same time take on every kind of ghost situation I could think of."[10] It was, in effect, Straub's first concerted effort to deconstruct the genre from within. In less than a decade, Straub had begun the series of interlinked "Blue Rose" stories and novels that would retain the sometimes gruesome tone of his earlier supernatural fiction in nonsupernatural narrative modes that borrowed far more freely from traditions of the crime novel (*Koko*, 1988; *Mystery*, 1990; *The Throat*, 1993) and the fairy tale ("The Juniper Tree," 1985; "Ashputtle," 1994) than from the traditions of genre horror. (At the same time, it might be noted, the police procedural crime thriller was moving aggressively into the realm of horror with such novels as Thomas Harris's 1988 *The Silence of the Lambs*, further blurring genre boundaries.) *The Throat*, it might be argued, is a genuine postgenre work, a horror novel that not only lacks supernatural horror, but lacks traditional horror scenes of any sort. By this point, Straub's authority and popularity were such that he continued to be honored for fantasy and horror even with works clearly more closely allied with crime fiction, if not with an even more diffuse American Gothic tradition (*Koko* won the World Fantasy Award in 1989 and *The Throat* a Bram Stoker Award in 1993).

Mr. X (1999), heralded as Straub's return to the realm of the supernatural, proved in its own way to be equally subversive of genre conventions, and is of interest here because of the Janus-like manner in which it addresses both the older, Lovecraftian tradition and the newer uses of horror. There is plenty of traditional horror in *Mr. X*, including a substantial and informed subplot involving Lovecraft and his Cthulhu mythos and Arthur Machen-like allusions to the survival of the god Pan, but there are also many elements that look beyond the conventions of genre, not the least of which is Straub's choice to make his protagonist and his family Black (without directly asserting this, a device coincidentally used a few years later by bestselling fantasy writer Neil Gaiman in his 2005 novel *Anansi Boys*), and to use jazz performance as a fairly complex central metaphor (Straub may be the only novelist around to include Lovecraft and jazz convincingly in the same novel). *Mr. X* is essentially a *doppelgänger* tale, and the main *doppelgänger* in question belongs to the narrator Ned Dunstan, a software programmer drawn back to his hometown of Edgerton, Illinois, because of forebodings about his mother Star, a sometime jazz singer who maintained a close relationship with Ned despite having long ago given him up to foster parents. Since childhood, Ned has experienced strange lapses of consciousness on his birthday, when he sometimes seems to be transported to another time and place. More recently, he has found himself occasionally mistaken for someone else—the classic *doppelgänger* plot point— and even finds himself accused of murder before he has been in Edgerton for long. Ned becomes involved with a number of local characters—various aunts and uncles, an assistant district attorney named Ashley who is investigating a powerful local developer named Stewart Hatch, a secretive landlady named Helen Janette, and most importantly Hatch's wife Laurie and her son Cobbie. In keeping with the shadow-figure motif, most of these characters are not quite who they seem to be, and even the town of Edgerton itself seems to have a dual identity, with its oddly out-of-place street names like Fish, Button, Treacle, and Wax, its Brazen Head hotel, and its ominous Veal Yard. Ned's own family history is even more mysterious, dating back at least to eighteenth-century Providence, where a long-abandoned family mansion came to be known as "the Shunned House" (allusions to Lovecraft permeate the novel). While in Edgerton, Ned discovers that his father of record is not his real father, a man named Edward Rinehart, and that a twin brother apparently had disappeared shortly after birth.

The father, Rinehart—the Mr. X of the title—provides the novel's second narrative voice, and unlike Ned, he *knows* that he's in a horror story, largely one of his own creation. Obsessed with Lovecraft's Cthulhu mythos, which he regards as a kind of divine revelation, Rinehart is one of Straub's most chilling creations—a sadistic murderer with supernatural psychic powers, self-styled Lord of Crime, and a bad horror story writer in the Lovecraft tradition. He is, in effect, a creature made of genre. Rinehart's story—and his narrative voice— provide a kind of grotesque mirror image of Ned's: Their respective youthful experiences at college and a military academy are pointedly juxtaposed, and Rinehart's contemptuous hatred of Star is as central a motivation as Ned's tacit devotion to her. It hardly comes as a surprise that Rinehart's mission in Edgerton is to destroy Ned. But Ned's own supernatural powers, together with those of his shadowy brother Robert, are sufficient to set the stage for an epic confrontation.

Despite several scenes of spectacularly gruesome murder, a deliberate evocation of Lovecraft's paranoid world-view, and a protagonist who seems, science fiction–like, to be able to travel through time, *Mr. X* is a complex novel that engages in an active and often witty critique of the horror genre while staking an authoritative claim to being part of it. Lovecraft, for example, functions partly as an emblem of horror's chronic looniness and partly as an inside joke for genre readers, even though Straub admits (in an afterword) that he has taken a few liberties with Lovecraft's publication history. But such allusions are crucial to the texture of the narrative, which—like all of Straub's best work— strives to add multiple tonalities to a genre best known for its one-note performances: the tragic and often treacherous family relationships, the detailed and richly textured portrait of the small southern Illinois town of Edgerton, and the persistent infusion of music into the narrative at both dramatic and structural levels, combine to give the novel a density of layers within which the conventions of genre horror are subsumed as merely another narrative resource. If Straub's *The Throat* moved into post-genre territory by forsaking both supernaturalism and graphic terror, *Mr. X* proves to be even more subversive by returning to the matter of horror and refusing to let it dictate the terms of the novel. This movement became even more apparent in his metafictional diptych *lost boy lost girl* (2003) and *In the Night Room* (2004), discussed elsewhere in this volume.

Fantasy without Fantasy

Always a more diffuse genre than either science fiction or horror, fantasy's emergence as a popular market can be dated almost exactly: May 1965, when the first U.S. paperback edition of the first volume of J. R. R. Tolkien's *Lord of the Rings* appeared. (This edition, from Ace Books, exploited a technicality in American copyright law that permitted the publisher to view the book as public domain and avoid paying royalties, but Ian and Betty Ballantine quickly met with Tolkien to arrange an "authorized edition," which appeared from Ballantine Books that October and—according to Betty Ballantine—benefited considerably from the controversy that had arisen over Ace's efforts to "cheat" Tolkien. The book was thus something of a literary *cause célèbre* even before the Ballantine edition appeared, which no doubt increased its profile in the general literary community.) Of course, individual fantasy writers had gained fame or notoriety before this, such as James Branch Cabell or Mervyn Peake (although their reputations had by now largely faded to cult-like status), and there were even earlier efforts to define fantasy as a popular genre, such as the pulp magazine *Unknown* (1939–1943; the title was changed to *Unknown Worlds* in 1941), created by science fiction editor John W. Campbell as a kind of companion to his *Astounding Science Fiction*, but for the most part fantasy, as a commercial category or a self-conscious tradition, had remained something of a muddle. The anthology series-cum-quarterly magazine *Avon Fantasy Reader*, edited by Donald A. Wollheim from 1947 to 1952, focused largely on the kind of supernatural horror fiction that had long characterized the pulp *Weird Tales*, while a 1951 paperback anthology called *The Saturday Evening Post Fantasy Stories* (edited by Barthold Fles) was in fact a mélange of science fiction, horror, and occult fiction. But Tolkien's immense success set off a flurry of activity among publishers to find new writers "in the Tolkien tradition" and—perhaps more important—to resurrect older works that could be viewed retroactively as a popular canon of "classics." Ballantine alone reprinted major works by Mervyn Peake, E. R. Eddison, David Lindsay, and Peter S. Beagle within three years of *The Lord of the Rings*, and in 1969 instituted its Adult Fantasy Series, which eventually ran to more than sixty titles, including those published prior to the series' official designation.

While a coherent idea of genre was never the series' strong point—it would be hard to guess what fans of Tolkien's hobbits would make of as crabbed and eccentric a work as Lindsay's *A Voyage to Arcturus*—there is little doubt that Ballantine's program, together with similarly aggressive lines of original fantasy titles from Ace and DAW, helped create a sense of a coherent market. But while the market tended to define itself in terms of works that bore at least a surface resemblance to Tolkien, such as Stephen R. Donaldson's double trilogy *The Chronicles of Thomas Covenant the Unbeliever* (1977–1983; a third series began in 2005), the genre itself was already radically unstable by the time it had gained a clear enough identity to come to the attention of literary theorists, most of whom (including Eric S. Rabkin, W. R. Irwin, and Rosemary Jackson) were hard pressed to describe it except to assert that it involved impossible beings or actions, maintained a particularly otherworldly tone, and subverted bourgeois expectations of narrative.[11] While both science fiction and horror could point to proto-works dating from the nineteenth or even eighteenth centuries, fantasy's late-blooming commercial identity *depended* on the archaeological discovery of such works; far more than its sister genres, it was a category constructed retroactively to meet the needs of a suddenly emergent market.

Yet one of the acknowledged canonical works of the field, dating from before Tolkien's trilogy, was Mervyn Peake's unique novel *Titus Groan* (1946), which was already violating one of the accepted terms of fantasy—namely, the presence of impossible worlds or beings. As exaggerated and unlikely as the world of the castle of Gormenghast is, with its bizarre population of grotesques (the servant Steerpike, the fat cook Swelter, the depressed Lord Sepulchrave), it is not explicitly an impossible world, and the events of the novel are not explicitly supernatural events. (The novel's two sequels, *Gormenghast* [1950] and *Titus Alone* [1959], are more problematical in this regard, as it becomes increasingly difficult to separate what might be fantasy from hallucinatory surrealism.) The fact that few readers seem to notice this, or be bothered by it, suggests that the overwhelming tone of the novel carries enough of the fantasy affect to override mere concerns of plot and setting. Almost before fantasy came to be defined as a genre, then, one of its classic texts had already violated the terms of that genre, creating a classic fantasy novel without material fantasy.

A more recent example of this violation seems to address much more deliberately the question of genre identity. Geoff Ryman's 1992 novel *Was* (British title "*Was...*"), described by its author as the work of a "fantasy writer who fell in love with realism," is set in a version of the American Midwest that seems strongly influenced by such naturalist writers as Hamlin Garland and Frank Norris, and on the surface offers few of the solaces of traditional fantasy. The novel's central conceit is that the Dorothy Gale (Gael in Ryman's novel) of L. Frank Baum's *Oz* books was an actual orphan in turn-of-the-century Kansas, sent with her dog Toto to live with her cruel Auntie Em and Uncle Henry and haunted by the memory of her brief happy earlier childhood in St. Louis, before her father disappeared and her mother died of diphtheria. Dorothy comes to think of her idyllic past as a place called Was. Sexually abused by her uncle Henry, she becomes a serious behavioral problem in school, until a visiting substitute teacher takes an interest in her and asks her to write about her life, and the land of Was. The substitute teacher is, of course, Baum himself, who goes on to appropriate large segments of Dorothy's tale into his famous novel. This narrative is intercut with two other narratives, one involving the childhood of the actress Judy Garland, and the other, more substantial narrative concerning a contemporary actor dying of AIDS who, in conversations with his therapist, becomes obsessed with the idea that Dorothy was real.

By an unlikely but fortuitous coincidence, the therapist who is working with the actor had been holding a summer job at a mental hospital in Kansas decades earlier when, during the first network television broadcast of the 1939 film *The Wizard of Oz*, in November 1956, one of the hospital's oldest inmates began claiming hysterically that the movie had stolen her life: She was, of course, the aged Dorothy, driven to madness by a long life of disappointment and sexual exploitation, and given to rambling on about a place called Was, and how you can't get there from Is. This key scene, which briefly unites the three plot lines of the narrative, is extremely powerful and lovely, but it is not fantasy. Nor is most of the rest of the novel, except perhaps for two brief episodes: one, when Dorothy finally runs away from home and has what appears to be a mystical encounter with a white buffalo, a mythic emblem of the lost American West; and another at the end of the novel, when the dying actor seems to disappear while searching for Dorothy. At the thematic center of the novel is the great fantasy *The Wizard of Oz* itself—as well as the 1939 Garland film—and much of the novel can be read as an extended meditation on the importance of fantasy in maintaining psychic equilibrium, especially in lives of extreme stress, but the novel is very nearly an anti-fantasy in its mode of presentation—as though Dorothy were the invention of Thomas Hardy rather than of Baum.

Interestingly, the contrasting landscapes in Ryman's novel echo the traditional contrast between realistic and fantasy worlds in Baum's novel: The bleak, gray Kansas of the real Dorothy is not dissimilar to the equally monochromatic Kansas in the opening chapter of *The Wizard of Oz,* while Dorothy's remembered childhood in Was is an obvious analog of Oz itself. Other fantasy worlds populate the novel in subtler ways: the unreal Hollywood life of Judy Garland contrasted with her own earlier childhood, the false Oz of the movie set, the promise of a broader world that briefly seems held out to Dorothy by the attractive, adventurous substitute teacher Baum, even the world beyond AIDS that haunts the young actor, who comes to conflate it with the myth of Dorothy. Structurally, many of the elements of classic fantasy are present in the novel—the youthful protagonist, the magical tutelary figure, the quest, the secondary world—but they are consistently undercut by the intrusion of realism, by reminders that, in Dorothy's words, you can't get there from Is. Ryman, an author who in other works has deliberately tested the boundaries of genre, shifting between politically charged realism, fantasy, and science fiction often in the same work, in *Was* seems to be out to explode the notion of genre altogether.[12]

None of this, of course, prevented *Was* from being nominated for the World Fantasy Award in 1993 as best fantasy novel of the year.[13] Interestingly enough, almost as if to underline the notion that fantasy as a genre had begun to evaporate into the broader spectrum of literature, *Was* was one of two non-fantasies on that final ballot. The other was Jane Yolen's *Briar Rose* (1992), a

Holocaust novel in which a young woman attempts to uncover the secrets of her late grandmother's life as a survivor, taking clues from the distorted version of "Sleeping Beauty" that the grandmother had told her and her sisters throughout childhood. Like Ryman, Yolen is a sophisticated writer with an acute understanding of the conventions of genre (earlier, she had written a time-travel fantasy about the Holocaust, *The Devil's Arithmetic* [1988]). But apart from its allusions to fairy tales, *Briar Rose* contains no supernatural events and, like Ryman's novel, it is meticulous in its historical realism, taking its readers to the survivors' camp established by the U.S. government in Fort Oswego, New York, to the concentration camp of Chelmno, to postwar Poland, and to contemporary Holyoke, Massachusetts—all far removed from any sort of fairyland. At its most fantastic, it's a very minimalist alternate history, positing that the grandmother might have survived a concentration camp from which there are no known women survivors. If it *is* a fantasy, it is a fantasy without fantasy.

Science Fiction and the Colonization of Genres

Unlike horror, which built upon a longstanding Gothic tradition and almost abruptly emerged as a blockbuster market genre in the 1970s, and unlike fantasy, which could lay a persuasive claim to being the dominant mode of fictional narrative for most of human history, science fiction, despite its healthy legacy throughout the nineteenth century, was essentially a *designed* genre after 1926, the year in which Hugo Gernsback launched *Amazing Stories*. It consisted of a set of available markets to which writers ostensibly would conform, rather than a tradition of narrative that eventually would find its markets. This inevitably placed serious constraints upon the ability of writers to expand the boundaries of the genre, and the field is rife with tales like that told by Daniel Keyes, author of the now-classic "Flowers for Algernon," about the insistence of editor Horace Gold to tack a "happy ending" onto the tragic story in order to make it more acceptable to the readership of *Galaxy Science Fiction*.[14] Because of the limitations of the market, the obtuseness of editors, the decline of the magazines, the growth of bestseller mentalities among publishers, and the incursion of paraliterary offshoots of the genre such as movie, TV, and game novelizations, science fiction writers periodically will publish essays mourning the recent or imminent death of the field (such essays appear only a little less frequently among horror writers and fantasy writers). What these essays are really mourning, upon closer inspection, is the declining market health of that self-invented and self-reflexive genre. They tend to offer little evidence that science fiction is actually disappearing—only that its consensus core is evaporating. Writers from "outside"—Doris Lessing, Marge Piercy, Margaret Atwood, Paul Theroux, John Updike, P. D. James, Jeanette Winterson, Philip Roth—freely appropriate its resources, while the notion of a common readership with a common reading background—once defined by the magazines and later by the paperback book publishers with regular science fiction lines—grows increasingly uncertain.[15]

Science Fiction Historicals

Writers have begun to respond to this uncertainty in a variety of ways, developing strategies for writing science fiction without writing in the *genre* of science fiction, just as Straub experimented in writing horror without horror, or Ryman fantasy without fantasy. One strategy is essentially to colonize another genre, using the tropes of science fiction as instrumentalities for moving the narrative into a different mode altogether. The time travel theme, for example, often has served as a convenient mechanism for constructing science fiction narratives that at the same time appropriate the protocols of historical fiction. A fictional group of time-traveling historians in twenty-first-century Oxford has provided Connie Willis with an angle of approach for several richly detailed historical fictions set in venues as diverse as London during the Blitz ("Fire Watch," 1982), a fourteenth-century village suffering from the Plague (*Doomsday Book*, 1992), or the 1889 Oxfordshire of Jerome K. Jerome (*To Say Nothing of the Dog*, 1998). An earlier novel, *Lincoln's Dreams* (1982), uses a kind of cross-time psychic connection to move the narrative into the era of the American Civil War. In each case, despite the science-fictional frame, the main narrative is constructed around the historical setting, which is the centerpiece of the novel and its *raison d'être*. Similarly, Kage Baker's series of novels and tales about a time-traveling "Company" involve settings as diverse as sixteenth-century Spain and England, eighteenth-century California, and the early days of Hollywood. Jack Dann, another writer with strong science fiction roots, moved even more directly into the realm of historical fiction with his novel *The Memory Cathedral: A Secret History of Leonardo da Vinci* (1995), which retains a claim to a science fiction identity through a speculative passage involving da Vinci's "lost" years; and with the Civil War novel *The Silent* (1998), whose connection to science fiction genre materials is even more vestigial.

A newer writer, Patricia Anthony, moved progressively further into historical fiction in two remarkable novels published in 1997 and 1998. The first, *God's Fires*, is set in a Portugal hovering between the late Inquisition and the beginnings of industrial democracy. Manoel Pessoa, a circuit-riding Jesuit, arrives in the village of Quintas to find it gripped by mysterious signs and portents: strange lights are seen in the sky, women claim to have been sexually assaulted by angels, a young virgin is apparently pregnant, another girl claims to have spoken with the Virgin Mary, a farmer's field is partially burnt and overgrown with huge, bloated potatoes. Soon an acorn-shaped spaceship is found and the two surviving aliens are captured and held in the local jail. And not long after that, the events in Quintas draw the attention of the Inquisition. Educated and humane, yet aware that his order is barely tolerated in Iberia, Pessoa forms an uneasy romantic alliance with another outsider, the Jewish herbalist Berenice Pinheiro (who herself occupies a middle ground between medievalism and modernity as a reputed "witch" whose knowledge of medicine derives largely from empirical observation). While almost everyone else sees the mysterious aliens as angels or demons—forcing them into an older cosmology—Pessoa suspects they may be something new in the world, and perhaps the harbingers of new ideas. This is certainly what they represent to the touchingly addled young King Alfonso, whose mind is strangely filled with images that we recognize as science, but that the Inquisition views as heresy, and in particular the Galilean heresy, which proves to be one of the central linchpins of the narrative. Despite the introduction of alien visitors, *God's Fires* is principally an historical novel that turns not on its science fiction conceit, but on its evocation of the unsettling play of conflicting ideas in an apocalyptic age—themes that seem ideologically appropriate to serious science fiction, but that are equally the stuff of intellectual history. "God save us from men with ideas," the villainous Inquisitor-General remarks at one point, summing up his terror of the destabilized world-view he sees in the work of Hobbes, Locke, and Galileo. But this conflict of world views is what the novel is really about, and the aliens whose spacecraft crashes in the village of Quintas—the principle science fiction elements of the novel—are used as no more than a lens through which to focus the essentially historical concerns of the narrative.

Anthony's next novel, *Flanders,* a brutal combat novel of the First World War, virtually does away with all fantastic apparatus except one, and that is attached to only one character: The epistolary narrator Travis Lee Stanhope, a Texas sharpshooter attached to a unit of the British Expeditionary Force, is gifted with second sight. His premonitions can save members of his unit from being in the wrong place at the wrong time while under artillery bombardment, and his recurrent dreams of an ornate cemetery and a girl in calico enable him to keep contact with the dead—and eventually to foresee the fates of the living (his own future, however, remains mercifully clouded in mist). It may be a mark of Anthony's cleverness that her sole concession to the supernatural takes the form of such an archaic trope; belief in second sight was so common in the era of spiritualism that it hardly disturbs the fabric of the tale's historical realism. But *Flanders* proves to be a transgenre novel in more senses than simply combing psychic powers with historical settings: The novel also freely appropriates the effects of horror fiction as well. Of course, a natural alliance exists between horror stories and war stories, an alliance that we have seen exploited by Peter Straub's depictions of the Vietnam War in *Koko* and *The Throat*. Anthony achieves a similar effect, investing all her strongly realized characters with a sense of impending doom (even Travis's name, with its obvious echo of the Alamo, seems to presage his fate) and putting her hero through a relentless parade of exploded, burning, disemboweled, decaying, rat-gnawed, and maggot-ridden bodies. With its surrealistic trench-warfare setting and its moments of supernatural insight, *Flanders* is a novel imbued with the sensibilities of science fiction, horror, and fantasy, but that aggressively colonizes the narrative territory of historical fiction and the combat novel.

British author Stephen Baxter, initially known for his universe- and millennia- spanning cosmic epics in the tradition of Arthur C. Clarke, moved even further than Anthony in the direction of literally incorporating full-scale historical fictions into an overarching science fiction context. Baxter's interest in exploring the possibilities of historical fiction was already clearly evident in his 2003 novel *Coalescent*, which traced centuries in the history of a British family, beginning in late Roman Britain, although it combines this saga with a contemporary family mystery, ends with a pair of chapters set on a distant planet, and leads to two sequels (*Exultant*, 2004, and *Respendent*, 2007) which are pure SF in Baxter's cosmological mode. His next series of novels, however, represents a far bolder experiment in developing historical fiction as literally a subset of science fiction. Titled "Time's Tapestry," this series began with *Emperor* in 2006, continued with *Conqueror* and *Navigator* in 2007, and concluded with *Weaver* in 2008. What is remarkable about this series is the manner in which each successive novel, set in a different period of British history, gradually brings a governing science fiction template toward the foreground, until by the final volume *Weaver* we realize that each of these historical episodes is actually subsumed into a science fiction narrative—even though the earlier novels in the series contain minimal overt fantastic elements. Essentially, Baxter has written a series of historical novels (or actually novellas, since the first three volumes in the series are comprised of ten discrete episodes) that retroactively are revealed to be science fiction, invoking time travel and alternate histories, as well as historical fiction.[16]

The first volume of "Time's Tapestry," *Emperor*, is essentially three novellas tracing a British family from 4 B.C. through the end of Roman rule. The sole clue to a science-fictional superstructure is a cryptic prophecy uttered in 4 B.C. by the dying mother of the family patriarch Nectovelin. Spoken in Latin—a language the woman could not possibly know—the prophecy foretells the coming of three emperors, the building of Hadrian's wall, and what is evidently the American Declaration of Independence (the prophecy refers to "life, liberty, and the pursuit of happiness"). While the meanings of most of these prophecies become clear after the events come to pass, the reference to the Declaration of Independence remains unexplained in the novel—suggesting that its meaning will become evident only in later volumes. The prophecies are preserved through generations of Nectovelin's family, covering the Roman invasion of Britain in A.D. 43, the building of Hadrian's wall in the second century A.D., and the fourth-century reign of Constantine, who proves to be a central figure in the prophecy's meaning. The novel ends with another birth and another prophecy, paralleling the opening, only now the prophecy is in yet a different tongue—Saxon—thus setting the stage for Baxter's next novel.

Conqueror, the second novel in the series, is organized around successive appearances of Halley's comet between A.D. 607 and 1066, and opens with a Saxon boy and a Norse soldier searching for that second prophecy from the end of *Emperor*, now some two hundred years old. They find it in the possession of the ancient Ambrosius, called the "last Roman," who explains that it predicts a great war and the rise of an Aryan empire—references immediately recognizable to twentieth-century readers—and that it is the work of the Weaver, "who sits in his palace of the future and sees all—and schemes to establish the new Rome."[17] Almost echoing the Hari Seldon of Isaac Asimov's *Foundation* stories (perhaps the most famous earlier example of science fiction appropriating historical narratives for its own ends), Ambrosius explains that the prophecy must be fulfilled exactly "if this shining future is to come to pass. Otherwise darkness will surely fall." The next three tales in the novel follow the prophecy through several centuries, including a Viking invasion, Alfred's defeat of the Danes, and the Norman invasion. Still another set of anomalies is introduced— detailed drawings of complex war machines produced by a near-autistic orphan, which, together with an account of Leif Erikson's westward voyages to discover Vinland and the first stirrings of the eastward Crusades, seem designed to set up the central conflict of Baxter's third volume, *Navigator*.

Navigator introduces yet another prophecy. In the ruins of a York laid waste by the Normans, a brutalized woman named Eadgyth speaks in a voice clearly not her own of a powerful figure called the Dove, who must be made to fly west rather than east. We eventually learn that this refers to Christopher Columbus. Those da Vinci–like war machines imagined by the autistic child in *Conqueror*, it turns out, are actually being built in Spain; one of Baxter's more villainous figures proposes to use them in an apocalyptic war against Islam, and if King Ferdinand can be persuaded to support Columbus's westward explorations rather than the eastern war, civilization may be saved. While this novel again features historical set pieces such as the Muslim Siege of Seville in 1248, the science fiction elements clearly move to the forefront. We learn that the mysterious Weaver from the future is engaged in a struggle with another figure called the Witness to alter history, as in Fritz Leiber's famous series of "Change War" tales. Other SF devices appear: A mysterious monk named Alfred may himself be a time traveler. A strange "amulet" shows up in thirteenth-century Jerusalem, apparently a voice recorder that when shattered reveals metal disks and other electronic bits. The superweapons from those drawings come to full fruition, with submarines, gatling-gun–like cannons, and flying machines being prepared for the holy war against the Muslims. The future represented by these weapons, one character speculates, is the result of the Weaver's meddling, while the Witness—possibly an inhabitant of that disastrous future—seeks to divert history in another direction: toward the discovery of a new world. By now, Baxter has set up so many possible alternate histories and made so explicit the theme of engineering history that his fourth volume will almost have to resolve into pure science fiction.

And so it does, but perhaps not in the manner we would expect. While it was clear that Baxter would reveal the identities of the Weaver and the Witness and how they managed to influence historical events and plant prophecies across time, his first surprise is in nearly dispatching both of these questions within the first few pages of *Weaver*. In the first place, the secret lies not in our future, nor even in our present, but in an alternate England during the early years of World War II. A brief prologue, set in an early computer lab at MIT in 1940, shows us how the first of the prophecies was transmitted into the past, involving something called a Differential Analyser, a brilliant young physicist (and former student of Gödel) with the rare ability to project his dreams along Gödelian closed timelike curves, and notions of time and consciousness that suggest Gödel, Husserl, and even J. W. Dunne.

Unlike the earlier novels, *Weaver* is a single tale in a single setting: England between 1940 and 1943. As such, it achieves a coherence and narrative suspense that makes it qualitatively different from the earlier volumes. Instead of choosing the episodic saga as his form, Baxter echoes the classic British Invasion scenarios that became so popular in the decades following George Chesney's "The Battle of Dorking" in 1871. Baxter's jonbar point, or fulcrum for alternate time streams, is a failed Dunkirk evacuation (historically, a Panzer general was actually positioned to attack the trapped British force, but didn't), which leads to Churchill falling from power and the Nazis mounting a land invasion of southern England and establishing a protectorate called Albion. The Nazis hope to capture Ben Kamen—that student of Gödel's whom we met back in the prologue—and use his wild talent to alter history and establish the ten-thousand-year Reich mentioned in the ancient prophecies. But despite the revelation that some of the manipulations of the past originated from this scenario, it's never entirely clear whether those distortions actually take hold, or the extent to which we are now invited to read those historical novels as themselves alternate histories leading to this point. In the end, the "Time's Tapestry" series evokes the central questions of the best alternate history tales: Is time malleable? Are we living in the wrong history? Do our choices matter? Such questions are among the key reasons readers tend to regard the alternate history tale as a subset of SF—rather than as fantasy—and Baxter may well have gone further than any other novelist toward suggesting that historical fiction may itself be a subset or special case of the alternate history subgenre.

Science Fiction Thrillers

Another genre that science fiction writers have been attempting to colonize with some regularity is that of the suspense thriller. Here the dissolution of genre boundaries is more subtle, since the imaginative material and narrative conventions of science fiction may be retained, while the plot, structure, and tone are borrowed from a mode of paranoid pursuit melodrama pioneered in espionage novels from John Buchan to Robert Ludlum. Initially, those novelists who seemed most successful—at least commercially—in effecting this merger were novelists whose starting point was the thriller rather than the science fiction tale: Robin Cook, Michael Crichton, and Peter Benchley are among the most prominent examples, with Crichton having based nearly his entire career on science fiction conceits. Occasionally, professional science fiction writers have ventured with some success into this arena (Frank Robinson's *The Power*, 1956; D. F. Jones' *Colossus*, 1966), but for the most part the very intellectual challenges that traditionally define an effective technological science fiction story seem to mitigate against the largely anti-intellectual (or at least anti-scientist), technologically ambivalent tone of the paranoid thriller. This may be a rare case where the most visible barriers separating two related genres lie in ideologies of power rather than in narrative mechanisms. Nevertheless, science fiction writers fairly consistently try to bridge the gap, sometimes very successfully (as with Greg Bear's 1999 novel *Darwin's Radio*, which freely uses the multiple viewpoints and globe-hopping locations of thriller fiction, but offers a solidly imagined evolutionary speculation as its thematic center; or Ken McLeod's 2007 *The Execution Channel*, which treats themes of terrorism and environmental catastrophe with an unusual degree of political sophistication), more often with mixed results (such as Ben Bova's *Death Dream* [1994] or Wil McCarthy's *Murder in the Solid State* [1996], novels you have most likely never heard of for this very reason).[18]

One science fiction writer who consistently tried to expand into the thriller market is Gregory Benford, one of the premiere hard SF writers of the last three decades; his most famous novel, *Timescape* (1980), was praised for its mainstream virtues, particularly its depiction of academic scientists at work in the 1960s, as well as its ingenious plot involving cross-time communication. In 1985, Benford published *Artifact*, a near-future archeological thriller involving the discovery of an ancient Minoan artifact that seems to contain some sort of alien singularity that, if released, could have catastrophic effects. Despite the sophisticated physics that goes into the explanation of the artifact (some of which is relegated to an appendix at the back of the novel), this central science-fictional device is for the most part reduced to the role of a MacGuffin (to use Alfred Hitchcock's term for an object whose sole purpose is to motivate characters) in what is primarily a novel of international political intrigue and adventure. Later, recognizing that novels like this were on the far edge of the genre in which he already had built a substantial reputation, Benford adopted the pseudonym Sterling Blake for his thriller *Chiller* (1993), a Robin Cook–style suspense novel involving cryonics.

In 1997, Benford returned again to this field under his own name with *Cosm*, which—despite another ingenious device at its center, again drawn solidly from theoretical physics (a chrome-like sphere accidentally created in a uranium nuclei experiment turns out to be a window into a newly created microuniverse—the "Cosm" of the title)—was sufficiently driven by a simple chase-and-pursuit plot that it briefly attracted the attention of Hollywood. But the novel is the result of two genres virtually laid one on top of the other, with the Cosm itself serving, on the one hand, as an inventive and evocative *novum* in the most traditional science fiction sense, and on the other as a thriller-MacGuffin like the artifact in *Artifact*. When the heroine, a Black physicist named Alicia Butterworth, removes the object from the laboratory at Brookhaven where it was created, she finds herself in the midst of an adventure tale involving fundamentalists, federal marshals, bureaucrats, and academic politics, while the provocative notion of a mini-universe evolving at a rate millions of time faster than our own takes a back seat to the cat-and-mouse pursuit plot. As in *Artifact*, Benford offers an afterword arguing for the plausibility of the physics involved, but for the purposes of the thriller aspect of the novel, the Cosm is for the most part simply a very strange object that might explode, like a smuggled atom bomb or a vial of deadly viruses.

Benford's most successful foray in transforming science-fictional materials into the materials of the commercial thriller is the novel *Eater*, published in early 2000. *Eater* seems almost a deliberate exercise in genre dissolution. It begins as an astronomical puzzle, and in rapid succession turns into a first-contact tale, a world-threatening disaster epic, a tragic romance, a space adventure, and an ontological fable that returns to one of Benford's favorite science fiction themes: the relation of organic to artificial intelligences in the universe. Benjamin Knowlton is a distinguished astrophysicist at the Mauna Kea observatory. His wife, an ex-astronaut, is suffering from late-stage terminal cancer as the novel opens. When a young colleague presents Knowlton with evidence of what appears to be a highly anomalous astronomical artifact—a repeating gamma ray burster—he is initially skeptical, but hesitant to discourage the enthusiasm of a younger, more idealistic scientist. One of the most impressive aspects of these early chapters is the manner in which Benford convincingly describes the real-life problems of science and science management; the varying styles of intellectual problem solving and reacting to new phenomena are an important part of the characterization of his major figures, and coping with scientific and political bureaucracies becomes an important survival skill as the plot unfolds.

The young scientist's measurements hold up, however, and the mysterious object—which has many of the characteristics of a black hole—is not only real, but is headed toward Earth at a startling rate. The object, which comes to be known as "Eater of All Things" because of its tendency, like a black hole, to consume objects in its path, proves to be intelligent—apparently the remnant of an ancient civilization that, when faced with doom at the hands of the black hole, downloaded itself into the singularity's magnetic fields and has been cruising the universe ever since, collecting samples from various civilizations. Now it demands the uploaded minds of several hundred humans—whom it identifies by name—to add to the collection. To underline the seriousness of its demands, it burns a huge swath across eastern North America, including the Washington, D.C., area. The scientists—who by now must contend with paranoid government bureaucracies as well as the all-powerful and possibly deranged alien—face the Abraham-like dilemma of whether to offer up the sacrifices. As a kind of supreme sacrifice, the dying astronaut volunteers to have her consciousness uploaded into a space vehicle, in the hopes that she can at least do some damage to the seemingly invincible alien. As do all seemingly invincible aliens, these have an Achilles heel waiting to be discovered, and while Benford's version of it is more sophisticated and intelligent than most, the final chapters of the novel veer toward crowd-pleasing escapades and uncomfortable echoes of far less sophisticated works, including such pop films as *Independence Day*, *Contact*, and *Armageddon*.

Eater works well enough as a science fiction novel, in terms of its scientist characters, the depiction of alien intelligence, and the nature of the central problem and solution, that it might seem perverse to cite it in the context of novels that test the boundaries of genre, or that contribute to the dissolution of their source genre. But the solid science fiction narrative at its core is repeatedly diluted by echoes of other genres—not only the thriller, but the epic disaster novel (which Benford had visited before with his 1980 *Shiva Descending*, co-authored with William Rotsler), the academic novel, and the mainstream novel of science, which Benford had blended effectively with a science-fictional con-

ceit in his classic *Timescape*. Still, the novel must be counted as a more successful hybrid of science fiction and the thriller than some prominent examples of
the reverse—novels by thriller writers seeking to exploit science-fictional plots
—such as James Patterson's *Where the Wind Blows* (1998) or Michael Crichton's *Timeline* (1999), both of which cavalierly violate the terms of their science fiction rationales in order to expediently deliver the next chapter-ending
cliffhanger.

Science Fiction/Science Fantasy/Fantasy

Finally, there is the most obvious candidate of all for science fiction's imperialist
impulses, the sister genre of fantasy. As we have already seen, the most important of the fantasy pulp magazines, *Unknown*, was founded by John W. Campbell, Jr., largely as a venue for fantastic stories that did not meet his rather
narrow technological criteria for *Astounding Science Fiction*, even though many
of these stories were from regular *Astounding* contributors. But Campbell's
materialistic bias tended to influence these writers toward a more highly rational, less numinous brand of fantasy that already, in 1939, had much in
common with science fiction. *Unknown*'s authors included Henry Kuttner,
L. Sprague de Camp, Eric Frank Russell, L. Ron Hubbard, Jack Williamson,
Theodore Sturgeon, and even Robert A. Heinlein, and their characteristic approach to fantasy was to treat it as a kind of alternative science, with its own
rigorous but internally consistent rules and a minimum of mythological supernaturalism. On several occasions, a fantasy template would be introduced and
developed only to be resolved, in sometimes clunky endings, as the work of
aliens interfering in human affairs. This, at least, was the central conceit of Eric
Frank Russell's Fortean novel *Sinister Barrier*, which was the lead story in the
first issue of *Unknown* in March 1939 and which to some extent set the tone for
the skeptical approach to fantasy that would characterize much of the magazine's fiction.[19] "They" (1940), for example, one of Heinlein's three contributions to the magazine, presents a classically paranoid vision of a world the
protagonist believes to be constructed entirely for his own benefit, only to
reveal in the closing paragraphs that the Dr. Hayward to whom he has been
revealing his suspicions is in fact a strange creature called "The Glaroon"
who indeed is supervising every aspect of his life as though it were a scientific experiment or military observation. Heinlein stops short of explaining in

science-fictional terms who or what the Glaroon is and what his motives are, but only this withheld explanation would seem to qualify the tale as fantasy. (Later, of course, Philip K. Dick would virtually make a career out of paranoid visions of reality resolved into science-fictional scenarios, and later still, films such as *The Truman Show* would exploit this basic fantasy in pop-media terms.[20])

"Rationalized fantasy" of one sort or another has been a common enough device over the years to earn no less than three definitions in John Clute and John Grant's *The Encyclopedia of Fantasy* (1997): works in which such fantasy elements as magic are given quasi-scientific rules, *Unknown*-style; works in which the fantasy elements are explained away altogether, and works in which fantasy elements are transmuted into SF tropes—elves or witches turning out to be mutants with psychic powers, for example, or the dragons of Anne Mc-Caffrey's *Pern* novels revealed as the product of genetic engineering.[21] This sort of device has been commonly used to rationalize aspects of supernatural horror as well, with trumped-up biomedical explanations for vampirism so common as to have generated a small but persistent narrative tradition of their own, from Richard Matheson's *I Am Legend* (1954) to Tim Powers's *The Stress of Her Regard* (1989) and Dan Simmons's *Children of Night* (1992). Works in what appears to be a fantasy landscape but is in fact a science-fictional world are even more common, and this kind of hybridization—sometimes called "science fantasy," in one of that term's various incarnations—has provided the template for some of the most powerful ongoing narrative traditions in either field: the romantic epic set in such a distant world that connections to our own are nearly unrecognizable, such as Jack Vance's *The Dying Earth* (1950), and its most important heir, Gene Wolfe's four-volume *The Book of the New Sun* (1980–1983) and its related series *The Book of the Long Sun* (1993–1996) and *The Book of the Short Sun* (1999–2001).[22] All these examples are what Mark W. Tiedemann calls "seed stories," which eventually give rise to the more radical genre-mixing of writers such as Jonathan Lethem, Jonathan Carroll, and Michael Swanwick.

Such narratively complex genre mixing, in which the narrative is not necessarily resolved according to the protocols of either fantasy or science fiction, is somewhat less common than rationalized fantasy. Some earlier experiments in this area were little more than crude tricks of marketing, such as Piers Anthony's "Apprentice Adept" series of novels, which began with *Split Infinity* (1980) and generated a number of sequels. Anthony's gimmick involved a protagonist who moves between the science fiction world of Proton and the fantasy world of Phaze; both worlds are portrayed in terms of the most generic clichés, and the narrative simply shifts between worlds at convenient points, like a juggling act. A much more provocative novel published the same year as *Split Infinity* is the British novelist Ian Watson's *The Gardens of Delight*, which ingeniously provides a science fiction rationale for what appears to be a purely spiritual landscape in the tradition of David Lindsay, in this case a planet whose exotic landscape and inhabitants seems to be a living realization of Hierony-mous Bosch's famous apocalyptic painting *The Garden of Earthly Delights*. (It is also worth noting that 1980 saw the publication of *The Shadow of the Torturer*, the first volume of Gene Wolfe's *The Book of the New Sun*.)

A writer who has made something of a career out of conflating such genre protocols is Sheri S. Tepper, whose first published novels, the *True Game* series (1983–1984) followed the pattern of science fantasy by introducing fantasy tropes into what was essentially a science fiction environment. Her 1991 novel *Beauty* freely combines elements of fairy tale (the Sleeping Beauty tale), histori-cal fiction (the fourteenth-century setting of the novel's opening), science fic-tion (the presence of time-travelers), and genre fantasy; and in later works, she has played deliberately with genre expectations. *A Plague of Angels* (1993) is one of her more successful novels in this regard, aggressively challenging the com-monly held genre assumptions that one can't mix spaceships and robots with dragons and ogres or place high-tech cities in the middle of medieval fairy-tale landscapes. Like Gene Wolfe, Tepper uses SF concepts to generate what appears to be a fantasy environment, and then gradually leaks out the science-fictional underpinnings so that the novel appears to shift genre as we're reading it. Science fantasy of this type is so easy to do badly ("Good Heavens! The oracle is a *computer!*") that when it works it's especially impressive—a way of asserting, as does the most effective postgenre writing, that the author and not the genre is in control of the material. But *A Plague of Angels* plays with this issue of authorial control in ways unusual even for this unusual genre.

Early on, the novel calls attention to its own textuality as we learn that a young girl named Orphan lives in an "archetypal village" where everyone ful-fills a traditional fairy-tale role: hero, oracle, miser, and so on. What seems odd is that the characters *know* that it's an archetypal village, and refer to it as such in the text. So do other characters, such as a farm boy named Abasio, who sets out hobbit-like to have an adventure and ends up in the violent and seedy city of Fantis. Dominated by youth gangs and plagued by drug abuse and immune-deficiency diseases, Fantis quickly reveals that this world is neither as innocent nor as pastoral as it seems. By the time we learn that the "witch" Ellel is seeking to dominate the world with the aid of an army of androids and weapons that she hopes to retrieve from a long-abandoned space station, the reader confidently assumes that the setting is a disguised SF environment, the novel a variety of rationalized fantasy. But then Tepper introduces the talking animals. Much of the appeal of *A Plague of Angels* comes from learning how and why this world came to be; much also comes from watching Tepper adroitly fit new pieces into her puzzle as the narrative progresses. We watch Abasio and Orphan grow from childhood to adulthood as their destinies gradually intertwine; we learn that neither is quite who they seem to be; and of course we learn from crucially placed clues that the world isn't what it seems to be, either. This rich background gives rise to a plot that on its surface is the simplest of fairy tales: the wicked witch pursuing the innocent orphan for nefarious purposes, while the farmer's son helps her evade capture and gradually enlists the aid of whole armies of allies, each with different strengths. The concluding epic battle fits easily with the traditions of both heroic fantasy and heroic science fiction, and even then we are still learning new and significant revelations about the world and the place of humans in it.

The final author who I would like to consider in terms of the increasingly complex relationship between fantasy, science fiction, and horror is the relatively young Sean Stewart, whose first experiment with genre expectations was the 1993 novel *Nobody's Son*. Like Tepper's *A Plague of Angels,* this novel begins in what appears to be a highly conventionalized fantasy world in which the title character, a commoner named Shielder's Mark, successfully exorcises the haunted "Ghostwood," which had foiled his society's greatest heroes, and then returns to claim as his prize the hand of the king's daughter. But there he confronts a court ridden with political intrigue and clearly annoyed by this upstart interloper. He finds that his real quest has yet to begin—overcoming his own intimidation and lack of education, and winning the respect of the court, the tomboyish Princess Gail, and her elegant lady-in-waiting Lissa. When he is awarded a dukedom, he finds himself thoroughly inept at managing affairs, and increasingly dependent on the politically savvy Lissa. His new bride even refuses to sleep with him, because she wants to put off having children. For most of the novel, it would seem that the fantasy setting is little more than a convenient backdrop for a coming-of-age tale with vivid, likeable characters, and indeed these characters are the novel's major strength. But then the fantasy reasserts itself as it becomes apparent that his initial heroic act has had the unforeseen consequence of releasing magic back into the world. For the reader, it comes as something of a surprise that this apparently generic fantasy world had ever lacked magic; the novel—which at first had deliberately undercut the happy-ever-after endings of traditional fairy tales with problems drawn from the realistic novel of manners (political rivalries, spousal rejection, financial management)—now reasserts its fantasy content in terms that have given it far greater depth. The novel shifts its genre footings twice: once by revisioning the happy ending of fairy tales and quest fantasies, then by reintroducing magic.

The return of magic to the world is also a central element in Stewart's remarkable series of novels (not really a trilogy, in terms of plot) that started with *Resurrection Man* (1995) and continued with *The Night Watch* (1997) and *Galveston* (2000), all of which share the premise that magic began to reassert itself in the Western world (there are strong suggestions it never really left China) following World War II, when Golems began to appear in the Nazi death camps. By the beginning of the twenty-first century, minotaurs bred of collective fear roam city streets, psychically sensitive "angels" assist police investigations, ghosts and dead bodies materialize out of nowhere, and the management of human affairs is increasingly given over to "krewes" associated with various supernatural figures or resurrected gods. Fragments of recognizable but altered history survive, however: Although John Kennedy was assassinated, a psychic helped avert the murder of Robert Kennedy, who became president. But not everything is changed. Poverty and street gangs still haunt the cities, and in a cleverly written conversation in *Resurrection Man* that succinctly interrogates the whole notion of alternate worlds, several characters wonder if the film *Star Wars* could ever have been made without the return of magic.

This alternate-world setting seems to place these novels clearly in what had become one of the most popular SF traditions during the 1980s and 1990s, but the very opening scene of *Resurrection Man* seems taken straight from the pages of supernatural horror, as the protagonist prepares to perform an autopsy on what appears to be his own dead body, which somehow materialized on his bedroom dresser. But soon we learn that this protagonist, Dante, seems himself to be a figure of fantasy, possessing some of the powers of an angel; furthermore, he is assisted by his ghost-like foster-brother Jet and his sister Sarah, a stand-up comedian. Dante views the corpse as an omen of his own impending death, and as the action unfolds during the following week—presumably Dante's last—he and his siblings uncover a series of dark secrets about their Hungarian-American family, Jet's birth, and a daughter who Sarah miscarried years earlier. Meanwhile, Laura Chen, a Chinese-American architect with whom Dante is secretly in love, becomes involved with the family after she discovers a break-in at Dante's apartment back in the city. Nearly all these characters have problems that, like those that undercut the fairy-tale atmosphere of *Nobody's Son*, derive from the realistic novel of character, but nearly all of their problems come to find symbolic analogues in the re-emergent magic of Stewart's world. Stewart's carefully balanced yet poetic style (at its most haunting in a series of interpolated comments by Jet on family photos that he has taken) gives this unusual plot something of the flavor of a mainstream family saga, as well as of mystery, horror, and fantasy (a mix of genres that would also work successfully in Stewart's unrelated 1998 novel *Mockingbird*).

While *Resurrection Man* is set in the very near future of this world, *The Night Watch* moves the action up to the late twenty-first century, when the magic is beginning to fade again. The Edmonton of *The Night Watch* is a city that has survived by dividing itself into magical and nonmagical districts, whereas Vancouver has fallen entirely under the sway of a phantasmagorical Chinatown. Something of these same contrasts are at work in *Galveston*, a setting chosen in part perhaps because of its borderland nature, an island that partakes of both New Orleans/Gulf coast culture and mainland Texas. The novel takes place mostly in 2028, midway between the two earlier novels, and introduces yet another set of science-fictional generic protocols: that of the post-apocalyptic novel in which society is reduced to a more primitive level of survival. For Joshua Cane and his family, the "flood" of magic seems a disaster comparable to the legendary 1900 Galveston hurricane in terms of the damage it has done to the human community. On parts of the Texas mainland, bands of marauders have turned to cannibalism, while tinkerers and mechanics like Josh's friend Ham try with increasing desperation to keep the small supply of automobiles running on makeshift parts and scavenged gasoline. The return of magic has not done twenty-first-century Texas much good at all, in fact, and Stewart doesn't miss many opportunities to point out how a return to an animistic world has created immense suffering.

Josh's father has long since disappeared after losing his house and all his money in a poker game, and his mother dies of diabetes from lack of insulin. Like his mother, Joshua is a pharmacist—a holdover from the world of scientific rationality—who is rapidly being reduced to becoming a herbalist, since the few remaining stores of "pre-Deluge" medicine are dwindling, forcing them to derive crude medicines from local plants and herbs. Josh is forced to amputate a ten-year-old boy's leg without anesthetic, even though Josh knows a small amount of penicillin would have cured him. After saving the wealthy debutante Sloane Gardner from an attack, he learns that her mother is also dying, but Sloane's idea of helping her derives not from medicine, but from magic. The magic in Galveston is centered around a kind of addictive refuge from reality called Mardi Gras, a tacky amalgam of Las Vegas sideshows and New Orleans carnivals that functions much the way virtual reality does in cyberpunk fiction. Mardis Gras is dominated by an incarnation of the god Momus, the Greek god of mockery. When Sloane disappears, the corrupt local sheriff Denton and his sadistic deputy manage to frame Josh and his friend Ham, sending them into exile shortly before a massive hurricane threatens the entire Texas gulf coast. The hurricane, the novel's major setpiece, effectively shifts the narrative into a survival-quest tale, with Josh and Ham, having to survive not only the storm but also the depredations of the cannibal-infested countryside before returning to Galveston for a climactic showdown with Denton, presented as an odd amalgam of magical fantasy and courtroom drama.

For most of its length, *Galveston* develops its narrative along the lines of a classic postcatastrophe tale, only Stewart's catastrophe is not drawn from the repertoire of sf—nuclear war or universal plague or purple clouds—but from fantasy. Stewart's choice of magic may well represent a conscious effort on his part to sabotage genre expectations, and the novel does this rather consistently, even offering a major natural disaster—a catastrophic hurricane—which turns his post-disaster world into a *post*-postdisaster world. With its high melodrama —pursuits and captures, heinous villains and goonish assistants, unrequited love, ladies in peril, and a huge, likeable, lumbering sidekick—*Galveston* is clearly the work of a writer familiar with a variety of genres and genre tropes, and not afraid to mix them freely.

Genre Implosion

"Fantasy is evaporating." At the risk of unseemly self-quotation, this is a sentence I found myself writing a few years ago in a review of the annual anthology *The Year's Best Fantasy and Horror*, edited by Ellen Datlow and Terri Windling (the anthology series remains the most effective and efficient way of following the developments of short fiction in these fields, and the lengthy introductions and summaries make them an important resource for the researcher as well as the casual reader). I meant to suggest not that the genre was in a state of collapse, but quite the opposite: that it had grown so diverse and ubiquitous that it seemed a central part of the fabric of contemporary culture—infiltrating other genres, the literary mainstream, otherwise conventional movies and TV programs, commercial art and advertising, music, theater, design, even pop ontology, as people showing no other outward signs of religious practice proclaim belief in angels, while Goths, Wiccans, Druids, Vampires, and Elves have their own websites and, in some cases, their own nightclubs and conventions. Fantasy, in other words, was in the air, like a mist. I could have said much the same thing about science fiction, and to a more limited extent about horror (which, of the three major fantastic genres, seems still to be struggling for identity). The writers who contribute to the evaporation of genre, who destabilize it by undermining our expectations and appropriating materials at will, with fiction shaped by individual vision rather than traditions or formulas, are the same writers who continually revitalize genre: A healthy genre, a healthy literature, is one at risk, one whose boundaries grow uncertain and whose foundations get wobbly. The authors discussed here—Straub, Benford, Baxter, Anthony, Ryman—are only the tip of a very large and imposing iceberg, and several more and lengthier essays could be devoted to those writers who, in the last decade or so, have moved even further along the postgenre path than some of those discussed here—Jonathan Lethem, Jonathan Carroll, Paul Auster, Paul Di Filippo, Kelly Link, China Miéville, M. Rickert, Jeffrey Ford, and Elizabeth Hand, to name only a few.[23]

But there is another aspect to the destabilization of genre that is far less sanguine, and at which I have only hinted. While on one end of the spectrum are these writers who strive to free genre materials from genre constraints, and in the vast center are authors who work with apparent contentment within a genre, testing its possibilities without contesting its terms, at the other end are writers for whom genre seems to be its own reference point, if not very nearly the whole of the literary universe. For every Peter Straub or Stephen King, the horror genre is populated by dozens of writers of fatally limited ambition, who are content—even eager—to recycle familiar tropes and effects in increasingly crabbed and self-referential works that appear in tiny-circulation magazines or as evanescent paperbacks, their apparent goal being not to enter dialogue with earlier horror writers, but simply to echo them: a kind of literary karaoke. Much the same is true of many current fantasy trilogists and franchise authors, except that they are far more likely to enjoy substantial financial rewards.

Science fiction writers who periodically proclaim the impending death of that genre cite as major culprits the flood of novelizations and franchises based on properties such as *Star Trek, Star Wars,* or *The X-Files,* which, it is claimed, divert the skills of talented novelists from their own work and crowd more imaginatively challenging science fiction off the bookstore shelves.[24] Publishing executives, drawn increasingly from the financial and marketing ranks of parent conglomerates, look only at prior sales records and pre-sold formula markets, further driving out fictions at the edges.

But there is at most limited evidence that any genre has been halted in its creative tracks by commercial franchises and corporate bottom lines; one might even argue that, as we saw at the beginning of this essay, popular genres owe at least a portion of their origins and growth to just such marketing decisions. But it is demonstrable that certain kinds of books, such as short story collections and experimental fictions, increasingly have shifted toward smaller, independent publishers.[25] Of greater concern than simple commercialism is the increasing self-referentiality of many genre texts, a narrowing of horizons that eventually leads to an accelerating inward spiral, resulting in a kind of genre implosion or collapse—virtually the opposite of the volatility represented by the more innovative and adventurous writers that has been the primary focus of this essay. Something very close to this happened in the horror field in the early 1990s, with designated mass-market imprints folding under the weight of too many novels that looked far too much like each other, or like replications of a handful of source texts. Genre implosion does not necessarily lead to the disappearance of a given genre, or even to a weakening of its market viability, but it can lead to atrophy and to a limited, self-contained readership, as happened with the Western novel after a half-century of dominance, with the series romance after a decade in which it grew to account for startling percentages of total paperbacks sold, and with the classical English-village murder mystery, which essentially devolved into a kind of puzzle recreation for a limited circle of devotees.

The fantastic genres, by virtue of the kinds of instability that I have attempted to delineate here in preliminary form, would seem to be less vulnerable to such genre-wide implosions—perhaps better able to sustain the depredations of formula abuse and rampant commercialization, but hardly immune to the damage from these forces. One can readily visualize a scenario in which science fiction, fantasy, and horror continue to evolve into postgenre modes of narrative discourse while leaving behind pools of comparatively degraded self-referential formula fictions. Already, it has become problematical to discuss in any meaningful way a "genre" that includes both Straub's *The Throat* and teenage slasher movies, both the novels of Sheri Tepper and *Star Wars* novelizations, both Sean Stewart and Robert Jordan. In fact, the term "genre" itself has accrued almost too many meanings to be useful: In one sense, it simply refers to market categories; in another, it refers to a set of literary and narrative conventions; in yet another, it refers to a collection of texts with perceived commonalities of affect and world view. To some extent, these problems affect all genres: The work of John Le Carré (and before him of Graham Greene) has never quite nestled comfortably within the conventions of the espionage thriller, nor have those of P. D. James or Scott Turow fit easily into the mystery genre. In a few cases, such as that of Raymond Chandler and the hardboiled novel, the very works that helped to define the genre far surpassed what would eventually become the terms and conventions of that genre. But the fantastic genres in particular seem evolutionary by their very nature: Science fiction must accommodate the shifting and often counterintuitive visions of base reality that science itself reflects; horror must accommodate the constantly transforming sources of the anxiety that it seeks to exploit; fantasy must accommodate the shifting dreams of a world no longer governed by the conventionalized desires of pastoral idealism. In the end, science fiction, fantasy, and horror are the genres that at their best, and by the very terms of the imaginative processes involved, transcend or supersede the old notions of genre. They are narrative modes that already have leaked into the atmosphere, that have escaped their own worst debilitations, and that have therefore survived.

three

Tales of Stasis and Chaos

first should explain that my use of the term "chaos" here has little to do with the relationship between scientific chaos theory and literature that we have seen in literally dozens of papers over the past few decades, such as in the work of scholars like N. Katherine Hayles. Instead, I am using the term "chaos" in its related but more traditional and generic sense of disunity and disorganization —the sort of chaos we experience everyday as we confront such terrifyingly enigmatic and unpredictable systems as, for example, tax laws or airline pricing schemes. Specifically, my use of this term was suggested by Greg Bear's 1998 novel *Foundation and Chaos*, the second book in a multi-author trilogy derived from Isaac Asimov's famous "Foundation" stories of the 1940s (the first, by Gregory Benford, appeared in 1997 and the third, by David Brin, in 1999). Far too often, novels based on other novels—or on movies, TV programs, or computer games—become automatic-pilot exercises, what we might term "accessory fictions" meant to sustain and highlight some larger product of the culture industry, the literary equivalent of a soundtrack album. But Bear, Benford, and Brin were already among the field's most eminent writers in the 1990s (known to fans as "the killer Bs"), and their trilogy, for all its clearly market-driven origins, did make some interesting efforts to reconsider and update some of Asimov's most important themes—which, given the canonical status of the original, are also among the most important themes of popular science fiction. Central among these—and central to Asimov's legacy in particular—are the oppositions of order and chaos, mind and nature, civilization and barbarism.

Bear's novel raises a question that has long fascinated me about the "Foundation" stories, particularly in a passage in which he describes the values that seem implicit in Asimov's corporatized future, values that would seem almost antithetical to commonly held views of science fiction itself: "Where once the human race had laughed and reveled in the absurd, in the products of pure imagination, they now earnestly pursued stasis."[1] Asimov's original stories concern the efforts of a brilliant mathematician, Hari Seldon, to save an enormous galactic empire from an extended Dark Age through the fictional predictive science of "psychohistory." Seldon's plan, which at times sounds much like a grant proposal gone berserk, consists mostly of compiling a universal encyclopedia, setting up elite institutes, and prerecording bits of annoyingly prescient advice to be played during historical crises long after his death. Originally published in *Astounding Science Fiction* between 1942 and 1950, augmented and collected into a trilogy in the 1950s, and voted the best science fiction series of all time by members of the 1966 World Science Fiction Convention, these five novelettes and four novellas eventually became a platform from which Asimov launched a series of bestselling sequels and prequels in the years before his death in 1992. The Foundation series has even shown up in the news from time to time; it was reported to be among the favorite works of former U.S. Speaker of the House Newt Gingrich, and in the mid-1990s it was cited as a principal inspiration for the Japanese Aum Shinrikyo ("supreme truth") cult, famous for releasing deadly nerve gas into Japan's subways in 1995. According to journalists David Kaplan and Andrew Marshall, the cult viewed itself as the embodiment of Asimov's Foundation and its guru Shoko Asahara as Hari Seldon—a much more direct connection than the more widely reported but tenuous link between Robert Heinlein and the Manson cult.[2]

Clearly, *The Foundation Trilogy* is one of the most popular and enduring classics of science fiction, influencing at least a few of its readers in ways that Asimov never could have anticipated. But why is it so popular? It contains almost no science, little technology (Asimov's original stories didn't even have robots), virtually no action and adventure, and characters who probably would disappear entirely from memory had they been given names like "Ben" or "Tom" instead of "Hari Seldon" or "Hober Mallow." And the underlying social and historical ideas, a kind of unholy alliance of Edward Gibbon and Karl Marx, have driven a few academic critics almost to intemperance.[3] Most significantly, as Bear's quotation indicates, it depicts a society whose survival seems to depend on controlled stasis, in apparent contradiction of science fiction's long-cherished view of itself as the "literature of change" and its celebration of the "sense of wonder." So part of what I want to explore is the question of why such a work, conceived during the early days of World War II and still spawning sequels decades later, should remain so compelling to so many readers for so long. Part of the answer, I believe, is that Asimov's famous work codifies and mythologizes a crisis of cultural identity that had been emergent not only in science fiction, but in American culture at large, long before he wrote his first story.

Consider, for example, the following passage:

In these seven years man had translated himself into a new universe which had no common scale of measurement with the old. He had entered a supersensual world, in which he could measure nothing except by chance collisions of movements imperceptible to his senses, perhaps even imperceptible to his instruments, but perceptive to each other, and so to some known ray at the end of the scale. Langley seemed prepared for anything, even for an indeterminable number of universes interfused—physics stark mad in metaphysics.

Historians undertake to arrange sequences,—called stories, or histories—assuming in silence a relation of cause and effect. These assumptions, hidden in the depths of dusty libraries, have been astounding, but commonly unconscious and childlike; so much so, that if any captious critic were to drag them to light, historians would probably reply, with one voice, that they had never supposed themselves required to know what they were talking about.[4]

This rather remarkable passage—which, among other things, seems eerily to anticipate some elements of quantum theory—comes not from the work of Asimov or any other science fiction writer, or even from a scientist. Instead, it comes from that most patrician of American autobiographies, *The Education of Henry Adams*, and it describes the differences the author perceived between the Chicago Columbian Exposition of 1893 and the Paris Exhibition of 1900. The Langley referred to in the passage is Smithsonian astronomer Samuel Pierpont Langley, who only four years earlier had built the first mechanically propelled flying machine, a steam-driven model airplane. In "The Dynamo and the Virgin," the book's most famous chapter, Adams sees the twentieth century— symbolized for him by the great dynamos on display at the Paris exhibition—as a kind of descent into multiplicity, a radical departure from the unity and continuity of the middle ages, which he had described in his earlier *Mont St.-Michel and Chartres* and which was symbolized by the Virgin, the cross, or the cathedral. By modern historical standards, Adams' view of the medieval world may seem somewhat idealized and schematic, but his sense of one of the fundamental tensions of modern thought seems prescient. Static versus dynamic models have become one of the central patterns of organizing theoretical debate in fields ranging from cosmology to neuroscience to history—and like many such broad-based cultural patterns, these models are reflected in popular literature as well.

In the study of the fantastic genres, it has already become something of a critical commonplace, however oversimplified, that stasis is the realm of fantasy and dynamism of science fiction: The unchanging feudal world is seen as the essential model for popular fantasy narratives in the mode of J. R. R. Tolkien or Stephen R. Donaldson, while dynamic industrialism becomes the model for classic American science fiction (those giant dynamos of Adams showed up repeatedly in early pulp SF illustrations).[5] More recently, we can see the global informational sphere as a template for postmodern forms of fiction and art, including cyberpunk and all its postcyberpunk redactions and spin-offs, including Vingean singularity fiction (which has nearly become a subgenre unto itself). As is always the case with common knowledge, such classifications are both too convenient and fatally reductive; after all, plenty of fantasy is modeled on shifting, ever-changing worlds (see David Lindsay's 1920 *A Voyage to Arcturus*, for example) and plenty of science fiction narratives celebrate a restoration of the status quo (such as the thrillers of Michael Crichton, which are essentially fictions of containment: a potentially massive science-fictional threat is introduced only to be heroically suppressed by the end of the novel, returning the world to "normal." Change is contained rather than celebrated). But the dichotomy of stasis and chaos seems significant in both fields, and indeed finds some form of expression in nearly all the popular genres. Furthermore, it may even provide clues as to how these genres organize themselves over time.

The term "supergenre" has been used by R. D. Mullen, Eric S. Rabkin, and others to describe clusters of genres with some common elements and some common readership, but that are formally quite distinct from one another.[6] The fantastic supergenre—as a trip to any large chain bookstore will quickly reveal—formally consists of the major genres of science fiction, fantasy, horror, and *Star Wars*. Another supergenre is the romance, which encompasses historical bodice-rippers, classic gothics, Danielle Steele soap operas, some chick-lit, and, increasingly, tales of heartstruck vampires or "paranormal romances," which in recent years have shown perhaps the healthiest market growth of any segment of fantastic literature, and which got their own "year's best" anthology in 2007. Yet another is espionage, which includes the traditional spy novel, the more chaos-driven international thriller, and the systems-obsessed techno-thriller—fiction that combines martial-arts lessons with tips on running nuclear submarines. And still another is what John Cawelti called the "social melodrama," a broad category of bestsellers that includes institutional novels (airports, hospitals, universities), geographical/historical sagas (almost anything by James Michener or Edward Rutherfurd), and some period melodramas (Ken Follett, Larry McMurtry). Some supergenres are almost moribund; consider frontier and wilderness fiction, which includes not only the Western, but the manly survival novel, the imperialist adventure tale, and (possibly a subdivision of the latter) the lost-civilizations story. To the extent that Westerns survive at all today as a vital genre, they have largely been subsumed into literary or mainstream fiction in the work of McMurtry, Cormac McCarthy, and a few others. (Why some genres bite the dust would be an interesting topic for another essay; my own suspicion is that such genres simply come to depend too heavily on a particular historical dynamic—say, the settling of the American West or the exploration of remote corners of the globe—which eventually plays itself out in the popular mind, or is supplanted by other fascinations.) Significant cross-breeding also takes place among genres, although most such works can be defined readily in terms of a "home" genre that determines marketing and readership. Hence, romance novels that involve elements of mystery, science fiction, or historical fiction remain almost unknown to readers of these other genres, and technothrillers that incorporate science fiction elements are seldom regarded by their core audience as having anything to do with science fiction.

If we look at virtually any of these supergenres, we find that works within them depict fictive worlds that tend to range along a spectrum between stability and chaos, and perhaps even that as a genre matures, its emerging idioms tend more toward worlds of chaos. The world of cyberpunk is far less orderly than that of classic Campbellian science fiction, which in turn is more dynamic and urbanized than that of the scientific romances of Wells and his contemporaries. Or take an example not part of the fantastic at all, the supergenre of crime fiction. In its classical form—the detective stories of Doyle, Christie, or Rinehart—we find what are basically tales of stasis disrupted by anomaly; the solution of a crime or series of crimes returns an essentially unspoiled world, say, the English village, to its prelapsarian condition. Crimes tend to occur one or two at a time, and criminal behavior is not a condition of life, but an invasion of it that must be explained. And in nearly all cases, the anomaly is resolved through a rigorous process of reason and observation; intellectual skill—from M. Dupin's "ratiocination" to Poirot's "little gray cells"—proves far more powerful than thuggish violence in this world, and the fictive world is constructed to be amenable to rational solutions. Many such novels are still being written today, of course—sometimes called "cozies" by enthusiasts—but now they must compete for shelf space with a wide variety of newer subtypes. My point is not that these new subtypes necessarily *replace* the older ones, but that they certainly do complicate them, and to some extent redefine readership and reader expectations: Genres, it seems, often evolve not through metamorphosis, but by accretion. In the later police procedurals of Georges Simenon, Ed McBain, Nicolas Freeling, and others, the world of the narrative is a little less unspoiled and a lot more dynamic. The detective is now a paid agent of society rather than an eccentric aristocrat, and by focusing on the institution of the police, these novels recognize that crime and aberrant behavior are conditions of society, rather than anomalies. Chaos is on the horizon, but at least the crimes still get solved.

America's next great contribution to the supergenre of crime was the hardboiled detective tradition of Dashiell Hammett, Raymond Chandler, or, later, Robert Parker or Robert Crais.[7] By now the world is nearly unsalvageable, a cauldron of corruption held at bay only by the individual integrity of Marlowe, Spade, Spenser, or Cole—the hero who, in Chandler's famous words, is "the best man in his world and a good enough man for any world."[8] The classic anecdote illustrating the aesthetic of chaos in this field—and the acceptance of such an aesthetic by the audience—is the familiar tale of the screenwriters for Raymond Chandler's *The Big Sleep*—William Faulkner and Leigh Brackett—growing so confused over who was supposed to have committed one of the murders in the story that they consulted Chandler himself—who also couldn't figure it out. But when the film was finally released with the murder still unexplained, no one complained.[9] The texture of this noir world was more important, it seemed, than the neat solution of its crimes. Chaos reigns, and what is more important, no one seems to mind very much.

But we aren't done yet. Next consider what Elmore Leonard, referring to his own work, simply calls the "crime novel"—a genre somewhere beyond hardboiled—tales of lowlife treachery in which the moral chaos of the world is unmitigated even by an honest private eye hero, and protagonists are likely to include shabby con men and venal grifters. Leonard is the current master of the form, but other examples might include Jim Thompson, Charles Willeford, George V. Higgins, more recently Dennis Lehane, George Pelecanos, Carl Hiaasen, and—to draw at least one example from film—Quentin Tarantino (who not surprisingly filmed a Leonard novel in 1997, as *Jackie Brown*). To visualize how broad the moral spectrum is in this one supergenre alone, consider the distance that we have covered from Agatha Christie to Elmore Leonard or Quentin Tarantino. Imagine Hercule Poirot cornering Samuel L. Jackson in Tarantino's *Pulp Fiction*. Or for that matter—to get back to the supergenre of the fantastic—try to conceive of an emblematic figure who would be equally at home in the various modes of fantasy, science fiction, horror, and cyberpunk. Such a fire-breathing, web-surfing, vampire hobbit from space might well be out there, but I haven't met her yet. A mature, evolved supergenre is much like a Burgess Shale of pop culture, encompassing a veritable explosion of forms and icons without entirely abandoning its fundamental structures.

The fantastic genres, of course, did not evolve with quite the linearity of crime fiction, but we can see something of this movement from stasis to chaos within individual fantastic genres, and even within particular themes. The social stability of the classical detective novel, for example, is roughly reflected in nineteenth-century vampire fiction, with its focus on anomalous Byronic figures such as Lord Ruthven or Dracula. In many ways, the version of England in Stoker's *Dracula* was even more stable than that of Dickens or Doyle—at least until those damned Eastern Europeans started coming over on the boat. (It may be no coincidence that *Dracula* gained popularity in 1897, at the height of the British craze for paranoid invasion literature that had begun in 1871 with George Chesney's *The Battle of Dorking*.) At least the threat of pollution was centered in a single figure, whose vanquishing could restore civilized order. But by the time of Richard Matheson's *I Am Legend* in 1954, the situation was exactly reversed, with a world of vampires trying to vanquish the lone surviving human—a situation also echoed in the ongoing spate of zombie movies such as George Romero's *Night of the Living Dead* series (1968–2008) or Danny Boyle's *28 Days Later* (2002) and its sequel *28 Weeks Later* (2007), not to mention the hugely successful 2007 film of the Matheson novel. In between, partway along the spectrum between the threat of the lone vampire and the vampire-dominated world, we have numerous works like Stephen King's *'Salem's Lot* (1975) that depict isolated communities or colonies of vampires, contained if not entirely vanquished, or novels like Octavia Butler's *Fledgling* (2005), in which they have co-existed for centuries as a hidden society within the larger culture. In fact, in a good deal of recent vampire fiction, cleansing the world of vampires would mean wiping out the Medicis, the entire British royal family, and most of the major figures of English romanticism—not to mention your neighbors down the hall and almost anyone with a sufficiently strange hairdo.

Like crime, vampirism becomes a condition of society, a subset of the population, even a hidden force in history.

And history, after all, is the shadow that hangs over this entire discussion of stasis and chaos. It may be no coincidence that as these genres reveal ever more dynamic and chaotic worlds, they also begin increasingly to explore historical themes and processes. Indeed, in the United States at least, popular genres have colonized historical fiction to such an extent that they threaten to supplant it entirely, at least in the genre marketplace. For decades, a major subtype of the romance novel was called the Regency romance (a term already so deracinated by the 1980s that Gore Vidal, in his novel *Duluth*, could describe a dimwitted romance writer who churned out mindless formula under the impression that she was writing "Hyatt Regency romances"). Historical detective stories, once the province of John Dickson Carr, Robert van Gulik, and a handful of others, have for some time been among the largest-selling and most rapidly growing subsets of the detective genre. Vampire fiction, as we have already noted, has long since appropriated settings from ancient Rome and Egypt to Renaissance Italy to Victorian England, along the way generating bestsellers from Anne Rice's famous series to Elizabeth Kostova's *The Historian* (2005).

In recent years, science fiction and fantasy seem to have been particularly imperialistic in colonizing what was once the realm of the historical novelist, in theme as well as in setting. Novelists such as Jack Dann, with *The Memory Cathedral* (1995) and *The Silent* (1998), or Patricia Anthony with *Flanders* (1998) offer minimal fantastic interpolation into their historical settings, despite the fact that their primary audience is likely to remain the science fiction readers who gave them their initial reputations.[10] In fact, I would argue that science fiction's near-obsession with history and historical forces may be a direct reflection of its attempts to develop strategies to address this tension between stasis and chaos. One of science fiction's core narratives is the tale of the static society destabilized; examples range from Wells's *The War of the Worlds* (1898) to Forster's "The Machine Stops" (1909), any number of revolt-in-dystopia tales, Heinlein's "Universe" (1941), Clarke's *The City and the Stars* (1956), and Aldiss's *The Malacia Tapestry* (1976; Aldiss's novel may seem more fantasy than science fiction, but it certainly is one of the most thoughtful speculations on what might happen if history just freezes up, and Aldiss himself was one of the first science fiction writers to explore the notion of static time as developed in the French *nouvelle roman* in the 1960s; see his 1968 novel *Report on Probability A*). In the destabilization tale, a society in stasis (Wells's middle-class Victorian England, Forster's vast underground complex, Clarke's automated city of Diaspar) is threatened by a destabilizing force (a Martian invasion, mechanical failure, a nonconforming rebel), with the usual effect that lessons are learned, and the narrative world is opened up to new possibilities. A major recent example of a fiction depicting such a static world disrupted by anomaly is Neal Stephenson's *Anathem* (2008), in which a monastic society of scientists and philosophers maintains itself virtually unchanged and isolated from the secular world for thousands of years, until the appearance of an alien spacecraft requires that some "avouts" leave the cloister to work with outsiders to defend the planet.

And of course this brings us back to that never-ending story with which we began: Asimov's *Foundation* series, with its blatant fantasy of history as little more than a set of statistical problems. Despite his reputation, Asimov was never one of science fiction's great inventors, but he was its single greatest apostle of management, and his dream of managing history, of reducing millennia of chaos to a few centuries through the science of statistics and a handful of strategically placed public service announcements, has proved to be one of the most seductive the genre has ever devised. If Henry Adams' historians "never supposed themselves required to know what they were talking about," Asimov's psychohistorians see themselves as directly answerable for their civilization's survival. Instead of a storyteller, the historian becomes an engineer, and a famously inexact discipline is brought happily into the fold of the laboratory sciences. This is even clearer in the work of A. E. van Vogt, whose own version of psychohistory in the stories that make up *The Voyage of the Space Beagle* (1950) is called Nexialism, and enables his hero to vanquish a succession of alien monsters—including the one that eventually metamorphosed into the film *Alien*—simply by applying his knowledge of Spenglerian historical cycles to the monster's behavior. (One of van Vogt's great inadvertent services to science fiction was his astonishing ability to rip away the cool surfaces of favorite genre ideas and reveal their underlying goofiness.) By the time Asimov and van Vogt were writing, it must have been clear to all but the most isolationist science fiction readers that the twentieth century, at least as envisioned by the utopianists of forty years earlier or Hugo Gernsback's happy engineers of only fifteen years earlier, simply wasn't working out—and that the culprit, the destroyer of these great mechanical dreams, was history.

So this soon became one of science fiction's grand, over-arching themes: the subjugation of chaos through the rationalization of history, of which Asimov's managerial model was only the most famous expression. Stasis, as a rule, is not a very attractive option for science-fictional worlds; it works against the central dynamic of the genre, which traditionally boasts of itself as the literature of change and dynamism. But chaos isn't a very attractive option either, for a genre that often claims to champion order and rationality. It becomes incumbent, then, for writers to find ways to mediate between unity and multiplicity, order and randomness, stasis and chaos. Various forms of social engineering, from Asimov's psychohistorians to near-utopian fictions by Kim Stanley Robinson and Greg Bear, to more ambiguous schemes for human transformation in novels like Joe Haldeman's *Forever Peace* (1997)—in which a technology initially designed as weaponry may hold the promise of eliminating war by increasing the capacity for empathy—may all be seen as attempts to mitigate chaos without returning to a totalizing world of imposed stasis.

The time-travel tale has also long been concerned with the reparability of history, from Mark Twain's *A Connecticut Yankee in King Arthur's Court* (1889) to L. Sprague de Camp's *Lest Darkness Fall* (1941), in which a time traveler undertakes to avert the Dark Ages, to any number of later examples. In Lisa Mason's *Summer of Love* (1994), the Haight-Ashbury of 1967 becomes a locus of future history. Connie Willis's deceptively antic *To Say Nothing of the Dog* (1998) features a missing cat threatening the historical timestream. The Second World War has practically become a sub-subgenre in this regard; two of many examples are J. R. Dunn's *Days of Cain* (1997), in which a future time traveler tries to liberate Auschwitz, and Christopher Priest's *The Separation* (2002)—one of the masterpieces of this theme—which depicts contrasting timelines, in one of which the war ended in May 1941. The moral of many time-travel tales, of course, is that history can't be repaired by visiting the past; it can only be damaged; witness Bradbury's famous proto-chaos-theory butterfly in "A Sound of Thunder" (1954), which gets squashed by a time traveler from the future to disastrous effect. But if we can't change the direction of the train we're on, we can wonder what it might have been like to change trains some time back; hence we get a growing array of "alternate history" tales, including retro-corrective fantasies in which things turn out more like they should have: NASA successfully lands a crew on Mars by 1989 (Stephen Baxter's *Voyage* [1997]), George H. W. Bush and Fidel Castro both end up as professional ballplayers in the 1959 World Series (John Kessel's "The Franchise" [1993]), or Columbus sails off the edge of the world (Philip José Farmer's "Sail On! Sail On!" [1952], which moves beyond alternate history to suggest an entire alternate cosmology). It's interesting to note that this fictive conceit, long regarded as little more than a parlor game by serious historians, is now a budding academic subspecialty called "counterfactual history," with its first conference at Ohio State in November 1997 and the entire tenth anniversary issue of the *Quarterly Journal of Military History* (1998) devoted to it.[11] Even bestselling literary novelists have gotten into the act, including Philip Roth with *The Plot Against America* (2004), depicting an antisemitic Lindbergh presidency and its effects on a family otherwise clearly modeled on Roth's own. (The fact that Roth and many of his reviewers claimed no knowledge of this tradition of alternate history may give some indication of how isolated much genre literature had become from what its advocates call the "mainstream".)

Still another variation is the "secret history," a subgenre whose rules dictate that the narrative violate no known historical facts, but that can do pretty much whatever it wants to in the interstices between those facts, proposing, in effect, an alternate story in place of the one we thought we knew. This gives us, for example, Dann's *The Memory Cathedral*, an account of the famous lost year in Leonardo da Vinci's life, and many of the works of Tim Powers, who has slyly inserted vampire-like lamia into the lives of Keats and Shelley and the cosmic struggles of the Fisher King into the sixteenth-century Siege of Vienna or the Las Vegas of gangster Bugsy Siegel.[12] On a somewhat cruder level, secret history—the idea that creepy forces are at work that we're never told about—gives us the films of Oliver Stone (*JFK, Nixon*), the television programs of Chris Carter (*The X-Files, Millennium*), and the entire supermarket tabloid newspaper industry, which offers us a world teeming with hidden tales, combining primitive science fiction conceits with Alice in Wonderland logic. (My favorite example, for which I am unfortunately dependent on memory, comes from a tabloid newspaper that some years ago ran a badly dummied photo that was pretty clearly a plastic model B-29 resting on a NASA photo of a moon crater, with the headline "World War II Bomber Found on Moon." A few weeks later, the same paper ran the same moon-crater photo, but without the model plane. The headline now was "World War II Bomber Found on Moon is Missing!" Panic favors the prepared mind.)

Secret history—the term used in *The Encyclopedia of Fantasy* is "fantasy of history"—cuts laterally across several genres, including espionage fiction, murder mysteries, and elements in certain works by mainstream novelists such as E. L. Doctorow, Robert Coover, or Edward Whittemore. Because it so easily slides into the realm of speculative nonfiction, secret history can be far more insidious than alternate history, and in its broadest definition includes such documents as the *Protocols of the Elders of Zion*, arguably the most destructive work of speculative fiction ever concocted, and various other false validations of paranoia and bigotry—not to mention a good many urban legends, such as the belief that various corporations (Procter and Gamble being the most famous victim, because of their moon-and-stars logo) are secretly controlled by satanists. But even here, we can see the text as mitigation of chaos: History may be controlled by the Jews, or by shadowy government conspiracies, or by mythical demi-gods hiding out in casinos, or even by the Masons, but at least it's controlled. And that, in turn, means that it's controllable.

Finally, science fiction offers two more options for dealing with the paradoxes of historical process: One is simply to escape history altogether, the other is to bomb it back to the stone age. Recent years have seen an increasing number of novels—and even an *X-Files* episode (by Tom Maddox and William Gibson)—in which characters upload their entire personalities into computer systems, leaving behind frail bodies and a deteriorating world in a kind of posthuman singularity. One of the most rigorous and impressive of these novels is Greg Egan's *Diaspora* (1997), which suggests that the external physical universe, with its plodding flow of time, may simply become unnecessary, while Dennis Danvers's *Circuits of Heaven* (1997) imagines that most people will cheerfully give up their bodies to live in a virtual replica of the real world, but with disease and death edited out.[13] Except for the technology, I'm not sure that such works are a significant step ahead of more mystical earlier treatments of escape from history, such as Arthur C. Clarke's *Childhood's End* (1953), in which humanity joins the Overmind, or Theodore Sturgeon's *More than Human* (1953), in which a group of misfits find a psychic home among other great minds of the past. Each, in its own way, anticipates the "singularity" fiction that became so popular in the early 2000s. In all these cases, the problem of confronting chaos and disintegration is neatly sidestepped by means of a kind of posthistorical nirvana.

"Posthistorical" is a term that has been applied, I think originally by Gene Wolfe, to one of the field's oldest and most time-honored means of dealing with the problem of history—namely, simply erasing the blackboard and starting over, whether it be through nuclear bombs, plagues, disasters, or the sheer weight of time.[14] This is the central conceit of scores of postcatastrophe tales, from Mary Shelley's *The Last Man* (1826) to George R. Stewart's *Earth Abides*

(1949), Walter M. Miller's *A Canticle for Leibowitz* (1959), and Russell Hoban's *Riddley Walker* (1980), and it figures in a number of far-future romances such as Jack Vance's *The Dying Earth* (1950) and Gene Wolfe's *The Book of the New Sun* (1980–1983). Artifacts and fragments of the old world may survive, but the inscribed narrative of which these fragments were a part is long forgotten, and they become incorporated in a new narrative, discontinuous with the old. In a perverse way, these tales of global disaster and distant medieval futures may be among science fiction's most reassuring texts, since they subvert the anxiety that Henry Adams felt by reversing the polarities of stasis and chaos in the master narrative: They begin with fragmented worlds and move toward some kind of order. In this sense, they become the genre's creation myths, reflecting Mircea Eliade's observation that we return to such myths because "life cannot be *repaired*, it can only be *re-created* by a return to sources."[15] Or, in the words of J. G. Ballard, the task of the apocalyptic novelist is "to confront the terrifying void of a patently meaningless universe by challenging it at its own game, to remake zero by provoking it in every conceivable way."[16]

Destroying the world, or the universe, may well be the endgame of science fiction's long, troubled affair with time and history, but what I have covered here hardly exhausts the genre's resources in this area, let alone the resources of allied fantastic genres. There are, for example, the cosmic epics of Olaf Stapledon, which present themselves as histories and which are echoed in contemporary writers as diverse as Stephen Baxter and Doris Lessing. There is the tradition of utopian and dystopian fiction, in which stasis begins as an ideal (with the classical utopianists) and ends as a nightmare (with Zamiatin and Orwell). Although utopian fiction for much of its history sought to be an active agent of change, the twentieth century has seen it largely supplanted by its sister genre of dystopian fiction, which tends to portray societies in which change is nearly impossible to achieve. Finally, there are the more recent, less easily classifiable postmodern fictions of Jonathan Lethem, Stepan Chapman, and others, that combine elements of a variety of genres to create surrealistic, Krazy Kat–like settings that have almost nothing in common, save for their annihilation of historical time. Such works often echo the long tradition of atemporal existentialist and absurdist mainstream fiction and drama, from Beckett and Sartre to Stoppard and Hiruko Marukami, in which stasis becomes a terrifying metaphor for historical and personal impotence.

Late in his autobiography, Henry Adams essentially gave up in his efforts to understand the multiplicity of the twentieth century through the lens of his classical education. "In the last synthesis," he declared, "order and anarchy were one, but . . . the unity was chaos," and the new generation of Americans born into what he now called a "multiverse" would need to think in terms of contradictions and indeterminacy.[17] (Although Adams probably borrowed the term "multiverse" from William James, it's interesting to note that decades later this became popular shorthand for describing a version of the many-worlds interpretation of quantum mechanics, and was particularly popularized by Michael Moorcock.) When Adams died in 1918, he still clung to his deterministic fear that history was forever beyond the influence of deliberate human action, and had begun to spin wildly out of control. His last major essay, "Letter to American Teachers of History," was the centerpiece of a book edited by his younger brother Brooks entitled *The Degradation of the Democratic Dogma* and published in 1919. More even than his brother, Brooks felt that the world, corrupted by capitalism and religion, was on the brink of an extended dark age of decay and destruction, and that the work of scholars and historians might at best mitigate the catastrophe, perhaps cut short the period of chaos. The following year, Isaac Asimov was born.

four

The Encounter with Fantasy

I f there is one thing the still-narrow body of literary scholarship devoted to fantasy has made clear, it is that whatever we are to call "fantasy" must first and foremost deal with the impossible. In a 1978 survey of several scholarly works on the subject, S. C. Fredericks noted that "there is general agreement among the critics that Fantasy constitutes what Irwin calls 'the literature of the impossible' . . ." and that fantasy writers "take as *their point of departure* the deliberate violation of norms and facts we regard as essential to our conventional conception of 'reality,' in order to create an imaginary counter-structure or counter-norm."[1] W. R. Irwin, to whom Fredericks refers, goes so far as to characterize fantasy as "antireal" and defines it as "a story based on and controlled by an overt violation of what is generally accepted as possibility; it is the narrative result of transforming the condition contrary to fact into 'fact' itself."[2] Eric S. Rabkin, in *The Fantastic in Literature,* makes "a direct reversal of ground rules" a condition of the fantastic and says of fantasy that "its polar opposite is Reality."[3] C. N. Manlove agrees that "a substantial and irreducible element of supernatural or impossible worlds, beings, or objects" is needed for fantasy, explaining that supernatural or impossible means "of another order of reality from that in which we exist and form our notions of possibility."[4] And in explaining his principle of inclusion for his bibliography *The Literature of Fantasy,* Roger C. Schlobin identifies the literature of fantasy as "that corpus in which the impossible is primary in its quantity or centrality."[5]

The criterion of the impossible, then, seems firmly in place in the academic study of fantasy literature; indeed, it may be the first principle generally agreed upon for the study of fantasy. The fantasy authors themselves seem to agree. Ray Bradbury, whose reputation as a science fiction writer often seems to overshadow his own avowed first love for fantasy, wrote that "each fantasy assaults and breaks a particular law" and "attempts to disrupt the physical world in order to bring change to the heart and mind."[6] C. S. Lewis, a literary scholar as well as a fantasist, defined literary fantasy (as opposed to psychological fantasy) as "any narrative that deals with impossibles and preternaturals."[7] And as long ago as 1890, two of the great Victorian masters of the fantastic tale, H. Rider Haggard and Andrew Lang, prefaced their ambitious fantasy sequel to the *Odyssey, The World's Desire*, with a poem that included the following lines:

Come with us, ye whose hearts are set
On this, the Present to forget;
Come read the things whereof ye know
They were not, and could not be so.[8]

Almost word for word, the modern author Samuel R. Delany echoes Haggard and Lang when he defines the "level of subjunctivity" of fantasy as "*could not have happened*."[9]

The notion of the impossible itself raises a number of intriguing questions, not all of which can be addressed adequately by the resources of literary scholarship. What, for example, are the psychological and cultural limits of what we regard as possible? How do we recognize the impossible when we encounter it in a work of art, and how do we decide that a particular impossible event or being signals an individual aesthetic structure rather than a private psychosis or a culturally accepted myth? What of a passage such as the following?

The Kingdom of Yr had a kind of neutral place which was called the Fourth Level. It was achieved only by accident and could not be reached by formula or an act of will. At the Fourth Level there was no emotion to endure, no past or future to grind against. There was no memory or possession of any self, nothing except dead facts which came unbidden when she needed them and which had no feeling attached to them.[10]

The passage is from Joanne Greenberg's fictionalized account of her own schizophrenia, *I Never Promised You a Rose Garden*, and while the passage clearly describes an "impossible" place and an at least unlikely state of being, the context in which it appears in the novel makes it clear that the novel itself is not a work of fantasy. Had Greenberg presented such schizophrenic fantasies unadorned by the essentially realistic account of hospitalization and psychotherapy that surrounds them, would she have written a fantasy? The obvious answer would seem to be no. Impossibility alone is not enough. As Fredericks observes, literary fantasy must serve a "reality-oriented function" and be deliberate and purposeful in the ways in which it diverges from cognitive reality.[11]

But the idea of a social or rhetorical motive for fantastic events also proves to be inadequate; otherwise, we would have to admit all sorts of myth systems and metaphorical conceits into the realm of fantasy. We cannot comfortably dismiss a Blackfoot creation myth as fantasy simply because its events and beings are "impossible" according to Western cosmology, nor can we protest the "impossibilities" of Dante's *Divine Comedy*. Such works are certainly "reality-oriented," intended at some level to describe and explain the workings of the world. These are the great public fantasies of other times and cultures, and what is "impossible" in them now was once accepted as possible, although they stand at the opposite end of the scale from the visions of an isolated psychotic. The notion of impossibility in fantasy, then, must lie somewhere toward the middle of this scale; it must be more public than the schizophrenic's hallucination, yet less universal than myth and religion. In fact, contemporary fantasy must engage in an implied compact between author and reader—an agreement that whatever impossibilities we encounter will be made significant to us, but will retain enough of their idiosyncratic nature that we still recognize them to be impossible.

Even as we delimit the nature of the impossible in fantasy, however, new complications arise. We might dismiss dream literature and surrealism—works such as Robert Coates' *The Eater of Darkness* (1926) or Raymond Roussel's *Impressions d'Afrique* (1910)—as being too void of meaningful referents, too much like the heavily unconscious fantasies of the schizophrenic for the middle ground we seek. But what are we to do with works such as Mervyn Peake's Gormenghast trilogy (1946–1959) or Peter Dickinson's *The Blue Hawk* (1976)— works that, except for their bizarre and unfamiliar settings and unusual characters, contain little or nothing that contravenes what we know to be possible? In the Gormenghast trilogy, notes Manlove, "Nothing 'supernatural' or magical by our standards is in fact present."[12] Manlove argues that the quality of "otherness" in such a work, the construction of its narrative without any direct referent to the known world, is sufficient that we may call it impossible; and the argument is persuasive, since these works certainly *feel* like fantasies and one comes away from them with the strong impression that one has been traveling in some impossible realm. But already one important factor in our criterion of impossibility shows signs of weakness, and that factor is what we might term the purely cognitive element. Cognition, at least as Darko Suvin uses the term in his characterization of science fiction, may be sufficient to enable us to recognize the limits of what is possible in a work of science fiction or historical fiction, but it often fails in aiding us to recognize the impossible that is fantasy.[13]

If the delineation of the cognitive element in science fiction has been one of the strengths of criticism in that field, it is a fallacy to assume that fantasy employs the same cognitive principle in reverse—that is, if science fiction deals with what we recognize as empirically possible, then fantasy must be what we recognize as empirically impossible. Such an approach ignores the strong affective element that accompanies and sometimes overpowers the cognitive in fantasy, and it fails to account for the ways in which fantasy narratives are carried forward. Cognitive recognition of specific impossibilities may serve to signal us that a given work is a fantasy, but it will not sustain us through multiple volumes of narrative—and in some cases, as with the Gormenghast trilogy, it is difficult to pinpoint any such cognitive impossibility at all.

When do we decide that we are reading something impossible? There are no ghosts, dragons, hobbits, or magical transitions between worlds in the Gormenghast trilogy, only an overriding sense of the grotesque and bizarre. Even when magical events and beings do show up in a fantasy, we expect that the author will keep them under control. A work that piles new impossibility upon new impossibility would be extremely taxing on the reader and in the end likely lead toward incoherence. Similarly, a work that is remarkably rich in invention and in which the terms of impossibility in the fantastic world are not made clear until late in the narrative—a work such as David Lindsay's *A Voyage to Arcturus* (1920)—is apt to be exhausting for most readers. On the other hand, a clear explication of the limits of the impossible can provide a convenient framework for a very accessible adventure story. Phyllis Eisenstein's *Born to Exile* (1978) maintains a tightly controlled level of cognitive impossibility; its hero can, in science-fictional terms, teleport, though she chooses to place him in a faux-medieval setting in which his talent functions essentially as magic. With no more in the way of cognitive impossibility than this, Eisenstein constructs a highly satisfying series of fantasy narratives. Our sense of being in a fantastic realm arises, it would seem, from some affective apprehension of the impossible rather than from this simple cognitive device—which by itself might even allow us to categorize the work as science fiction.

An interesting principle begins to emerge: We cannot, it is apparent, simply use our recognition of cognitive impossibility to "test" for fantasy, at least not in the same way that we can use our recognition of what is possible to test our acceptance of a work of science fiction. Another way of stating the difference between science fiction and fantasy is that science fiction has a relationship with the world of today; whether works are set in the past or the future, the reader has an implicit or explicit awareness of a relationship with the contemporary world. Fantasy offers a clean break with reality; settings and characters may be analogous with the "real" world, particularly in historical fantasy, but the rules that govern fantasy worlds are not necessarily consistent with our notion of reality. Recognition of the possible can and often does sustain a reader throughout a work of science fiction, and part of the thrill of reading what is often referred to as "hard" science fiction arises from discovering just how far our concepts of the possible can be stretched. In many works of science fiction, a single glaring impossibility may burst the balloon of the narrative, but a glaring "possibility" in fantasy disturbs us not at all. In fact, the further we progress in a fantasy narrative, the less we expect in the way of new impossible marvels; once the ground rules have been laid, a *deus ex machina* in fantasy is as intrusive as in any other kind of fiction. Nor can a standard adventure novel be made into a true fantasy by informing us at the outset that we are in a mythic world or time, no more than a fantasy can be transformed into realistic fiction by tacking on to the ending a tired phrase like "And then I awoke in my room."

Does this mean that the criterion of impossibility isn't a useful way of identifying works of fantasy? After all, by the time we begin the second volume of Tolkien's *Lord of the Rings* or the third or fourth volume of Roger Zelazny's "Amber" series, we are entrenched in the author's symbolic universe and do not expect many new "impossibilities" to occur, although we might well expect new inventions consistent with the impossibilities that we have already accepted. Yet it would be absurd to suggest that only the first volume of these or other fantasy series qualify as true fantasies simply because it is in those inaugural volumes that our primary dislocation of what we take to be possible occurs. Once a dragon takes flight in a work of fantasy, or a unicorn talks, or a wardrobe becomes a forest, we are not apt to be much impressed to witness the same thing for a second or third time. But in an effective fantasy work, we do not lose our sense of the wondrous or impossible even long after all the marvels have been introduced and the magic has become commonplace. To account for such works, we must move beyond the simple criterion of cognitive impossibility and examine such elements as tone and setting—elements that help to construct what we might call the affective sense of the impossible.

To use a term that has been explored by both Freud and Gaston Bachelard, fantasy is in many ways closer to daydreaming or reverie than to cognitive thought, and as Bachelard observes, "Dreaming reveries and thinking thoughts are certainly two disciplines which are hard to reconcile."[14] The reason Bachelard gives for this is that cognitive thought is based in what he calls our "reality function":

The demands of our *reality function* require that we adapt to reality, that we constitute ourselves as a reality and that we manufacture works which are realities. But doesn't reverie, by its very essence, liberate us from the reality function? From the moment *it* is considered in all its simplicity, it is perfectly evident that reverie bears witness to a normal, useful *irreality function* which keeps the human psyche on the fringe of all the brutality of a hostile and foreign non-self.[15]

Bachelard's "irreality function," which he explores in greater depth using the resources of phenomenology and Jungian theory, approaches closely what I have called the affective sense of the impossible. And since reality, in the words of Peter L. Berger and Thomas Luckmann, is socially constructed, it follows that the irreality of fantasy must gain some of its power from socially determined notions of what is possible and impossible. "Finite provinces of meaning" is the term Berger and Luckmann employ to describe the alternate realities of art, religion, and myth; and the term might well be applied in a more limited sense to describe the impossible worlds of artistic fantasy.[16]

Meaning is an essential factor in the irreality function of fantasy; it is what lends the fantasy something resembling Clive Bell's "significant form" and what sustains our interest in the impossible long after our cognitive apprehension of impossibilities has passed, long after we have resolved the momentary hesitation or irresolution that Todorov calls "the fantastic."[17] This is hardly a revolutionary thought; any work of art must hold out the promise of some significant meaning and form if we are to retain interest in it, especially in the face of manifest impossibilities. But in fantasy, the sources of meaning, the ideational structures of the narrative, are essential in molding our attitude toward the impossible and in controlling the depth of our response to it. In some kinds of fantasy, the ideational structure is very close to what we might expect from more conventional kinds of fiction. What is commonly (and often surprisingly accurately) called "sword-and-sorcery" fiction—a genre most closely associated with authors such as Fritz Leiber (who is said to have coined the term) and Robert E. Howard—seems to me in many ways closer to historical fiction and science fiction than other kinds of fantasy. Its ideational structure is primarily technological and political, as the very term "sword-and-sorcery" suggests. A sword, after all, is a tool, and however primitive, it is an implement of technological weaponry. Sorcery is a causal system analogous to science, its rules often so circumscribed that this genre of fiction has managed to give birth to a series of popular games that thoroughly reverse the process of discovery that we ordinarily associate with fantasy: Instead of discovering the rules and limits of the impossible through induction, by following the action of a fantasy narrative, many of these sword-and-sorcery war-gamers prefer to work deductively, learning the rules of the game at the outset and reducing the narrative itself literally to the level of play. It is not surprising that sword-and-sorcery tends on the one hand toward historical fiction (as with Poul Anderson's *The Last Viking*) and on the other toward science fiction (as with Anne McCaffrey's Dragonrider series). Meaning, whether in Dungeons & Dragons or in sword and sorcery, arises from the same sort of fundamental concerns about how the world works, and what you can then do within it. In conversation, editor David G. Hartwell has referred to such rule-bound fantasy fiction as "sword-and-sorcery procedurals."

Other kinds of fantasy deal with issues more commonly associated with fairy tales and *Bildungsroman*—issues such as education, personality, morality, duty, family, social relations, and other aspects of human development. Protagonists in these fantasies more often achieve control over self than over environment (although the self may take many forms in a fantastic world), and the ideational structure is psychological. As Bachelard observes of reveries, "They situate us in a world and not in a society."[18] And the objects, events, and beings that we encounter in this fantastic world—however impossible—must exist in a fullness of affect that enables us to respond to them as though they were real. A contrast with science fiction may be helpful here. In much science fiction, the fantastic environment is subordinated to a rationalized purpose, and the elements of that environment relate to the science fiction reader in much the same way that elements of reality relate to the scientist. They are, to use Ernest Schachtel's phrase, "objects-of-use": "The scientist, in these cases, looks at the object with one or more hypotheses and with the purpose of his research in mind and thus 'uses' the object to corroborate or disprove a hypothesis, but does not encounter the object as such, in its own fullness."[19] The perceptual world of science fiction, then, is significant in that its objects are subject to manipulation and control; they are a means to an end. If the furnishings of our room begin to disappear, as they are apt to do in a Philip K. Dick novel, we soon will learn that it is not really the impossible that is happening but rather some sort of sophisticated yet understandable manipulation of these objects, or our perception of them, for some equally understandable end. In science fiction, objects, landscapes, and even characters are often stripped of all but those qualities that eventually will serve some cognitive purpose; this is why many readers who do not like science fiction sometimes complain of its "flatness," "coldness," or "lack of affect" (although such accusations are certainly not always justified).

In fantasy, another kind of "stripping" often takes place, and we may encounter objects reduced not to their usefulness, but rather to their affective significance. It is at first a little disconcerting to read through five volumes of Roger Zelazny's "Amber" series and learn so little about Amber itself. We are told early in the series that "Amber was the greatest city which had ever existed or ever would exist" and that "every other city, everywhere, every other city that existed was but a reflection of a shadow of some phase of Amber."[20] But Amber itself often seems to have no population other than its royal family and their hired minions, no streets, no economy, no network of social organization. For Zelazny's purposes, such aspects of the city are nonessential and may be distracting. Amber exists not like cities in science fiction, which function to show us the problems and promises of technology or population control or some other such issue; rather it exists as an emotional archetype. All we really need know of Amber are its power, its order, and its beauty; what does not tend to reinforce this primary affective response can be dispensed with. Similarly, we do not need to know much about the history, design, or function of the magic wardrobe in C. S. Lewis's *The Lion, the Witch, and the Wardrobe* (1950), since it is primarily an emblem of curiosity and mystery, a place to be explored. Nor do we look for an account of the biology of the Nazgul in Tolkien's *Lord of the Rings* (although inevitably fans have tried to do so), since the fearfulness of this creation is quite sufficient to account for its presence in a fantasy.

At this point, we might be tempted to conclude that our original problems concerning the criterion of the impossible in fantasy have been pretty much resolved, and that fantasy manages to sustain our interest in impossible worlds simply by making these worlds emotionally meaningful to us. This is indeed true of some kinds of fantasy, but it does not enable us to distinguish serious fantasy from the purely sensational kinds of narratives that sometimes are allied to it, such as pornography, whimsy, or horror. It may be that a single affective attitude controls a fantastic narrative to the extent that it maintains our interest, but in the most successful serious fantasies, a whole range of emotional experience is apt to be explored, and we cannot depend on a particular affective construct to sustain our acceptance of the impossible. When a particular affective construct so dominates a work of fantastic literature that we find ourselves waiting for the same emotional sensation to be repeated in different guises, we are no longer in a fully realized fantastic world, but in a world of formula fiction—one that many readers celebrate and sustain through volume after volume of similar adventures. The objects and events in this world are apt to become again "objects-of-use," repeatedly manipulated by the author in the service of a single dominant emotional tone. Thorne Smith's delightful *The Night Life of the Gods* (1931) is full of impossible happenings and mythological figures, but all are subordinated to a screwball comic tone that controls the whole work. H. P. Lovecraft's "shuggoths" and elder gods may be impressive creations in their own right, but once they have served Lovecraft's primary purpose of giving us a thrill of horror or disgust or awe, they must be hauled offstage or, equally characteristic of Lovecraft, the story must end. Just as Smith's work can be more aptly labeled comedy than fantasy, so might Lovecraft's be more aptly labeled horror fiction.

Comedy and horror may of course be elements in any fantasy, but we cannot depend on them as controlling elements. Here another distinction from Manlove may be helpful:

Two broad classes of fantasy may be distinguished: "comic" or "escapist," and "imaginative" fantasy. The line of division is simple enough: it is between fancy versus imagination, where "fanciful" works are those carrying either no deeper meaning or one lacking in vitality . . . Any number of Waste Lands, broken lances, grails, Eucharistic or baptismal symbols may appear in a story without that story having any potent meaning.[21]

Manlove may be borrowing the terms "fancy" and "imagination" from one of the authors he discusses in his study, George MacDonald, who drew much the same distinction more than eighty years earlier. Of the creation of fantastic worlds and beings, MacDonald wrote:

When such forms are new embodiments of old truths, we call them products of the Imagination; when they are mere inventions, however lovely, I should call them the work of the Fancy. . . .

. . . you may, if *you will*, call Imagination the tailor that cuts her [Truth's] garments to fit her, and Fancy his journeyman that puts the pieces of them together, or perhaps at most embroiders their button-holes.[22]

Such a distinction between fancy and imagination suggests that in works of true imagination we can expect an ideational structure that goes far deeper than the controlling tone of the work, that is in fact based in what Manlove calls "deeper meaning" and MacDonald "old truths."

What these deeper meanings and old truths are may vary widely from one author to another, ranging from the Christian Platonism of C. S. Lewis to the blend of Gnosticism and Teutonic philosophy that underlies the work of David Lindsay. What gives credence to such systems in fantasy is the manner in which the fantasist forges a unity between them and the affective structures we have already discussed. This does not mean that fantasy is limited to being didactic or allegorical, but it does imply that at the center of these works of imagination (as opposed to fancy) must be a core of what might best be called *belief*. Belief in fantasy—what Tolkien calls "Secondary Belief" to distinguish it from the primary belief in experiential reality—arises from the conjunction of psychological affect and ideational structure, and as Tolkien notes, it is quite a different thing from Coleridge's "willing suspension of disbelief."[23] Put another way, belief is what enables genuine emotions to be aroused from impossible circumstances, not unlike Marianne Moore's familiar description of poetry as "imaginary gardens with real toads in them." Moore's observation in her poem "Spenser's Ireland," that one is not free until one is "made captive by supreme belief," is also apt.

Fantasy indeed tries to set us free by making us captive to belief, but since the kind of belief that is peculiar to fantasy arises as much from affect as from cognition, it is not necessary for us to share an author's philosophies or beliefs for us to accept and "believe in" their embodiment in the narrative. We need not be Christians to be impressed by the strength and kindness of C. S. Lewis's Aslan; we need not be in agreement with Jesse Weston's sometimes shaky hypotheses about hero myths to enjoy their embodiment in Roger Zelazny's Amber series. In Patricia A. McKillip's *The Forgotten Beasts of Eld* (1974), we can accept the final transformation of the hideous monster Blammor into the beautiful Liralen bird without necessarily agreeing with the identity of creative and destructive passions that such a metaphor implies. In all of these narratives, affect and tone transform such ideational constructs into events and beings that are fully consistent with the author's created universe.

Fantasy authors who are most successful at creating this kind of belief attempt neither to allegorize their own systems of belief nor to subordinate those systems to sensation. Instead, they achieve a balanced tension—perhaps more properly a dialectic—between cognition and affect, between moralism and passion, between the impossible and the inevitable. They do not merely construct metaphors for a preconceived reality, or if they do, the power of the metaphors is apt to transform the nature of those preconceptions into something new. At their most ambitious, these fantasists resemble the painter Peter Copping in David Lindsay's *Devil's Tor*:

Only, what every painter worth his salt is trying to present—probably without knowing it—is neither beauty, nor life, nor truth (charming words, all of them!) . . . but . . . the *whole universe*—at one stroke. By means, necessarily, of *action*. That is symbolism in a nutshell. Nothing exists apart, but only the universe exists. Whatever individual person or thing I paint must stand, not for itself, but for the entire scheme.[24]

The notion of symbolism that Lindsay introduces (for the character Copping likely is speaking with Lindsay's voice here) provides us with the final clue as to how to deal with the impossible in fantasy. Underlying the belief in the fantastic world itself, which, as we have found, arises from the union of idea and affect, is a deeper belief in the fundamental reality that this world expresses. I use the term "expresses" rather than "represents" because many of the finest fantasy writers correctly have rejected the notion that their work is in any sense mere allegory or apologue—"a wall decoration with a label attached," in the words of Lindsay's Peter Copping.[25] For these writers, the fantasy world does not symbolize the experiential world but rather co-exists with it; each world, in the words of George MacDonald, is "the human being turned inside out," "a sensuous analysis of humanity."[26] C. S. Lewis, in *The Allegory of Love*, calls this attitude "sacramentalism or symbolism" and describes it as "almost the opposite of allegory": "The allegorist leaves the given—his own passions—to talk of that which is confessedly less real, which is a fiction. The symbolist leaves the given to find that which is more real. To put the difference in another way, for the symbolist it is we who are the allegory."[27]

One might object to the apologetic for idealism that is implied in Lewis's formulation and thinly disguised in his own fiction, but if the fantasy author successfully integrates idea and affect to achieve a primary level of belief in the work, this deeper level of belief will emerge naturally, without constricting the work or reducing it to overt didacticism. When the primary level of belief falters (as I believe it does from time to time in both Lewis's *Perelandra* and his *That Hideous Strength*), the deeper belief overpowers it, and we have at best a very entertaining homiletic. But in the best works of fantasy, ranging from the rigorous intellectuality of Lindsay's *A Voyage to Arcturus* to the delicate lyricism of Peter Beagle's *The Last Unicorn,* this deeper belief is so much of a piece with the created world that the question of "meaning" becomes a phenomenological rather than a literary one.

This discussion has of necessity been rather abstract, and unfortunately has not permitted room for detailed investigations of particular works. But it does suggest a kind of structure for the reading of fantasy that enables us to posit an answer to our original question of how fantasy not only sustains our interest in the impossible, but finally wins our belief and reveals that the impossible is, after all, the real. Briefly summarized, this structure is as follows:

1. *cognition of the impossible* in which we realize, usually early on in a fantasy, that the accepted ground rules of our reality are in some significant way being contravened;

2. *location of the impossible,* or the awareness that this contravention of reality lies somewhere between private psychological fantasy and culturally shared myth (although in works such as Evangeline Walton's Mabinogion novels or T. H. White's *Once and Future King* the public myths of earlier cultures may be transformed into fantasies for our time);

3. *delimitation of the impossible,* which assures us that the work is under control and that some underlying system places constraints on what may happen in this fantastic world;

4. *feeling of the impossible,* or the affective sense of "otherness" (as opposed to horror's "outsidedness") or "irreality" that assures our continued emotional investment in this world even after new marvels have ceased to appear;

5. *awareness of affective significance,* which sets the work apart from mere speculation or sensationalism by promising that this emotional investment, once made, will be rewarded by some underlying affective order;

6. *awareness of cognitive significance,* or "deeper meaning," which in effect refocuses our cognitive concerns away from the surface impossibilities of the narrative and toward an emerging ideational structure;

7. *belief* in the fantastic world, arising from the interaction between affective and cognitive significance; and

8. *deeper belief,* which permits certain fantasy works to become analogues of inner experience virtually as valid as events of the "real world," and which express the author's own most fundamental convictions.

Not all fantasies, of course, will carry the reader successfully through all these stages of experience, and not all will try. At worst, a fantasy will not carry us much beyond the initial recognition that what we are reading is impossible;

at best, it will lead us to a further recognition that these surface impossibilities constitute a necessary strategy for approaching some profound and intense reality. For such works, "the impossible" may be little more than a surface structure; the works themselves concern things that could not be more real. Fantasies that successfully lead us all the way to this deeper belief are still rare, despite the illustrious history of fantastic literature; perhaps, indeed, taking us that far is the most fantasy can do. If so, that is still a great deal to ask of any literature.

Afterword

Since this essay originally appeared, the body of critical literature on fantasy has blossomed, but the criterion of the impossible remains firmly in place in formal definitions of the genre. In one of the most influential studies of the 1990s, *Strategies of Fantasy*, Brian Attebery offers the attractive notion that fantasy is best regarded as what logicians call a "fuzzy set," readily definable at its center but blurring at the edges. Still, he writes, "The essential content is the impossible, or, as I put it in *The Fantasy Tradition in American Literature*, 'some violation of what the author clearly believes to be natural law' . . . there is general agreement that some such violation is essential to fantasy."[28] Another highly influential work—notable because of the dozens of theoretical and taxonomical propositions scattered among its hundreds of reference entries—is John Clute and John Grant's *The Encyclopedia of Fantasy* (1999), which offers the following as a working definition: "A fantasy text is a self-coherent narrative. When set in this world, it tells a story which is impossible in the world as we perceive it . . . when set in an otherworld, that otherworld will be impossible, though stories set there may be possible in its terms."[29]

At the same time, an increasing number of authors have developed ingenious strategies for subverting, bending, or confusing our notions of the boundary between the possible and the impossible, from the genetically engineered alien dragons in Anne McCaffrey's ongoing series of Pern novels to the afterburner-assisted part-mechanical dragons of Michael Swanwick's *The Iron Dragon's Daughter* (1993). Swanwick's semi-sequel, *The Dragons of Babel* (2008), combines figures drawn from Sumerian, Scandinavian, African, and Japanese myth and folklore with allusions that seem intended to confound the "impossibility" of the setting. His fantasy Babylon features Frank Lloyd Wright lounges,

saloons with framed pictures of Muhammad Ali, Bowie knives, gas chromato-
graphs, dumpsters, Kawasaki motorcycles and Mercedes and BMW automobiles, Pepsis, McDonalds, Marlboros, Zippo lighters, Hermes bags (for carrying
runes), Hard Rock Café t-shirts and Givenchy gowns—allusions that in a science fiction novel would seem to violate a basic writers' workshop principle
sometimes called "Brand Name Fever," but that here serve to undermine any
assumptions we may bring to his created world. Palace courtiers check their
Blackberries and PDAS, while animate stone lions discuss Faulkner and Tolstoy and wise old women quote Mary McCarthy. Swanwick is far from the
only author testing these boundaries—Ted Chiang, Kelly Link, China Miéville,
Jeffrey Ford, and M. Rickert are among others who come to mind—but his
work may serve as one of the most dramatic and critically informed examples.

As far as the structure of reading fantasy is concerned—the question of how
fantasy texts draw the reader in beyond the introduction of initial marvels—two
of the most important recent studies are John Clute's *The Darkening Garden: A
Short Lexicon of Horror* and Farah Mendlesohn's *Rhetorics of Fantasy*. Clute's
"lexicon" is actually a collection of thirty short essays on various concepts
that he associates with horror fiction, and in part builds upon a proposed
four-part "grammar" for fantasy narratives—"wrongness," "thinning," "recognition," and "healing"—which he earlier developed in his entry on fantasy in
The Encyclopedia of Fantasy;[30] here he revises "healing" to "return" and offers
a parallel structure for horror fiction—"sighting," "thickening," "revel," and
"aftermath." While the details of Clute's developing system are too complex to
summarize here (like Northrop Frye, he also parallels each four-part grammar
to corresponding seasons, with fantasy beginning in autumn and horror in
spring), his proposals are most illuminating when viewed as a means of structuring the experience of reading a text, though they take a much different
approach from that proposed in this essay. Mendlesohn, who rather pointedly
avoids the question of defining fantasy as a genre or mode, suggests a typology
of fantasy narratives based largely on "the reader's relationship to the framework."[31] She classifies fantasies as "portal-quest," "immersive," "intrusion," and
"liminal," with an added fifth chapter on "irregulars," or texts that subvert,
question, or evade the taxonomy that she has proposed. The portal-quest fantasy involves a fantastic world entered through a one-way portal (such as C. S.
Lewis's *The Lion, the Witch, and the Wardrobe*); immersive fantasy takes place
entirely within an imagined world (and thus is allied to science fiction); intrusion involves the fantastic invading our own world (and thus may be allied to

horror); the liminal happens when the level of fantasy may be indeterminate and the reader's experience may seem at odds with that of the characters (her lead examples are Hope Mirrlees and Mervyn Peake). Both Clute's and Mendlesohn's ideas are far more comprehensive than the limited reader-response structure proposed in this essay, which limits itself mostly to the apprehension of the impossible, but both are equally reader-centered.

five

The Artifact as Icon in Science Fiction

S cience fiction, like many forms of popular literature, boasts a repertoire of recurring images that are emblematic of the major concerns and underlying anxieties of the genre. The most familiar of these icons, such as the intelligent machine, the spaceship, the alien or monster, and the futuristic city, gain power from their peculiar property of both revealing knowledge and withholding it; they are familiar, while at the same time they remain estranged from us in some significant aspect. The robot, for example, is supposed to operate by understandable mechanical and electronic principles and frequently is portrayed in a pseudohuman form, but is clearly not human and its "intelligence" is therefore of an alien kind. (A more extensive exploration of such "icons" is the focus of my *The Known and the Unknown: The Iconography of Science Fiction*.) Many of these science-fictional icons derive from both mythological and technological sources; there is room in the history of the spaceship for Icarus as well as Robert Goddard. In fact, many readers of science fiction have come to regard the genre as having an oddly bifurcated history, drawing at once on ancient myth and modern technology, on pop culture and arcane science. Science fiction does owe a great deal to the mediating and formulizing influences of earlier forms of popular narrative, and it shares at least one of its most enduring icons with narrative formulas as diverse as the Gothic romance, the horror story, modern fantasy, the mystery, and the espionage novel. This is the icon of the artifact, and the means by which science fiction has appropriated this image and invested it with new meanings is an interesting study in how a particular genre adopts and transforms broader conventions of popular narrative.

I am taking "artifact" to mean not just any manufactured object, but rather (in the more popular archaeological sense) as a manufactured object embedding evidence of some specific (usually remote) time and place, and invested with some indeterminate value—be it material, pedagogical, or spiritual—to those who receive or discover it in some other time or place. The artifact implies and interacts with three distinct historical systems: the system surrounding its manufacture, the system of its own history, and the system of the receiving culture. If either of the first two systems is unknown or insufficiently understood, the artifact also implies a mystery, and a mystery particularly well suited to the dynamic of science fiction. Like other SF icons, it partakes of the known (the circumstances surrounding its discovery and its observable characteristics) and the unknown (the circumstances surrounding its creation and its history). The solution to this mystery almost always involves decoding or "dissecting" the artifact itself; as folklorist Henry Glassie writes,

Dissected, the artifact becomes understandable: its parts, past, and associations become traceable: the artifact can be viewed as the product and source of meaning. The assignation of meaning to a thing brings it value in the same way to the people who make and use it and to the people who study it. A thing is only a thing until a man wanders into the picture and begins relating the thing to other things; then, the thing becomes an icon. . . . The conceptualization of associations, relations, and meaning is the recognition of the thing's functions and of the icon's powers.[1]

Glassie is writing primarily of the artifacts of folk culture, but his observations might as well apply to the imaginary artifacts that so liberally populate popular fiction. Even at its most mundane—a potsherd or an arrowhead—the artifact carries with it a wealth of associations, invites speculation, and implies whole systems of thought, alien cultures, and historical processes. At its most ambitious, the imaginary artifact in science fiction may embed many of the genre's most popular icons—it may be a spacecraft, a machine, a city, a marvelous invention—and thus it becomes emblematic of the systematic "sense of wonder" that many regard as the genre's most potent source of appeal.

While the artifact may seem a natural device for science fiction, there is nevertheless evidence that this icon entered the genre gradually, even though it had long been a staple in many forms of popular literature. The vast, complex artifacts in Arthur C. Clarke's *Rendezvous with Rama* (1974), Larry Niven's *Ringworld* (1970), Bob Shaw's *Orbitsville* (1975), Gregory Benford's *In the Ocean of Night* (1978), or even films like *Star Trek: The Motion Picture* are fairly recent developments (although one can find evidence of this trend as early as the 1930s with such stories as Raymond Z. Gallun's "Derelict" [1935]). Earlier science fiction artifacts, such as the interplanetary communications device that is the "crystal egg" of H. G. Wells's 1897 story by that title, have almost as much in common with the magical amulets of fantasy as with imaginary technological marvels, particularly when one looks at the narratives in which they are presented. In the case of "The Crystal Egg," for example, the mysterious crystal through which one can somehow observe the landscape of Mars is discovered in a "little and very grimy-looking" curio shop, which is familiar to us now through a long tradition of "magic shop" fantasies, pioneered by H. G. Wells and John Collier, and which continues to the present day in such stories as Harlan Ellison's "Djinn, No Chaser" (1982), Bruce Sterling's "The Little Magic Shop" (1987), Jeffrey Ford's "Jupiter's Skull" (2004), Terry Pratchett's *Soul Music* (1995) and *The Light Fantastic* (1987), and films such as *Gremlins* (1984).

Fantasy is not the only other popular genre to make use of the artifact as a plot device—the mystery tradition would hardly be the same without Wilkie Collins's *The Moonstone* or Dashiell Hammett's *The Maltese Falcon*—but the most likely genre in which to trace the origins of the artifact as used in science fiction is the late Gothic tale of the supernatural. There seems little that is even remotely "science fictional" about such bizarre early Gothic irrationalities as the giant helmet in Horace Walpole's *The Castle of Otranto* (1757) or such folkloristic amulets as George MacDonald's "The Golden Key" (1867), but by the time we get to the mysterious chest filled with family artifacts that leads to the quest in H. Rider Haggard's *She* (1887), we are much closer to a "science-fictional" treatment of the artifact. Haggard seemed fascinated by the science of archaeology, which was experiencing a "golden age" as he was writing, and he devotes considerable time to describing the translation of the ancient potsherd that reveals the history of Kallikrates. The artifact is thus presented as an object that will yield to rational scrutiny, and not merely as a magical treasure or Hitchcockian "MacGuffin." Indeed, the Victorian fascination with archaeology in general, which had been stimulated by Schliemann's excavations at Troy in 1870, helped provide a new scientific validation for the narrative use of artifacts that might otherwise have belonged merely to the "cursed object" tradition of Gothic romance.

Only three years after the appearance of *She*, Arthur Machen published a tale that provides an excellent example of this "scientization" of the Gothic, and that points directly toward later authors who would considerably broaden the potential uses of the artifact as icon. "The Novel of the Black Seal," an episode in Machen's *The Three Impostors* (1895), describes the adventures of a professor who is drawn into a web of mysteries involving the "little people" associated with a mysterious stone seal that is inscribed with unknown characters and said to date from the time of the Babylonians. The professor encounters a rural idiot boy who seems to speak the language of the little people, and eventually comes upon a kind of Rosetta stone that enables him to translate the mysterious inscription and (presumably) to make contact with the little people themselves. The professor, needless to say, disappears, and his tale is related by a young woman, who is assured by one of the company to whom she is telling the story that the "most extraordinary circumstances in your account are in perfect harmony with the very latest scientific theories."[2] They are not, of course, but the fact that Machen chose to offer us this assurance suggests that, while by no means a science fiction writer, he at least found value in suggesting the possibility of a scientific explanation for the artifact and the events surrounding it. Historical and archaeological detail also surround a similar black stone artifact in David Lindsay's *Devil's Tor* (1932), in which the two halves of the broken artifact, which is presumably of extraterrestrial origin and which was split apart in antiquity, are reunited and reveal hidden truths to a man and woman who realize they are destined to found a new race.

Machen's story was much admired by H. P. Lovecraft, who devoted two pages to it in his *Supernatural Horror in Literature* (1945, though originally composed in 1927). The extent to which Machen's notion of an ancient, inhuman society surviving in the wilds of Britain may have influenced Lovecraft's own famous "mythos" is a matter of speculation for Lovecraft students, but it is evident that Lovecraft's fiction made extensive use of the artifact as a means of providing a link between the modern world and the ancient, cosmic monstrosities that so fascinated him. What is often overlooked, however, is the extent to which Lovecraft developed such artifacts into more "science-fictional" images by connecting them to vast sweeps of space and time and to a number of patterns of science fiction imagery.

As early as 1917, with "Dagon," Lovecraft had made use of the artifact as evidence that earlier races once may have ruled the Earth, but it is in his later tales, most notably *At the Mountains of Madness* (1931) and "The Shadow Out of Time" (1935), that he begins to exploit the full potential of the artifact as a science fiction icon. These stories concern ancient stone ruins discovered in Western Australia and Antarctica that give evidence of a technologically advanced "great race" that long ago ruled the cosmos. Because of this race's power to project their minds anywhere in space and time, they remain a threat even today (particularly to those with an inclination to meddle into Things Best Left Unseen). But Lovecraft's "great race" is not Machen's mythic "little people"; it is, instead, a technological civilization that built vast machines and cities, mastered travel through time and space, and made contact with alien races on Venus and a moon of Jupiter. The artifact—in this case, the ruins of ancient stone cities in remote corners of the Earth—is no longer merely a gateway to the past, or to a lost civilization, or to the world of faerie. Instead, it has become a link between the known world and the vast unknown universe that is science fiction's stock in trade.

Lovecraft even underlines the science-fictional nature of his concept with (rather limp) references to Einstein and relativity as a means of explaining the possibility of psychic travel through space and time. (Colin Wilson, in his later Lovecraft *pastiches—The Mind Parasites* [1967], *The Philosopher's Stone* [1969], and *The Space Vampires* [1976]—consciously emphasized the science-fictional nature of the Lovecraftian artifact, even to the extent of replacing it with a derelict alien spacecraft in *The Space Vampires.* And Stephen King's *The Tommyknockers* [1987], with its buried alien spacecraft mysteriously altering those who find it, also might be viewed as a science fictionalization of Lovecraftian horror.) Lovecraft's followers did not hesitate to exploit endlessly the convention of the artifact as gateway to space and time, and the number of mysterious objects that lead to grisly ends is legion in the pulp fantastic fiction of the thirties and forties. Inevitably, a few real artifacts get roped into the mythos as well, and Donald Wandrei in *The Web of Easter Island* (1948) managed to connect *both* Stonehenge and the Easter Island monoliths with a mysterious green figurine that eats people.

This notion of alien artifacts already on Earth became a fairly common one even in Lovecraft's era, receiving (for one example) a somewhat Charles Fortean treatment in R. DeWitt Miller's "Within the Pyramid" (*Astounding,* 1937), in which a mysterious alien pyramid is discovered in the Central American jungle; the pattern has recurred with some regularity to the present (see the discussion of Michael Crichton's *Sphere* [1987] below). The most widely familiar examples include Stanley Kubrick's film *2001: A Space Odyssey* (1968), based on Arthur C. Clarke's 1951 story "The Sentinel" (in which the artifact is actually found on the moon, but is given a sister artifact on Earth in the film); and Kurt Vonnegut, Jr.'s *The Sirens of Titan* (1959), in which various wonders of the world (the Egyptian pyramids, the Great Wall of China, and the like), are revealed as messages from an alien civilization to explorers stranded on a moon of Jupiter. Indeed, the idea seemed so inviting that it eventually gave rise in the 1970s to the cult of Erich von Däniken and his ancient astronauts, in which science fiction scenarios were presented as nonfiction, and rewarded with a much greater degree of commercial success than were many of the original stories about such alien visitors. I have argued in *The Known and the Unknown* that the power of a given icon to embed cultural anxieties becomes evident when the icon eventually "breaks free" of particular fictional contexts and gains currency in the popular culture at large (toy robots being a simple example).[3] The success of von Däniken and his followers suggests that much the same thing already has happened with the icon of the artifact.

Perhaps because of this appropriation of the traditional artifact by the general culture, many science fiction artifacts have tended toward the monumental, the metaphorical, or the bizarre. It is no longer enough that the discovered artifacts give evidence of an alien civilization, or provide a mystery with which to ignite the plot. Instead, the artifact itself moves to center stage, embedding the major thematic concerns particular to the work in which it appears, as well as stirring the general "sense of wonder" that such artifacts traditionally have evoked. As English science fiction writer Kenneth Bulmer has written, "many and wonderful have been the alien artefacts [sic] dug up, discovered drifting in space, or falling to Earth. The hard bustle of Solterran technology contrasts forcefully with the romance and mystery of weird alien artifacts on abandoned worlds orbiting chill and distant stars."[4]

One of the first works to explore this radically polysemic function of the artifact was Algis Budrys' novel *Rogue Moon* (1960), which describes the discovery of an inexplicable alien labyrinth on the Moon. After repeated forays into the labyrinth have resulted in the deaths of several volunteers, a matter-transmitting device, capable of recreating an exact replica of a person or object (without destroying the original), is used to project replicas of volunteers to receiving stations on both the Earth and on the Moon, near the labyrinth. Both "copies" of the individual involved can remain in telepathic contact for a short time. The time can be extended if the Earthbound "copy" experiences sensory deprivation—thus receiving only the sensory stimuli experienced by the "copy" on the Moon, and consequently seeming to experience the labyrinth without physical danger. All of these volunteers, however, are driven insane by the trauma of death when their duplicates in the labyrinth are killed. Hawks, the scientist in charge of the experiment, sets out to find a volunteer so enamored of death that he might withstand the psychological trauma. Since the novel is set in an otherwise contemporary 1959, this complex of science-fictional ideas that provides the novel's backdrop may be a bit much for some readers. I have often suspected that *Rogue Moon* may not have received the attention it deserves simply because the notion that space travel, matter transmission, alien intelligences, and telepathy all might have been known secretly to the scientists of Eisenhower's day seems dizzyingly paranoid. Yet it soon becomes clear that all this hardware is necessary to set up the story that Budrys wants to tell, and the bravura with which he launches into it, skimming past the vast implications of each of these discoveries or inventions in favor of more epistemological questions, is admirable. The science fiction hardware, however, serves another function. By establishing a narrative premise built on several of the favorite tropes of "hard SF," Budrys lulls the reader into expecting a hard SF solution—the novel looks as though it's going to be an elaborate Asimovian "puzzle story"—and when Budrys's more harshly existential concerns become apparent, their impact is intensified. In this sense, the novel is far ahead of its time for genre science fiction; Budrys is in effect doing for the technological puzzle story what Stanislaw Lem would do later for the alien intelligence story or Philip K. Dick for the "alternate reality" story.[5] And in so doing, Budrys discovers entirely new uses for the icon of the artifact.

The artifact in this case is a structure that first appears to us as a group of "black obsidian blocks" that might have come out of a Lovecraft story. Later, we find that no two people entering the artifact see quite the same thing, and that the most arbitrary actions—kneeling while facing north, raising the left hand above the shoulder, writing the word "yes"—can result in bizarre and horrible deaths. When Barker, the daredevil volunteer who represents Hawks's last-ditch attempt to find someone who can withstand the experience of death, comes out of the maze for the first time, he describes it as "Alice in Wonderland with teeth."[6] Barker, who initially is presented as almost a parody of a macho pulp hero, obsessed with his own bravery and heroism, is nearly devastated not by the experience of death, but by its meaninglessness: "Hawks, it didn't care! I was *nothing* to it!" he exclaims. Hawks later explains to Barker,

You couldn't say to yourself, as you died, that you had misinterpreted the rules, or failed to obey them, or tried to overcome them. There were no rules. No one had found them out. You died ignorant of what killed you. And there had been no crowd to applaud your skill or mourn your fate. A giant hand reached down and plucked you from the board—for what reason, no one knows. Suddenly, you knew that where you were was not a ski-slope at all, and all your skills were nothing. You saw, as clearly as anyone could ever see it, the undisguised face of the unknown universe.[7]

Barker, whose life has been defined by ritual and action, only gradually comes to understand the implications of this "unknown universe," and when (accompanied by Hawks) he finally traverses the entire labyrinth successfully, he emerges feeling an undefined sense of loss. Hawks, on the other hand, realizes that the meaning of the artifact lies in what it does to us, not in who built it or why. In a startlingly touching passage for what is in many ways a harsh novel, Hawks explains to his lover Elizabeth the remarkable paradox that mind should even exist in an entropic universe, and concludes by remembering how, as a child, he had transformed a winter landscape into a "wonderland" by squinting so that his tears created a radiance around all things. It was, he asserts, a world made not by the universe, but by himself, and it was a world unrecoverable except through memory. (The reference to "wonderland" echoes ironically Barker's earlier allusion to the artifact as "Alice in Wonderland with teeth.")

The alien artifact itself is never "explained" in the terms that we had been led to expect earlier in the novel—or for that matter by the conventions of science fiction—and in fact no explanation could do the image justice. The artifact behaves toward us as capriciously as the universe itself does, and by letting the image stand as an emblem for all that we seek to understand, Budrys transforms the icon into something considerably more powerful than it might otherwise have been. His original (and preferred) title for the novel was *The Death Machine*, and that title—given the various ways that death figures in the novel, from Barker's bravura to another character's cancer to Hawks' concern over what memories will be lost when he dies—might refer to the universe itself as well as to the artifact.

Budrys's complex novel may have paved the way for a wide variety of more metaphorical science fiction works, including Harlan Ellison's "I Have No Mouth, and I Must Scream" (1967), which also concerns a labyrinthine structure (the interior of a computer) that kills people in horrifying ways; J. G. Ballard's "The Terminal Beach" (1964), with its desolate landscape of deserted bunkers and its desperate central character; and Gregory Benford's *Against Infinity* (1983), in which a mysterious alien machine threatens colonists on Ganymede. Benford, in fact, has returned to the theme of the artifact more consistently than probably any of his generation of major science fiction writers. Before the "Aleph" of *Against Infinity* came the "Snark" of *In the Ocean of Night*, and after it came the artifact of *Artifact* (1985).

Benford's artifacts, like Budrys's, are important chiefly as catalysts for the development of ideas and characters rather than as puzzles for the reader to solve. Nigel Walmsley's discovery, in *In the Ocean of Night*—that the asteroid Icarus is actually an ancient alien spacecraft—sets up situations that unfold not only throughout that novel, but through its sequel, *Across the Sea of Suns* (1984). *In the Ocean of Night* is structured around the discovery of three alien artifacts. Fifteen years after his experience with Icarus, Walmsley encounters and is able to communicate with another alien spacecraft, called the *Snark*, which proves to be an emissary from a machine civilization that reveals to Walmsley that organic life is rare and precious in the universe. Four years later, the discovery of a wrecked alien craft on the Moon brings Walmsley into contact with alien intelligence for a third time. We eventually learn that all these events are connected, that the *Snark* had in fact been summoned on a distress call from Icarus, and in turn activated the artifact on the Moon. Walmsley becomes a pariah of sorts following his first two encounters; in both cases, he was ordered to destroy the artifact and in both cases he refused to do so until he had gained as much information as he could from it. His involvement with the third artifact, therefore, is somewhat controversial even though his role is merely that of a computer and language systems specialist, and even though he has become something of a celebrity as the only human to have made contact with an alien civilization. Walmsley again manages to be on the receiving end when the alien message comes through on the computer terminal, and his vision of life and the physical universe is transformed in a way that alienates him from the rest of humanity (this alienation becomes a major factor in *Across the Sea of Suns*).

In many ways, Walmsley's experience with the alien artifacts changes him in a way similar to that of Barker in *Rogue Moon*. But Benford has also incorporated elements of Clarke's "The Sentinel" and *2001*, and he even brings Bigfoot into his story in a way that vaguely parodies von Däniken. He is clearly experimenting with the various roles that the icon of the artifact can play in science fiction narratives, and even though the artifacts themselves become less enigmatic as we learn more about the machine societies that dominate the universe (and that become the focus of the later novels in this series, *Great Sky River* [1987], *Tides of Light* [1989], and *Furious Gulf* [1994]), the message and meaning of the artifacts remain as inchoate and spiritual as in Budrys' novel.

In *Artifact*, Benford returns to a more conventional narrative use of the icon, which in this case is a cube of black granite with a strange amber cone embedded in it. (There seems little doubt, by this point, that black stone is the material of choice for fictional artifacts.) The object is found during an excavation by American archaeologists of a Mycenaean tomb, and its discovery sets off a fast-moving tale of international intrigue and academic politics as a Greek archaeologist-colonel schemes to reclaim the object from the Americans, who have smuggled it to the United States for tests. Although the mode of the novel is that of the international thriller, the artifact itself is ingeniously imagined, and serves as the focal point for the novel's developing concerns about archaeology, physics, and myth. Physicists find that inside the artifact is a singularity—a miniature black hole—that has remained in equilibrium within its granite casing during the centuries since its burial with the Mycenaean king who "trapped" it. With its golden "horn" and subterranean environment, in fact, the artifact may even have given rise to the legend of the Minotaur. Needless to say, the singularity's equilibrium is disturbed when it is stolen back from the American laboratory by Greek agents, and it begins to travel through the Earth to seek its twin in Greece. Various improbable adventures lead to a fiery conclusion worthy of Indiana Jones. While Benford was clearly having fun with this novel by casting it in the form of a "mainstream" bestseller, he was also imaginatively experimenting with the icon of the artifact, and managed to invent one that, while neither the product of alien intelligence nor of supernatural forces, nevertheless displays the properties of both. As he says in his "Technical Afterword," he used the artifact to reveal to us the strangeness of the universe described by modern physics, and to say, "See how *odd* the world could be?"[8]

Despite these ambitious transformations of the icon in Budrys, Benford, and others, the more conventional science fiction artifact is alive and well. Take for example the derelict spaceship—of the sort that triggers the action of Benford's Nigel Walmsley novels—which has undergone some spectacular embroidery, as in Fred Saberhagen's series of "Berserker" stories about ferocious automated warships roaming the universe millennia after their creators apparently have disappeared. More important are a number of novels that combine the idea of the alien artifact with that of space habitats. The notion of human habitats in space was first seriously advanced by Konstantin Tsiolkovsky in 1903 and developed further in 1929 by J. D. Bernal (who suggested hollowing out asteroids for habitation, an idea that has since had a long life in science fiction). This inevitably led to the speculation that some advanced alien civilization already may have built such habitats and abandoned them, leaving them waiting for some future Heinrich Schliemann or Howard Carter to discover their riches. When Freeman Dyson in 1959 developed Bernal's ideas even further into the notion of a myriad of habitats virtually enclosing a star—the so-called

"Dyson sphere"—the invitation to science fiction writers seemed all too clear. Larry Niven's *Ringworld* (1970) described a partial Dyson sphere in the form of a massive ring-shaped habitat encircling a star at a distance of some 90 million miles, and with a width of a million miles, giving the artifact a total usable surface some three million times that of the Earth. While *Ringworld* provides the setting for an exciting quest-adventure involving humans and aliens, the artifact itself remains a mystery in the best tradition of technological puzzle stories. In 1980, Niven published a sequel, *The Ringworld Engineers*, which resolved the mystery introduced in the earlier novel and gave Niven (with the aid of readers fascinated with the concept, who had written to him with all sorts of calculations involving Ringworld) an opportunity to examine further some of the engineering problems of his imaginary artifact.

Not to be outdone, the English author Bob Shaw published *Orbitsville* (1975), concerning a *complete* Dyson sphere—a solid shell encircling a star and providing on its inner surface a usable land mass some five *billion* times that of Earth. As in *Ringworld*, the artifact itself is such a marvelous conception that it might sustain any sort of narrative, but Shaw's tale hardly does justice to the conception. Whereas Niven was able to place his narrative within the context of his galaxy-sweeping "Known Space" series and further distract us with endless tidbits of engineering lore, Shaw is less technical and provides less of a context for his tale. Marvelous as it is, Shaw's Orbitsville becomes in the end little more than a pawn in a trust-busting action: By providing a virtually infinite supply of land, it destroys the monopoly on space colonization held by a powerful multi-national organization whose vindictive president is the hero's nemesis. Shaw is aware of the social implications of a potentially infinite and hospitable frontier for colonization and even suggests that Orbitsville might be an elaborate behavior-control device for disarming the territorial imperative that inevitably leads to conflict in technological civilizations. He fails to explore this fully, however, and his second Orbitsville novel, *Orbitsville Departure* (1983)—despite a brief focus on the purpose of Orbitsville—is concerned primarily with the depopulated Earth following massive emigration to the new lands.[9]

It is not surprising that some of science fiction's old masters would turn to this theme as well, albeit on a more modest scale, and indeed Arthur C. Clarke's *Rendezvous with Rama* deals with an artifact "only" thirty miles long by twelve across. Rama is the astronomical name given to this mysterious cylindrical body that drifts into the solar system and is explored by astronauts from Earth; it is a testament to Clarke's skill as a novelist that he can make such an artifact as fascinating in its own way as the spectacular artifacts of Niven and Shaw. By setting his novel in a closely imagined near-future world and keeping the action within the solar system, Clarke—like Benford—is able to take advantage of the romance of archaeological exploration and discovery as well as the romance of hard science, and *Rendezvous with Rama is* replete with allusions to Howard Carter and even Captain Cook. Most of the narrative involves the exploration of the apparently abandoned interior of the artificial habitat, which provides Clarke the opportunity to set up and resolve a number of ingenious problems— each of which carries with it a Jules Verne–like lesson in scientific principles. The scientific detail is invariably engrossing, and the repeated pattern of puzzles and solutions should satisfy any reader's taste for popular science. But the pattern serves another function as well: Like the hard-science apparatus of *Rogue Moon,* it establishes an expectation in the reader that the greatest of these puzzles—Rama itself—also will yield a solution. And it does, in a way; when Rama changes trajectory near the Sun, it becomes apparent that the artifact has used the solar system as nothing more than a refueling stop, and that the Ramans themselves, whatever their purpose, are unconcerned with and proba- bly unaware of humanity. Thus, the scientific ingenuity that has been the novel's hallmark receives an ironic comeuppance in the novel's conclusion. Rama departs, having grown from a tantalizing mystery into an adventure- filled landscape and finally into a monument to the universe's indifference. Like the universe, Rama can be explored and measured, but not explained or understood.

Clarke's novel enjoyed several weeks on national bestseller lists, suggesting perhaps that the icon holds a fascination for many readers not familiar with its rich science fiction heritage.[10] Further evidence of this is Michael Crichton's *Sphere* (1987), which also spent several weeks in bestsellerdom. Crichton has made something of a career out of recycling aging science fiction plots into blockbuster suspense novels, and *Sphere* combines elements as diverse as Jules Verne's *Twenty Thousand Leagues Under the Sea* (1870), Stanislaw Lem's *Solaris* (1961), Frank M. Robinson's *The Power* (1956), John W Campbell, Jr.'s "Who Goes There?" (1937, and the basis for two later films titled *The Thing),* and the film *Forbidden Planet* (1956). In Crichton's novel, an enormous spacecraft dis- covered on the ocean floor is found to have come from the future, where (when?) it was designed to travel through a black hole. Something went wrong during its journey, and it "returned" to a different part of space-time—some three hundred years in the past. The team sent to explore the derelict discovers an alien artifact, a huge silver sphere, apparently captured by the ship during its passage through the black hole. After some members of the team enter the sphere, strange "manifestations"—similar to those in Lem's *Solaris*—begin to plague the undersea habitat where the team is stationed. Like the machines built by the alien "Krell" in *Forbidden Planet,* the sphere apparently gives humans the power to project their unconscious fears into reality, and like "Who Goes There?" much of the suspense derives from not knowing which members of the team represent the alien power, as they are killed off one by one. Finally, the protagonist learns that he, too, must enter the sphere to gain "the power," and when he does so the plot shifts into a contest of telekinetic powers similar to that in the Robinson novel. There is even a brief echo of *Rogue Moon* when a character speculates on the unknowability of the alien sphere by comparing the discovery of it to an intelligent space bacterium discovering a communications satellite and wondering if the satellite was designed as a "test" for bacterium (a character in Budrys's novel makes the same speculation about the artifact, using the analogy of a beetle in a discarded tomato can). Crichton's novel is naive science fiction—characters pause in the most stressful situations to give little lectures on everything from relativity to giant squids (which menace the habitat *à la* Verne)—but highly effective suspense writing, which exploits many of the traditions of the science fiction artifact to good effect.

In several of the works that we have been examining—especially those by Budrys, Benford, and Clarke—the artifact is a condition for transformative experiences. As Clarke writes of one of his explorers, "He was going not only where no one had ever been before, but also where no one would ever go again. In all of history he would be the only human being to visit the southern regions of Rama."[11] When Barker makes a similar observation in *Rogue Moon,* Hawks asks him, "Perhaps you've become a man in your own right?"[12] For all its power as an image of the intersection of the known and the unknown, the artifact is also a mirror, a kind of locus of identity for the characters who encounter it. This aspect of the icon is more familiar to us in fantasy than in science fiction; Jorge Luis Borges, for example, was fond of describing magical artifacts that become obsessions for his characters—such as the tiny sphere that contains the universe in "The Aleph" (1945), the magical coin cursed with unforgettability in "The Zahir" (*A Personal Anthology,* 1961) or the disk of Odin in "The Disk" (*The Book of Sand,* 1978). Charles Williams is another example of an author for whom artifacts are a convenient means of exploring something else, in this case the nature of love and spirituality—the Stone of First Matter, for example, in

Many Dimensions (1931), or the magical tarot deck in *The Greater Trumps* (1932). And the number of artifacts associated with feats of endurance and tests of worthiness in modern fantasy—in the tradition of J. R. R. Tolkien's *Lord of the Rings* (1954–1955)—is considerable.

A discussion of artifacts in modern fantasy would be another essay entirely, but it might be worthwhile to examine a fantasy story that addresses the iconic value of the artifact directly. Harlan Ellison's "Grail" (1981) concerns a young man who throughout his life has been obsessed with a quest for "True Love." In Saigon in 1968—an ironically appropriate setting to begin a quest for an unattainable dream—his dying lover tells him of an object, excavated at Knossos in 1900 and lost since 1946, that is the literal embodiment of his ideal. She also teaches him how to summon demons to assist him in searching for the object. He devotes the next twelve years of his life to tracking down the "grail," and finally locates it in the penthouse apartment of a dying millionaire. The object, absurdly, turns out to be a gaudy, eighteen-inch-high loving cup with the words "True Love" engraved in flowery script on its face. Inside the cup, he sees reflected the faces of all the women he has loved or been infatuated by, and one face—"the most unforgettable face he had ever seen"—that he does not recognize.[13] He realizes that, although his true love exists, he will never know her; that the moment of that knowledge is the peak of his life, and that this is the curse he has received from bargaining with demons.

Ellison's artifact is at once a garish parody of all the artifacts of science fiction stories and a strangely moving embodiment of their power. The artifact reminds us, paradoxically, of all that we know and all that we will never know; it at once expands and diminishes us, connects us to the universe while alienating us from it, and promises both the resolution of mystery and its continuation. I have wondered if the appeal of the artifact as a persistent feature of fantastic literature might not be that, in some way, this icon serves as the literature's image of *itself*. If "hard science fiction" promises a knowable universe, then its artifacts will finally be knowable. If horror stories seek to exploit our most paranoid fantasies, then the artifacts of horror fiction will validate that paranoia. And if a story aspires to philosophical fiction, then its artifacts are likely to raise unanswered questions. It might be said that when an artifact appears in fantastic fiction, the function of that artifact in the narrative will be analogous to the function of the narrative itself. Certainly the artifact in science fiction has a history of thematic transformations leading to even greater complexity and richness that, at its best, reflects the growth and development of the genre as a whole.

Afterword

The artifact has remained such a ubiquitous staple of science fiction and fantasy, and of popular culture in general, that it's almost fruitless to try to track the myriad ways in which it has been used since this essay originally was written. One particular variety of artifact has become such a convention in science fiction that it earned its own entry in John Clute and Peter Nicholls's *Encyclopedia of Science Fiction*: the "Big Dumb Object," a term possibly coined by critic Roz Kaveny to describe the sorts of vast constructs mentioned above in novels such as *Rendezvous with Rama* and *Orbitsville*.[14] In fact, a self-imposed challenge seems to have emerged among science fiction writers to see who could imagine the most colossal dumb object of all; one candidate is the Great Attractor that is the title object in Stephen Baxter's 1994 novel *Ring*, an alien construct so vast that it draws entire galaxies toward it. A few, almost random, examples of the variety of alien artifacts in more recent fiction might include Robert Charles Wilson's *Mysterium* (1994), involving a secret government project to investigate a strange and deadly alien artifact that originally had been discovered in Turkey in 1989 and kept secret; Alastair Reynolds's *Revelation Space* (2000), whose title is drawn from the radically distorted pocket of spacetime that surrounds a bizarre alien artifact known as the "shrouds"; Ken Macleod's *Newton's Wake* (2004), with its vast artifact of immense power that draws the novel's characters together in complex ways; or Tobias Buckell's *Crystal Rain* (2006), in which a long-lost artifact of power called the *Ma Wi Jung* serves as a kind of MacGuffin for the novel's characters.

An increasingly common use of the artifact is as a gateway or portal to other parts of the universe, or to other universes entirely—a device that offers a dual advantage to writers, at once enabling them to take advantage of the emotional resonance of the Big Dumb Object and to elide the physics problem imposed by faster-than-light travel. This turns the artifact into a means to tell a particular story, rather than an iconic end in itself, and suggests that the artifact is becoming so domesticated and familiar an image that it need not serve as a source of wonder itself, but can become merely a gateway to wonder. The first, and still among the most famous treatments of this theme, is Frederik Pohl's *Gateway* (1977), although the notion gained its widest popular currency through the 1994 film *Stargate* and the enduring TV and media franchise that followed. Other recent uses of such portals include Tricia Sullivan's *Lethe* (1995), which echoes the Pohl novel in that a mysterious object on the edge of the solar system contains a series of "gates," one of which may lead to a habitable world, and Robert Charles Wilson's *Spin* (2005) and *Axis* (2007), in which vast, arch-like structures on Earth provide instantaneous transportation to a distant planet. Novels in which the gateway is to an alternate world (as opposed to a distant planet) range from the essentially young-adult focus of Steven Gould's *Wildside* (1996) to the political and social satire of Paul McAuley's *Cowboy Angels* (2007). The portal to another world—whether presented as an alien artifact or not—has become one of the most commonplace of science fiction icons in the past few decades, though it has been such a fixture of fantasy narratives so long that Farah Mendlesohn, in *Rhetorics of Fantasy*, could identify the "portal-quest" fantasy as one of the main subtypes of the genre. In fantasy, of course, the portal has long been domesticated in this sense; the wardrobe in C. S. Lewis's *The Lion, the Witch, and the Wardrobe* (1950), for example, is hardly viewed by readers as the main source of wonder in the novel, but rather as a romantic and mysterious object that serves as a means of getting to Narnia. Perhaps the same sort of thing is happening in science fiction.

This, in turn, raises the broader issue of how and when a classic icon of science fiction such as the artifact becomes merely an enabling plot device or narrative convention. The rocket or spaceship, for example, often was treated as an object of wonder in early science fiction, and retained some of its magical panache as late as Ray Bradbury's *The Martian Chronicles* (1950). But by the time Bradbury was writing, the spaceship had become an almost mundane convention of the genre. Similarly, H. G. Wells's time machine was described in awestruck detail in *The Time Machine*, but has become such a widespread convention that many recent stories hardly bother to describe the device itself at all. As the ever-increasing vastness of alien artifacts in novels like Stephen Baxter's *Ring* suggests, science fiction has a way of continually increasing the ante on its own "sense of wonder."

six

The Remaking of Zero

I n Ray Bradbury's 1950 short story "The Highway," Hernando, a poor Mexican farmer who lives beside a highway from the United States, enjoying such
odd fruits of this link to technology as sandals made from tire rubber and a
bowl made from a hubcap, is startled by the sudden appearance of cars speed-
ing northward in great numbers, all filled with mysteriously panic-stricken
American tourists returning home. At the end of the flood comes an aging
Ford, packed with young Americans who stop at Hernando's shack to ask for
water for their failing radiator. The driver explains the exodus: "The war!" he
shouts, "It's come, the atom war, the end of the world!"—the tourists are all
trying to return to their families. After the young people leave, Hernando
prepares to resume his plowing. When his wife asks him what has happened, he
replies, "It's nothing," and sets out with burro and plow, pausing to muse,
"What do they mean, 'the world?' "[1]

This little parable of nuclear holocaust—it's hardly realistic speculation,
since Hernando's life obviously will be altered in radical ways that he is unaware
of—raises in Bradbury's best elliptical form some fundamental issues of stories
that begin at or near the "end of the world." Bradbury suggests that Hernando's
simple and apparently self-sufficient world will continue much as it has (although, one assumes, without the interruption of tourists), while the "world"
that has been destroyed is the world of technology and profligate wealth represented by the highway. As in most postcatastrophe fiction, the "end of the
world" signifies the end of a way of life, the end of a culture and its system of
beliefs—but not the actual destruction of the planet or its population (although
this population may be reduced severely). For this reason, it is perhaps most
helpful to regard such stories as tales of cosmological displacement: the old
concept of "world" is destroyed and a new one must be built in its place.
Economic and political systems, beliefs, and behavior patterns are destroyed,

but more often than not the Earth abides, and so, at least in part, does human-ity. This type of "end of the world" has occurred fairly often in human history, most obviously in such dramatic genocides as the destruction of Native Ameri-can civilizations or the Nazi death camps, but also, in a broader sense, such historical movements as urbanization or the Industrial Revolution. Often these endtimes are associated with new technologies or the introduction of tech-nologically superior weaponry, and in fact many of the apocalyptic anxieties of the post–World War II period arose from just such a technological innovation: nuclear weapons. But in the fiction of catastrophe, the world often is trans-formed by a reversal of this historical process: technologies are *removed* from the world, rather than new ones being introduced as in conventional under-standings of the forward movement of history. Much of the impact of such fiction arises from the speculations that it offers about the effects of the loss of technology on machine-dependent populations—such as the tourists flowing past Hernando in "The Highway."

Bradbury's story reveals a number of themes common to post-holocaust fiction. The highway represents the mobility of a society that contrasts sharply with Hernando's own deep relationship with his plot of land by the river; the larger society, no longer as mobile, will have to learn quickly the value of such a relationship. Technology appears in the story in four guises. First, the "big long black cars heading north" suggest a whole complex of industrial civilization: the availability of mechanics; the dependability of industries that produce and transport gasoline, rubber, metal, and plastic; the efficiency of governments in maintaining roads and bridges. After this initial flood of well-kept cars has passed, a second, more ominous image of the same technology appears: the dilapidated Ford, its top gone and its radiator boiling over. While this machine is part of the same society that produced the earlier ones, dependence upon it has clearly become precarious. As it wears out, the car no longer offers protec-tion from such discomforts of the natural world as rain, and it must be repaired frequently by whatever means are available—in this case, well-water from a farm. Significantly, the Ford is driven by young people, since it is the young who will have to make do with such machines in the remnants of a mechanical civilization that has lost the means to service and maintain its machines.

But the story contains a yet more ominous image of what is to come for these young people. At the bottom of the river that runs by Hernando's hut lie the remains of a big American car that had crashed there years earlier. Some-times the wreck is visible, and sometimes it is obscured by the muddy waters; in a few years the sediment of the river will cover it entirely. From this wreck, Hernando has salvaged the tire from which he carved his rubber sandals, just as his hubcap-bowl has been salvaged from a hubcap that had flown off another car. These images suggest what may become of technology after even the old Fords are gone: The machines themselves will be turned into raw materials, their parts stripped for primitive implements and clothing before they are reclaimed by the natural world.

A fourth image of technology suggests what might happen still later, when even salvaging the remnants of technology is insufficient. This image, the last in the story, is one of life and hope: Hernando sets his plow in the furrowed soil and begins tilling the land. It is at this point that he wonders, "What do they mean, 'the world?'" and the question is an appropriate one, since Hernando's present world resembles closely the world that may come to pass after industrial technology has faded altogether and the survivors are forced to return to that most basic of all machines, the plow. In the end, Bradbury's story is perversely optimistic in its suggestion of a return to a simpler, less complex life. Such a vision is presented also in Bradbury's *The Martian Chronicles* (1950), in which the Martian colonists, like the Americans in "The Highway," return home *en masse* at the outbreak of nuclear war on Earth. One family, however, escapes *to* Mars, and there the father ceremonially burns such symbols of the old world as stocks and bonds. This suggestion of starting a new world symbolically cleansed of the sins of the old is not only in keeping with earlier millenarian traditions, but is also common in literary works that begin at or near the world-ending events.[2] As we shall see later, one of the richest of such novels, George R. Stewart's *Earth Abides* (1949), conforms closely to the postapocalypse pattern we find in Bradbury's "The Highway."

Although the very notion of beginning a narrative with a "world-ending" event seems perverse, especially if the underlying tone of the novel is going to be optimistic, such a fantasy is very much in line with millenarian thought. As Mircea Eliade writes, "the idea of the destruction of the World is not, basically, pessimistic."[3] Norman Cohn has traced medieval millenarian movements to the unrest, disorientation, and anxiety of the rootless poor who sought to improve their lives but found little cause for hope in existing social and economic structures. While contemporary science-fictional versions of the end of the world differ in key respects from these earlier millenarianists—few involve supernatural agencies, for example (although the most popular millennialist series of the 1990s, Tim LaHaye and Jerry B. Jenkins's *Left Behind* novels, was so

steeped in Christian fundamentalism it could hardly count as science fiction)—
they often share the belief that a new order can come about only through a
complete destruction of the old. In Eliade's terms, "life cannot be *repaired*, it
can only be *re-created* by a return to sources."[4] Or, in the words of J. G. Ballard,
one of science fiction's master catastrophists, "I believe that the catastrophe
story, whoever may tell it, represents a constructive and positive act by the
imagination rather than a negative one, an attempt to confront the terrifying
void of a patently meaningless universe by challenging it at its own game, to
remake zero by provoking it in every conceivable way."[5] After surviving a mysterious plague that all but wipes out humanity, the protagonist of Stewart's *Earth
Abides* thinks, "Now we have finished with the past. . . . This is the Moment
Zero, and we stand between two eras. Now the new life begins. Now we com-
mence the Year One."[6]

The promise inherent in the idea of "remaking zero" is certainly one of the
reasons the post-apocalyptic story has survived as long as it has, and in so many
guises. On the simple level of narrative action, the prospect of a depopulated
world in which humanity is reduced to a more elemental struggle with nature
provides a convenient arena for the sort of heroic action that is constrained in
the corporate, technological world that we know. The "true" values of individual effort and courage are allowed to emerge once again, and power flows
eventually, after initial conflicts over such resources as weapons or stockpiled
food, to those who possess these attributes—to a "natural aristocracy" unin-
hibited by the previous world's political and economic complexities. (Perhaps,
in this sense, the ancestry of the modern disaster novel should include James
Fenimore Cooper, whose works also depict the emergence of a new aristocracy
in the wilderness of a new world where the conventions and constraints of the
old have been supplanted by new imperatives.) This simplification of relationships also permits a simplification of the forces of good and evil, making it
possible to depict a world of easily discernible heroes and villains. Thus, in
terms of the action story, the notion of starting the world over is appealing.
Furthermore, end-of-the-world stories provide a convenient means of exploring at least two of science fiction's favorite themes—the impact of technology
on human behavior, and the relationship of humanity to its environment—
without necessitating the sometimes cumbersome narrative apparatus usually
associated with these themes. The impact of technology on human behavior is
most often dealt with through the introduction of new technologies into fictional worlds—robots, time machines, spacecraft, computers, and the like. But

the problems of developing both the details of the new technology and the details of the fictional world create a rather complex dialectic for the reader, who must try to understand the impact of a fictional technology on a fictional world and draw from that some insights concerning our own world and our own technology. By *removing* familiar technology from a familiar world, however, the end-of-the-world story simplifies this dialectic considerably, allowing the author to explore issues of technology and society by speculating on the effects of their loss.[7] A number of science fiction stories—including E. M. Forster's "The Machine Stops" (1909), S. S. Held's "The Death of Iron" (1932), Kit Pedler and Gerry Davis's *Mutant 59: The Plastic Eaters* (1972, based in part on an earlier episode of the *Doomwatch* TV series), and Kevin J. Anderson and Doug Beason's *Ill Wind* (1995)—construct the entire catastrophe around the failure of machines; the latter three stories concern worldwide plagues that affect only machine parts such as iron and plastic.

The other significant science fiction theme made accessible in post-apocalyptic fiction is that of humanity's relationship to its environment, or its alienation from that environment. As with new technologies, new and strange environments are likely to require a great deal of narrative exposition concerning alien planets, climates, and the like; in the post-holocaust story, this problem can be circumvented by defamiliarizing familiar environments through the transformations wrought by the disaster. A city emptied of its people, whether through nuclear disaster or disease or environmental catastrophe, becomes a strange and alien place. Similarly, a pastoral landscape becomes a foreboding wasteland by the implied danger of holocaust survivors reduced to savagery, disfigured by radiation, or given to strange new beliefs. Leigh Brackett's *The Long Tomorrow* (1955) and John Wyndham's *Re-Birth* (1955) depict wasteland journeys detailed with such geographical verisimilitude that they can be traced on current maps of North America; the territory is familiar, and yet so alien that we have no idea what it may contain. Robert Merle's *Malevil* (1972) spends much time before the holocaust detailing the landscape surrounding the ancient fortress of Malevil, so that we can better appreciate the devastating transformation this landscape has undergone. Generally, geography is an important recurrent element in post-holocaust narratives, and almost always it serves to establish a link between the strange new environment and the world we know.

Related to these familiar science fiction themes is what is probably the fundamental reason for the emotional power of post-holocaust narratives: the mythic power inherent in the very conception of a remade world. The sources of mythic power in this genre are at least threefold, for in most post-holocaust narratives we see the re-emergence of chaos into the experiential world (and the attendant opportunities this provides for ritualistic heroic action); the reinforcement of cultural values through the triumph of these values in a final, decisive "battle of the Elect"; and the assurance of racial survival despite the most overwhelming odds—a kind of "denial of death" on a cultural rather than individual level.

By "the re-emergence of chaos" I mean the return of Nature as a material adversary in the narrative. The subduing of chaos is a fundamental activity of technology, and perhaps of culture. But the arena for this confrontation moves ever outward; once the natural environment of Earth has been subdued, Nature becomes outer space, or alien planets. But the post-catastrophe tale brings this confrontation with Nature closer to home; in these stories chaos may lie just beyond the limits of the village, or outside the family circle, or—especially with "last man on Earth" stories—around the next corner. In M. P. Shiel's *The Purple Cloud* (1901), the struggle is even internalized; the question is not merely whether Adam Jeffson, apparently the last man on Earth, can master the immense environment he inherits, but whether what he calls the "White" forces of his own mind can master the destructive and chaotic "Black" forces that cause him to burn great cities and nearly kill the only surviving woman. Mythic heroic action depends partly upon confrontation with chaos, and the post-holocaust world repeatedly provides opportunities for such confrontations, between the characters and their environment as well as between individuals.

But such confrontation is meaningful only if it can be associated with a set of values, and the reinforcement of such values is another mythic function of the post-holocaust tale. In fact, such tales often become openly didactic, pitting diametrically opposed value systems against one another in a final battle for supremacy. Once the "evil" antagonists are vanquished, such narratives seem to say, the evil values they represent will disappear, making it possible for the new world to evolve toward greater perfection than the old. One of the most didactic of such novels, Alfred Noyes' *No Other Man* (1940), pits the devout Catholic protagonist against the mad scientist Marduk (whose very name suggests pre-Christian Babylon), only to vanquish Marduk and thus validate the superiority of religious over scientist thought. Only slightly less didactic is Alfred Coppel's *Dark December* (1960), in which the opposed value systems are both military: the conscientious and professional but guilt-ridden (because of his role in the nuclear war as a missile officer) Gavin against the psychopathic, fascistic Collingwood, who sees the devastated environment as an opportunity for men like himself to rise to power. (Of course, Collingwood eventually falls off a bridge.) In Merle's *Malevil,* following the holocaust of nuclear chain-reactions, the rationalistic communal life of Malevil castle under the direction of Emmanuel Comte comes into conflict with an oppressive theocracy imposed on a neighboring village by the hypocritical false priest Fulbert le Naud. The ensuing struggle for supremacy not only validates the humanism of Malevil's system, but also indirectly validates the need for technology, since the struggle convinces the inhabitants of Malevil that they must begin research into the reinvention of weapons in order to protect their interests and values—despite their acute awareness of what the technology of weaponry can ultimately lead to.

A third mythic function of the fictional end of the world is that, ironically, it provides some reassurance of survival. In fact, most such fictions that we conveniently label "end of the world" stories are in fact quite the opposite, and dwell on the *survival* of key representative individuals and in some cases key institutions (such as the family) as well. It might be more accurate to label such fictions "almost-the-end-of-the-world" fictions, or "end-of-most-of-the-world" fictions, but works that describe a complete annihilation of the planet and all human life are comparatively rare. And even among this small group of works, such as Poe's "Conversation of Eiros and Charmion" (1839), there is some promise at least of spiritual survival. Eliade has suggested that old-fashioned millennialism has suffered under the threat of nuclear holocaust; that modern Western thought does not hold out much hope for survival and re-generation. "In the thought of the West this End will be total and final; it will not be followed by a new Creation of the World."[8] But the fiction of catastrophe belies this, and does provide some reassurance against nuclear anxiety. With the exception of a few works such as Mordecai Roshwald's *Level 7* (1959) and Nevil Shute's *On the Beach* (1957), most nuclear holocaust stories assure us that humanity can rebuild against the most staggering odds—and the same is true for other types of catastrophe tales as well. This promise of survival redeems even the bleakest of endtime fictions. Wilson Tucker's *The Long Loud Silence* (1952), for example, details the growing brutality of its protagonist in a shattered world. In terms of the survival of values that we discussed earlier, there is nothing much promising about Corporal Russell Gary, who finally rejects all human companionship and—in the novel's unpublished original ending—even apparently resorts to cannibalism.[9] A similar bleakness and apparent destruction of values, leading again to cannibalism, characterizes Harlan Ellison's "A

Boy and His Dog" (1969). But each of these fictions holds out the promise of survival, and Ellison's even perversely suggests that values, too, will survive, even if they are comparatively trivial and sentimental ones. After all, Ellison's protagonist says after making a meal of his lover to keep his pet dog from starving, "A boy loves his dog" (254).

Whether these stories aspire to adventure, to thematically powerful science fiction, or to a mythic template for cultural rebirth, stories that begin at the end of the world have evolved a fairly characteristic five-part narrative formula over the years. The formula may be varied in many ways, with some elements expanded to fill nearly the whole narrative, others skipped, and new ones added, but there are commonly five large stages of action: (1) the experience or discovery of the cataclysm; (2) the journey through the wasteland created by the cataclysm; (3) settlement and establishment of a new community; (4) the re-emergence of the wilderness as antagonist; and (5) a final, decisive battle or struggle to determine which values shall prevail in the new world. While this formula describes specifically works that begin with the cataclysm itself, elements of it are found in narratives that begin before the holocaust or in ones that begin long after. Let's consider each of these stages in turn.

1. Experience or Discovery of the Cataclysm

Works that begin at the end of the world usually limit their viewpoint to that of one or two central characters, and the manner in which the cataclysm is revealed to these characters traditionally takes one of two forms: Either the central character is isolated from others when the event occurs, and thus has no immediate knowledge of it, or the character witnesses the event indirectly from a relatively safe vantage point. The former case, in which part of the drama is the character's gradual discovery of the nature and extent of the disaster, includes Shiel's *The Purple Cloud* (and Ranald MacDougall's considerably different 1958 film from this novel, *The World, the Flesh, and the Devil*), Noyes' *No Other Man* (which coincidentally also was considered briefly for filming by Frank Capra), and Stewart's *Earth Abides*. Of these, only the Shiel novel attempts to forge a direct moral link between the protagonist's symbolic isolation from human society and the destruction of humanity. Adam Jeffson is off discovering the North Pole when the strange volcanic gas kills all of humanity, but he achieves his goal only by committing a series of murders; furthermore, he describes himself from childhood as being "separate, special, marked for—something."[10] Jeffson sees his subsequent isolation alternately as a monumental punishment for his evil deeds and as a monumental reward for his being "special." He is cursed by loneliness and madness, but he also inherits the Earth and founds a new race—resembling one of the Nietzschean supermen of Shiel's later fiction. Stewart and Noyes each provide some moral justification for the survival of their protagonists; in *Earth Abides,* Isherwood Williams is helplessly recovering from a snakebite while on an ecological expedition in the woods, and in *No Other Man,* Mark Adams is trapped in a wrecked enemy submarine where he had been held captive. In each case, the character is relieved somewhat of the responsibility of being isolated, since the isolation is enforced by external circumstances. But in neither case is a direct moral link established between the actions of the survivors and the destruction of the rest of humanity.

Stories in which the survivors witness the cataclysm from a protected vantage point are somewhat more common. The protagonists of both Roshwald's *Level 7* (1959) and Coppel's *Dark December* (1960) are military personnel stationed in underground bunkers. Philip Wylie's *The End of the Dream* (1972) and Kate Wilhelm's *Where Late the Sweet Birds Sang* (1976) both portray isolated strongholds specifically designed to withstand the impending ecological catastrophes. The central characters of Merle's *Malevil* happen to be gathered in a deep wine cellar whose stone walls protect them from the firestorm, and the collision of Earth with another planet is witnessed from aboard a spaceship by characters in Philip Wylie and Edwin Balmer's *When Worlds Collide* (1933). In S. Fowler Wright's *Deluge* (1928) and John Bowen's *After the Rain* (1958), the good fortune of being on high ground or finding boats save the protagonists from worldwide floods. Geography also protects the survivors of nuclear war in Pat Frank's *Alas, Babylon* (1959) and Wilson Tucker's *The Long Loud Silence* (1952); both novels begin in small towns isolated from major target areas. And in one of the few openly comic treatments of this theme, Robert Lewis Taylor's *Adrift in a Boneyard* (1947), a mysterious thunderclap annihilates everyone except a family in their car on the way to the theater—clearly suggesting the family was deliberately "chosen" for survival. (Although the two novels may seem odd bedfellows, *Adrift in a Boneyard* shares with *The Purple Cloud* the implication that the end of the world is brought about largely to force moral choices upon the main characters of the novel.)

2. Journey through the Wasteland

Perhaps because of its implicit mythic aspect, the journey through the waste-land is often one of the most important elements in end-of-the-world fictions; occasionally—as with Robert Crane's *Hero's Walk* (1954) or Roger Zelazny's *Damnation Alley* (1969)—it occupies virtually the whole of the novel. But ex-tensive journeys also figure in the works mentioned by Noyes, Shiel, Wright, Coppel, Stewart, Taylor, Tucker, Brackett, and Wyndham. Such journeys serve two major functions: to provide an overview and confirmation of the disaster, and to serve as a kind of purgation of despair on the part of the central character. The longest such purgation, in Shiel's *The Purple Cloud*, takes Adam Jefferson through decades of madness and destructiveness. In the Noyes and Taylor novels, the journeys also serve to satirize the trivial aspects of pre-holocaust life by revealing people caught up in petty matters at the time of death. On his cross-country journey, Stewart's protagonist sees the various ways that people may relate to their environment, most poignantly observed in the contrast between a self-subsistent Black farm family and a hopelessly technology-dependent Manhattan couple trying to survive in an empty but still mostly functioning New York.

In Coppel's *Dark December* and Wright's *The Deluge,* the journey is moti-vated by the desire to reunite families separated by the cataclysm, with despair mitigated by the increasingly irrational hope that a wife or husband has some-how also survived. Such hope also motivates some of the survivors in Shute's *On the Beach* (1957) and Frank's *Alas, Babylon.* In Tucker's *The Long Loud Silence,* Brackett's *The Long Tomorrow,* and Wyndham's *Re-Birth,* rumors of a better society somewhere beyond the wasteland motivate the journey. And in nearly all these novels, the search for additional survivors with whom one might establish a new community is a central motivation for the journey.

But the journey has another aspect, too: the promise of new frontiers, of exploring a new or remade world. In Philip Wylie and Edwin Balmer's *After Worlds Collide,* which begins following the destruction of the Earth, the world to be explored is literally a new planet where the survivors hope to settle (although the ruins of an ancient technological civilization make it seem curi-ously like the landscape of a future Earth). But even Earthbound disaster fic-tions suggest that the frontiers have been remade, especially if we remember that the classical nineteenth-century definition of "frontier" was based on low population density rather than simply whether an area had once been explored. These new frontiers thus might include even urban areas. Despair is once again mitigated, then, by the hope, restored by cataclysm, of renewed patterns of growth and exploration, and by the sense of immense freedom that comes from being able to choose openly where and how one will live. Shiel's Adam Jeffson does not hesitate to make himself at home in various palaces (the illustrations accompanying the original appearance of *The Purple Cloud* in *The Royal Magazine* even portray him as a sort of Oriental potentate), and the family in Taylor's *Adrift in a Boneyard* quickly takes advantage of the situation to move into the mansion of an eccentric millionaire, enjoying the security that this provides against ravaging animals and such luxuries as a fine wine cellar.

3. Settlement and Establishment of a Community

Following the confirmation of the cataclysm brought about by the wasteland journey comes the establishment of a permanent settlement that will be the basis of the new community and, by extension, of the new civilization. In Shiel's *The Purple Cloud,* in which there are only two survivors, this community has to be defined rather loosely, but the novel nonetheless provides the archetype for post-disaster communities, which are frequently associated with the "marriage" of the protagonist, and hence with the prospect of a new family and eventually a new community. Contrary to many readers' memories of *The Purple Cloud,* Jeffson's discovery of the sole surviving woman, Leda, occurs scarcely more than two-thirds of the way through the narrative, and it is Leda who causes him to cease his restless, destructive wandering and to settle with her: At the end of the novel, when in despair he deliberately abandons her to return to England, her telephone message that the purple cloud has reappeared on the horizon causes him to flee back to protect her. It is practically Jeffson's first motivated action since the cataclysm, and the motivation is that of protectiveness and preservation. Jeffson is clearly thinking of a good location for a settled community by the end of the novel. Both Stewart's *Earth Abides* and Wright's *Deluge* also associate the founding of the new community with a woman; in the Stewart novel the new community accretes around Isherwood Williams and his newly found wife Emily, while in the Wright novel the community is associated with the simple values of Mary Wittels, an almost archetypal "wise woman" who nurses the wife of the protagonist back to health and is eventually instrumental in reuniting them. Their reunion, we are led to believe throughout the novel, is the single action most necessary to validate the stability of the new community. In Frank's *Alas, Babylon* and Merle's *Malevil*, both novels in which the symbolic journey is confined to short exploratory trips in the immediate neighborhood, the growing internal stability of the community occupies a larger role in the narrative. In *Alas, Babylon*, the journey motif is effectively replaced by a local ham radio operator who provides the necessary confirmation of the disaster by monitoring messages from other parts of the world. The narrative thus can focus on the challenges that the small Florida community of Fort Repose faces in obtaining necessary supplies and defending itself from looters. *Malevil*, perhaps the most determinedly localized of all post-holocaust novels, establishes at the outset the isolated, almost medieval aspect of the French countryside surrounding the small village of La Roque and focuses throughout on the problem of establishing a new social contract and the need for authority. It is interesting that both of these novels, with their paramount concern for the integrity of the village, end with the rediscovery of the necessity for military organizations and weapons, despite their demonstration of the dangers inherent in such institutions.

The novel that perhaps most clearly and thoughtfully explores the relationship between the outward journey and the community is Wilhelm's *Where Late the Sweet Birds Sang*. In this novel, the integrity of the community is intensified by the presence of large numbers of human clones, who form social groups among those cloned from the same "donors." These "clone families" develop intense empathic relationships with one another, but when the necessity arises to make journeys to urban areas for supplies, they suffer a kind of separation anxiety like that experienced during early childhood. As a result, the journeys nearly fail, and the community is forced to turn for guidance to an "outsider," a child born without the genetic permission of the community who has learned the techniques of wilderness survival as a result of his isolation. The dangers of a community turned too much inward are emphasized even more strongly at the end of the novel when this outsider, Mark, establishes a community of "exiles" that survives long after the community of clones has failed. Mark's community, it is suggested, may mark a return to savagery compared with the protectiveness of the clone village, but it also represents the dynamic interaction with the environment that must take place in order to rebuild. Civilization cannot be preserved; it must be rebuilt.

4. The Re-Emergence of the Wilderness

Within the idea of "wilderness" I include not only the encroachments of the natural world on the community—the proliferation of rats, wild animals, or disease, and the erosion of such technological support systems as roads and electricity through weather, fire, earthquakes, and vegetation growth—but also the challenges brought on by fellow survivors, who commonly revert to savagery and thus threaten the stability of the frontier-type settlement. In many post-holocaust novels, the first great challenge to the survivors, once they have formed a community, lies in making the difficult transition from dependence on the detritus of the destroyed civilization—for example, raiding grocery stores for prepackaged foods—to reinventing an agricultural and mining economy that confronts the wilderness on its own terms. Hence, in *Alas, Babylon,* a major triumph of the survivors is discovering a natural source of salt to preserve meat following the loss of electrical refrigeration; in *Malevil,* a triumphant moment occurs with the successful raising of a small wheat crop. Stewart's *Earth Abides* details, through separate expository passages presented apart from the main narrative, the various ways in which natural forces over the years destroy the remnants of civilization upon which the survivors are initially dependent; and a continuing theme in Wilhelm's *Where Late the Sweet Birds Sang* is the growing inability of the isolated community to remain self-sufficient in the midst of the growing wilderness.

Traditionally, with the wilderness comes the savage, and savagery in post-holocaust tales usually takes the form of individuals or groups who, rather than attempting to form stable communities of their own, scavenge in predatory bands across the countryside, threatening what stable communities have been established. Often, these roving bands are presented with some sympathy; one of the most traumatic moments in *Malevil* follows the massacre of such a starving band, whose pillaging of the wheat crop threatens the survival of the community at Malevil. Similarly, *Alas, Babylon* features the reluctant murder of outsiders; in both novels, the event teaches the community the necessity of military and police authority as an essential part of the social contract. Other kinds of "savages," though, are presented less sympathetically: These are often individuals who, fulfilling personal fantasies of power, represent a moral viewpoint antithetical to that of the novel's main characters. Wright, in *The Deluge,* goes to great pains to explain how weak or repressed individuals—accountants and government functionaries in the pre-catastrophe world—find in the new world a chance to seize power by whatever means available, resulting in make-shift governments sometimes derived from democracy, sometimes from meritocracy, most often by simple warlord-style bullying. Marxism, or anything that resembles it, generally does not fare well in these novels (*Malevil*, in particular, which features a Marxist as one of the secondary characters, repeatedly demonstrates the failures of this character's schemes in reorganizing the new society). But novels in which the antagonists threatening the community represent a strong moral viewpoint usually do not associate such characters with the wilderness; such characters, instead, prepare us for the decisive moral battle discussed below.

5. The Decisive Battle of the Elect

This phrase, borrowed from Norman Cohn (who sees it as an aspect of Marxist and National Socialist fantasies as well as of medieval millenarianism), may seem a rather melodramatic description of the struggle between good and evil that concludes many post-holocaust narratives, but in some cases it is scarcely an exaggeration.[11] Marduk in Noyes' *No Other Man*, Collingwood in Coppel's *Dark December*, and Fulbert le Naud in Merle's *Malevil* are figures of almost consummate evil, direct descendants of the "Black powers" that threaten to overwhelm Jeffson in Shiel's *The Purple Cloud*. These are false prophets whose potential victory would transform not merely a community or an historical movement, but the entire future of the human race—and in a few cases, such as Bowen's *After the Rain*, these prophets literally set themselves up as gods, as self-consciously supernatural figures in the mythology of the age to come. "You had better begin by worshipping me," says the villainous Arthur to his subordinates in *After the Rain*. "What is recorded of your behaviour will live on as revealed religion."[12] In Stephen King's *The Stand* (1978), which begins with an influenza pandemic that nearly annihilates the human race, Randy Flagg is a figure of consummate, archetypal evil, the "rough beast" of Yeats's "Second Coming"; and preparations for the final, cosmic battle against him make up the bulk of the very lengthy novel.

Much of what is so threatening about these evil figures lies in the recognition on the part of the reader—and usually on the part of the protagonist as well—of how much they have in common with us. In Shiel, this identification of good and evil is internalized: The struggle for dominance takes place within the mind of Adam Jeffson himself. Coppel's *Dark December* is not far removed from this. "I am you and you are me," says Collingwood to the protagonist Gavin. "We're two sides of the same coin. . . . Yin and Yang, if you prefer."[13] Gavin realizes that such taunts from Collingwood nearly tempt him to murder—which, of course, would be an ironic triumph for Collingwood's point of view. Gavin hates Collingwood most of all, he says, "for making me what I could feel myself becoming."[14] Similarly, the protagonist Martin in Wright's *Deluge* finds himself fearfully aware that he is adopting the strategies and duplicities of the "savages" he is fighting; and in Merle's *Malevil*, Emmanuel Comte is compelled to imitate some of the actions of his rival Fulbert le Naud—such as making himself a false abbé in a religion he does not fully accept to counter the sway that the false priest le Naud holds over the villagers. Clarke, the narrator of Bowen's *After the Rain*, is nearly swayed by Arthur's bizarre arguments, at least until Arthur's madness becomes undeniable. But in each of these cases, a fatal ideological or moral flaw finally separates the protagonist from his opponent. In *Dark December*, Collingwood eventually reveals himself as nothing less than an agent of Chaos ("Chaos is the natural condition of man," Collingwood claims), his rationalism nothing more than a front for a vicious brand of fascism.[15] Arthur's flaw in *After the Rain* is his obsession with natural selection and his reductive view of humans as nothing more than reasoning animals. "Imagination," he says, "is the enemy . . . when we have destroyed it, we shall have proved ourselves worthy of survival."[16] In both *Malevil* and *Deluge,* the sadism and sexual excesses of the villains are revealed as self-indulgent and wasteful, while sometimes apparently similar actions on the part of the hero are revealed to be part of a larger plan for the survival of the human race.

Other novels present this final struggle less as a moral confrontation than as a simple ideological argument. The culminating battle in Wylie and Balmer's *After Worlds Collide* turns out to be a struggle between democracy and communism after the survivors of a destroyed Earth find themselves competing with another band of survivors, from communist nations, for dominance of the new planet. Larry Niven and Jerry Pournelle's *Lucifer's Hammer* (1977), Brackett's *The Long Tomorrow,* and a number of other works seek to validate the importance of science and technology in the face of post-holocaust neo-Luddite movements. Noyes' *No Other Man* may be the closest thing we have to the same story told from the neo-Luddites' point of view; in this novel, the apparently last surviving scientist, Marduk, is done in shortly before the two protagonists join a band of Franciscan monks. Wilhelm's *Where Late the Sweet Birds Sang,* in the end, seems to be a validation of sexual reproduction over technological cloning—hardly a burning issue at this point in history—but in a larger sense, the novel also demonstrates the necessity of interacting with the environment rather than withdrawing from it protectively, as the community of clones attempts to do.

This five-part structure for post-holocaust tales might seem a bit mechanical, but it appears less so when regarded in terms of a representative novel of this kind. There is probably no better candidate than George R. Stewart's *Earth Abides,* winner of the 1951 International Fantasy Award and one of the most fully realized accounts in all science fiction of a massive catastrophe and the evolution toward a new culture that follows. The novel has not received the attention it deserves among students of science fiction, perhaps in part because it came from outside the genre; indeed, the origins of the novel seem to lie less in the tradition of science fiction catastrophes than in Stewart's own abiding concern with natural forces that seem almost willfully directed against human society. In two earlier novels, *Storm* (1941) and *Fire* (1948), Stewart presents these elemental forces as narrative protagonists. His studies of Western American history also often focus on natural catastrophes, while other anthropologically oriented novels reveal his concern with the way that societies evolve. But only in *Earth Abides,* freed from the constraints of historicism, was Stewart able to explore fully the themes of nature, myth, and society that his other works tended toward.

The title of the novel comes from Ecclesiastes 1:4—"one generation goeth, and another cometh, but the earth abideth forever"—and the action of the novel is in many ways a dramatization of the philosophy of that most oddly agnostic of the books of the Bible. Isherwood Williams, a young ecologist, suffers a rattlesnake bite while alone in the mountains and gradually recovers both from the snakebite and from another, inexplicable illness. Upon returning to a nearby village, he finds no other humans; but week-old newspapers tell him that a virulent new disease has attacked virtually the entire world population. Ish begins his wasteland journey by taking possession of a car and traveling to San Francisco, where he finds few survivors but observes that the automated processes of civilization, such as electric street lights and running water, continue to function, adding an eerie note of irony to the cataclysm. Still not certain of the extent of the catastrophe, Ish begins a transcontinental trek through the Southwest, the Plains, and the Midwest. In Arkansas, he finds a Black farm family continuing much as they had before the disaster, figures reminiscent of the Mexican family in Bradbury's "The Highway." For them, the world has not really ended at all. But at the end of Ish's journey, in New York, he meets a couple gamely trying to maintain a technology-dependent urban lifestyle amid the vast resources of an empty Manhattan. This couple, Ish realizes, provides a dramatic contrast to the Black farmers and probably will be unable to survive once the automatic processes begin to break down and the wilderness begins to reassert itself. Having thus confirmed the range of the cataclysm, Ish returns to California "to establish his life."[17] He adopts a dog named Princess—the first, slight indication of the new community—and locates himself in a place convenient to libraries and food supplies. In his despair, he seeks solace in books, but finds it only in the Bible and specifically in Ecclesiastes, with its "curious way of striking the naturalistic note, of sensing the problem of the individual against the universe."[18] Only when he meets and falls in love with another survivor, however—a Black woman named Em—does the third phase of the narrative, the establishment of a community, really begin. The nature and values of this future community are strongly hinted at by the interracial marriage that begins it.

Ish and Em begin to raise a family and take in other survivors, but the re-emergence of the wilderness—the fourth phase of our formula—threatens the budding community from the start. Plagues of ants are followed by plagues of rats from the nearby city and, in the years that follow, insects, crows, and even mountain lions reclaim the territory they had lost to the advance of human civilization. Later, elk appear, balancing the threatening image of the mountain lions with a more uplifting image of wildness. Forest fires rage out of control with no one to fight them; a mild earthquake destroys many of the remaining buildings; and diseases that might once have been routine inconveniences—including the common cold—grow potentially fatal and threaten the community, which nevertheless grows and begins to think of itself as a tribe.

Fighting the encroachments of the wilderness eventually ceases to be the aging Ish's main concern, however. "After twenty-one years . . . the world had fairly well adjusted itself, and further changes were too slow to call for day-to-day or even month-to-month observation. Now, however, the problem of society—its adjustment and reconstitution—had moved to the fore, and become his chief interest."[19] The struggle to determine which values shall prevail in the new world occupies the entire second half of *Earth Abides,* and this struggle takes on a much more complex and ambivalent form than it does in such novels as Coppel's *Dark December* or Noyes' *No Other Man.* The struggle takes place on two fronts. The first, and more traditional, follows another wasteland journey, undertaken by explorers of the second generation sent out by the community to see how others have fared in the two decades since the catastrophe. Returning, the young men bring with them Charlie, who comes as close as any character in the novel to representing the kind of evil usually associated with the battle of the Elect. Charlie threatens to corrupt the youth of the community and is described by one elder as being as "rotten inside as a ten-day fish"—literally as well as figuratively, since Charlie is a carrier of venereal disease.[20] The elders of the community discuss banishing Charlie, but decide that the only safe route is to execute him. The execution is carried out reluctantly, but not before Charlie's venereal disease spreads throughout the community killing, among others, Ish's son and chosen successor Joey, the only child of the new generation who has learned to read. The community thus assures its survival against the kind of evil Charlie represents—but at the same time it loses, in the person of Joey, its only real link with the pre-catastrophe culture and the values that culture represented.

The profound struggle of the last half of the novel revolves around Joey's death. Ish has struggled for years to transmit, through education, the values and traditions of the pre-catastrophe world, but early on he found his repeated imprecations about the need for science and social institutions coming to be regarded as a kind of eccentric obsession, much respected but little attended to by the youth of the community—with the sole exception of Joey. Ish's attempts to train the young people to become self-sufficient repeatedly fail, and he has so strongly tried to inculcate the value of certain symbols of the old world—such as the university library located nearby—that these symbols become totemic. Ish himself unwittingly evolves into a tribal priest, venerated for the magical knowledge that he possesses but brutally pinched and tormented when this knowledge fails because the younger members of the tribe no longer perceive the rationalistic basis for this knowledge. Eventually, as an old man, Ish comes to realize that the tribe is indeed becoming more self-sufficient, not because of his teachings, but because of the "forces and pressures" that cause a society to evolve in the first place. "A tribe is like a child," an ancient Ish says to his only surviving friend, Ezra. "You can show it the way by which it should grow up, and perhaps you can direct it a little, but in the end the child will go his own way, and so will the tribe."[21]

In an essay on *Earth Abides,* Willis E. McNelly has noted that the names "Ish" and "Em" derive from Hebrew words meaning "man" and "mother."[22] This and myriad other details invite a heavily mythic interpretation of the novel, with Ish and Em standing not for a simplistic equivalent of Adam and Eve, as they might in lesser post-holocaust novels, but for a broad range of human institutions. On the broadest level, Ish and Em are indeed Adam and Eve, and their adventure is the adventure of the human species. But they also stand for a culture, since despite their failure to inculcate codes of values deliberately, they profoundly influence the behavior of generations to come. At increasingly narrower levels, they also stand for the tribe, for the family, and even for the individual, and the basic five-part structure we have used to explore this novel reveals new meanings when regarded in each of these separate contexts. And it may be that these complex levels of potential meaning account for the remarkable power and richness of all the best post-holocaust novels. In the broadest sense, such novels are epics of the power of humanity to remain dominant in the universe. Read this way, the cataclysm is literally a new creation or genesis, the period of exploration a dispersion or exodus, the establishing of a community the invention of a social contract, the emergence of the wilderness a testing of that social contract, and the final battle of the Elect a confirmation of permanence. At the tribal or family level, the five-part structure becomes the separation from existing family structures through cataclysm, the journey in search of new family members, the founding of the new family in a settled community, the struggle to maintain the family against the encroachments of disorder, and the final battle to preserve the sanctity and integrity of the family from "evil" forces that would pollute or destroy it. The story may even be viewed on a level of individual psychology, as an epic of individuation: the cataclysm becomes the birth trauma, the journey a period of growth and exploration leading toward ego development, the establishment of the community the growing awareness of the super-ego, the emerging wilderness the threat of the unconscious, and the final battle the triumph of the emerging personality over forces that would subsume or disintegrate it. To narrowly allegorize any of these novels according to such a system would be dangerously reductive, but to ignore such potential meanings altogether would be reductive in an entirely different way. *Earth Abides* supports each of these readings at least in part, as suggested by Ish's comparison, late in the novel, of the tribe both with human society in general and with the growth of an individual child. Perhaps, after all, the profoundest question we can ask of such novels is that simple question of Hernando's in Bradbury's "The Highway": "What do they mean, 'the world?' " And perhaps it is for all these reasons that fic-

tions that begin with cataclysm often include some of the most strangely lumi-
nous visions of affirmation in the whole of fantastic literature.

Afterword

For reasons not at all surprising, apocalyptic fiction underwent a resurgence
during the periods of the two World Wars, and probably had its longest sustained run as a major science fiction theme during the Cold War era, when
visions of nuclear annihilation informed everything from foreign policy to
electoral politics, city planning, and elementary school education (with its
famous 1951 "Duck and Cover" Civil Defense film instructing children on how
to protect themselves from atomic bombs). As the Cold War waned, so did
nuclear catastrophe as a dominant subtheme of science fiction, replaced to
some extent by apocalypses driven by the growing environmental movement
(one of the most extreme of which was Philip Wylie's posthumously published
The End of the Dream [1972]), or by newer anticipated threats such as space-
plagues, nanotechnology, black holes, global warming, and asteroid strikes.

After 2000, however, possibly influenced by pandemics, the terrorist attacks
of 9/11, and widely publicized climatological disasters such as Hurricane Ka-
trina or the 2004 Indian Ocean tsunami, apocalyptic visions underwent another resurgence, including popular films such as *28 Days Later* (2002; sequel in
2007 as *28 Weeks Later*), *The Day After Tomorrow* (2004), *The Children of Men*
(2006, based on P. D. James's 1992 novel), and *I Am Legend* (2007, based on the
1954 novel by Richard Matheson), TV series such as *The Stand* (1994, based on
Stephen King's 1978 novel), or *Jericho* (2006–2008), which directly resurrects
the theme of nuclear war. A 2008 anthology titled *Wastelands: Stories of Life
after Apocalypse*, edited by John Joseph Adams, collected twenty-two stories
on this theme, all but six of them originally published after 1990. Perhaps
most notable was a blossoming of interest in the theme in literary and bestselling fiction—what science fiction readers and writers call the "mainstream"—
with apocalypse serving as the background for a variety of novels such as
Margaret Atwood's *Oryx and Crake* (2003), Chris Adrian's *The Children's Hospital* (2006), Matthew Sharpe's *Jamestown* (2007), or Nick Harkaway's *The
Gone-Away World* (2008). Among the most successful of these novels, which
directly address the sort of survival scenarios discussed in this essay, are Cormac McCarthy's Pulitzer Prize–winning bestseller *The Road* (2006) (which was

certainly among the darkest and most unusual selections for TV host Oprah Winfrey's book club), and British novelist Jim Crace's *The Pesthouse* (2007). Interestingly, each begins with a strikingly similar premise: Two decent and caring people, the rest of their families dead, trying to make their way across the devastated landscape of what was once America, avoiding brutal slavetakers and thieves, while hoping to reach the ocean that they believe will somehow represent their salvation.

In McCarthy's case, the two are a nameless father and son, armed only with a gun with three bullets (two of which are meant to serve as a last resort) making their way through a burned-out world toward the ocean while trying to find occasional food and shelter and avoiding the roving bands of feral cannibals and violent paramilitary groups. The boy's mother killed herself shortly after the event, and the boy has known no other world, although his father sometimes tells him, in brief fragments, about life before the unspecified disaster. McCarthy shows little interest in writing a cautionary tale, and is so disdainful of the actual causes of this nuclear winter landscape that he barely alludes to it: "The clocks stopped at 1:17. A long shear of light and then a series of low concussions" (45). It could as easily be a nuclear war or an asteroid strike, and what later clues he offers—such as an image of corpses frozen into a melted roadway, suggesting that firestorms continued long after the initial event had sent refugees on the road—clearly are intended more as nightmare dressings than as backstory. In effect, he has taken the raw iconography of the apocalyptic tale, but left out the learning: We never know more than what the father and son trekking through this burnt landscape know, and they're never going to learn much. But for all the gruesome tableaus they encounter along the way—a headless gutted baby roasting on a spit, a group of emaciated people kept trapped in a basement as food—the novel still portrays fitful efforts at starting new communities, and even ends on a faint note of hope. Most important, it portrays much the same kind of polarization of good and evil discussed in this essay, contrasting the boy's unquestioning trust in his dad and the father's fierce but understated love for the boy with the feral brutality of many of the characters they encounter along the road. Although hints appear of the five-part structure that I've described in this essay, McCarthy focuses almost entirely on the journey through the wasteland, with occasional suggestions of abortive efforts to start communities, but in the context of an unremittingly bleak vision.

Crace's novel is also a love story of a sort, set in an almost medievalized future America not unlike many of those discussed earlier. The novel opens with a small-scale apocalypse of its own: a rain-drenched hillside collapses into a lake, stirring up poisonous gases that wipe out all life in the village of Ferrytown, which had gained prosperity by providing river crossings to refugees trying to make their way eastward to find passage to Europe, escaping the plague-stricken and ruined America. The only two survivors are Franklin Lopez, a traveler whose knee injury had forced him to remain on high ground while his brother Jackson sought help in the village, and Margaret, an unmarried woman quarantined to a hilltop "pesthouse" after contracting the "flux," a usually fatal disease whose symptoms resemble bubonic plague. After he helps nurse her back to health, she joins him on his eastward quest (this reversal of the historical westward frontier movement is pointed and obvious), and it's not long before they fall in with other refugees. When their little community is raided by an outlaw band led by the brutal Captain Chief (a near-stereotype of post-apocalyptic literature; the self-appointed warlord), Franklin is enslaved and Margaret left behind, eventually inheriting (or more accurately, stealing) a baby and ending up in a religious commune called the Finger Baptists. This repressive but efficient community, though reminiscent of some of the survivalist camps in earlier novels, is perhaps Crace's most original invention. But when Captain Chief's crew, with Franklin in tow, show up at the Finger Baptist redoubt, the novel takes an unlikely turn toward a chase-and-pursuit adventure, as Franklin and Margaret reunite, steal a couple of horses, and take off for the coast.

Crace's avowed effort to invert, subvert, and revise the classic American frontier narrative while offering a critique of what he regarded as overly optimistic science fiction ends up both reconstructing a frontier narrative and recapitulating the familiar science fiction theme we've discussed throughout this essay. While Franklin and Margaret are both touching and sympathetic characters, trying to learn how to love each other in a society that, for all its anarchy and chaos, seems weirdly puritanical and familiar, the main attraction of *The Pesthouse* is Crace's graceful prose and his unerring feel for the rhythms of nature, both of which at time recall Stewart's *Earth Abides,* and which suggest that the imperative to remake the damaged world remains powerful more than a half-century after it emerged as a classic subtheme of science fiction.

seven

Frontiers in Space

y title is borrowed from a 1955 paperback science fiction anthology,
edited by Everett F. Bleiler and T. E. Dikty, which bears on its back cover
the claim that science fiction has "opened new frontiers to the pioneer hero,
given him new worlds to conquer and marvellous means to conquer them."
Such claims were endemic among science fiction publications of the period, as
publishers sought to position the recently emergent science fiction book market in the context of other, more-established genres such as Westerns or mysteries (a similar strategy involved describing the genre as "a different kind of
mystery thrill," in the words of another paperback cover).[1] A few years later,
another paperback advertised, "Centuries have passed since man first set out
across the uncharted seas of his own World. But the same urgent spirit that
drove men on journeys from which they knew they might never return is still
tugging and pushing. And now the restless questing of mankind has sent him
out across the unknown seas of space."[2] Such comments might fairly be said to
represent the marketing of science fiction rather than the fiction itself, but they
do serve to illustrate a widely held popular belief concerning the relationship of
science fiction with the concept of the frontier, a belief that often has been
expressed by science fiction writers and fans, and has even been the subject of a
number of academic studies.[3]

The basic tenets of this belief are as follows: For centuries, such genres of
fantastic literature as the imaginary voyage and the utopia had thrived upon
people's fascination with the uncharted regions of the globe. In America, this
fascination became focused upon the Western frontier—not quite uncharted or
even unsettled, but still an arena for the kind of heroic individualism that increasingly seemed to be disappearing in the urbanized and industrialized East.
With the closing of that frontier, the popular audience sought promises of yet-
new areas to explore, and science fiction gained popularity as a kind of literature

that not only offered new frontiers but did so without sacrificing the technological idealism that equally had come to characterize industrial America. Science fiction offered its audience both the machine and the wilderness—in fact
made them interdependent—and thus opened for exploration the Moon, other
planets, and finally other stars. Popular culture had found itself an infinite
frontier, or "the final frontier," as TV's *Star Trek* had it.

According to this view, science fiction was almost inevitably an outgrowth of
frontier fiction. Indeed, the growth of popular science fiction did coincide to
some extent with the closing of the American frontier, and a great many science
fiction works portray frontier societies as arenas for individual heroism. The
term "space opera," coined by science fiction fan and writer Wilson Tucker in
1941 to describe the hackneyed cosmic adventure epics of pulp magazines in the
1930s, seems to insist on a relationship between such stories and the "horse
operas" of the same period.[4] But even before Tucker, the connection seemed
evident to even a casual reader of the pulps. Bernard De Voto, himself a widely
respected historian of the West, clearly made the connection in what was surely
one of the first accounts of pulp science fiction to appear in a literary magazine
(*Harper's*, September 1939):

The science thus discussed is idiotic beyond any possibility of exaggeration, but the
point is that in this kind of fiction the bending of light or Heisenberg's formula is
equivalent to the sheriff of the horse opera fanning his gun, the heroine of the sex
pulp taking off her dress. . . . These stories are more maturely written than those in the
cowboy pulps, for example, if only in that they use longer words and more involved
sentences. Their conventions and narrative formulas are also less primitive than the
chase-with-sixshooters of the horse operas. Some of them are, to be sure, just that
chase rephrased in terms of death rays, with heroic earthmen overcoming malign Ven-
usians on the last page, but the majority of them forgo melodrama in favor of exegesis.
They fulfill the hopeless dream of detective-story writers: they are a kind of fiction in
which explanation is action.[5]

As if to demonstrate this relationship once and for all, a little-known pulp
writer named Guy Archette (pseudonym of Chester S. Geier) was able to transform a Western into a science fiction story by changing only a few key words
and publishing it in *Amazing Stories* in 1953.[6] Such a view necessarily over-
simplifies the nature of science fiction and of popular literature in general.
While it is true that much science fiction deals with the colonization of other
worlds, most of it does not, and this theme is only one among dozens that have

evolved during the long course of the genre's history. While it is also true that popular science fiction in America developed close upon the end of the frontier period—around the turn of the century—so did the Western and the urban crime story. And while it is probably true that popular literature sought ways of dealing with the narrowing arenas for heroic adventure on Earth, science fiction was far from the only response to this need. The "lost race" novel, the jungle adventure tale, the prehistoric romance—even the tale of universal cataclysm, which provides a kind of "frontier" by returning much of the Earth to a depopulated wilderness (see "The Remaking of Zero" elsewhere in this volume)—all enjoyed vogues during the late nineteenth and early twentieth centuries. Utopian fiction also began to appear with increasing frequency in America during this period, and at least one of the authors of such fiction— William Dean Howells—believed that the utopian story was late in coming to America because of the presence of a frontier to absorb and deflect utopian impulses.[7] Nor is it entirely accurate to view the history of science fiction solely in terms of the pulp-magazine phenomenon that began before the turn of the twentieth century and eventually gave the genre its present name. In recent years, much research has been done on the science-fictional elements in works of Hawthorne, Poe, Melville, Fitz-James O'Brien, Thomas Wentworth Higginson, and others, and one curious observation that derives from all this work is that such early science fiction overlaps very little with the body of frontier literature that began with captivity narratives and became most clearly defined in the works of James Fenimore Cooper.[8] While it might be argued that the appeal of such frontier literature has much in common with the later appeal of such science fiction works as Ray Bradbury's *The Martian Chronicles* (1950)— the notion of settling a new land, of finding a new kind of democracy, of evolving a "natural aristocracy" based on assimilation with the new environment, of escaping the ills of urban life—it's also important to remember that works such as Bradbury's came relatively late in the history of science fiction, that Bradbury himself (at least) was deliberately attempting to recreate a frontier experience in his stories, and that the science fiction of the nineteenth century expressed comparatively few such concerns.[9]

In fact, it might well be argued that the first real confluence of science fiction themes with the literature of the frontier did not occur until the advent of the dime novel. Edward S. Ellis's *The Huge Hunter: Or, The Steam Man of the Prairies* (1868) generally is credited as the first of the dime novels to introduce the "marvelous inventions" theme that later would become such a staple of the genre in the "Frank Reade, Jr." series (which also virtually plagiarized this novel in the 1876 *Frank Reade and His Steam Man of the Plains*).[10] As Everett F. Bleiler describes the formula of these early science fiction adventures, "a boy genius invents something that is not too far removed from the science and technology of the day, and then has adventures which usually could have happened just as well without the invention."[11] While this is generally true of Ellis's novel as well—most of the novel is given over to Indian chases, buffalo hunts, and mining expeditions—*The Steam Man of the Prairies* is nevertheless interesting for both what it does and what it doesn't tell us about the relationship of science-fictional ideas to the notion of the frontier. Ellis was a New Jersey school administrator whose 1860 *Seth Jones* had been one of the first works to prove the immense potential of the Western dime novel as a popular literary form. A popularizer of American history who apparently drew much of his inspiration from James Fenimore Cooper, he never experimented with science fiction before or after *The Steam Man*. But elements of the novel show some awareness of what the basic appeal of popular science fiction eventually would be, and there is some evidence that well-known modern science fiction writers such as Robert A. Heinlein were familiar with this story in one of its many incarnations.[12]

The Steam Man concerns a ten-foot steam-driven iron robot (which looks suspiciously African American in at least two of the illustrated editions, and which likely was inspired by an actual "steam man" patented by Newark inventor Zadoch Deddrick in early 1868) designed by a lovable but deformed boy-genius. (Already, echoes of the later Heinlein are apparent, since one of Heinlein's most popular stories for *Astounding Science Fiction*, "Waldo" [1942], also concerned a crippled boy-genius who invents remarkable devices for increasing his strength.) Some of the inspiration for the idea of the steam man becomes apparent when a New Englander, upon first seeing the machine, claims that he had had a similar idea "ever since [he] went through Colt's pistol factory in Hartford."[13] Despite the detail that Ellis lavishes upon his descriptions of the operation and maintenance of the machine—not actually a robot so much as a humanoid steam-engine—it is really good only as a substitute horse, pulling a specially designed wagon at speeds up to sixty miles an hour (although for safety's sake the boy seldom drives it above twenty). The boy makes friends with a "strong, hardy, bronzed trapper," who invites him to take the machine west. The steam man is shipped to Independence, Missouri, from where it is taken out upon the prairies to frighten Indians, assist in gold mining, and hunt buffalo. Even though the device eventually proves of limited use—it can only go forward over flat terrain, and it can't work in the rain—the boy's ingenuity finally saves his party from a band of hostile Indians when he devises a means of converting the steam man into a moving bomb, which wipes out the Indians.

While there is little portrayal of frontier society as such in this tale, there might have been something naively appealing to Ellis's nineteenth-century audience about the idea of bringing a single item of technology to bear upon such disparate undertakings as Indian extermination, buffalo hunting, and gold mining. It would be easy to read the steam man as a metaphor for the railroad, but it seems unlikely that Ellis and his readers were as concerned with metaphor as they were with the fantasy of using technology as a way of bringing adventure into the life of a weak and disadvantaged urban youth. This appeal later would characterize much juvenile and pulp science fiction, from the Tom Swift stories of "Victor Appleton" to the "space operas" of the pulps in the 1930s. And the notion of a young technologist solving a problem by thinking of a new way to use his machine—turning it into a bomb—was a remarkable anticipation of the ingenious engineer-hero of much later science fiction. At the very least, the story is significant in showing how a dangerous wilderness may be conquered by an urban boy with technical training as well as by the traditional frontier hero.

At the same time, the story is a long way from modern science fiction, and a long way from presenting any substantial notion of a frontier other than the pop culture Wild West. It would take a long time for science fiction to translate the American frontier to other worlds and still longer for it to treat "outer space" or the galaxy as frontiers in themselves. In fact, the relatively sophisticated technique of exploring social issues through the presentation of frontier-like societies on other planets was rather late in coming to science fiction, and the young genre had to pass through a number of important transitions before the intellectual scaffolding for such a theme would be fully in place.

The first such transition involved the dislocation of the frontier from the American West into "science-fictional" settings, and for this no better example can be found than in the work of Edgar Rice Burroughs. Whereas Ellis and a few other writers (notably Luis Senarens in his "Frank Reade, Jr." series) enthusiastically shipped marvels of technological invention westward, it was quite another thing to imagine entirely new frontiers. Burroughs, with his "interplanetary romances," represented an important shift from introducing imaginary machines into an existing wilderness to creating a completely imaginary environment. Other planets had been seen before in fiction, to be sure, but for the most part they were settings for utopian fantasies (as in Percy Greg's *Across the Zodiac* [1880]) or for confrontations between technological superpowers (as in Garrett P. Serviss's *Edison's Conquest of Mars* [1898]). Burroughs's "Barsoom," in contrast, clearly was intended as a setting for adventure. Burroughs, who had served for a time in the U.S. Seventh Cavalry and was familiar with the American West, found a way of returning the frontier hero to his roots, so to speak; rather than giving his characters technical superiority, he placed them in environments that served effectively as new kinds of frontiers. In a sense, it made little difference whether these environments were Mars, Africa, Venus, or the interior of the Earth—Burroughs was almost certainly influenced by the "lost civilization" motif popularized by H. Rider Haggard and his imitators— but from the point of view of science fiction history, his choice of Mars as a setting for his earliest successes was undeniably significant. As Paul A. Carter notes, "John Carter's initial impression—that Mars is a place not so very different from Arizona—has decisively influenced all subsequent interplanetary fiction. When Americans land on another world, it seems, they expect it to resemble the American West."[14]

Burroughs' John Carter first appeared in "Under the Moons of Mars" in *The All-Story Magazine* in 1912. In 1917, this was retitled *A Princess of Mars* for its book publication. Carter, a Virginia aristocrat and veteran of the Civil War, is an almost supernatural figure at the book's outset, never seeming to age and living over a hundred years by his own account. He undertakes a prospecting expedition with his friend Capt. James K. Powell in Arizona in 1866 (described as a professional mining engineer, Powell almost inevitably calls to mind explorer John Wesley Powell). After the two of them strike gold, Powell is killed in an Indian attack and Carter is pursued to an isolated cave, from which— perhaps with the aid of ancient Indian magic—he somehow projects himself to Mars by simply staring at it in the Arizona sky. Burroughs' description of the moonlit Arizona landscape is telling: It is "as though one were catching for the first time a glimpse of some dead and forgotten world, so different is it from the aspect of any other spot on earth."[15] The Mars to which Carter transports himself is indeed such a "forgotten world," and if it is not dead, it is dying. Remnants of a once-great technological society struggle to keep the atmosphere intact with great machines, while warring races of various colors dominate the mostly barren landscape. If Burroughs was borrowing from the literature of the frontier, it was not from later myths of the West as garden but from earlier visions of a Great American Desert that, as Henry Nash Smith writes, "throws the hero back in upon himself and accentuates his terrible and sublime isolation. He is an anarchic and self-contained atom—alone in a hostile, or at best a neutral, universe."[16] John Carter's Mars is not a land fit for settlers, and no settlers will follow him. It is not a new land, but a decaying one, and in most conventional senses it is not a frontier at all. But his adventures there—a repeating cycle of pursuit, capture, escape, and trial by battle—bear a noticeable resemblance to the adventures of the early fictional frontier heroes; and some of the races that he encounters—notably the fifteen-foot-tall, bellicose "green men," serve narrative roles not unlike the Plains Indians of earlier Western lore. Onto this basic frame, Burroughs has grafted elements of the "lost race" novel, with its beautiful princesses, and elements of the "marvelous invention" story, with its atmosphere generators and flying machines. The mixture proved enormously successful for the next several decades, and if it did not quite treat outer space as a "new frontier," it at least opened it up as a likely arena for frontier-like adventures and as a means of keeping alive some of America's favorite myths about its self-sufficient frontier heroes.

Popular genres may evolve in many ways: formulas may become more variable, style more refined, characters and themes more complex. Early pulp science fiction seems to have evolved through a simple process of accretion. To the basic adventure-story template were added marvelous inventions, interplanetary settings, lost races, princesses, scientists, aliens, spies—practically everything popular fiction had to offer, each piled on with none of the older conventions retired to make way. The formulaic, episodic adventure structure of Burroughs' novels resembles the structure of such earlier dime-novel series as Frank Reade and Tom Swift, but whereas the latter concerned young scientific geniuses using their wits to escape perils on Earth, Burroughs reinstated the traditional masculine hero and moved the setting to other planets. From here, it was only a series of steps to combine all these elements into the figure of a young, masculine, scientific genius-hero whose domain was not merely other planets but the entire universe. This almost uncontrolled proliferation of devices and character types culminated in the "space opera."

Less than three years after "Under the Moons of Mars" appeared in magazine form, E. E. Smith (who would later famously sign his name "E. E. Smith, Ph.D." even though his doctorate was in food chemistry and he was a doughnut-mix specialist by profession) began writing the first of what eventually would become known as science fiction's "space operas." Unable to find a market for his story of a brilliant scientist who ranges throughout the universe destroying whole planets to spread civilization and win the hand of his sweetheart, Smith did not publish *The Skylark of Space* until after the advent of the first pulp science fiction magazine, Hugo Gernsback's *Amazing Stories*, in 1926. The novel was serialized in 1928 and immediately spawned a host of sequels and imitators. (The subtitle of the first sequel, *Skylark Three* [1930], was "the tale of the galactic cruise which ushered in universal civilization.") While much Wild West flavor hangs about Smith's astonishingly naive (and, according to some, cryptofascist) tales, he did little to add to the science fiction myth of the frontier beyond expanding the scope of Burroughs's other planets to include entire galaxies, and Burroughs's multiple races to include endless varieties of alien civilizations. Nevertheless, his "space opera" helped outline the broad canvas upon which future science fiction would draw its increasingly sophisticated portraits of colonization and conflict.

While space opera became a familiar staple of pulp science fiction throughout the 1930s, the genre as a whole began to undergo a widely documented sea-change when John W. Campbell, Jr., assumed the editorship of *Astounding Stories* in September 1937. Arguably, it was Campbell's strong editorial hand that eventually forced science fiction writers to think more systematically and rationally about what "frontiers in space" might be like. Although Campbell himself had written space operas in his youth, as an editor he demanded narratively realistic treatments of carefully worked-out scientific and social concepts. Stories began to appear that seemed to share common assumptions about future human expansion into the universe, and authors such as Robert A. Heinlein were encouraged to place their stories in the context of an overall "future history." Eventually, such tales became sufficiently codified that at least one historian of the genre, Donald A. Wollheim, later was able to identify what he called a consensus "cosmogony," or future history, underlying much of the science fiction of the 1940s and 1950s. This future history involved voyages to the Moon and planets, followed by interstellar flights, the rise of a "galactic empire," the dominance and later decline of this empire, a period of "interregnum" or reversion to barbarism, the evolution of a more stable galactic civilization, and finally a "Challenge to God."[17] If many stories of the Campbell years were so codified, the codex for them was almost certainly Isaac Asimov's series of "Foundation" stories that appeared in *Astounding* between 1942 and 1950. "What the Foundation series did was to create the point of departure for the full cosmogony of science fiction future history," wrote Wollheim.[18]

Asimov's ambitious borrowing from Edward Gibbon provided a context for science fiction that incorporates all sorts of opportunities for frontier narratives, even though Asimov's own series hardly falls under this rubric.

This "consensus future history" provides the next major transition leading toward modern science fiction frontier narratives. If Burroughs moved the frontier hero to other planets, and Smith crossbred him with the superscientist and moved him across the universe, these *Astounding* stories provided him with the essential context for all real frontier narratives—a history. The myths about American history that underlay the fiction of the American frontier could not be adapted wholesale to the needs of science fiction, and it took the genre some twenty or thirty years to construct its own historical myth, drawn loosely not only from Gibbon but from parts of Toynbee and Spengler as well. Ironically, this development gave science fiction an opportunity to speculate intelligently upon the meaning of the frontier at the same time that it isolated the genre from other types of popular fiction and made it appear increasingly inaccessible to all but the most devoted readers; while a Western enthusiast could follow Burroughs with no trouble, and could read space opera with only a little extra suspension of disbelief, this same reader might have more difficulty with stories whose common assumptions about scientific and technical advances seemed to be shared only with an initiated readership. Confined by the magazine format to short stories, series, and serial novels, popular American science fiction provided its authors few opportunities to construct an extended epic of space frontiers, and the epic evolved instead as a series of what Patrick Parrinder called "epic fables"—short tales depicting episodes in an unfolding galactic epic whose broad outlines were familiar only to regular readers of the genre.[19] To examine one of these "epic fables" is to discover in large measure what was happening to the idea of the frontier within the emerging historical myth of Campbellian science fiction. A widely anthologized story that is often cited as a "touchstone" for such fiction—Tom Godwin's "The Cold Equations" (*Astounding Science Fiction*, 1954)—is also coincidentally (perhaps) written by a Western native and former prospector who lived in Nevada. Little else is known about Godwin, and his science fiction output was limited to a few other stories and novels, but if ever an author can be said to have established a reputation based on a single short story, it is Godwin. What's more curious about the story is its reputation as the archetypal "hard science fiction story"—the kind of science fiction story built around real physical laws and accurate calculations—even though there is very little "hard science" in it. In fact, it is a frontier story that attempts to find in science a rationale for some cherished traditional myths that are not too far removed from those of Burroughs or even Edward Ellis. It attempts to tell us that it is the nature of the universe itself, and the "cold equations" that describe that universe, that determine a value system based on masculine ideals and stoic behavior, a value system that clearly echoes the rugged ethos of the Wild West.

Much of the popular impact of the story undoubtedly derives from its disarmingly simple plot: A young girl stowaway aboard a spaceship learns that she must be jettisoned because her additional weight will exhaust the carefully calculated fuel supply before the ship can land safely. The spaceship in this case is a one-man "Emergency Dispatch Ship" on a rescue mission bearing serum to a frontier outpost on a remote planet. Barton, the pilot of the ship, is a fair example of what had become of the frontier hero in science fiction: He is "inured to the sight of death, long since accustomed to it and to viewing the dying of another man with an objective lack of emotion."[20] Thus it is without hesitation that Barton, upon detecting the presence of a stowaway, prepares to jettison his unknown passenger in accordance with strict regulations, and in order to save himself and the outpost to which he is bringing medicine. The story is set up in such a way that the law of the frontier becomes a law of physics, and the values of the frontier become principles of science: Environmental determinism is carried to such an extreme that no one is really responsible for his or her individual actions. The interweaving of frontier and scientific imagery underline this world view: "It was a law not of men's choosing but made imperative by the circumstances of the space frontier"; "she was of Earth and had not realized that the laws of the space frontier must, of necessity, be as hard and relentless as the environment that gave them birth"; "H amount of fuel will not power an EDS with a mass of m plus x safely to its destination"; and so on.[21] And, within the context of the story's contrivances, there is little arguing with this bleak and deterministic view. Frontier settlements are visited by large space cruisers only according to fixed schedules, and any emergencies must be handled by the small EDS craft dispatched from the larger ships. Using liquid rocket fuel rather than the complex atomic mechanisms of the cruisers, these ships are given only sufficient fuel for a one-way mission (the pilots, presumably, must wait for the next scheduled cruiser stop to return), and that fuel is allocated carefully by computer. Additional weight will result in insufficient fuel for landing, and the ship will crash. No allowance for stowaways is possible, but of course the stowaway herself doesn't know this. Much of the appeal of the story, in fact, may derive from the apparently scientific cast it gives to the familiar hardboiled line, repeated by Barton, that "That's the way it is."[22]

Godwin's complication, such as it is, involves making the stowaway a young girl, which permits him to exploit the sentimental potential of this world view while at the same time reasserting its masculine values. "She belonged in that world of soft winds and warm suns, music and moonlight and gracious manners and not on the hard, bleak frontier."[23] The girl is a poor teenager hoping to visit her brother, who has been sending money home to help her take courses in linguistics, which, presumably, will make her employable on the settled planets. Her brother—one of six men in a settlement whose disease serum had been destroyed, significantly, by a tornado from the "Western sea"—is like Barton, one of the "men of the frontier" who "had long ago learned the bitter futility of cursing the forces that would destroy them for the forces were blind and deaf." By sentimentalizing his woman character, Godwin can proceed easily to show how she has no place in a harsh Newtonian universe. The myth of coldly rational science has been merged with the myth of the boys' book; the whole universe becomes a heroic, masculine arena, and it's nobody's fault. The Western desert is made infinite.

Like the American frontier, however, the space frontier is as much a creation of economics as of environment. Godwin reveals little of the economics of a society that would institute such draconian regulations regarding fuel (it is never dearly explained why the EDS ships are designed with no emergency fuel supply), but we can pick up enough hints to discover that it is an essentially capitalist society that exploits its frontier in familiar ways: The girl's parents barely eke out a living from their small shop, she has to pay for the education that will make her employable, and the money to pay for it is sent by her brother. She wears sandals made of cheap imitation "Vegan leather," and practices her language on a "native girl" who works as a cleaning lady on the space cruiser. In a later story, "The Last Victory," Godwin postulates an oppressive society founded in "Technogration" (a portmanteau of "technology" and "integration") from which rugged individualists called "Outlanders" seek to escape on the space frontier. The fear of racial mixing in the latter story is as evident as the fear of women in "The Cold Equations"; in both cases, space is the last hope of white male hegemony, and in both cases, this doctrine is heavily disguised through sentimentality and the appeal to science.

No one claims that Godwin is one of the great writers of science fiction, but he is interesting precisely because he lacks the distinguishing idiosyncrasies of more prolific writers such as Robert A. Heinlein or Isaac Asimov, who have also dealt with frontiers in their fiction.[24] While it probably is unfair to characterize Godwin's work—as some have—as purely the outgrowth of editor John Campbell's beliefs or of a consensus future history emerging from science fiction tropes, a story like "The Cold Equations" does have much in common with other science fiction stories of its period in its view of frontier life and economics. It represents a view that, although harshly criticized in the fiction of relatively anomalous (in terms of the Campbell tradition) writers like Ray Bradbury, is in most ways characteristic of science fiction's view of other worlds once these worlds came to be viewed as frontiers for colonizing rather than merely as arenas for swashbuckling action. Godwin's significant variation on the problem-solving formula of much Campbellian science fiction is that he posits a frontier so uncompromising that even the ingenuity of trained spacemen cannot provide a solution.

David Mogen (in *Wilderness Visions*) has observed that treatments of the frontier in modern science fiction tend to be either metaphorical or literal. Ray Bradbury, in *The Martian Chronicles* (1950), is an example of a metaphorical writer who pays little attention to the possible conditions of life on other planets, whereas the Campbell school of "hard" science fiction—which includes Tom Godwin—views the movement into space as a kind of extension of the manifest destiny myth of American expansion, focusing largely on the problem-solving aspects of life in a hostile wilderness. A classic story of this type is Isaac Asimov's "The Martian Way" (1952), which deals with a conflict between Martian settlers and the Earth over water rights (the Martians import small amounts of water from Earth, and this leads to their being targeted by a demagogic politician clearly modeled on Joseph McCarthy). The "Martian way" of responding to this threat is to tow an enormous iceberg from the asteroid belt to Mars and offer to sell water to Earth. The industrious pioneer spirit exemplified by this dramatic and risky undertaking, Asimov implies, is the spirit that eventually will lead to the colonization of the universe. Asimov's story is significant in that it introduces, albeit simplistically, a large-scale economic theme into its considerations of the frontier. Economic concerns generally had not been addressed adequately in Campbellian science fiction (as evidenced by "The Cold Equations"), and when they were addressed, it was often in the context of a satirical utopia (such as depicted in Eric Frank Russell's ". . . And Then There Were None" [1951]). With the rise of *Galaxy* magazine in the early 1950s, economic satire became popular, largely through the works of

Frederik Pohl and C. M. Kornbluth, most notably with their depiction of a world dominated by advertising agencies in *The Space Merchants* (1953; first published in *Galaxy* magazine as "Gravy Planet," 1952). Even in this work, however, the view of the space frontier as safety valve for the industrious and independent-minded persisted.

This growing awareness of the necessary economic relations between the frontier and the Earth eventually began to evolve formulas of its own. One such formula, apparent in "The Martian Way" and in several other works by Asimov and Robert A. Heinlein, depicts fundamentalist or politically conservative groups opposing the idea of expansion into space either in principle or because of the need to address resource shortages on Earth. (Ironically, the argument that resources devoted to space travel could better be directed toward domestic problems emerged as a stereotype of right-wing thinking in science fiction at about the same time that it was beginning to emerge as a liberal issue in American politics.) Another formula, almost the direct opposite of the first, sees the frontier as an arena for capitalist exploitation. In *The Space Merchants*, a project to colonize Venus is undertaken by corporations as a way of tempting settlers to relocate to a hostile environment in order to support an over-expanded economy on Earth (although eventually the project is co-opted by "Conservationists," who seek to colonize Venus in the name of the more traditional science fiction virtues of freedom and human hegemony in the universe).

Selling the frontier became a fairly common theme in science fiction, one often used to bitterly satiric purposes. In C. M. Kornbluth's "The Marching Morons" (1951), for example, a future society threatened by overbreeding of imbeciles is "saved" when a businessman from the present awakes from suspended animation and concocts a vicious scheme to dispose of the excess population in space by convincing them that they are emigrating to a promising new world. In Philip K. Dick's *Do Androids Dream of Electric Sheep* (1968), people are urged to relocate from a dying Earth by a massive advertising campaign that even promises personal slaves, or androids, to those choosing to emigrate to Mars (some of this propaganda is retained in Ridley Scott's very different 1982 film based on the novel, *Blade Runner*).

A few authors, such as Ursula K. Le Guin (in "The Word for World Is Forest" [1972]), focused on the alien societies subjugated under capitalist imperialism in stories clearly influenced by the American experience in Vietnam (as well as by the history of white/Native American relationships), and by the re-evaluation of a number of cherished American myths in light of that experience. This growing awareness of complex economic and social issues informed the work of a number of writers using frontier themes, including not only Le Guin, but Samuel R. Delany, Joanna Russ, James Tiptree, Jr., and perhaps most notably Kim Stanley Robinson, whose Mars trilogy (*Red Mars,* 1992; *Green Mars,* 1993; *Blue Mars,* 1996; with a follow-up collection of related stories, *The Martians,* 1999) represents perhaps the most exhaustive fictional account of the colonization and eventually terraforming of a planetary frontier. Robinson's work is possibly the most self-conscious treatment of Mars as a utopian frontier since Bradbury's *The Martian Chronicles;* one of the main characters in *Red Mars,* the semi-legendary first man on Mars, is even named John Boone, and at one point finds himself under investigation by a bureaucrat named Sam Houston. When Boone undertakes a long exploration of the emerging Martian colonies years after he first set foot on the planet in 2019, it carries echoes of his near-namesake's explorations of Kentucky. Martian colonization is pushed forward by a twenty-first-century version of trading companies called transnationals and by the pressure of growing population, exacerbated by the discovery (initially among the Martian colonists) of a technique to extend the human life span. Meanwhile, back east, the Earth is rapidly sinking into economic and ecological chaos. Mars holds out the only hope for a new start, and in the speech that opens the novel, Boone sounds almost like de Tocqueville in his assertion that the new world is producing not merely an extension of the old, but an entirely new social order and a new kind of human. By the time the trilogy is finished, leaping centuries forward in the third volume to give us a picture of a lushly terraformed Mars, Robinson will have revisited nearly all the historical and philosophical issues surrounding the transformation of the frontier, from geological explorations to underground movements (a significant character in the later volumes is called Coyote), and even an extended constitutional convention (in *Green Mars*) attempting to unite the various Martian cultural factions into a united government that eventually succeeds in liberating itself from Earth.

But as the more purely adventurous frontiers give way to fictions of the philosophy of history, as in Robinson, science fiction's "consensus" view of the space frontier survives in the work of "hard" science fiction writers, although even here we see a greater degree of sophistication about the social implications of such frontiers and the economic conditions that might underlie them. A novel that combines much of the classic mythology of space opera frontiers with the political, economic, and literary complexity of later works is Gregory

Benford's *Against Infinity* (1983), drawing as it does on both the traditions of Campbellian science fiction—which was waning in influence when Benford's novel appeared—and on the broader traditions of the American *bildungsroman* and the modernist literary techniques that were increasingly evident in the growing "literariness" of the genre. Benford's novel, appearing only a year before William Gibson's phenomenally influential *Neuromancer* would usher in the age of cyberpunk and redefine frontiers in an increasingly posthuman sense, provides an illuminating perspective on earlier science fiction frontiers and is an excellent example of how the emerging science fiction of the period neither entirely broke free of its genre precedents nor was subsumed by them.

Against Infinity is modeled closely on William Faulkner's classic 1942 novella "The Bear," so much so that some initial readers regarded it as a *tour de force* of little significance on its own merits. To be sure, the ingenuity with which Benford transforms Faulkner's bear hunt into a search for an alien artifact on a moon of Jupiter is impressive, but the tale was archetypal even when Faulkner told it. Benford's use of this classic structure provides him with an opportunity to demonstrate how the resources of science fiction can enlarge upon and extend some deep-rooted American myths of maturation and confrontation with the wilderness. Set on the moon Ganymede, the novel is organized in six parts, the first five of which roughly parallel the five parts of Faulkner's novella, and the sixth of which extends the theme of the frontier to incorporate broader "science-fictional" concerns—not only of the infinitely receding frontier represented by the physical universe but of the scientific and even metaphysical frontiers represented by the unusual nature of an alien artifact called "the Aleph." (In this latter regard, Benford borrows as much from Jorge Luis Borges as from Faulkner; Borges' 1945 story "The Aleph" also concerns an artifact that seems to contain infinity.) The basic story concerns the coming of age of a boy named Manuel Lopez, who first sees the legendary Aleph when he is thirteen. The Aleph itself is one of those marvelous inventions of pure alienness that science fiction sometimes is capable of producing—an apparently unstoppable "thing" that for decades has burrowed unpredictably throughout Ganymede, sometimes disrupting settlements and wreaking havoc with human attempts to "terraform" the satellite into a habitable world. ("Terraforming" is a concept borrowed from Campbellian science fiction, and although the notion of altering planetary environments had been used earlier and may even have its roots in nineteenth-century dreams of turning the "Great American Desert" into a garden, the word itself was coined by Jack Williamson in a story published in

1942.) Over the next several years, Manuel repeatedly encounters the Aleph until finally, under the tutelage of an aging pioneer named Matt Bohles (who appeared as a teenager in Benford's 1975 novel *Jupiter Project*, set nearly a century earlier) and with the aid of a mechanically enhanced part-human animal known as Eagle (parallel to the hunting dog in Faulkner's tale), he is able to immobilize it. Benford's plot is so rich in science fiction invention—terraforming, mechanically reinforced animals with enhanced IQs, alien artifacts, space colonies, and more—that it may seem daunting to readers not familiar with science fiction. But its significance derives in large part from the degree to which it does allude to the traditions of the genre. Apart from some passages of Faulknerian prose, the first two-thirds of the novel might easily be read as an interplanetary adventure firmly in the tradition of John W. Campbell, Jr.'s *Astounding Science Fiction*.

The last two parts of the novel, however, provide a perspective that often is lacking in such fiction. Part IV, like part IV of Faulkner's novella, is set some years later and provides historical and social background for what went before. Manuel has moved from the frontier settlement of Sidon to the city of Hiruko, where he encounters the effects of the socialist doctrines that have come to dominate Earth society when two men demand possessions from him as part of a legislated redistribution of wealth. A colleague explains to him that socialism on Earth evolved out of the contradictions inherent in capitalism, but that the socialist system itself—while efficient at handling the overpopulated condition of Earth—must expand into new worlds to maintain efficient production of goods, and this in turn breeds a new kind of capitalism at the frontier. "So we get humankind—with refined, humanitarian socialism in the older, crowded core. And capitalism sprouting up like weeds at the edge."[25] The frontier society of which Manuel has been a part, then, is less the product of a dream of conquering new worlds than of economic forces. Like Isaac McCaslin in Faulkner's "The Bear," Manuel learns that his inheritance is tainted. His mentor—the propertyless Matt Bohles who had lived more than a century in the colonies around Jupiter and who apparently had no family ties (the figure of Sam Fathers from "The Bear")—is a social anomaly rather than a harbinger of a regenerated society. And the Aleph itself has been reduced to an object of scientific research nearly resembling a museum piece. It is at this point, appropriately, that Manuel learns that his estranged father has died.

Returning to Sidon, Manuel encounters Earthmen visiting Ganymede to conduct research on the Aleph, and comes to realize that "*They came here out of duty. Not from a yearning, but because their commonweal decided. They're priests, not explorers*."[26] At Sidon, the frontier is giving way to civilization, even though the settlement's random sprawl still contrasts with the orderly grids of Hiruko. After the funeral, Manuel learns an odd fact about his military father: Earlier in the novel, Colonel Lopez had seemed to represent the order of civilization in contrast to Matt Bohles's pioneering spirit of independence. Now Manuel learns that the hunts that eventually brought down the Aleph had been financed by his father for years at a loss to the settlement's economy, not only to give the men something to do in contrast to their oppressive settlement life but for "the thing itself." This "pioneering spirit," then, was alive in Manuel's father as well as in Bohles: perhaps it was not purely an anomaly.

The final section of the book begins, as did the first chapter, with an expedition from Sidon settlement in search of the Aleph. Now new domes have grown up, an atmosphere is becoming evident on the satellite, and there is talk of the mechanized animals creating a new underclass in society, "yet another source for the forward tilt of capitalism."[27] Manuel accompanies an Earth scientist doing research on the Aleph and learns that the Aleph has revealed secrets as challenging to physics as the space frontier itself is to society: It continually rebuilds itself at the atomic level, "like something restlessly remaking itself, forever discontented."[28] It reveals, in fact, that the physical laws governing the universe may themselves undergo evolutionary change. "Nothing remains, nothing is held constant," as the scientist explains to Manuel.[29] At the same time, the Aleph seems to contain all it has encountered, like the Aleph of Jewish legend: Venturing inside it, Manuel finds images of Matt and of himself, stored from his earlier encounter with the artifact. Shortly after, an earthquake resulting from the stresses imposed by the terraforming process kills the scientist and nearly destroys the settlement. "The land ruled now, not men."[30]

Manuel realizes that years earlier—at the time of Matt's death—"he had joined forever the other side—the wilderness, the opening outward, the undomesticated, the country of the old dead time."[31] The "killing" of the Aleph not only accompanied the death of Matt, it prefigured the death of Manuel's father as well and committed the boy to a new way of thinking, dominated neither by the economic structures of his society nor by the scientific mode of its progress. "Out here, forging some understanding was not a matter of guessing and then testing, like a scientist, but of listening; waiting; witnessing the slow certain sway of worlds, the rhythms of gravity and ice. . . ."[32] The universe resolves itself into a series of dialectical frontiers at various levels: Economic systems generate new patterns as a result of internal stresses, stresses in the crust of a planet build and rebuild it into a kind of ongoing dialogue between what humanity seeks with its terraforming and what nature will permit, and stresses at the sub-atomic level of matter itself—such as within the Aleph—suggest a universe forever remade and never completely understandable, but one that will always draw certain individuals into its vastness. *Against Infinity* suggests as few other novels have that "frontiers" in science fiction are multiplex and have the potential of encompassing such diverse themes as economic expansion, particle physics, planetary exploration, and the ancient myth of the hunt. If Burroughs's John Carter could not quite handle such frontiers, neither could John W. Campbell's scientists and engineers. But, Benford suggests, humanity seems to have a way of producing the individuals it needs for the new frontiers it encounters, and in the end, it is this optimism that links his work most firmly with those earlier traditions. That perhaps is the defining characteristic of the genre's persistent return to the frontier.

PART II

writers

As the preceding essays have argued, genres do not always behave as expected, and this may be particularly true of the fantastic genres. And, as I hope my various examples have made clear, the reason for this is that *writers* do not always behave as expected, and are not always comfortable within the perceived strictures of the genres to which, by circumstance or marketing, they have found themselves assigned. As I mentioned in "Malebolge, or the Ordnance of Genre," writers often have used the term "ghetto" to describe the sense of entrapment they may feel as a result of being categorized as a horror writer, science fiction writer, or fantasy writer, and some writers bristle at such labels altogether. Given the tendency of publishers and booksellers to market by category, the tendency of readers to organize themselves into affinity groups, and even the tendency of librarians to shelve fiction according the special interests of patrons, this complaint is hard to dismiss. An experienced science fiction writer turning to mainstream realistic fiction may find herself very nearly in the position of a first-time novelist, and may even be warned by her agent against making such a risky move in the first place.

While a great many successful and talented writers are comfortable continuing to work within their market niches, they are by and large not the ones I've been focusing on in this book. Of the authors I *have* been discussing, however, I plead guilty to the charge of contributing in some small measure to that ongoing ghettoization by treating these writers as exemplars of the very arguments that I have been making about the instability of the fantastic genres. On the one hand, I'm claiming that such authors seek to stretch or escape the strictures of genre altogether;

on the other I'm saying, isn't this interesting in what it tells us about these genres? I would not blame any of these authors for shaking their heads and muttering, "You can't win." The three essays that follow represent something of an effort to redress that imbalance by focusing first on the authors, and only secondarily on the genres they generally are thought to inhabit. While genre considerations are hardly absent from these essays, the focus here is more on technique and angle of vision—even on the lives of the authors themselves—than on the manipulation of specific conventions. These are authors for whom genre is not a space to inhabit, but a collection of tools and resources to be drawn upon along with the myriad other tools and resources available to the makers of contemporary fiction.

eight

The Lives of Fantasists

Unser Leben ist kein Traum, aber es soll und wird viellicht einer werden.
[Our life is no dream; but it ought to become one, and perhaps will.]
—Novalis (Friedrich von Hardenburg), as quoted in George MacDonald's
Phantastes (1859)

And do not rely on the fact that in your life, circumscribed, regulated, and
prosaic, there are no such spectacular and terrifying things.
—C. P. Cavafy, "Theodotus," as quoted in Elizabeth Hand's *Last Summer at
Mars Hill* (1998)

When one looks at the published memoirs and autobiographical sketches written by science fiction and fantasy authors, often for the benefit of their fans—the sort of thing collected in Brian Aldiss and Harry Harrison's *Hell's Cartographers* (1975) or Martin Greenberg's *Fantastic Lives: Autobiographical Essays by Notable Science Fiction Writers* (1981)—one initially is struck by the relative thinness and lack of genuine introspection of many of the essays. Typically, such pieces read as a variety of Augustinian conversion tales, depicting a precocious childhood, often solitary and bookish, sometimes sickly, sometimes featuring battles with parents to get into the adult sections of the library, and characteristically leading toward a moment of revelation. Here are three examples from *Hell's Cartographers*: "And then came Hugo Gernsback"; "Then I saw and bought an issue of something called *Amazing Stories*"; "So science fiction entered into and began warping my life from an early age."[1] In one of the still comparatively rare autobiographies of SF writers, *Wonder's Child: My Life in Science Fiction*, Jack Williamson ends a chapter with the following cliffhanger:

Something else happened, however, in the spring of 1926, the first year I was out of high school. Something that changed my life. Hugo Gernsback launched a new pulp magazine, filled with reprinted stories by Jules Verne and H. G. Wells and A. Merritt and Edgar Rice Burroughs, stories he called "scientifiction."

The magazine was *Amazing Stories*.[2]

Following these road-to-Damascus moments, however, these memoirs and autobiographies seldom become genuine testaments, instead amounting to not much more than narrative resumés, filled with anecdotes of encounters with fellow writers and editors and often with almost obsessively detailed accounts of sales figures and payments; one comes away with the sense that (a) science fiction writers all clearly remember the first SF story they read, and (b) they keep really good tax records.

To be fair, Williamson does go on to describe his bouts of depression and his encounters with psychology—he may have been the first SF writer to undergo full psychoanalysis—and he drops tantalizing hints as to how this may have affected the darker moments of his fiction. And the science fiction world has produced a handful of other genuinely thoughtful autobiographies, such as Brian Aldiss's *The Twinkling of an Eye* (1998). But the most famous of all science fiction autobiographies, the fifteen-hundred-odd pages of Isaac Asimov's *In Memory Yet Green* (1979) and *In Joy Still Felt* (1980) are monuments to the unexamined ego, filled with astonishingly minute details that reveal remarkably little about the man or his fiction and seem almost intended to obfuscate; even the poem that provided these titles turns out to be a fake, written by Asimov himself specifically to generate the titles. Only much later, literally on his deathbed, did Asimov revisit his life in another massive volume, *I. Asimov: A Memoir* (1994), with fragmentary—but one feels more unmediated—meditations on his work and his career. Similarly, Robert Bloch's 1995 autobiography *Once around the Bloch* is essentially an extended version of one of his legendarily funny con speeches, Frederik Pohl's *The Way the Future Was* (1978) is mostly an engaging insider's history of much of American science fiction, and Piers Anthony's 1988 *Bio of an Ogre* features more cranky score-settling than genuine introspection.

Perhaps we shouldn't expect more; after all, as I mentioned, for the most part these are celeb memoirs, written more to satisfy the curiosity of fans than to draw us deeper into the authors' works and worldviews. And we can, if we wish to play games of psychological criticism, draw our own conclusions, speculating for example on how Asimov's own self-confessed agoraphobia and love of Manhattan translated into the contained urban environments of *The Caves of Steel* (1954) or *The Naked Sun* (1957), much as an earlier generation of psychological critics found sources for Kafka's "The Hunger Artist" (1922) or *The Trial* (1925) in his vegetarianism or his stultifying office job. But I'm not certain this will lead us to understand the complex and often inchoate relationships between the stuff of an author's life and the stuff of his or her fiction, particularly when that fiction is cast in a fantastic or nonrealistic mode. We might have better luck if we look at those novels by SF or fantasy writers that we already know (from introductions, interviews, or self-evident subject matter) to be overtly autobiographical—J.G. Ballard's *Empire of the Sun* (1981), for example, or Brian Aldiss's *Forgotten Life* (1989) or *Remembrance Day* (1993), or Ray Bradbury's *Dandelion Wine* (1957), or Joe Haldeman's *War Year* (1972). The first of these certainly explains a lot about where all those drained swimming pools and low-flying aircraft in Ballard's fiction came from, just as the Bradbury reveals the sources of his Midwestern landscapes, some of them transplanted to Mars, in his long-lost Waukegan childhood. Haldeman's book, following the more or less traditional arc of the tour-of-duty novel, provides us a baseline account of the experiences in Vietnam that would inform so much of his later fiction. The Aldiss novels reveal much not only about Aldiss's landscapes, but about the sources of his characters (nearly all the major characters in *Forgotten Life* turn out to be avatars of Aldiss's own multiple identities as war veteran, writer, son and husband, and Oxford institution). But these novels are not even science fiction or fantasy, and what we can learn from them about how the stuff of writers' lives becomes the stuff of the fantastic is available to us only through inference, or through a kind of triangulation with what we already know of the author's other works. There are probably many seeds of doctoral dissertations here, and some probably have already been written, but such an approach still doesn't tell us much about the central question of what transformative mechanisms SF and fantasy *in particular* have to offer to the storying of lives.

One way to approach this question is to look at SF or fantasy stories that are self-consciously autobiographical, without becoming fictionalized memoirs. The identifiable tradition of using devices of the fantastic to "thicken and intensify" (to use Rudy Rucker's phrase) the materials of lived experience from time to time has even given rise to manifestos—not uncommon in science fiction. In 1983, the *Bulletin of the Science Fiction Writers of America* published Rudy Rucker's "Transrealist Manifesto" arguing not only for the use of personal experience in fiction, but for actually featuring the author—under his or her own name—as a character. This is something Rucker himself has done in *Saucer Wisdom* (1999); it was done by J. G. Ballard in *Crash* (1974) and more recently by James Patrick Kelly in "Daemon" (1987), China Miéville in "Reports of Certain Events in London" (2004), and Paul Park and Jeffrey Ford in a number of stories. (Damien Broderick later extended Rucker's ideas in a much more disciplined way in his 2000 academic study *Transrealist Fiction: Writing in the Slipstream of Science.*) More recently, the "Mundane Manifesto" concocted in 2004 by Geoff Ryman and a group of young writers at the Clarion Writers' Workshop seems intended as a kind of science fiction version of filmmaker Lars von Trier's "Dogme" movement, eschewing such conventions and devices as interstellar travel, aliens, alternate universes, magic, or time travel, thus presumably forcing writers toward a discipline more firmly rooted in credible experience, and toward the use of fantastic elements clearly derived from such experience, although it stops short of advocating specifically autobiographical material.

In an essay that Kelly later wrote about his story "Daemon," which involves a strange encounter with a fellow student at the Clarion Science Fiction Writers' Workshop (which Kelly actually attended in 1974), he noted that the story confused many readers when it first appeared, because "in the foreground of this autobiographical structure, I presented an entirely fictional plot. Yes, I did go to the Clarion Writers Workshop in 1974, but I met no Celeste there. Nothing that happens in this story ever really occurred—thank God! But the challenge I set myself here was to imagine something fantastic that could realistically happen to a boring guy like yours truly."[3] If we set aside such self-imposed technical challenges, Kelly seems to suggest that one reason writers might include fictionalized versions of themselves could be due to a sort of Walter Mitty-esque character-envy—fictional characters, after all, get to live through more challenging, difficult, and powerful events than are likely to intrude upon the presumably quotidian existence of the writer, no matter how many colorful past experiences and occupations might be documented in the promotional bios on the flyleaves of their novels. Such writers may well be asking themselves in print how they would hold up under the sorts of stresses that they regularly impose on their characters—there is certainly a long tradition of stories about writers being.drawn out of their lives into fantastic worlds (Fredric Brown's 1949 novel *What Mad Universe* is a fairly early example in SF)—but, as we shall see shortly, the reverse also may be true, with fictionalized versions of self sometimes functioning as a means of framing and ordering the challenging, difficult, or powerful events of the writer's own life.

Long before transrealist or mundane manifestoes, writers were drawing on autobiographical material for fantastic and genre fiction, and occasionally, like Kelly, they have written essays or books about it. In a remarkable book called *Algernon, Charlie and I: A Writer's Journey* (1999), Daniel Keyes constructs what amounts to an autobiography of a single story, his classic 1959 "Flowers for Algernon." In it, Keyes details how virtually every element of that story derived from particular events in his own experience—the trauma of dissecting what turned out to be a pregnant mouse in a college biology class, his discovery the same day of the poetry of Algernon Charles Swinburne, his work in a bagel bakery similar to the bakery that his character Charlie Gordon works in, his frustration in dealing with psychology professors and analysts, and most tellingly an encounter with one of his students in a "special modified English" class that Keyes was teaching in a Brooklyn high school in 1957: Recognizing that he has been placed in a class for slow learners, the student plaintively tells Keyes, "I want to be smart."[4] By then, Keyes already had been toying with the idea of writing a story based on the notion of artificially increased intelligence, inspired loosely by H. G. Wells's "The Man Who Could Work Miracles" (1936), but what is particularly revealing is how this idea repeatedly had failed to jell. In retrospect, Keyes's trouble may have been due partly to his efforts to conceptualize it in terms of the familiar conventions of genre fiction: In one iteration, the central character is the subject of a military experiment, in another he's a criminal who keeps getting caught because of his own stupidity, in another he's a punk school dropout. It wasn't until Keyes opened up the tale to his own experiences that the writing began to flow.

We could cite many earlier examples—Zenna Henderson's "People" stories (a career-long series that began in 1952), for example, based on her own childhood in rural Mormon communities and her long-time experience as a schoolteacher in Arizona, or Clifford Simak's stories and novels featuring crusty individualists in rural Wisconsin settings similar to his own childhood home, or much of Theodore Sturgeon's fiction, such as the novel *The Dreaming Jewels* (1950), the autobiographical elements of which didn't become fully clear until the publication in 1993 of his painful memoir of his step-father, *Argyll*. Even Paul Linebarger's bizarrely romantic far-future "Cordwainer Smith" stories can be seen as outpicturings of his globetrotting childhood and colorful diplomatic and military career, especially when read in conjunction with his more directly autobiographical novels *Ria* (1947) and *Carola* (1949). But relatively few explications of source material for any SF story are as comprehensive as Keyes's memoir.

None of these writers, however, took the interpenetration of the fantastical and autobiographical quite as far, or quite as explicitly, as did Philip K. Dick, whose increasingly self-obsessed work is the most likely model for the sorts of transformative fictions that Rucker calls for in the "Transrealist Manifesto." Dick is far too involved a subject to get into much detail about here—his later work may represent the most complex interpenetration of life and art in all of modern science fiction—but there is a certain irony in that, when Dick attempted to portray aspects of his life and relationships in realistic novels such as *Confessions of a Crap Artist* (1975), *In Milton Lumpky Territory* (1985), or *The Broken Bubble* (1989), he was unable even to get these novels published during his lifetime, while the same relationships and anxieties transformed into science-fictional imagery yielded such novels as *Martian Time-Slip* (1964), *Three Stigmata of Palmer Eldritch* (1964), *Ubik* (1969), and *A Scanner Darkly* (1977). By the time of the so-called Valis Trilogy—*Valis* (1981), *The Divine Invasion* (1981), and *The Transmigration of Timothy Archer* (1982, although Dick never intended this to be part of his original planned trilogy)—he clearly was seeking through fiction, and through fantastic fiction in particular, a means to order the increasingly disordered nature of his own self-perception following his famous visionary experience of March 1974. The character Horselover Fat in *Valis*—a punning translation of Dick's own name—can even be read as a kind of mediation between the ordering power of art and the dissociation of nightmare. But neither Dick's own philosophical meditations in his famous "Exegesis," nor his mainstream novels, nor even his earlier science fiction, could achieve quite the sense of transcendence (of both real life and of genre protocols) that emerges from this odd interpenetration of invented and personal fantasy.[5]

But Dick, who in many senses lived inside a science-fictional world during the last decade of his life, is hardly a useful model for exploring the conscious interface between the fantastic and the personal. As significant as his body of work is, much of its importance to our present discussion is in the manner in which it contributed to a broadening of the very nature of science fiction and fantasy, or at least in the potential of these genres to explore and interrogate more personal concerns. Some writers roughly contemporaneous with Dick may have used similar devices—Ballard in *Crash*, for example—but there was a certain self-conscious literary archness about such devices in the work of Ballard and other New Wave writers; with Dick we instead get almost a sense of desperation, as though narrative voice might somehow provide a frame for the unframeable. And it is this *rawness*, this sense of ordered but not fully mediated experience, that has become increasing evident in the work of several excellent writers in the last couple of decades, although generally more in fantasy and horror than in genre science fiction. It might be useful, then, to examine a few specific examples of how such frames might serve to mediate personal experience—including, in some cases, what horror writers (including Peter Straub, discussed in the following chapter) have described as "extreme experience."

One example of an author who has drawn powerfully on such extreme experience is Elizabeth Hand, whose initial reputation as a science fiction novelist has been nearly overwhelmed by the continuing popularity of her 1994 fantasy novel *Waking the Moon* and the critical praise earned by this and later fantasy novels. Hand often has located her fictions in transformed versions of her own places. Her childhood home in Yonkers, New York, and the nearby village of Katonah became the Kamensic Village of the story "Last Summer at Mars Hill" (1994) and the 1999 novel *Black Light* (which also draws on her experiences in the New York post-Warhol punk scene, as does the 2007 novel *Generation Loss*); her grandparents' house in Yonkers became the rambling mansion Lazyland in the underrated millennial novel *Glimmering* (1997) and a source for the family house in "Illyria" (2007); her experiences as a student at Catholic University in Washington, D.C., provided *Waking the Moon* (1995) with the convincing authenticity of a college memoir despite its spectacular return-of-the-goddess plot, and figured prominently in her story "Wonderwall" (2004); her lakeside cottage in Maine became an inspiration for the setting of the novella "The Least Trumps"(2002); the Camden Town neighborhood where she stays while in London figures prominently in *Mortal Love* and "Cleopatra Brimstone." It's the latter novella, originally published in 2001 and later included in her collections *Bibliomancy* (2003) and *Saffron and Brimstone* (2006), which most tellingly examines how the devices of the fantastic might serve to frame extreme experience. Hand's protagonist, a young woman fascinated by entomology, is brutally assaulted while at college by a rapist who insistently orders her to "Try to get away." Never fully dealing with the rape during her months of convalescence at her parents' home, she eventually moves to London, where she volunteers as an entomology assistant at Regent's Zoo while haunting the clubs of Camden Town in the persona of Cleopatra Brimstone, a name taken from a species of butterfly. In this transformed state, she captures a series of young men as though they were specimens, urging them to "Try to get away" as she magically causes them to metamorphose into varieties of moths and butterflies. It's a beautifully dark tale, and in the note accompanying it in *Bibliomancy* Hand explains that it's her first direct attempt to write about her own abduction and rape years earlier in the Washington, D.C., area.[6]

Hand has written other explicitly autobiographical tales by her own account—a road trip in "On the Town Route" (1989); the death of a friend in "Pavane for a Prince of the Air" (2002)—but never in such an aggressively transformative way.

But this transformative function of the fantastic is not in any sense limited to cases of extreme trauma. Jeffrey Ford, a writer whose genre roots are so fluid that he's managed to win both the World Fantasy Award and the Edgar Award from the Mystery Writers of America, has also drawn on explicitly biographical material, from the bar he used to frequent and its haunting painting in "A Night in the Tropics" (2004) to his childhood catechism lessons in "Creation" (2002), his experiences as a Long Island clammer in "The Trentino Kid" (2004), his mother's death in "Present from the Past" (2003), and his own career as a writer in "Bright Morning" (2002).[7] Perhaps the fullest use of such material is his long story "Botch Town" in his 2006 collection *The Empire of Ice Cream*, later expanded into the 2008 novel *The Shadow Year*. Narrated by a sixth-grader in a working-class Long Island community in the late 1960s much like Ford's own, the story and the novel read like an authentic and moving celebration of childhood. But the story that to me most clearly demonstrates the ordering potential of the fantastic is "The Honeyed Knot" (2001), included in his collection *The Fantasy Writer's Assistant and Other Stories* (2002). Ford is a writing professor at a community college in New Jersey, and insists that this tale is "99.9 percent true."[8] His narrator, also named Jeff Ford and also a writing professor at a community college in New Jersey, recalls a student from years earlier who, while still in his class, raped and murdered a little girl, leaving Ford vaguely guilt-ridden over having failed to detect warning signs in the obscure symbolism of the student's writing. Much later, a middle-aged woman, Mrs. Apes, enters his class and writes bizarre accounts of a magical world overseen by a spirit named Avramody. Pressed to write about issues in her own life, she describes two events: a brutal beating from her husband that led to a near-death experience in the hospital (wandering the hospital corridors in a kind of spirit trance, she was saved by "a little girl down in the hospital morgue in the basement"), and the death of her own teenage daughter who was struck by a car. She also tells Ford that her writing tells her he'll "find a buck in the road," and that night, driving home, he indeed strikes and apparently kills a deer with an odd-shaped antler, which with its dying breath makes a sound eerily like a human word, but one which he can't quite place. But he sees the exact word in the next essay from Mrs. Apes: Ayuwea, which she explains was the name of her daughter. Meanwhile, Ford's son reports having seen a wild buck that eerily matches the description of the one Ford hit, and eventually Ford sees the animal himself near the college parking lot. Adding to the mystery, the college librarian as a favor tracks down the name Avramody from Mrs. Apes's fantastic cosmology, finding initially that it was the name of a fifteenth-century cleric whose book *The Honeyed Knot* (the title a metaphor for the complex but ultimately beneficent tangle of human relations) influenced the Puritans— but also that it was the name of the little girl murdered by Ford's student years earlier.

I've spent a bit more time describing this story because it seems to me to centrally concern some of the issues at the heart of this discussion, and because it specifically addresses the act of writing as framing. The magical world that Mrs. Apes concocts in her formless essays—the narrator calls them "visionary testaments," and they sound very much like a literary equivalent of the kind of obsessive outsider art associated with figures like Henry Darger—provides a means for her to cope with the tragedies of her own life, and we can guess that the little girl she met in the hospital morgue during her near-death experience might be the same little girl that Ford's student had murdered years earlier, hence the coincidence of the name Avramody. The deer, killed like Mrs. Apes's daughter (whose name it seems to pronounce) but living on in the tale, is at once fantastical and real, offering the narrator a kind of transcendent insight into the complex design of human relationships described by the fifteeenth-century Avramody as "the honeyed knot." As true as the tale may be in Ford's own view, it partakes of the conventions of the ghost story as well as those of the more mainstream tradition of the disturbed-student tale, the most famous example of which is Lionel Trilling's 1943 story "Of This Time, Of That Place" (in which the disturbed but brilliant student was long thought to have been Allen Ginsburg—who had been a student of Trilling's—although Ginsberg himself denied it). I'm not arguing that Ford's story, which pointedly uses devices of the fantastic to move outside the frame of received experience, is necessarily superior to Trilling's classic, which is a very different tale, but simply that it serves as an example of how the techniques and devices of fantastic writing can provide to the dissociations of raw experience a kind of narrative closure, or at the very least a frame—the honey in the knot, so to speak.

Of course, literally dozens of other writers have employed the resources of fantasy, horror, or science fiction as means of framing experience, sometimes in radically different ways from those I've described here. Some who come to mind immediately—and this list is deliberately wildly diverse—are Graham Joyce, whose childhood and family figure prominently in *The Facts of Life* (2002) and *The Limits of Enchantment* (2005); Kim Stanley Robinson, whose near-future science fiction in *Forty Signs of Rain* (2004), *Fifty Degrees Below* (2005), and *Sixty Days and Counting* (2006) draws on his own experiences as a father and his awareness of the workings of the Washington science bureaucracy; Harlan Ellison, who transforms pieces of his life and career repeatedly, notably in stories like "Jeffty is Five" (1977) and "All the Lies That Are My Life" (1980), and who sometimes would publish the same narrative as a story in one context and a memoir in another; Thomas M. Disch, whose Midwestern boyhood provided the template for fantasy in *On Wings of Song* (1979); even mainstream novelists like Doris Lessing, who (in a Worldcon guest of honor speech) described her tale of a decaying near-future England *Memoirs of a Survivor* (1974) as an "attempt at an autobiography" or Philip Roth, whose *The Plot against America* (2004) details his own childhood—using his real family names and narrated by an adult named Philip Roth looking back—transferred into a world in which Lindbergh was elected president and Nazi-style anti-semitism begins to infect the United States.[9]

At the beginning of this essay are two quotations on the transformative nature of art, chosen not by me but by prominent fantasy writers who, a century and a half apart, found in them a particular resonance. George Mac-Donald, heavily influenced by German Romantics like Novalis and their fervent notions of art as literal transcendence, spent most of his writing career and gained most of his contemporary fame as what we would describe today as a Scottish regional novelist. Today, he is remembered almost entirely for two remarkable fantasy novels that he wrote at the very beginning and very end of his career—*Phantastes* (1859) and *Lilith* (1895). Both embodied deeply felt and profoundly poetic versions of episodes from his own life that never achieved such transformative expressions in his more realistic novels; both expressed an inchoate desire, expressed in the words of Novalis, that art might literally make life more dreamlike. Elizabeth Hand's choice of the Cavafy poem suggests a different strategy: Art, instead of changing life into a dream, can unpack what is already "spectacular and terrifying" within it. These are very different uses of fantasy, to be sure, but in each case the devices of the unreal can frame experience in ways otherwise unavailable to the writer, otherwise invisible to the reader, otherwise merely the stuff of life.

nine

Peter Straub and the New Horror

with Amelia Beamer

Horror is a house that horror has already moved out of.
—Peter Straub, "Horror's House"

Horror has always been a notoriously difficult genre to define. Sometimes it's described in simple terms of formulaic conventions of plot and character (often conflating fiction and film), sometimes entirely in terms of its so-called "affect" (horror is whatever scares you). As has often been noted, it's the only popular genre actually named after the fear, terror, and similar emotions intended to be produced in the reader.[1] Film scholar Linda Williams identifies horror (at least in film) as what she calls a "body genre"—a genre intended to produce a literal bodily response in the audience. Her other examples were melodrama (intended to cause weeping) and pornography (arousal), though we might add comedy (laughter) to this list. Even Terry Heller, whose 1987 study *The Delights of Terror* remains one of the more sophisticated theoretical discussions of literary horror, described his topic as "a group of works that seem to share the main purpose of frightening their readers."[2] The website of the Horror Writers Association (formerly Horror Writers of America), a professional writers' association, proclaims that horror's "only true requirement is that it elicit an emotional reaction that includes some aspect of fear or dread."[3] It's possible that this traditional single-minded approach to horror even dates back to Poe himself, who in a famous 1842 review of Hawthorne's *Twice-Told Tales*, argued in favor of a kind of short fiction characterized by "a certain unique or single *effect* to be wrought out," and that every single word or sentence in a tale should lead inevitably to the "outbringing of this effect."[4]

But horror, or at least horror writing of any degree of narrative complexity, has never really been limited to a single effect—or affect—and it might be argued that such a single-minded approach to sensation almost catastrophically narrowed the range of the field, leading it toward self-parody during the commercial boom and bust cycle of the 1970s and 1980s. Even then, however, a small but highly visible group of "literary" horror writers sought to expand and deepen the narrative possibilities of the field and in recent years, in both literature and the media, this newer sort of horror has experienced a kind of rebirth, one example of which is Peter Straub's 2008 anthology *Poe's Children: The New Horror*, published in advance of the two hundredth anniversary of Poe's birth and including several contemporary writers and stories not generally associated with horror as a genre (Dan Chaon, Kelly Link, M. Rickert, John Crowley, M. John Harrison, Ellen Klages). Another sign of this rebirth is the diffusion of horror tropes into other modes, from comedy to romance to literary fiction. On the media side, this might be viewed as the *Buffy*ization of horror (from Joss Whedon's highly complex and successful TV series *Buffy the Vampire Slayer*, 1997–2003), with horror tropes repurposed as comedy or even romance, to much commercial success in the case of *Buffy* and certain of its successors. The "paranormal romance" has even grown into a commercially viable subgenre of its own in the wake of this trend, with its own formulas, its own websites, its own awards, and (as of 2006) even its own annual "best of" anthology.[5]

An intriguing theoretical model of traditional horror as a genre or mode of storytelling can be found in John Clute's 2006 book, *The Darkening Garden: A Short Lexicon of Horror*. It's a fairly powerful model. In attempting to elucidate a vocabulary for understanding horror, using mostly terms of his own invention, Clute defines horror as following a recognizable grammar or structure, comparable to the passage of the four seasons ending in winter. "Sighting," or "a glimpse of terror to come," is related to Freud's uncanny, and hooks the protagonist into the emerging narrative; "thickening," which begins to realize the portents of sighting, moves the unwilling protagonist deeper into the "suffocating tangle of plot"; "revel," occurs when "the field of the world is reversed" and the terrifying truth is made manifest; and "aftermath" represents the recognition that the newly revealed world is "no longer storyable," and that the story must end.[6] Innumerable examples of horror in both fiction and film subscribe to Clute's frankly prescriptive system, which offers far more useful ways of reading than can be described in simple terms of affect or narrative formula. Clute's model is not the only template for horror fiction, of course, but it is among the most provocative, and it provides a starting point for our own argument about the increasingly complex uses of the material of horror in recent works by Peter Straub and other writers.

We want to explore a body of fiction for which traditional horror provides a kind of foundational substrate, but which takes Clute's notion of "aftermath" in some fundamentally different directions. This is the kind of fiction that Peter Straub refers to when he says, "horror is a house that horror has already moved out of."[7] It is, to a great extent, fiction that eschews the language and strictures of traditional horror, that is not satisfied with effects, but that is not shy about occasionally using these effects, manipulating and transforming familiar tropes, and repositioning horror in the context of a narrative movement that denies the closure of the traditional horror dynamic. The works of Peter Straub and a number of other contemporary writers characteristically open up where traditional horror shuts down; in the face of what Clute calls "vastation," they seek to find room for something like the sacred. This revisionist approach to horror breaks through both horror and fantasy tropes to arrive at a kind of transcendence: a heightened sense of reality laced with deeper, more difficult, and more powerful meanings than are available through traditional narrative techniques or genre protocols. Such an "opening up," or sense of transcendence, is achieved not only through the portrayal of extreme emotional states—the familiar stuff of much horror—but also by the use of deliberate narrative devices, including unreliable narrators, stories-within-stories, metatextual layering of narratives, shifting points of view, self-conscious allusiveness, and often surprising dissonances of tone and style. Traditional horror, in contrast, tends to be narratively conservative, characteristically narrowing the potential for meaningful action in a world only gradually revealed to be damaged, reduced, terrifying—in John Clute's term, "a Cloaca down which the raw world pours."[8] The damaged world is still revealed in this kind of transcendental horror, but far from serving as climax, the revelation only hints at further revelations beyond; a novel such as Straub's *lost boy lost girl* begins with the emotional devastation of serial murders and a suicide, but seeks to move its central character beyond this toward some sort of accommodation, possibly even toward some version of grace. Material horror (the actual effects mentioned in those earlier definitions) becomes as much a function of angle of vision, or point of view, as of raw sensation.

Manipulating point of view, of course, has long been a familiar technique in classic horror—witness *Dracula* or *The Strange Case of Dr. Jekyll and Mr. Hyde*—and there are numerous such antecedents for these techniques. Many of the key techniques of this new or "transcendental" horror, we readily admit, are not entirely new, while others clearly reflect both postmodern techniques such as narrative instability and self-reflexivity, and modernist concerns such as psychological realism, allusiveness, and stylistic complexity. In fact, it is in large part this expansion of horror to include these aspects of modernism and post-modernism that enabled Straub and a few other writers to survive the collapse of the genre horror market, with its traditional Gothic strictures, and to incorporate elements of it into a more contemporary mode of writing, which in many cases barely resembles genre horror at all, despite the occasional presence of these familiar trappings.

* * *

Peter Straub, as noted earlier in this volume, consciously explored many of the conventional tropes of the genre in such novels as *Ghost Story* (1979) and *Floating Dragon* (1983), novels that might be discussed profitably in terms of Clute's prescriptive definition of horror. Beginning with *Koko* in 1988, however, Straub deliberately set out to expand the possibilities of horror within the context of the contemporary novel. With its two related novels *Mystery* (1990) and *The Throat* (1993), *Koko* launched an exploration of a complex personal mythology—the "Blue Rose" stories—in which the conventions of supernatural horror are clearly subsumed to the effects of personal traumas ranging from a violent childhood event to the experience of the Vietnam War, and to his characters' quests to transcend, or at least accommodate, these powerful events. Ironically, as Bill Sheehan points out, Straub's most realistic work is what eventually gained him the greatest recognition within the fantasy community: both *Koko* and "The Ghost Village"—a reworked episode from *The Throat*—became his first works to win World Fantasy Awards, and yet both are stories without significant fantastic content.[9]

During this same period, Straub's other short fiction also began to reflect this harsh realism and to reconsider or reposition the materials of horror in distinctive new ways. In three of his most powerful stories, published within a few years of each other between 1988 and 1994, he explores various mechanisms for coping with such childhood damage or trauma. "The Juniper Tree" (1988), "The Buffalo Hunter" (1990), and "Bunny is Good Bread" (1994) all begin in worlds that, for the protagonists, are already desolate. "The Juniper Tree" and "Bunny Is Good Bread" both concern young boys who suffer at the hands of insensitive and brutal fathers and who end up spending their afternoons in local movie theaters where they suffer sexual abuse at the hands of local child-predators. In the case of "Bunny is Good Bread," the young Fee Bandolier is even forced to watch his mother gruesomely and gradually die after a brutal beating from his father (who later is revealed to be a serial murderer as well). In both tales, the movies that the boys watch become entangled with their own stories and their notions of their own identities. And both stories end with abrupt leaps decades into the future, in which we learn that the first-person narrator of "The Juniper Tree" has become a respected novelist, while the boy Fee from "Bunny is Good Bread" goes on to commit brutal rapes and murders before enlisting in the Special Forces for service in Vietnam.

Straub depicts essentially the same extreme experience—child abuse—as leading toward a serial murderer in one story and a novelist in the other. The characters' capacity, or lack of capacity, for transcendence is evidenced in what they do with their lives after these childhood nightmares. The unnamed narrator in "The Juniper Tree" uses the plots of the movies playing during his victimization in the movie theater to integrate this devastating experience into the undamaged portion of his life—using fiction as a means of healing. On the other hand, Fee Bandolier in "Bunny is Good Bread" fails to heal from similar horrific experiences and instead finds in his own tragedies a template for revenge against the damaged world, expressed in the form of serial murders (significantly, the film he watches is an imaginary *noir* revenge melodrama, while the narrator of "The Juniper Tree" sees the actual 1949 film *Chicago Deadline*, about a newspaper writer). Another important difference between the two stories is the narrative approach: The first-person narrator goes on to a successful life, while the more distanced Fee, described in third-person narration, fails to do so.

Ironically, however, neither of these stories involves aspects of supernatural horror, and it's the long novella "The Buffalo Hunter" that combines a more traditional horror-story ending with a rare effort to directly portray transcendent experience. In this story, the protagonist Bobby Bunting is already an adult in his thirties, having long ago moved away from home to work as a data clerk in an anonymous New York corporation. However, Bobby is still unable to cope with a father who declared him a "fuck-up," saying that he was "never going to amount to anything in this world." As in "Bunny Is Good Bread," Bobby's mother is dying, suffering from an unspecified illness causing lapses of consciousness, and Bobby's father resists paying a doctor for treatment. Bobby is aware of some vague catastrophe in his past, but "his life depended on keeping this knowledge locked inside him." He has developed some odd habits, such as drinking vodka from baby bottles, but his most remarkable means of escape turns out to be an ability to enter the worlds of the books he is reading—first a Luke Short Western titled *The Buffalo Hunter*, later Raymond Chandler's *The Lady in the Lake*, and eventually Tolstoy's *Anna Karenina*. This selection of books itself may say something about the necessity of moving beyond the limits of genre, but Bobby's most remarkable experience occurs shortly after his encounter with Chandler's world: On his way to work, a sudden ray of sunlight falls on him, and the world falls silent. "His eyes had been washed clean of habit, and he *saw*."

It was as if all of life had gloriously opened itself before him. If he could have moved, he would have fallen to his knees with thanks. For long, long seconds after the lightning faded, everything blazed and burned with life. Being streamed from every particle of the world—wood, metal, glass, or flesh. Cars, fire hydrants, the concrete and crushed stones of the road, each individual raindrop, all contained the same living substance that Bunting himself contained—and this was what was significant about himself and them. If Bunting had been religious, he would have felt that he had been given a direct, unmediated vision of God: since he was not, his experience was of the sacredness of the world itself.[10]

As Bill Sheehan writes in *At the Foot of the Story Tree*, this passage may be "one of the clearest, most naked expressions found anywhere in Straub's work of a belief in the existence of sacred, transcendental mysteries."[11] At the very least, it's one of the few occasions where Straub has attempted to dramatize such a belief in terms of a particular character's moment of insight, although he has spoken of it in interviews, and in later fiction—as we shall see—he has sought to develop means of conveying such a notion more indirectly to the reader solely through narrative technique. But Bunting's vision, and even the transcendence that he derives from fiction, is not enough to save him: While in the world of *Anna Karenina*, he steps in front of a train like Anna herself. The story's final section portrays Bobby's building superintendent admitting his recently widowed father into the blood-spattered room where Bobby had been found horribly crushed and mutilated, "like he got hit by a truck."[12]

Between Bobby, Fee Bandolier, and the unnamed narrator of "The Juniper Tree," we are presented with three possible responses to childhood horror: turning into a monster (Fee), escaping into a world of artifice and possible transcendence (Bobby), and becoming a successful novelist (the narrator of "The Juniper Tree"). But "The Juniper Tree" and "Bunny is Good Bread" turn out to be connected in other ways as well. "The Juniper Tree," according to the afterword in Straub's collection *Houses without Doors* (1990), is one of two stories actually written by Tim Underhill (the other is "The Blue Rose," another tale of childhood violence). Underhill later shows up in Straub's major novels *Koko* (1988) and *The Throat* (1993), as the central point-of-view character. These stories, Straub tells us, "represent the first part of Underhill's efforts to comprehend violence and evil by wrapping them in his own imagination."[13] Fee Bandolier also shows up again in *The Throat*, under the guise of the mysterious and genuinely terrifying Franklin Batchelor, a renegade officer apparently modeled on Joseph Conrad's Kurtz from *Heart of Darkness* (1899), almost certainly one of the ur-texts of transcendental horror.[14]

Tim Underhill turns out to be a central figure in much of Straub's fiction, and the one who most often grapples with the paradoxical relationship between horror and the transcendent. This struggle is made more overt in Straub's remarkable pair of recent novels concerning Underhill's grief over his nephew's disappearance. Both *lost boy lost girl* (2003) and *In the Night Room* (2004) combine moving explorations of character with playfully postmodern narrative techniques and powerfully evocative themes, including the nature of evil and the ways in which reality and personal identity are constructed. In *lost boy lost girl*, Underhill returns from New York to his childhood home of Millhaven upon the suicide of his sister-in-law, and soon faces the disappearance of his beloved nephew Mark as well. Learning that Mark had become obsessed with the abandoned house of a serial killer named Kalendar, whose many victims apparently included his own young daughter, Underhill begins to fear that Mark has fallen victim to a second serial killer currently terrorizing the city. Mark is never exactly found, but Straub provides an ending that seems to represent a kind of transcendent escape into cyberspace. Underhill gets an e-mail from Mark directing him to a website where Mark, in the company of Kalendar's daughter—who somehow survived after all—is seen walking romantically on a beach, with lowering clouds in the distance: The eponymous lost boy and girl seeming to live on safely in a kind of cyberspace afterlife. But the novel's internal logic shows this escape to be false, and this is made explicit in *In the Night Room*, when we learn that *lost boy lost girl* is yet another of Tim Underhill's fictions. Underhill, whom we recognize as a fictive shadow of Straub himself, consistently (and sometimes tragically) searches for the hints of transcendence that he wants to believe lie behind the traumas of life, from childhood violence to the Vietnam war. The fact that he is portrayed as an

author thus takes on added significance, as he seeks to discover this transcendence through his own fiction. But in a sense that fiction is never more
than an approximation of the insights that he wants to convey; portraying a
character having a transcendent moment, or offering an apparently transcendent denouement for a character, merely externalizes a fundamentally internal
struggle. Straub, whom we may assume is a somewhat shrewder novelist than
Underhill, seeks to deliver the sensation directly to the reader at the level of
narrative technique, and his most important experiments in this direction are
found in these two novels.

The books are hardly conventional horror or fantasy by any genre standards,
and in fact are pointed experiments in the manipulation of point of view. *In the
Night Room* begins with what seem to be dual plotlines, one involving Underhill receiving creepy e-mails from dead people and encountering a bizarrely
frightening fan, the other involving a children's book author named Willie who
recently has married an ominously secretive financier; interestingly, Willie's
most famous book is also titled *In the Night Room*. Soon, however, we realize
that the chapters involving Willie are part of a novel that Underhill is writing,
and that the mysterious events in his life are the result of a supernatural agency,
perhaps the ghost of the murderer Kalendar, who felt unjustly maligned by
Underhill's previous novel *lost boy lost girl*. To complicate matters further,
Willie finds herself transported into Underhill's "real" world by an Oz-like
whirlwind, and the two of them set out for Millhaven to restore a balance and
perhaps learn the true fate of Kalendar's daughter Lily.

The indeterminate nature of reality is a central inquiry in these books, and it
may be seen in various elements, including that deranged fan who tells Underhill that he compulsively collects multiple copies of the same books, looking for
the "real" book, on the theory that the print run of each book includes a few
copies of the "correct" book that the author had actually intended to write. But
even this fan, Jasper Dan Kohle, turns out to be something other than what he
seems (his name is an anagram of the murderer Joseph Kalendar). In one truly
remarkable chapter, we are thrust into a completely different story in which we
meet a Hardy Boys–type teen detective named Teddy Barton who suddenly
realizes that he will never solve the mystery he is working on, and will in fact
never do anything new again. Teddy's world has collapsed mid-narrative when
his author (another character from the same Underhill novel that created
Willie) is killed. While the notion of the embedded tale may be a familiar one
from the history of earlier Gothic fiction, few novels have situated the reader so

boldly within these fictional worlds-within-worlds, and in Straub's hands the technique more closely resembles the reality-testing fictions of Philip K. Dick than earlier Gothic traditions.

These metatextual and metafictional chapters, anagrams, and coded messages repeatedly create a feeling of revelatory horror, for both Underhill and the reader: Underhill's cryptic e-mail messages and his encounter with Kohle are genuinely unnerving, as is Willie's devastating realization that she is a fictional character (who, in a nice touch, must constantly eat candy in order to keep from disappearing altogether). *In the Night Room* invites us to read it as deconstructing *lost boy lost girl*, revealing the latter as a wish-fulfillment narrative by a grieving author and thus casting doubt on narrative reliability in the newer novel as well. Straub plants only a few clues in *lost boy lost girl* to suggest how the narrator is playing with reality—most notably through a single chapter that pointedly switches to first person in an otherwise third person novel. *In the Night Room,* however is explicit in manipulating the levels of narrative reality, with characters emerging from books written by other characters and, at least in one case, the Teddy Barton chapter, a character living within a novel written by another character who *himself* is a character in a Tim Underhill novel! Reality, we are reminded repeatedly, is conditional, contingent, indeterminate—a function of the stories we tell to describe it. The various narrative effects are central both to generating the feeling of horror and to implying the more nebulous idea of transcendence, the notion that at the heart of the horror is some kind of emotional truth, a truth that Straub hopes to make manifest to the reader even when it isn't immediately apparent to his characters.

The deliberate misdirections in these novels are closely related to what we are calling "transcendence." Such transcendence is not mere insight, not just a matter of puzzling out the epistemology of the narrative, but creates the much more disturbing epiphany that arises from glimpsing a reality that neither the characters (nor the reader) are fully prepared to deal with. When Willie gradually comes to realize that she is a fictional character somehow transported into a "real" world, her sense of disorientation is one the reader can readily identify with, because we ourselves have experienced the same disorientation upon making the discovery a few chapters earlier. While many examples of this occur in *In the Night Room*, the core revelation and the dramatic center of the book is the discovery that Lily Kalendar was in fact not murdered by her father, as Underhill realizes when he sees a glimpse of the real Lily through a window. It seems to be one of the few moments of irreducible reality given to Underhill in either of the novels—until we remember that we are still trapped in Underhill's viewpoint, and the most we can claim with confidence is that Underhill *believes* he has found the core reality of his largely self-constructed tale. For the reader, given what we now know of the reliability of Underhill's viewpoint, the "core" remains contingent (see our discussion of "contingency of worlds" in the essay that follows, "Twenty-First-Century Stories").

Straub's narrative techniques in *In The Night Room* and *lost boy lost girl* call into question both the nature of fantasy and the nature of narrative reality and serve as a meditation on the purposes, methods, and limits of fiction as a way to frame experience, particularly when that experience involves extreme or traumatic emotional events. And the past doesn't ever go away, whether it erupts in the form of e-mails from the dead or the unlikely survival of Lily Kalendar. As Underhill says in *Koko*, "deep down, the things that happened to you never stop happening."[15] Straub has drawn repeatedly upon personal experience in his fiction, and has discussed the auto accident that he suffered at age seven, with repeated hospitalizations and a long convalescence that essentially ended his childhood. Additionally, as Straub discussed in an unusually candid interview in *Locus* magazine in 2006, some of his bleakest stories, "Bunny is Good Bread" and "The Juniper Tree," also draw from personal memories of childhood abuse, which he only recovered and confirmed later in life—giving a particular poignancy to a comment made by the narrator of "The Juniper Tree," that [I] knew that I had *something to remember* without knowing what it was."[16] These very difficult, very powerful, and very traumatic experiences shaped Straub's life, but to speak of them only in terms of how they inform his fiction is to risk falling into the trap of purely psychological interpretation. In Straub's work, the damaged world is an *a priori* condition, and the narrative uses extreme experience and experimental storytelling techniques to work through the implications of this world, in the same way that talking about damaging experiences can help one accept and transcend those experiences. The sheer extremity and personal nature of such events, and the difficulty of describing them, are central to the notion of transcendence in horror.

* * *

"Transcendence" is admittedly a nebulous and elusive concept. It can refer to a moment of revelation given a character (as with Bobby in "The Buffalo Hunter"), an interpretation of events by a narrator who may or may not be reliable (as with Tim Underhill), or to a state of mind that the author strives to convey to the reader through the manipulation of narrative technique. Straub described the difficulties with trying to elucidate it in an interview with *Locus* magazine in 1994:

In fiction, you cannot write about transcendence. You can't even talk about it right, because the words we use are inadequate for the things they're supposed to be invoking. What you can do, if you're good enough and you're paying enough attention, is lead the reader along a path of extremity, so that he has at least some dim notion of what it's like to be truly terrified for an extended period of time, or to be really jolted by some unexpected and miserable experience. At moments of terrible terror and extremity, one can experience a sort of clarity. Nobody would want to go through the aftermath or the consequences, but at those moments, one sometimes can really see. And *then* next to that you can put something about the other half of that experience—what you might see, what you might experience, that you could carry with you later when you're healing.[17]

Straub is not the only contemporary writer of the fantastic to think along these lines, and for the remainder of this discussion we want to suggest how a number of newer writers—writers whose careers began well after Straub's—have addressed similar issues. China Miéville also discussed transcendence in a recent *Locus* interview: "As [Clute] says, horror has to do with the numinous, the uncovering of the terrible truth that is there under the everyday. That is only another articulation of uncovering the *transcendent* truth under the everyday."[18]

Transcendence may be especially difficult to write about, as Straub says, because it cannot be described or evoked directly; instead, it's something such fiction triangulates and infers, though never fully articulates. It's also a term that comes bearing a fair amount of baggage, from Emersonian philosophy to New Age idealism. In our sense, however, it's something of a precipice, perhaps a descendant of Longinus's notions of the sublime as reconsidered by Edmund Burke, who wrote, "Whatever is fitted in any sort to excite the ideas of pain, and danger, that is to say, whatever is in any sort terrible, or is conversant about terrible objects, or operates in a manner analogous to terror, is a source of the sublime; that is, it is productive of the strongest emotion which the mind is capable of feeling."[19] The notion of the sublime as a potential function of terror is a staple of Gothic criticism, often associated with something like Clute's "vastation" or the Lovecraftian awareness of a vast, cold, indifferent universe or of the terrors lurking beneath the surface of everyday life. The questions Straub raises are: What happens next? What lies beyond the moment of recognition? If horror is not an end in itself, what is it part of, and how can fiction even begin to approach that?

Of course, Straub is not alone in asking these questions. Miéville, for example, from his New Crobuzon novels to his short fiction to his young adult novel *Un Lun Dun* (2007), has brought a veritable arsenal of techniques, ranging from surrealism to Dickensian social realism to comedy, to the task of exploring the revelatory nature of extreme or grotesque events and characters. Miéville's fiction was widely associated with a vaguely defined movement called "the New Weird," which was debated on a now-defunct discussion board in England in the early 2000s, but which was defined more broadly than what we are discussing here. Miéville himself cited such horror writers as H. P. Lovecraft and Clark Ashton Smith among the precursors of the New Weird, a movement that also included substantial elements of science fiction, fantasy, and surrealism. His insight suggests significant links between notions of transcendence and elements of more traditional Gothic fiction.

A number of other current writers working in similar modes—many of them included in Straub's *Poe's Children* anthology—are often reviewed simply as fantasists, or even as mainstream writers, and are seldom discussed in terms of horror. Yet Kelly Link often uses such traditional horror tropes as zombies and ghosts, even when, as in "The Hortlak," she subverts these tropes in comedic or absurdist ways. In the case of "The Hortlak," the story elements include harmless but uncommunicative zombies frequenting a convenience store, an animal shelter employee who gives dogs a last car ride before euthanizing them, and a store clerk whose pajamas reveal the secret lives of unrelated characters. The recurring themes of death and loss of control generate a deeply terrifying feeling, but one that can hardly be described as affect horror, and one that implies meanings just out of reach. Characteristically shifting between mundane reality and fantastic events, sometimes within the same paragraph, Link is another writer who repeatedly suggests the notion of a reality beyond experience. Similarly, M. Rickert's "Map of Dreams" begins and ends with a mother whose six-year-old daughter is gunned down by a crazed sniper on a New York streetcorner, and while the intervening narrative takes the grieving mother through episodes involving time travel and Australian aboriginal dreamtime, the central triggering event is one of pure horror, a mother watching her own child's death. Another writer who sometimes works in this mode is Jeffrey Ford, whose story "A Night in the Tropics" begins as a childhood memory, but then embeds what is essentially a horror tale about a cursed chess set, as the adult narrator returns to the bar and meets a hooligan from his childhood. Point of view is crucial; while a traditional horror writer might have been satisfied with the tale of the chess set, Ford frames it as an almost nostalgic tale from the narrator's childhood, again involving the persistence of the past and the hint of a darker meaning—a technique that Ford has used to great effect in many of his tales.

Link, Rickert, Ford, and Elizabeth Hand are among the writers discussed in the next essay, "Twenty-First-Century Stories," but we could readily cite additional examples from the work of Miéville, Graham Joyce, Brian Evenson, Tim Powers, Joe Hill, M. John Harrison, Dan Chaon, Margo Lanagan, Neil Gaiman, Christopher Priest, or any number of others—or for that matter we could look backward toward Robert Louis Stevenson, Joseph Conrad, Arthur Machen, John Collier, Roald Dahl, Shirley Jackson, and others who have demonstrated a common interest in adapting the materials of horror to a mode of fiction that, directly or indirectly, aspires to evoke transcendence. These are not writers who "transcend" their genres—a misuse of the term that demeans both the genre and its alleged transcenders—but rather writers who incorporate genre materials among a complex of other narrative resources, often producing fiction that seems to defy any sort of traditional genre reading protocols at all. In the work of many such writers, we may encounter ghosts, zombies, demons, succubi, brutal murderers, or supernatural events, but their stories are rarely *derived* from these elements, and rarely identify themselves as horror tales; to paraphrase a Taoist apothegm, horror that says it's horror is not new horror. For the most part, such fiction is not in any sense a conscious literary movement, and in fact it may well be regarded more usefully as a reading protocol or a critical approach than as a readily definable group of works or authors. If that's the case, a great many stories that we haven't even attempted to touch on might yield to such a reading. As these stories and writers remind us through their continual reinvention and recombination of the materials and techniques of both genre and mainstream narratives, we must learn not how to read horror—we already know how to do that—but to read *through* horror to seek the source of the stories' more complex mysteries. If horror has moved out of its old house, it behooves us to follow.

ten

Twenty-First-Century Stories

with Amelia Beamer

Does a story inhabit a genre, or does genre inhabit a story? While such a question might at first seem to confuse questions of market with questions of aesthetics—after all, for decades some writers having been submitting their work to identifiable genre magazines, anthologies, and publishing lists, while others have been using similar materials in stories published outside of these venues—it nevertheless underlies a fascinating dialogue that has emerged in the last decade or two in various essays, reviews, anthologies, conference papers, blogs, interviews, and panel discussions, mostly in the arena of fantastic literature and its familiar genres of fantasy, horror, and science fiction. It's also one of the crucial questions surrounding the recent evolution of these genres and their materials, and it has given rise to a panoply of new terms: Slipstream. Interstitial. Transrealism. New Weird. Nonrealist fiction. New Wave Fabulist. Postmodern fantasy. Postgenre fiction. Cross-genre. Span fiction. Artists without Borders. New Humanist. Fantastika. Liminal fantasy. Transcendental Horror. (Okay, we ourselves made that last one up, as a way of trying to approach the fiction of Peter Straub in the preceding essay, which insistently led us into the territory that we propose to explore here.) While we easily could devote an entire essay simply to cataloguing and parsing these various terms, doing so would seem to validate the very practice our purpose is to avoid: namely, the growing tendency to replace meaningful critical discourse with ingenious tagging. Some of these labels, like "span fiction" (suggested by Peter Brigg in a 2002 book on intersections of mainstream and science fiction) frankly don't seem to have gone anywhere. Others, like "slipstream," have altered their meaning through time and usage (John Clute's entry on it in his and Peter Nicholls' 1993 *Encyclopedia of Science Fiction* related it to a kind of "commercial piggybacking" on the part of nongenre writers using SF tropes—quite different from contemporary usage, which we'll discuss a bit later). Still others are accidents; "New

Wave Fabulist" was concocted by Bradford Morrow merely as a label for a special issue of the journal *Conjunctions* edited by Peter Straub in 2002, and has since taken on a life of its own, often misattributed to Straub (for example the 2006 anthology *Paraspheres*, edited by Rusty Morrison and Ken Keegan, is subtitled "Fabulist and New Wave Fabulist Stories"). And yet others, such as "interstitial," come complete with organizations, conferences, auctions, art shows, and anthologies.[1]

Suffice to say that a bewildering array of terms has been suggested to describe recent fiction outside the traditional categories of the fantastic, and that some of these terms are being promoted and treated as actual literary movements. We've come a long way since Michael Swanwick, writing in *Asimov's* in 1986, could note, "The generation I want to talk about hasn't been named yet."[2] By now it has been named with a vengeance. Let's take "slipstream" as an example, since many of the stories that we're discussing in this essay have been called slipstream. The original term, meaning a region of low pressure and forward suction in the wake of a fast-moving vehicle, provides an obvious source for the "piggybacking" that Clute referred to back in 1993. Jeff Prucher, in his *Brave New Words: The Oxford Dictionary of Science Fiction*, traces the first use of "slipstream" as a back-formation to a Bruce Sterling piece in *SF Eye* in 1989, where he proposes it as shorthand for what he describes as "novels of Postmodern sensibility."[3] But the word is also a parody of "mainstream," according to Bruce Sterling in that same essay (in a column called *Catscan*). It's difficult to trace when "mainstream" became a kind of derogatory code term among genre writers, but its first use in critical discourse about science fiction is likely an essay by Rosalie Moore, "Science Fiction and the Main Stream," which appeared in Reginald Bretnor's early critical anthology *Modern Science Fiction: Its Meaning and Its Future*, in 1953. To everyone else, it's just general fiction—anything shelved in the Fiction & Literature section at your local chain bookstore.

By 2003, in a column in *Asimov's*, James Patrick Kelly could describe slipstream as "a type of writing that crosses genre boundaries in and out of science fiction." He suggested that it's a conscious strategy on the part of a number of authors and identified three in particular—Kelly Link, Karen Joy Fowler, and Carol Emshwiller—as the "muses" of the movement.[4] And by 2006, it had all coalesced to the point where Kelly, with his collaborator John Kessel, could edit a slipstream anthology, *Feeling Very Strange*, only now they defined it as an effect rather than a genre, characterized by a violation of the tenets of realism, an abjuration of specific genre identity, "playful postmodernism," and above all the quality of (another term from Sterling) "feeling very strange."[5] In Kelly's terms, slipstream is

a literary effect—in the same way that horror or comedy are literary effects achieved by many different kinds of dissimilar stories. What is that effect? We borrowed the term cognitive dissonance from the psychologists. When we are presented with two contradictory cognitions—impressions, feelings, beliefs—we experience cognitive dissonance, a kind of psychic discomfort that we normally try to ease by discounting one of the cognitions as false or illusory and promoting the other to reality . . . We think that what slipstream stories do is to embrace cognitive dissonance.[6]

Kessel added, "Many people feel that the world doesn't make sense according to the structures that held during the twentieth century." By way of example, he described a story by M. Rickert, "You Have Never Been Here," as follows: "It is both clearly written and profoundly disorienting. It does not resolve itself easily into any simple category. At times it seems like a dream. At times it seems like a dystopian fantasy. At times it seems to be a rational story told from the point of view of a madman. Just when you think you've got it figured out, it takes a left turn. Yet it does not feel arbitrary. This story makes me feel very strange."[7] Kelly and Kessel's much-discussed anthology included not only the slipstream "muses" Link, Emshwiller, and Fowler, but also newer writers such as Rickert and Benjamin Rosenbaum, writers with "mainstream" credentials such as Michael Chabon and Jonathan Lethem, and comparative old-timers such as Sterling and Howard Waldrop (not to mention Emshwiller herself, who had been doing something like this since the 1950s). Specific reference to any privileged association with science fiction in particular was omitted from this new definition. Slipstream was no longer viewed as an offshoot of genre SF, but as a mode of writing that might allude freely to all the genres of the fantastic, sometimes even within the same story.

The following year, Christopher Priest, in an essay on *Ice* by Anna Kavan, revisited the issue of how slipstream had moved beyond science fiction, identifying it as a movement that arose during the late 1980s in the United States,

originally an attempt to identify a certain kind of ambitious science fiction, which lay outside the familiar pulp-magazine tropes of space travel, alien invasions, time travel, and so on . . . [O]ther writers, who were outside the SF genre, but whose work could conceivably fit into the wider definition allowed by slipstream, were summoned in support. So Angela Carter, Paul Auster, Haruki Murakami, Jorge Luis Borges and William

S. Burroughs were some of the writers invoked in this case. . . . The best way to understand slipstream is to think of it as a state of mind, or a particular approach, one that is outside of all categorization. It is in essence indefinable, but slipstream induces a sense of "otherness" in the audience, like a glimpse into a distorting mirror, perhaps, or a view of familiar sights and objects from an unfamiliar perspective.[8]

Where science fiction tends to resolve toward explanations, however unlikely, slipstream, according to Priest, "shifts science (and its effects) into the realm of the unconscious mind, into metaphor, into emotion, into symbols."[9]

So slipstream may be the first of these terms to gain wide discussion in the twenty-first century, but what of "interstitial" and "New Wave Fabulist" and all the others? Unsurprisingly, these various movements also claim many of the same authors identified as slipstream, and claim many of the same characteristics. Several "slipstream" writers show up in that Straub-edited "New Wave Fabulist" issue of *Conjunctions*, or in Jeff and Anne VanderMeer's *The New Weird* anthology in 2008, and a number of younger writers appeared in *Interfictions* (2007), from the Interstitial Arts Foundation and edited by Delia Sherman and Theodora Goss. The Interstitial Arts Foundation website, by the way, defines "interstitial art" as "art made in the interstices between genres and categories. It is art that flourishes in the borderlands between different disciplines, mediums, and cultures. It is art that crosses borders, made by artists who refuse to be constrained by category labels."[10] As stirring as this anthem-like definition may sound, it's a definition based not on any set of identifiable characteristics, but rather on exclusion: Just like some definitions for slipstream, interstitial is precisely *not* something that we can point to, although we can readily point to what it isn't. In traditional categorical terms, it's not *something* but rather *something else*. It's a definition that harks back to one of the conditions of slipstream stories mentioned by Kelly and Kessel: "they are not science fiction stories, traditional fantasies, dreams, historical fantasies, or alternate histories."[11]

We're not trying to argue the usefulness or necessity of snazzy new terms to describe snazzy new fiction; all such terms can serve to identify affinity groups, literary movements, marketing niches, or convenient ways to group and understand stories, and they may well be helpful for readers seeking to find stories of a certain type. However, we do want to examine the odd fact that these definitions tend to focus far more on what these stories are *not* rather than on what they are. Is it really useful to have a genre that is essentially indefinable, or definable only in terms of what it is not? Slipstream is not "about" any particular material content, even in the broad conventional sense of science fiction being about the possible and fantasy about the impossible. In a purely rhetorical sense, this is a very strange way to go about defining a new movement: The very act of claiming that a story is not genre science fiction or fantasy or horror, or that an artist refuses to be constrained by category labels, seems more likely to validate and valorize those labels than to overcome them.

Why approach these stories in terms of such received categories at all? When Shirley Jackson, arguably one of the major ancestors of the kind of fiction we're simply calling "twenty-first-century stories," published her collection *The Lottery: The Adventures of James Harris* in 1949 (the subtitle later was dropped), *New York Times* reviewer Donald Barr merely emphasized her "very effective talent as an ironist" and mentioned her use of the macabre, but paid no attention at all to the stories' genre content or lack thereof.[12] More important, describing these works of fiction in such categorical terms seems to violate the rhetorical and aesthetic imperatives by which fiction is created in the first place; many of the authors mentioned have indicated in interviews and essays that their methods involve following the internal logic of the story at hand—which may or may not involve the deployment of genre materials—rather than setting out to write stories that are unclassifiable in traditional terms. "I certainly had no intention of resisting categories when I started writing," Kelly Link told an interviewer. "I submitted my work to genre magazines. Being published in magazines like *Fence* and *Conjunctions* came as a surprise to me, and I'm not being disingenuous when I say that."[13] Nor are we trying to be disingenuous by titling this piece "Twenty-First-Century Stories" rather than adopting any of the labels we've discussed, or suggesting any new ones. Our title is, if anything, an anti-label. We refer back to Kessel's comment that "the world doesn't make sense according to the structures that held during the 20th century," and note that, while critics and writers were commenting on this trend as early as the 1980s, a virtual blossoming of these stories has occurred in the new century; nearly all the stories we discuss here (and certainly all of the story collections) were published after 2000.

We would like to propose that many stories claimed by slipstream, interstitial, and other movements can be explored in terms of specific narrative and rhetorical strategies, that these stories in fact have identifiable *features*. Our main examples—M. Rickert, Elizabeth Hand, Theodora Goss, Kelly Link, and Jeffrey Ford—use genre materials without limiting themselves to genre forms or structures, and draw freely on both modernist and postmodernist literary techniques. The choice of these writers is somewhat arbitrary, and we could include a variety of others (see the preceding essay), but these writers offer a variety of recurring approaches and methods that seem to provide a useful entrée into an exploration of this new fiction. Thematically, their stories often are charged with grief, loss, nostalgia, and irreconcilable change, but often attain a feeling of wonder, insight, and hope—even transcendence. Themes of tragic romance are common, although no one would reasonably associate these fictions with romance as a genre. Often, some strategies in these stories recall young adult or even children's fiction.[14] Writers like Ford, Rickert, Goss, Link, and Hand—all early- to midcareer writers—are developing a new, twenty-first-century paradigm, a fiction beyond postmodernism, a fiction for the unstoryable, or as yet unstoried, new century. Choosing broadly from the narrative toolbox, such tales are often metafictional, with self-aware and emotionally powerful storyteller voices. Unlike the often coolly ironic surfaces of much postmodern fiction, they are often funny or heartbreaking, although they are comfortable with mystery and irresolution—which is not to say that they have no plot or story; unlike some postmodern or contemporary mainstream fiction, these narratives tend to have plots and characters, not just style and voice.

Most important, despite their lack of clear genre markers and their unconventional approach to even traditional narrative elements as plot, character, and setting, these tales "do not feel arbitrary" (as Kessel said of Rickert's story) nor particularly performative. At their best, they achieve a kind of emotional and aesthetic coherence of a sort that is rare in contemporary fiction, and particularly in the kinds of fantastic fiction that have been associated with popular genres. For the remainder of this essay, we will suggest a number of recurrent techniques and characteristics that help this fiction achieve such coherence, and that seem to provide some commonalities between the work of writers who, on the surface at least, differ widely in their influences, style, and narrative modes and who, as far as we know, don't even identify themselves as being part of the same group. The characteristics we're suggesting are hardly exclusive to these writers, and the list of techniques is neither exhaustive nor prescriptive. Many of the features we're describing are not even particularly innovative—some are familiar from the long history of the modernist short story; some are drawn from techniques specific to science fiction, fantasy, or horror; some can be found in a range of postmodernist or experimental fiction. Our argument is not that any particular technique can serve as a litmus test for this sort of twenty-first century fiction, but rather that the manner in which these techniques are combined and recombined can yield insights about the nature of such fiction.

Slippage

These stories freely draw on the furniture of horror, fantasy, or science fiction, as well as the conventions of domestic realism, memoir, surrealism, even non-fiction. Stories may offer what appear to be clear genre markers, but then shift among genres in midstream—almost giving a literal meaning to "slipstream." For example, M. Rickert's novella "Map of Dreams" begins like a horror story: The protagonist Annie Merchant's six-year-old daughter is gunned down by a crazed sniper on a New York streetcorner.[15] Another of the sniper's victims is a physicist involved in quantum theory, and for a while the story seems to be turning into science fiction as Annie grows obsessed with the notion that she might find her daughter in an alternate timestream. She convinces herself that the physicist's widower has found the secret of time travel, and tracks him down to a remote part of Australia. Now the science fiction gives way to a mythical fantasy involving aboriginal dreamtime, as Annie finds herself aided in her quest by figures from different periods of Australian history; she eventually returns to New York just before the shooting, facing a classic grandfather paradox while returning the tale to its original horrific situation. Each successive genre iteration subsumes those that had gone before, resulting in a tale that is profoundly unsettling in its mode yet remarkably coherent in its final effect.

Another example, Jeffrey Ford's "A Night in the Tropics" begins with a nostalgic childhood recollection of a painting in a neighborhood bar, in which a character that very much resembles Ford himself—a writer and community college teacher—returns to visit as an adult.[16] But as the bartender relates a lengthy story about a cursed chess set, the tale-within-a-tale becomes a classic horror story, only to unite the two modes into a single tale at the end. Kelly Link's "Pretty Monsters" begins disarmingly as a kind of teen romance—a girl named Clementine Cleary, who has had a crush on the handsome Cabell Meadows since first grade, determines to win him over once and for all after he saves her from drowning. As the tale unfolds, we realize that the story is actually contained in a book being read by a girl named Lee, who is involved in a far more unsettling teen story in which a foreign student at a high school is abducted (along with her younger sister) for a harrowing initiation "ordeal." Each of these stories then takes an unexpected turn toward supernatural horror, both involving werewolves, and neither offers a clear resolution. Furthermore, both eventually are subsumed into a *third* tale involving two sisters reading a book together in a bedroom in an isolated country house—the story they're reading is apparently Lee's—and this tale too resolves into a werewolf tale.

Horror is the genre that provides the most significant patterns of imagery in these tales, even though the materials of horror are often wryly subverted, and few would claim these three interlocked tales as genre horror stories. In other stories, Link writes of haunted houses ("Stone Animals"), zombies ("The Hortlak," "Some Zombie Contingency Plans"), ghosts, witches, and the devil ("The Great Divorce," "Catskin," "Lull"), but often with a distinctly ironic or comic edge—her zombies are more like nebbishes than monsters—while Ford's work includes ghosts ("The Trentino Kid"), serial killers (*The Shadow Year*), monsters ("The Beautiful Gelreesh"), and ancient curses ("A Night in the Tropics"), but often filters these through a haze of memory and nostalgia.

Theodora Goss's "Miss Emily Gray" and "Conrad" might well qualify as horror stories, at least of the Shirley Jackson variety. In the former, Miss Gray is a seductive governess who takes over an entire family, apparently engineering the death of the father and son and chillingly explaining to the surviving daughter, "I was sent to make come true your heart's desire."[17] In the latter story, she's a nurse in collusion with an aunt whom the title character Conrad is convinced is trying to poison him. Rickert also achieves a Shirley Jackson–like flavor in her story "Bread and Bombs," which begins in a sunny town where the fourth graders have just started summer vacation, but quickly turns ominous as we realize that this is a science-fictional post-terrorist world of continuous war in which the refugee neighbors become targets of a horrendous act. Her other tales feature child abuse ("The Harrowing"), murderers ("Many Voices") including child murderers ("Map of Dreams," "The Chambered Fruit"), and ghosts ("More Beautiful than You"). Elizabeth Hand's "Cleopatra Brimstone," discussed earlier in "The Lives of Fantasists," concerns a rape victim and entomologist who becomes a vengeful denizen of London's punk nightclub scene, although its supernatural elements are hardly the only source of the tale's governing emotion, which is never far removed from the very real-world sexual assault that is its motivating event. Hand's "Calypso in Berlin" involves a predatory artist of similar supernatural abilities, but again the horror is far from an end in itself. In fact, each of these stories, in its own way, slips free of the expectations associated with the genre machinery that they so freely appropriate, whether from science fiction, fantasy, horror, or the domestic realism associated with what is called "mainstream."

Domesticity

The kings and rings and spells and bells of traditional genre fantasy are comparatively rare in these tales, although not entirely unknown. We already have seen how Rickert's "Map of Dreams" begins in contemporary New York or "Bread and Bombs" in a suburban community during school vacation, Ford's "A Night in the Tropics" in a neighborhood bar, Link's "Lull" with an unhappy married couple. Link is one of the authors who most consistently and most effectively makes use of the furniture of domestic realism. "Stone Animals," with its family recently moved into a suburban house—disaffected wife, unhappy children, and preoccupied commuter husband— might well be borrowing a page from John Cheever's suburban *angst*, until various household items—the TV, the coffeemaker, even a toothbrush—start to act haunted, and a growing population of rabbits begins keeping vigil in the front yard.[18] "Magic for Beginners" begins with the familiar situation of a group of teenage friends sharing an obsession with a TV show called *The Library*—except that this show appears according to no fixed schedule and on no particular station, with a different cast of actors every time. The story focuses on a boy named Jeremy Mars, whose goofy father writes horror stories about giant spiders and badly reupholsters sofas, and whose relationship with Jeremy's mother is falling apart. As Jeremy and his mother go on a road trip, the story develops into a reality-testing tale involving a phone booth in Las Vegas that Jeremy has been calling in order to talk to what might be a character from *The Library*. In "The Great Divorce," a husband who has married a dead wife (and has two dead children with her) tries to work out the problems in his marriage by taking the family to Disneyland. The characters and events may be fantastical, but the settings and anxieties are those of domestic realism. Even one of Link's most famous zombie tales, "The Hortlak," is set largely in an all-night convenience store, and is about clerks and customers as much as zombies—and the zombies themselves aren't terribly different from actual late-night convenience-store customers, with their disorientation, lack of usable money, and unarticulated but intense needs.

As we saw in "The Lives of Fantasists," many of Ford's and Hand's stories draw on autobiographical material to lend the tales a quotidian texture that often evokes the tone of remembered experience. Ford, in stories like *The Shadow Year*," "The Honeyed Knot," "The Trentino Kid," and "Bright Morning," employs realistic settings drawn from his childhood on Long Island or his teaching career in New Jersey, and even as purely fantastical a tale as "The Annals of Eelik-Ok" (depicting in high heroic terms the vastly accelerated life cycle of tiny fairies who take up residence in sand castles built on the beach by children) is framed as a manuscript discovered inside a conch shell by a five-year-old girl roaming a beach in New Jersey in 1999. Hand may have introduced ancient goddesses and mythological figures into her work, but a key trademark of her fiction is her vivid rendering of similarly autobiographical settings—Yonkers, New York ("Illyria"), coastal Maine ("The Least Trumps," *Generation Loss*, "Winter's Wife"), or the District of Columbia ("Wonderwall," *Waking the Moon*).

In virtually all these cases, the fantastic or supernatural elements emerge less as an intrusion into this domesticity (as in conventional horror fiction) than as a hidden dimension of it, sometimes represented in Hand's stories through images of walls: a wall in a Manhattan loft that turns into an immense slab of rock in 1999's *Black Light*; a wall in a hidden London lane in 2004's *Mortal Love* that reveals to the poet Swinburne a seductive green world beyond; a wall in a hidden attic room in the novella "Illyria" that hides a magical miniature theater; a Minoan fresco in "The Saffron Gatherers" that serves as another window into a lost world; an apartment wall in 2004's "Wonderwall" on which a quotation from Rimbaud, painted years earlier, bleeds through each successive layer of paint. The protagonist of the latter story obsesses over how to "tear through the wall that separated me from that other world, the real world, the one I glimpsed in books and music, the world I wanted to claim for myself."[19] As in magic realism, the marvelous is presented not in opposition to domestic realism, but as a subtext of it.

Contingency of Worlds

Not only are the narrative and genre markers slippery, the fictive worlds themselves are inherently unstable in many of these tales—that is, in a formally logical sense, they are neither purely possible nor purely impossible, and may shift among levels of possible reality. Samuel R. Delany's famous essay "About

5,750 Words" distinguished between what he called levels of "subjunctivity" in various modes of fiction, associating "*could have happened*" with naturalistic fiction, "*could not have happened*" with fantasy, and "*have not happened*" with science fiction.[20] It's not uncommon for the stories we are discussing to shift freely among these modes, sometimes with no "base" level of narrative at all, or only what's implied by the storyteller's own voice (which is not necessarily trustworthy).

Jeffrey Ford's "Under the Bottom of the Lake" (2007) begins with a writer describing his efforts to discover his story, which he imagines is contained in "a bubble of rose-colored glass" in a grotto beneath the bottom of a lake. As baroque as this particular image may be, the initial situation of a writer seeking a tale is familiar and realistic (even bordering on cliché). Soon the author realizes that he must create a character to release the story, and he invents a teenage girl named Emily, on the way to the cemetery to visit her recently deceased grandmother's grave, accompanied by her boyfriend Vincent. Their story shifts into a more fantastical, alternate-history mode as they come upon the mausoleum of a wealthy local resident named Cake who made his fortune from inventing a heroin-like painkiller used on the battlefield in a war much like World War II—and who had fallen in love with Emily's grandmother, fascinated by her talent for origami. The story shifts again into a more aggressively fantastical mode as we're offered a vision of Vincent's father as a young man, finding a many-colored bird in a cage in the woods and shooting it with an arrow, after which its feathers burst into flame; and a story of an ancient wizard who taught Cake the secrets of negating pain in exchange for his soul—which he then placed into a many-colored bird. All these levels of fantasy and reality eventually are united in the image of the tale trapped in the rose-colored glass with which the story began, and which Emily and Vincent discover when they follow a hidden tunnel beneath Cake's tomb. As they emerge from this dreamlike fantasy back to the surface, they find that Cake's tomb has cracked open, that his skeleton contains a feather where the heart should be, and, in the hand, folded paper figures of the story's main images. In one reading of this conclusion, the feather serves as a fairly conventional bit of evidence to validate the fantastic tale we've just heard; in, another, it's an image of the writer-narrator (who has by now backed out of the tale altogether) finally discovering his tale. The story is at once a fantasy of magical birds and wizards, and an account of the process of storymaking.

In Kelly Link's "Lull," unhappy middle-aged parents call a phone number offering a storytelling service and request a story about the Devil and a cheerleader. In the story they are told, time runs backwards. The cheerleader is waiting for the arrival of her parents, whom she has never met, and recalling her kids, long since returned to the womb. The Devil asks the cheerleader for a story, and she tells one about a couple with the same names as a man and his estranged wife in the frame story. The woman, Susan, clones multiple copies of herself, and talks about the impending arrival of aliens. She asks her husband, Ed, to tell her a story, and he in turn makes up a short tale about a couple and a time machine. By the time we get back to the frame story, the internal stories have wrought irrevocable damage to Ed and Susan's relationship (or perhaps just revealed the damage already there), and time has stopped. The story shifts so freely among its narrative levels that the reader is never quite certain as to which is the "base" narrative, or if there is one at all.

Another Link story, "The Faery Handbag," deals with the tentative beginnings of romance among a group of contemporary urban young people, but soon focuses on the narrator and her grandmother Zofia, who escaped from an obscure eastern European country with a magic handbag made of dogskin, which once sheltered Zofia's entire village from a pogrom-like raid. After the narrator tells her boyfriend Jake—who's obsessed with Houdini-like escapes—about the handbag, he disappears, and then the handbag itself disappears when Zofia falls ill and dies. The narrator is left searching for the lost handbag and her lost love, uncertain as to which world is really hers.

Shifts in Point of View, Setting, or Chronology

These stories often achieve a disorienting effect by suddenly shifting from one character's point of view to another's, or by startling breaks in setting or chronology. Kelly Link's "Stone Animals" moves freely from the commuter husband's viewpoint, to that of the disaffected wife, the real estate agent, and the individual children. Theodora Goss's "The Rapid Advance of Sorrow," a dark, existential fable of entropy, alternates a legend of a fabulous Siberian city named Sorrow with a convincingly detailed account of a strange *anomie* that overcomes students in contemporary Budapest, and perhaps around the world, while her "Singing of Mount Abora" alternates the legend of a famed dulcimer-maker's niece who marries the Cloud Dragon with a tale of the romantic entanglements of a contemporary graduate student in Boston trying to complete her thesis on Samuel Taylor Coleridge, whose poem "Kubla Khan" provides the source mythology of the legend. Elizabeth Hand's novel *Generation Loss* begins with a grimly naturalistic account of its narrator Cass's failed photography career in New York and her descent into drug abuse and promiscuity, then abruptly shifts to Maine more than twenty years later, signaling a shift in narrative mode from realism to mystery thriller. Hand's novella "Illyria" similarly vaults the narrative decades forward in its last few pages, lending a distinctly elegiac tone to the romance at its center and shifting the fantasy element away from center stage (quite literally, since the main fantasy element is a magical toy theater).

Jeffrey Ford, too, frequently makes effective use of memory as a narrative device, along with point-of-view shifts. "The Annals of Eelin-Ok" begins with the narrator's memory of something he was told as a child, then shifts to the tale of the five-year-old girl finding the conch shell on the beach, then finally arrives at the central narrative of the sand-fairies. "The Beautiful Gelreesh" begins as a kind of medieval legend about a half-human, half-canine monster who uses his talent for empathy and pity to lure his victims to death, after which he devours their bodies, but the tale only comes into focus when the point of view shifts forward centuries to that of a graduate student trying to uncover the legendary gelreesh's remains, in a device similar to that of Goss's "Singing of Mount Abora." And, as we noted earlier, several Ford stories—"Jupiter's Skull," "The Weight of Words," The Empire of Ice Cream," *The Shadow Year*—are told from the point of view of a narrator remembering events decades past, as though trying to subsume the eruption of the fantastic into the stuff of memory or legend.

Denial of Resolution

Not only do many of the stories we're describing resist conventional modes of closure; they also resist what we might think of as genre resolution—they often don't "settle" into one genre or another. Despite the presence of multiple and sometimes conflicting genre markers, the stories are seldom controlled by such markers; science fiction tropes do not necessarily signal a rationalistic science fiction resolution, and fantasy or horror tropes—or even the conventions of domestic realism—do not necessarily mean that the story will satisfy expectations associated with those genres. Kelly Link, in a recent interview, said "I prefer reading fiction that resists easy interpretation, or which can be reread in such a way that it's a different story each time."[21] Similarly, her character Carly in "Some Zombie Contingency Plans," invoking art forms that might serve as useful analogues to this fiction, says " 'I like concerts. Jazz. Improvisational comedy. I like stuff that isn't the same every time you look at it."[22] Carly's own story can serve as an illustration: On the simplest level, it can be viewed as a tale of a girl who throws a party at her parents' house in the suburbs (the domestic setting again) while her parents are out of the country. There she meets an ex-convict who introduces himself as Will (but is also variously called Soap, Art, and eventually Wolverine) who possibly seduces her, robs the house, and kidnaps her little brother. But such a reading would be almost catastrophically reductive of a complex tale that spins off a variety of improvisations, like jazz solos or comedy riffs, involving zombie movies, art museums, prisons, soap, icebergs, and bicycles, organized largely around Will (or Soap's) obsession with the zombie contingency plans of the title, reflected in a couple of interpolated scenes that read like parodies of zombie films. Almost none of these improvised tales are resolved in the story's indeterminate conclusion, but all contribute to the comic sensibility and unity of theme of the story.

We've noted how these authors may comfortably use materials from multiple genres, but to classify these stories as horror or fantasy or science fiction would be to radically oversimplify their effect, or to deliberately misread them—either by dismissing some of the contradictory narrative markers, or by imposing genre markers from outside the story. To this extent, we're in agreement with the advocates of slipstream or interstitiality; these tales employ genres without necessarily inhabiting them. In the penultimate episode of Goss's "The Rose in Twelve Petals," after the sleeping beauty princess has been asleep for a century, the prince finally appears, driving a bulldozer and looking forward to a break for beer and sandwiches. "What did you expect?" Goss writes. "Things change in a hundred years."[23] The prince, it seems, is now living in the Socialist Union of Britannia, from which royal titles have long been abolished. Far from being an invitation to recast the entire story in near-future science-fictional terms, this shift introduces another of the multiple narrative modes that Goss employs, including fairy tales, alternate history, and genre fantasy, to explore this otherwise overfamiliar tale. By the same token, the embedded narratives with clones, aliens, and time travel in Link's "Lull" are not enough to make a case for reading the entire story as science fiction, any more than the zombies of "The Hortlak" or the summer-camp monster of "Monster" transform these tales into genre horror. We can say the same for Rickert's "Journey into the Kingdom" with its embedded ghost story, or Ford's "Night in the Tropics" with its embedded horror story.

Story as Agency

While tales-within-tales date back centuries if not millennia, the specific technique that we are referring to here involves embedded or "braided" tales that often serve a fractal or dialogic role—they comment on, resonate with, or reveal additional information about the surface narrative, almost functioning like characters in the wider tale. We already have seen how Link's "Lull" involves a story told by a cheerleader within a story about the devil told by a phone service within the frame narrative, how her "Pretty Monsters" creates two stories in dialogue with one another before braiding them into a third tale that closes the narrative, or how Jeffrey Ford's "Under the Bottom of the Lake" interlaces stories of a writer seeking his tale with those of teenagers visiting a cemetery, an entrepreneur inventing an addictive painkiller, and an ancient wizard. M. Rickert's "Journey into the Kingdom" begins with a young man named Alex reading an "artist's statement" accompanying a series of innocuous paintings (collectively titled "Journey into the Kingdom") on display in a coffee shop. The notebook, titled "An Imitation Life," contains an account narrated by Agatha, the daughter of lighthouse keepers whose father has died in a boating accident, who meets a series of ghosts, including that of her father. The ghost of a sailor named Ezekiel relates his own tale of his life as the son of a Murano glassmaker, who becomes jealous of the boy's talent and who is eventually murdered by the boy in an act of self-protection. Against the wishes of her mother, Agatha falls in love with Ezekiel, becoming a ghost and gaining the ghostly ability to suck breath from the living with a kiss. Her mother becomes her first victim, after which Agatha flees to a distant city, takes up painting, and gets the job in the coffee shop, thus returning the narrative to its apparent surface level. But in fact there is yet another narrative enveloping all these—the story of Alex himself, the young man who reads the notebook and becomes morbidly infatuated with the coffee shop barista who says she has written the notebook but claims it's merely a story. Alex recently has suffered the loss of his wife Tessie to cancer, after which "he felt in danger of floating away or disappearing," and he tells this to Agatha when he finally persuades her to accompany him on a kind of date.[24]

What appears to be turning into a romantic tale shifts yet again when Alex, having invited Agatha for dinner, ties her up, watches a bit of TV with her, and finally drives her to a pier and throws her in the water. In the story's conclusion, Agatha returns like a figure from an EC horror comic, dripping wet; she admits that he was "right about everything," and finally offers the breath-stealing kiss that will end his suffering.[25] Each of the major tales embedded in the story— Alex's, Agatha's, and Ezekiel's—echoes and illuminates the themes and events of the others.

In one of the most accomplished examples of the story-as-dialogue technique, "Cold Fires," Rickert begins by describing a spectacularly cold winter in the locutions of a tall tale: "It was so cold birds fell from the sky like tossed rocks, frozen except for their tiny eyes, which focused on the sun as if trying to understand its betrayal."[26] A man and woman isolated in a remote house decide to tell each other stories, which at first appear to be wildly unrelated. The woman tells of her great-great grandmother, whose pirate husband brings home a strange blonde girl who is thoroughly incompetent as a maid but who seems to have a magical affinity for strawberries. While the husband is away on a long pirating expedition, the townspeople make plans to try the girl as a witch, but then the husband returns with a shipload of irresistible strawberries and soon builds a fortune selling them, until the strawberry girl—who may be the maternal ancestor of the woman telling the story, since both the girl and the pirate's wife become pregnant—suddenly disappears. The man in turn describes a time years earlier when he took a job curating a small art museum whose founder, Emile Castor, had obsessively painted thousand of crude portraits of a particular woman. Trying to escape the depression of being surrounded by so much bad art, the curator finds himself in a bed-and-breakfast that features a brilliantly nuanced painting of the same woman, which he learns was also painted by Castor. The bed-and-breakfast owner and his wife relate the story of Castor and the woman he loved, and of his efforts to create an icon for her in a local church, which turns out to be another great work of art. Each of the two tales ends in a kind of moral: the woman saying, "if ever you should wake and find me gone, it is not an expression of lack of affection for you, but rather, her witchy blood that is to be blamed," and the man, at the end of his tale, saying, "when you find me sad and ask what's on my mind, or when I am quiet and cannot explain to you the reason, there it is. If I had never seen the paintings, maybe I would be a happy man."[27] The counterpoint of these two disparate tales of abandonment and devotion tell us all we need to know about the two unnamed narrators, and creates their story as well, although that story is never developed explicitly beyond those two brief morals and a brief coda explaining how the two survived the remainder of the winter in their ice-covered cottage.

The Storyteller's Voice

As should be apparent from the frequency with which characters in these stories tell each other tales, the storyteller's voice is often a paramount feature, both in the surface level and in embedded narratives. The voice calls attention to itself—and thus to the author's assertion of control—in a number of ways, including direct addresses to the reader and allusions to earlier storytelling traditions such as myths and fairy tales. Goss's "The Rose in Twelve Petals" tells the Sleeping Beauty story from twelve viewpoints (including those of the spinning wheel and the tower). In the space of a few pages, Goss moves from fairy-tale redaction to whimsical historical fiction to poetic meditation and finally to a kind of offhand SF, without losing consistency of tone or theme. Her story "In the Forest of Forgetting" similarly uses a fairy-tale tone and setting: A cancer patient is exploring a forest, meeting a witch, knight, princess, and so on, and questioning each about her own name. The names that she's given are allegories of her roles in life: Patient, Daughter, Wife, Mother, casting her as a figure in various kinds of stories.

We've already noted how the problem of a storyteller discovering his tale is central to Jeffrey Ford's "Under the Bottom of the Lake." Rickert, in her collection *Map of Dreams*, takes this a step further by presenting the bereaved mother of her lead story "Map of Dreams," Annie Merchant, as the author of the remaining tales in the collection. Kelly Link, for her part, sometimes addresses the reader in the ingratiating tones of a gossipy teenager. "The Wrong Grave" concerns a boy who, in a fit of romance, places a sheaf of his poems into the coffin of his dead girlfriend, then later has second thoughts and digs up the grave to retrieve them. When he finds a strange girl in the grave, the narrator comments: "You might think at certain points in this story that I'm being hard on Miles, that I'm not sympathetic to his situation. This isn't true. I'm as fond of Miles as I am of anyone else. I don't think he's any stupider or any bit less special or remarkable than—for example—you. Anyone might accidentally dig up the wrong grave. It's a mistake anyone could make."[28]

Allusions to specific storytelling modes of myth or legend are also common in such fiction. Ford often has visited mythological themes. "Boatman's Holiday" reconsiders the myth of Charon, while "The Cosmology of the Wider World" concerns Belius the minotaur, born to a human family and seemingly fated to a life of exile and alienation until he somehow is translated into the "wider world" of sentient animals, which he seeks to understand by writing a vast cosmological treatise. "Creation" revisits the legend of the Golem, "The Green Word" invokes the medieval legend of the green man, and "The Beautiful Gelreesh" and "The Annals of Eelin-Ok" invent their own legends. Rickert offers variations on the myths of Leda and the swan ("Leda") and Persephone ("The Chambered Fruit," "Map of Dreams"), and even plays with the Nativity story in "Peace in Suburbia." Hand offers a whole series of myth redactions in her remarkable story suite "The Lost Domain," which includes four variations on themes involving muses and nymphs: "Kronia," "Calypso in Berlin," "Echo," and "The Saffron Gatherers," while her earlier fiction includes stories that feature avatars of Circe, Dionysus, and Ariadne (notably in her most underappreciated novel, *Black Light*), Euripides' Bacchae (in the story "The Bacchae") or Pan ("The Boy in the Tree"). Her most famous novel, *Waking the Moon*, brings the ancient pre-Minoan cult of the goddess into a college campus in contemporary Washington, D.C.

Themes of Art and Artifice

In addition to all the devices we've mentioned that remind us in various ways that the story is a told or made thing, many of these tales remind us of their artifice through the recurring use of art and artists as themes and subjects. Rickert's characters include painters ("The Chambered Fruit," "Journey into the Kingdom," "Cold Fires"), sculptors ("The Girl Who Ate Butterflies"), glassmakers ("Journey into the Kingdom" again), and singers ("Moorina of the Seals"); Goss's include children's book writers ("In the Forest of Forgetting," "Pip and the Fairies"), painters ("Letters from Budapest"), musicians ("The Wings of Meister Wilhelm"), ballerinas ("Death Comes for Ervina"). Hand's characters include actresses and singers ("Illyria"), photographers (*Generation Loss*), writers ("The Saffron Gatherers," "Pavane for a Prince of the Air"), a tattoo artist ("The Least Trumps"), painters ("Calypso in Berlin"), rock musicians, and even kids' TV performers ("Chip Crockett's Christmas Carol"). She also has written a perceptive essay on "outsider" artist Henry Darger.[29] Ford's characters include poets ("Jupiter's Skull"), painters ("Coffins on the River"), writers ("A Night in the Tropics," "Under the Bottom of the Lake," "The Fantasy Writer's Assistant"), musicians ("The Empire of Ice Cream"), a lighting designer ("Man of Light"); Link's include writers ("Magic for Beginners," "Most of My Friends are Two-Thirds Water") and even cellists ("Louise's Ghost"). Interestingly, both Hand, in "The Least Trumps," and Goss, in "Pip and the Fairies," have written stories about characters who had as children served as models for figures in children's books written by their mothers, and who now struggle to deal with that heritage as they discover their own artistic identities, thus doubling or tripling the allusions to artifice. In some ways recalling the real-life struggles of Christopher Milne (whose father used him as a model for Christopher Robin in his Pooh novels), these are more importantly stories about people trapped in stories. Artifice is not always what we escape to; sometimes it's also what we must escape *from*.

The Writing Process

Some of the authors discussed here have said in interviews or essays that they are consciously playing with genre materials, while others claim not to know where a story is going as they write it. M. Rickert said, "I know I'm not a very clever writer and I'm not an intellectual writer, but I'm an emotional writer, and that's something I can work with. When I'm starting out to write, a lot of times I don't know where things are going to go and I'm not clear about what the lead character's voice has to say. I might write a sentence that has three things happening that couldn't all be happening at the same time. Eventually I'll have a clearer picture of what's going on, and I'll crop out the extra things. And then at *some* point, I usually grab a new sheet of paper (I write longhand) and I have the ending: I know what I'm writing towards. It doesn't feel like 'ideas'—it feels true."[30] For Elizabeth Hand, art is a very conscious focus. In a *Locus* interview, she said, "Art is one of the means we have of reaching transcendence, a method for achieving an ecstatic experience, and that's what I'm most interested in writing about. An earlier version [of the 2007 novel *Generation Loss*], when it was going to be a straight horror novel, was going to revolve around music (electronica, techno), but with music even outsider artists can get turned into commodities very quickly, so I wanted to take somebody who was a little more outside that loop." She continues,

Short stories are much easier for me to produce [than novels]—I tend to write them at a white heat. Often it's "the lady or the tiger?", a binary process where I have two endings in mind. One will generally be the happy, transcendent, uplifting ending, and the other the terrible, awful, ambivalent ending. I wrote "The Least Trumps" in about two weeks with two endings in my head, and literally did not know which I'd use until the day before I finished it. But by the time I got to that point, one seemed more right than the other. It's not a traditionally happy, feel-good ending so much as a potentially *redemptive* one: having the world open up for the central character, rather than close down.[31]

Hand's writing process seems to be much like Rickert's in that the "right" ending is an emotional focus, dictated by the needs of the story rather than by considerations of genre expectations or markets, or by conscious attempts to subvert those expectations. In such cases, genre becomes essentially irrelevant to the writing process.

Kelly Link, discussing the state of the field, offered a dual perspective from her role as editor and publisher as well as writer: "Reading for the fantasy half of the Year's Best anthology [Link and her husband Gavin Grant assumed co-editorship of *The Year's Best Fantasy and Horror* with Ellen Datlow in 2004], Gavin and I have noticed that the best collections aren't straight fantasy, straight horror, or straight science fiction. Writers recombine or tease out elements of all of these genres to really good effect. . . . It's good news—for writers like me at least—that mainstream and genre are colliding so productively."[32] As with Rickert and Hand, her reading protocols seem to be based on the cognitive and emotional effects of stories, rather than genre conventions:

I have this theory that it's possible to read mainstream fiction as if it were science fiction. Or maybe what I mean is that if you're a science fiction fan, everything comes filtered through that lens. Certain mainstream books with no discernable fantastic content make me happy, satisfy me as a reader in the same way that genre work will. . . . Even in the most traditional, heart-of-genre fantasy and science fiction, there's something about the way the fantastic interacts with the style of the author, with the way that characters encounter the world, that pulls me right in.[33]

This from someone who declared herself a science fiction writer in a 2002 *Locus* interview, saying: "I finally decided that everything I write was SF, whether or not it had science fiction in it" and who has responded repeatedly to interviews by simply describing her fiction as "sf."[34]

Conclusions

In the same 1989 essay in which he offered that early definition of slipstream, Bruce Sterling quoted an interview with Carter Scholz about the literary significance of genre literature: "In the 60s and 70s, Scholz opines, sf had a chance to become a worthy literature; now that chance has passed. Why? Because other writers have now learned to adapt sf's best techniques to their own ends."[35] While we've chosen to talk about writers who publish in genre magazines and presses and often identify themselves with the genre community (such terms as "slipstream," "interstitial," and the others generally came from *within* this community), we might as easily have examined the work of contemporary "mainstream" writers borrowing genre trappings—Aimee Bender, Junot Diaz, Michael Chabon, Dan Chaon, Brian Evenson—or on the long and unexamined string of authors who predated and influenced the movement—Shirley Jackson, Donald Barthelme, Avram Davidson, Roald Dahl, Harlan Ellison—some of whom are known primarily as genre writers, some of whom are almost never mentioned in genre histories or critical studies.[36]

Part of what we are arguing is that a term such as "mainstream" is as archaic as the other, more familiar genre labels, and is as imprecise as all those new movement labels with which we began. As China Miéville said, "any act of artistic labeling is as much to do with reclamation as with categorization. To look at past writers in a new way, to reclaim writers who have been forgotten, to announce the necessary forgetting of writers who have been remembered—this is part of the process. It is as much argumentative archaeology as it is ongoing taxonomy."[37] Miéville's point is crucial to understanding the origins of this twenty-first-century aesthetic. Historically, new movements in fiction have been characterized largely in terms of some version of Harold Bloom's anxiety of influence—the need to overcome the past, to cast off old strictures, to proclaim revolution. Modernism reacts against the narrative conventions of classic storytelling, postmodernism reacts against the formalism and perceived elitism of modernism, the New Wavers and cyberpunks react against the narrative formulas of genre fiction, the post–New Wave or post-cyberpunk seek ways to reclaim those formulas, and so on. The indeterminacy in these twenty-first-century stories—in terms of slippery genre markers, contingent worlds, self-conscious narrative devices and aesthetics—may well be no more than a post-postmodern narrative iteration of Keats's negative capability in its original sense, as he defined it in his famous 1817 letter: "I mean Negative Capability, that is when man is capable of being in uncertainties, Mysteries, doubts, without any irritable reaching after fact and reason."[38]

As we hope we have shown, the new aesthetic is based less in a rejection of earlier forms than in a celebration of them, what Jonathan Lethem calls the *ecstasy* of influence—a willingness to borrow tropes, language, techniques from almost anywhere—genre fiction, literary modernism, popular culture, *avant-garde* experimentalism, fable and folklore, as well as from alternate modes such as music, film, theater, so-called "outsider art," graphic novels, painting, or photography—and to incorporate them into an eclectic new mode that quite properly resists labeling and libeling. This is why we're simply calling them twenty-first-century stories, rather than something post-tacular and meta-tastic—although we were at times reminded of a line from rapper M. C. Lars, himself an exemplar of a recombinant movement known as nerdcore hip-hop: "Did I say postmodern? That was a lie! I've been post-postmodern since junior high!"

PART III

critics and criticism

By now, astute readers will have noticed that the ten preceding essays are not exactly governed by a single overarching critical methodology or theory. This is partly due to the variety of venues and times in which they were originally written and partly to the very slipperiness of the material under discussion, but it's also in part quite deliberate. This book does not purport to propose a theory of the fantastic in literature. At best, it tries to demonstrate a variety of approaches—some thematic, some historical, some technical—that might be useful in contextualizing those specific works and specific traditions that I have been referring to—out of convenience—as the fantastic genres. Those approaches are influenced in part by my formal academic work as a professor, in part by my years as a reviewer for *Locus* magazine, in part simply by my responses as a reader.

But that very variety of approaches reflects another interesting problem about these genres, namely, how are we supposed to talk about them meaningfully if they won't hold still? As Amelia Beamer and I mentioned in "Twenty-First-Century Stories," these fictions often do not readily yield all their riches to the traditional tools of literary analysis inherited largely from Victorian traditions of domestic realism and from modernism, nor do they yield entirely to genre-based discussions of theme, convention, or formula. They eventually may require a kind of critical discourse as polysemic as the fiction itself. And, like the fiction itself, that discourse has been evolving in the criticism of science fiction, fantasy, and horror over the last several decades, drawing on a variety of traditions and methodologies that I attempt to outline, in crude form, in this final essay, which is in part a bibliographical essay and in part an argument for a synthesis of critical discourses sufficiently malleable to address the fluidity that I have been arguing has increasingly come to characterize the most interesting examples of fantastic literature.

eleven

Pilgrims of the Fall

Since 1970, the Science Fiction Research Association (SFRA) has presented an annual award, the Pilgrim, for lifetime achievements in science fiction scholarship, and since 1986 another academic organization, the International Association for the Fantastic in the Arts (IAFA), has presented a similar annual career award for the somewhat more broadly defined field of scholarship in "the fantastic." While the genres of fantastic literature in general—science fiction, fantasy, horror—have become known for a bewildering plethora of awards, these two in particular can be interesting for the ways in which they reveal the multiple discourses and venues that have come to comprise the critical dialogue in this field. The relationship between the arts of fantastic literature and the arts of scholarly inquiry has long been a vaguely distrustful one from both directions; some might dismissively call it a marriage of convenience born out of the science fiction or fantasy writer's yearning for acceptance in the literary community and the academic's need for fresh critical material. But in fact, both the Pilgrim and IAFA awards appeared rather late in the game, after decades of spirited debate and amateur scholarship (in the root meaning of "amateur" as "lover") had established a tradition of critical discourse almost entirely in isolation from both mainstream literary culture and the imprimatur of the academy. In order to understand how this tradition came into confrontation with the world of more formal academic scholarship in the 1970s—and how it eventually gave rise to a new kind of synthesis of critical discourse in the work of critics such as John Clute—it might first be helpful to trace briefly the early development of both writer- and fan-based criticism and that of academic scholars.

From the beginning of the pulp era, letter columns such as "The Eyrie" in *Weird Tales* (founded 1923), "Discussions" in *Amazing Stories* (1926), "The Reader Speaks" in *Wonder Stories* (1929), and "Science Discussions" (later "Brass

Tacks") in *Astounding Stories* (1930) debated the merits of stories from previous issues, as well as artwork, editorials, layout, scientific and pseudoscientific matters, and—inevitably—the nature and characteristics of "scientifiction" as a genre (although a term like "genre" would have seemed radically out of place in such columns). It did not take long for correspondence with the magazines and with each other to seem inadequate for some fans, and individually produced fanzines began to appear by 1930, with organized fan meetings and conventions only a few years behind. The science fiction folk culture, with its passion for neologisms and grand debates, was under way—and since many of these early fans became professional authors themselves, the vocabulary of fandom became conflated in part with the vocabulary of the professional author, and in turn with the vocabulary of the publishing industry. "SF" (or the earlier "stf" for "scientifiction") became shorthand for science fiction, and "space opera," "sword and sorcery," and "hard SF" for specific themes or subtypes. Later academic critics, confronted with this makeshift critical tradition that had grown in virtual isolation from (and innocent of) any conventional literary or critical discourse, found themselves in an almost unprecedented situation, effectively inheriting a literary tradition that came complete with its own idiosyncratic critical lexicon, even though a few of the pioneer scholars in the field had themselves long been involved in fandom; both Everett Bleiler and Thomas D. Clareson, for example, were members of "First Fandom," a loose organization of fans who had been active in the field since the early days of organized fandom.[1]

Perhaps the most significant critical work to emerge from the early fan publications concerned itself more with fantasy than with science fiction. H. P. Lovecraft's long essay, *Supernatural Horror in Literature*, was first commissioned for an amateur publication in 1924 and later revised for a fanzine in the 1930s (although the fanzine folded, and the essay finally appeared in the 1939 omnibus volume, *The Outsider and Others*, from Arkham House—a publishing house that itself originated from the devotion of Lovecraft fans August Derleth and Donald Wandrei). Lovecraft's work was in part derivative of earlier studies and was as resolutely eccentric as his fiction, but it brought to fandom a tradition of what Lovecraft himself would no doubt have termed "gentlemanly scholarship" and demonstrated that works of academic significance could emerge from the community of pulp magazines and fan writers. Later fan undertakings would range from ambitious philosophical histories of the genre (such as Alexei and Cory Panshin's *The World Beyond the Hill: Science Fiction and the Quest for Transcendence* [1989]) to highly specialized references (such as a 1968 concordance to the works of E. E. Smith[2]), many of them taking advantage of private collections, correspondence, interviews, and other sources not readily available to academic scholars, at least not until libraries such as those at the University of California at Riverside and the University of Liverpool began to amass significant collections including fanzines and authors' papers, in the 1980s and 1990s.

After World War II, as science fiction began to move from the exclusive province of magazines into the bookstores and libraries, and as the pulp era eventually died, more thoughtful book reviews and occasional surveys of the field began to appear in the professional magazines as well as in the fan press. In 1947, Lloyd Arthur Eshbach edited for his newly formed Fantasy Press a symposium of articles by well-known science fiction authors *Of Worlds Beyond: The Science of Science Fiction Writing* (probably the first book-length treatment of modern science fiction). The most noteworthy contribution to this symposium, Robert A. Heinlein's "On the Writing of Speculative Fiction," raised important questions about the proper name of the genre (Heinlein preferred "speculative fiction") and about the role of extrapolation (which remains one of the key buzzwords of the field and eventually became the title of an academic journal). Jack Williamson's "The Logic of Fantasy" discussed a number of principles that he saw as governing internal consistency in a fantastic story and anticipated more formal attempts to describe the genre by later critics. Other essays, by John Taine (Eric Temple Bell), A. E. Van Vogt, L. Sprague de Camp, Edward E. Smith, and John W. Campbell, Jr., focused more narrowly on how to write stories—and indeed, the general thrust of the volume was that of a writers' handbook. Nevertheless, *Of Worlds Beyond* was significant to the development of science fiction criticism.

Fantasy criticism, on the other hand, already had begun to infiltrate the groves of academe, at least in England. In 1939, while he was working on the trilogy that would perhaps do more than any other single work to place fantasy study in the university curriculum (for better or worse), the Oxford philologist J. R. R. Tolkien delivered a lecture titled "On Fairy-Stories" at the University of St. Andrews. Later expanded for inclusion in an Oxford University Press volume in honor of Tolkien's friend (and fellow fantasist) Charles Williams— published in 1947, the same year as *Of Worlds Beyond*— this lecture outlined a number of concepts that since have become staples in fantasy theory. Beginning by attempting to define (largely by exclusion) the fairy story, Tolkien soon focuses on the term "Faerie" itself, identifying this as the "Perilous Realm," the general details of atmosphere and setting that reveal a sense of the supernatural, a magical view of nature, and a "Mirror of scorn and pity" toward humanity. Such a "secondary world" demands literary or "secondary belief," and the artist who creates such a world becomes, on the model of the deity, a "sub-creator."[3]

Such fantasy, argued Tolkien, offers four principal psychological functions for the reader. Fantasy itself is the first of these—the purest form of human creativity, and one that enhances rather than undermines reason, since it depends on the reader's exercise in distinguishing the real from the not-real. "Recovery" is Tolkien's term for the "regaining of a clear view" or an innocent perspective; and "escape" is a kind of coping mechanism exemplified by the symbolic escape from death embodied in many fairy stories. Finally, "consolation" is provided by the tale's happy ending, or "eucatastrophe." Overall, these effects give rise to a sense of "joy" not unlike the joy of religious revelation. (Tolkien even suggests the Gospels as a kind of mythic model for the fairy-tale form.) A later psychoanalytic critic, Bruno Bettelheim, adopted Tolkien's four-part reader-response structure in his controversial 1976 study of fairy tales, *The Uses of Enchantment,* and later critics and writers have often responded to Tolkien's framework by adopting or rejecting it. (The writer China Miéville, for example, vehemently rejected the notion of consolation as a function of fantasy in a 2002 interview with *Locus* magazine.)[4] In either case, these writers and critics recognized the value in Tolkien's effort to develop a critical vocabulary specific to fantasy, and his invented or adapted terminology is an important precursor to later terminologies we see in critics such as Clute (who included an entry on "Eucatastrophe" in his *Encyclopedia of Fantasy,* which otherwise largely eschewed Tolkien's terminology in favor of it its own).

The same volume of *Essays Presented to Charles Williams* in which "On Fairy-Stories" first saw print also included a shorter essay by Tolkien's fellow-Inkling, C. S. Lewis. Lewis's famous "space trilogy" (*Out of the Silent Planet,* 1938; *Perelandra* 1943; *That Hideous Strength,* 1945) had given him what was at the time a wider reputation as a fantasist than Tolkien's, and his still-earlier classic study of medieval narrative tradition (*The Allegory of Love,* 1936) had laid out a number of ideas that would become crucial to modern approaches to fantasy—for example, Lewis's distinction between allegorical and "symbolic" narratives, the latter symbolizing aspects of a higher reality rather than of the experiential world. Lewis also traced the gradual "liberation" of fantasy narratives from their allegorical justifications, giving rise to stories in which the imagination becomes largely its own reward. Lewis's "On Stories," which appeared in the Oxford University Press volume, carried this argument further by postulating that "story" serves a liberating function quite apart from its embodiment in a particular rhetorical mode, and cited fantasy as the purest form of storytelling. More than Tolkien, Lewis brought his ideas to bear on works that since have come to be regarded as part of the canon of modern fantasy—William Morris' *The Well at the World's End* (1896), David Lindsay's *A Voyage to Arcturus* (1920), E. R. Eddison's *The Worm Ouroboros* (1922)—and thus helped to establish that canon as well. In later essays, Lewis defended fantasy in the context of his own fiction, of children's literature, and of science fiction (although he came to view the latter as a mechanistic degradation of mythic storytelling). His 1961 *An Experiment in Criticism*—the "experiment" was his suggestion to suspend evaluative criticism for a while and let reader response dictate the relative power of works of literature—included chapters on myth, fantasy, and realism. Myth he viewed as the most powerful of all stories, not only because of its numinous quality but because of its extraliterary appeal, its sense of inevitability, and its fantastic elements. "Fantasy" and "realism," he argued, are both confusing and misused terms—"fantasy" because of its various psychological and cultural meanings, "realism" because it may refer either to "realism of content" (verisimilitude) or "realism of presentation" (internal consistency and believability).

Formal academic attention to science fiction is also generally agreed to have begun in 1947, with the publication of J. O. Bailey's historical study *Pilgrims through Space and Time: Trends and Patterns in Scientific and Utopian Fiction* (after which the Science Fiction Research Association's Pilgrim Award was named). Written originally as a 1934 doctoral dissertation and published not by a university press but by a New York bookseller, Bailey's work is in two parts: a historical survey that outlines the prehistory of the genres, focuses heavily on the period 1870–1915, and appends a chapter on post-1915 science fiction; and a section that attempts to identify various narrative characteristics and themes of the genre ("Inhabitants of a Strange World," "The Voyage Through Space," "Invasion from a Strange Planet," "Destructive Warfare"). Although the book's rather mechanical taxonomizing of concepts provides little in the way of a coherent critical approach, and although some members of the fan community objected at the time to the short shrift given magazine science fiction, Bailey's work did much to establish the groundwork for historical studies of the genre. Together with Everett Bleiler's lengthy bibliography, *The Checklist of Fantastic Literature*, which appeared the following year (also from a small specialty press,

Shasta), it also helped establish a canon of early works, provided evidence of a long and significant tradition of science fiction writing, and developed a context for the discussion of emerging trends and themes.

Bailey's study might have had greater impact at the time had it not come up against the distrust of some fans who viewed him as an "outsider." "Inside" and "outside" had by the 1940s already become significant categories to readers of science fiction when discussing critical treatments of the genre; perhaps sensitive to a scathing 1939 essay in *Harper's* in which mainstream critic Bernard DeVoto attacked the pulps, readers had become wary of any attention tendered by "academics" or "literary types" (especially if they were not American: William L. Hamling devoted an entire editorial in a 1953 issue of the science fiction magazine *Imagination* to a sneering attack on an essay about science fiction by the Polish writer Stanislaw Lem, then virtually unknown to American readers).[5] At the same time, writers and editors within the genre seemed anxious to capitalize on such "outside" attention, and *The Magazine of Fantasy and Science Fiction* did not hesitate throughout the 1950s to parade on its back cover endorsements from such cultural icons as Clifton Fadiman, Orville Prescott, Basil Davenport, and even Louis Armstrong. Davenport himself occasionally reviewed science fiction for the *New York Times* and wrote a short study of the genre in 1955, *Inquiry into Science Fiction*, in which he discussed with some sophistication questions of definition, the distinction between science fiction and fantasy, and such subgenres as space opera, "scientific science fiction," and speculative science fiction.

A literary essay by a mainstream figure that was somewhat similar to Davenport's, but far more widely discussed, was Kingsley Amis's *New Maps of Hell* (1960), based on a series of lectures given at Princeton University. Again raising questions of definition and the relationship to fantasy, Amis begins with a breezy survey of the early history of the genre and settles in to base his defense of it largely on the satirical and dystopian works that emerged from *Galaxy* magazine in the 1950s, and in particular on works by Ray Bradbury, Robert Sheckley, and Frederik Pohl (whom Amis characterized as "the most consistently able writer science fiction, in the modern sense, has yet produced").[6] By focusing on science fiction largely as a satirical mode, Amis was able to link the modern genre directly with a respectable literary tradition; by focusing on contemporary works, he was able to draw attention to science fiction as a vital ongoing phenomenon and not as a curiosity of literary history or popular culture. For these reasons (as well as Amis's reputation as a novelist), *New Maps of Hell* probably had greater impact outside the genre than any earlier critical work—and its influence within the genre was assured by its being reprinted by Ballantine Books in its mass-market series of science fiction paperbacks, the first critical study to gain such a distinction.

Meanwhile, "inside" criticism and theory developed in books as well as magazines. Following Eshbach's lead, Reginald Bretnor edited three collections of original essays on science fiction in 1953, 1974, and 1976. The first of these, *Modern Science Fiction: Its Meaning and Its Future*, was a comprehensive attempt to assess the status of the genre in 1953, with contributions from John W. Campbell, Jr., Anthony Boucher, Isaac Asimov, Arthur C. Clarke, Philip Wylie, Fletcher Pratt, L. Sprague de Camp, and others. The collection introduced a number of definitions of the genre and raised a number of issues—including relationships to the mainstream, "social science fiction," religious themes, and the influence of publishers—that would remain key topics for discussion in later scholarship. Bretnor's second collection, *Science Fiction Today and Tomorrow*, reassessed the field from the vantage point of 1974 and featured essays by Pohl, Frank Herbert, Theodore Sturgeon, James Gunn, Gordon R. Dickson, Jack Williamson, Poul Anderson, and a number of other writers. While some of these essays covered the same ground as the earlier collection, others focused more on the growing acceptance of science fiction as literature (and the concomitant need for critical methods and vocabularies), while still others focused more on technique. Bretnor's third collection, *The Craft of Science Fiction*, emphasized technique in particular, although several of the essays contained valuable critical and historical insights.

L. Sprague de Camp's *Science Fiction Handbook* appeared in 1953, and the anonymously edited collection (with an introduction by Basil Davenport) *The Science Fiction Novel: Imagination and Social Criticism* based on talks by major writers at the University of Chicago, in 1959. While de Camp's book (revised and reissued in 1975) is very much a how-to manual, the Davenport collection of essays by Heinlein, C. M. Kornbluth, Alfred Bester, and Robert Bloch was one of the first to raise questions regarding what might be called the "social conscience" (or lack of it) in the genre. Kornbluth's essay in particular comments on the failure of the genre to fully realize its potential, and this attitude of critical self-examination is evident in the other essays as well. Although a slim volume, this collection is representative of a maturing self-awareness that was also reflected in the magazine criticism of Damon Knight and James Blish.

Magazine criticism, in fact, was perhaps even more important in establishing a common set of critical assumptions and critical vocabularies than the various books of essays mentioned. Blish published a four-part survey of "The Science in Science Fiction" in 1951 and 1952 issues of the pulp magazine *Science Fiction Quarterly*, and James Gunn published several articles (derived from his master's thesis) on "The Philosophy of Science Fiction" and "The Plot-forms of Science Fiction" in *Dynamic Science Fiction* in 1953 and 1954. Such essays drew both on the authors' academic training and on their familiarity with the genre as readers and authors, and thus represent the earliest attempts at deriving a critical vocabulary for the genre that both "insiders" and "outsiders" could use. Blish, with his assessments of magazine fiction, and Knight, with his reviews published in the professional magazines, each held the genre to rigorous standards of critical analysis during the crucial years of science fiction's broadening recognition in the early 1950s, identifying major themes and concepts with a clarity that is still valuable.[7] The importance of the genre's major internal critics in establishing a context for later science fiction and fantasy criticism cannot be overestimated, although it remains surprising how few academic researchers are familiar with the work of these critic/reviewers. From the synoptic early reviews of the pulps and early digest magazines (sometimes with several books neatly disposed of in a simple paragraph or even on a chart), genre reviewing emerged as a significant body of critical work in its own right, with Joanna Russ and Algis Budrys (both of whom also contributed to academic publications) the most notable examples of the 1960s and 1970s. Budrys's reviews in *Galaxy* and later *The Magazine of Fantasy and Science Fiction* often digress into critical theory and inevitably seek to establish a context for the book under discussion, and his essay "Paradise Charted" was among the most insightful short surveys of the development of science fiction to that period.[8] Russ, whose reviews appeared in *The Magazine of Fantasy and Science Fiction* between 1966 and 1980, offered acerbic and often prescient insights during a particularly volatile period that included the New Wave, and, together with her essays in academic journals such as *Extrapolation*, helped lay the groundwork for later feminist critiques of the field.[9]

Despite the presence of such acute critics as Blish, Knight, Russ, and Budrys (all eventually received the Pilgrim Award except Blish, who died only a few years after it was established), the magazines did not entirely forgo the celebratory and often defensive traditions of earlier fan criticism. Sam Moskowitz's sketches of major writers in the genre, originally published in magazines and gathered into two volumes in 1963 (*Explorers of the Infinite*) and 1966 (*Seekers of*

Tomorrow), tended distinctly toward uncritical celebration and dogged source-hunting, sometimes sacrificing accuracy of detail for the dramatic anecdote and often treating sources of information as proprietary secrets. Yet these volumes were read widely and were for a considerable time virtually the only published source of biographical data about a number of writers. More important than these volumes, as works of scholarship, are Moskowitz's various historical anthologies of early science fiction that began appearing in the late 1960s, such as *Under the Moons of Mars; A History and Anthology of "the Scientific Romance" in the Munsey Magazines, 1912–1920* (1970), and *Science Fiction by Gaslight: A History and Anthology of Science Fiction in the Popular Magazines, 1891–1911* (1968).

Probably the first academic study of science fiction to be published under the imprimatur of a university press was Robert M. Philmus's *Into the Unknown: The Evolution of Science Fiction from Francis Godwin to H. G. Wells*, published by the University of California Press in 1970, the same year the Pilgrim Award was first presented to J. O. Bailey. Oxford University Press already had published H. Bruce Franklin's anthology *Future Perfect: American Science Fiction of the Nineteenth Century*, with its extensive critical commentary in 1966, but Philmus' book was exclusively a critical and historical study, more carefully researched and theoretically coherent than similar material covered in Bailey's 1947 volume. Later in the 1970s, academic studies of science fiction began to appear with increasing regularity. Bowling Green University Popular Press issued Thomas D. Clareson's *SF: The Other Side of Realism*, a collection of essays by various hands, in 1971: and Clareson's *Science Fiction Criticism: An Annotated Checklist* appeared from Kent State University Press in 1972, the first extensive bibliography of writings about science fiction. Clareson, a fan-turned-academic who had been involved in the first Modern Language Association seminars on science fiction and who founded the journal *Extrapolation*, continued to edit volumes of essays throughout the 1970s, and contributed much valuable research of his own concerning the early history of American science fiction and the lost-race narrative in particular, culminating in *Some Kind of Paradise: The Emergence of American Science Fiction* (1985). David Ketterer's *New Worlds for Old: The Apocalyptic Imagination, Science Fiction, and American Literature* (1974) was one of the first theoretically rigorous attempts to locate science fiction in a tradition of literary discourse (what Ketterer called the "apocalyptic"); and in 1975, David Samuelson's *Visions of Tomorrow* provided detailed readings of six classic science fiction novels, demonstrating con-

vincingly that the best science fiction could stand up to the kind of sophisticated textual and thematic analysis traditionally associated with the realistic
novel. That same year saw the appearance of a slim volume by Robert Scholes, a
renowned critic whose interest in narrative had brought him increasingly closer
to the genre over a number of years. *Structural Fabulation*, based on a series of
lectures delivered at Notre Dame, contained broad theoretical proclamations
and limited analysis of individual works, but it did demonstrate that science
fiction was beginning to draw the attention of the critical "establishment,"
much in the same way that Kingsley Amis's 1960 volume seemed to represent
the attention of the literary mainstream. Scholes, too, found it necessary to
approach the genre in terms of his own invention, adapting his earlier "fabulation" to a more genre-specific usage.

By the late 1970s, enough of a body of academic criticism had been established that it no longer seemed necessary for each new volume to be com-
prehensively theoretical or historical in scope. Paul A. Carter's *The Creation of
Tomorrow* (1977) focused exclusively on the history of American magazine
science fiction, while Walter Meyers' *Aliens and Linguists* (1980) dealt with
language in science fiction, Patricia Warrick's *The Cybernetic Imagination in
Science Fiction* (1980) with artificial intelligence, Warren Wagar's *Terminal Visions* (1982) with eschatological themes, and Casey Fredericks' *The Future of
Eternity* with mythologies and myth systems. Theoretical models for the discussion of the genre were presented by Darko Suvin (*Metamorphoses of Science
Fiction* [1979]), Gary K. Wolfe (*The Known and the Unknown: The Iconography
of .Science Fiction* [1979]), and Mark Rose (*Alien Encounters* [1981]). Of these
studies, the most widely discussed and debated has undoubtedly been Suvin's.
Defining the essential quality of science fiction as "cognitive estrangement,"
Suvin provides a carefully reasoned argument for setting the genre apart from
related genres of fantastic literature and for treating utopian fiction as a subgenre. He is careful to place science fiction in the context of an intellectual
tradition of sociopolitical thought and, in the second half of his volume, ana-
lyzes this tradition in terms of the early history of the genre in both Europe and
America. His work is significant not only for bringing to science fiction the
methods of structuralist and Marxist literary analysis (and for bringing science
fiction in turn to the attention of these disciplines), but also for the attention
it pays to Eastern European science fiction and the utopian tradition. While
a number of readers, particularly outside of academia, complained of Suvin's
dense style, the rigor of his methodology helped to set new standards for

the discussion of science fiction in the context of intellectual history—and his trademark term, "cognitive estrangement," entered the lexicon of genre criticism.

Two equally rigorous and challenging critics emerged during this time from within the genre. Samuel R. Delany and Brian W. Aldiss. Delany's critical writings, initially collected in *The Jewel-Hinged Jaw* (1977), *The American Shore* (1978), and *Starboard Wine* (1984), focus largely on the kinds of language that make up fantastic narratives and the evolution of conventional ways of reading, or "protocols," that enable the reader to relate such language meaningfully to experience. Delany's frequently brilliant, often pyrotechnic approach to criticism draws equally on the highly personal experiences of a young fan turned author and on extensive study of European post-structuralist modes of analysis. More than any other critic of this period, Delany showed promise of bridging the gap between "inside" and "outside," but his essays have not always been as widely or well received as they deserve (part of the problem, too, is their relative inaccessibility from having been published in originally hardbound editions by specialty presses, although Wesleyan University Press began publishing several volumes of his critical writing in the 1990s.) Aldiss, already one of England's most distinguished novelists, published his *Billion Year Spree: The True History of Science Fiction* in 1973, with its influential argument that the real founder of science fiction was Mary Shelley, and the book quickly came to be regarded as the standard one-volume history of the field, and the basis for much subsequent debate on the nature and historiography of the field. Together with David Wingrove, Aldiss considerably expanded his study in 1986 under the title *Trillion Year Spree: The History of Science Fiction*, but with his most contentious arguments about the early history of the field remaining mostly intact. Aldiss also published a number of critical essay collections that often focused on science fiction.

This dramatic blossoming of science fiction and fantasy scholarship, termed "the academic awakening" in a chapbook edited by Willis E. McNelly for the College English Association in 1974, soon turned into something resembling a flood. Series of individual author studies appeared both from small presses such as Starmont House, Borgo, or Taplinger and from academic houses or university presses such as Oxford, Southern Illinois, Georgia, Indiana, and Greenwood. The collection of critical essays, at the time a relatively minor factor in more traditional areas of literary scholarship (such as, for example, Victorian studies), became a principal outlet for the scholarship of science fiction and fantasy, to the extent that by 1982 more original essays were appearing in such volumes than in all the scholarly journals in the field combined. Students and teachers from the thousand-odd science fiction and fantasy classes suddenly being taught on campuses all over the world besieged librarians for basic reference material, only to find that even the most respected genre authors were excluded from standard literary reference works. The resulting demand created a small but significant library and scholarly market for reference books on the teaching of fantastic genres, general guides or introductions, and more theoretical critical and historical works. Three major scholarly journals (*Extrapolation*, *Science-Fiction Studies*, and *Foundation*) appeared between 1959 and 1971, and the early issues of these journals—like the various reference books, teaching guides, and handbooks—tended to include contributions from fans, writers, and independent scholars as well as from university-based academics and younger scholars just entering the field.

Perhaps the most dramatic examples of this exploitation of the emerging library market were the Salem Press *Surveys* of science fiction and fantasy, which appeared in 1979 and 1983 and consisted of a total of 1,000 "essay-reviews" with a combined total of over 5,000 pages of critical commentary from something like 150 contributors, including fan scholars such as Sam Moskowitz and David Pringle, fans-turned-academics like Thomas Clareson or T. A. Shippey, writers like Brian Aldiss and James Gunn, and independent scholars like John Clute, as well as many of the newer generation of university scholars and theorists such as Darko Suvin or Brian Attebery. About the same time, Peter Nicholls and John Clute produced the first edition of *The Science Fiction Encyclopedia* in 1979. Later revised and hugely expanded in 1993 as *The Encyclopedia of Science Fiction*, it became what is still the standard one-volume reference work in the field. Clute and Nicholls each eventually received Pilgrim Awards, and Clute also received the Distinguished Scholarship Award from the International Association for the Fantastic in the Arts.

While many of the essays that appeared in these journals, collections, and reference works were excellent by any standards, others were hastily produced and seemed to give credence to fears within the science fiction and fantasy community that academia was opportunistic and exploitative; that academics were less interested in doing serious research in the field than in seeking tenure. Such concerns were expressed repeatedly during the 1970s not only by fans, but by professional writers and editors including Lloyd Biggle, Jr., William Tenn, and Lester del Rey. While their fears that the involvement of academia might somehow "damage" science fiction now seem rather naive, some of the specific concerns they expressed were not entirely without foundation. The extreme statement of this position was made by Algis Budrys in a controversial review in the January 1983 *Magazine of Fantasy and Science Fiction*, where he stated flatly that "the formal scholarship of speculative fiction is, taken in the whole, worthless."[10] In addition to accusing academics of being intellectually incestuous and of not doing adequate primary research, Budrys claimed that an essay by Harold Bloom in the volume under review was "not directed at anyone outside a tight circle who all share the same vocabulary and the same library." The would-be literary scholar, Budrys argued, is forced to read more criticism than actual literature, or would be in danger of losing "his grip on the nomenclature."[11]

* * *

This is essentially the context, and the controversy, into which the SFRA Pilgrim Award and later the IAFA Distinguished Scholarship Award were introduced in the 1970s and 1980s—a proliferation of academic scholarship, some valuable and some bandwagon-jumping, met by an often skeptical response from "in-house" writers, critics, and fans, who by then had been working toward a critical dialogue on fantastic literature for decades in fanzines, magazine letter columns, bibliographies, reference works, and small-press books. The early Pilgrim Awards managed to evade the controversy by honoring authors of pioneering studies like the Bailey's 1947 *Pilgrims through Space and Time* (for which the award was named) and Nicholson's 1948 *Voyages to the Moon* (the 1971 award), even though neither of these scholars did significant additional work in the field. Soon, however, the Pilgrim Award list began to reflect the variety of communities of discourse from which science fiction criticism derived, recognizing professional writer-critics (Damon Knight, Brian Aldiss, Joanna Russ, Ursula K. Le Guin, L. Sprague de Camp, Brian Stableford, Algis Budrys); writers who had bridged into academia (Jack Williamson, James Gunn, Samuel R. Delany); scholars whose work was done essentially as fans (Sam Moskowitz, Mike Ashley, Everett Bleiler); academic literary historians (I. F. Clarke, Thomas D. Clareson); bibliographers (Neil Barron, Hal W. Hall); literary theorists (Fredric Jameson, Darko Suvin); and academic scholars who had built their primary careers around science fiction (George Slusser, David Ketterer, David Samuelson). Beginning in 1986, the IAFA Distinguished Scholarship Awards took a wider purview that reflected an even broader variety of critics, including scholars of Gothic and horror fiction (Devendra Varma, S. T. Joshi); fairy tales and folklore (Jack Zipes); children's literature (Peter Hunt); and even translation (Marcial Souto). Five critics have received both the IAFA and SFRA awards (Aldiss, Stableford, Clute, H. Bruce Franklin, and Gary K. Wolfe), but it's Clute—an independent critic and scholar whose major reference books *The Encyclopedia of Science Fiction* and *The Encyclopedia of Fantasy*, produced without benefit of university affiliation, are nevertheless major benchmarks of scholarship in the field—whose career raises the most interesting questions about the various modes and venues in which fantastic literature is discussed, and how they relate to each other today, when we can still find significant remnants of these various critical communities (the past few years alone have seen significant studies by writers such as Gwyneth Jones, Barry Malzberg, and Damien Broderick; writer-academics like Adam Roberts; and academics such as Brian Attebery, Roger Luckhurst, Edward James, and Farah Mendlesohn). Most important, Clute's work, eccentric though it may seem, holds what may be the greatest promise of a synthesis among these various communities.

Although Clute had been reviewing professionally since 1966, it was not until his first collection of reviews and essays, *Strokes*, appeared in 1988 that his work became fully embroiled in the controversies of discourse regarding science fiction and fantasy. The book came in for a fairly scathing (if entertaining) review by Rob Latham in the academic *Journal of the Fantastic in the Arts*, the journal of the IAFA. Disdainfully labeling Clute a "journalistic commentator" and repeatedly alluding to the "journalistic" contexts in which Clute's work had largely appeared, Latham assailed Clute's "obfuscatory smoke blowing," and concluded that the book is "deeply disappointing as criticism"—largely because Clute apparently lacked a clearly articulated theoretical base, specifically a "fairly comprehensive command of recent (postmodern) theory, the only framework capable of resolving all the paradoxes spawned by the binary logic of Clute's modernist humanism."[12] Even worse, "Clute's own critical practice has largely remained tied to the immediate, short-term concerns of generic production"; that is, he wrote *book reviews*. Latham has since become one of the most distinguished scholars in the field, who later wrote incisive and favorable reviews of Clute's work in *The Encyclopedia of Science Fiction* and *The Encyclopedia of Fantasy*, and it might seem a bit of intemperate exhumation to quote that old review here, if it hadn't already taken on something of a life of its own in the emerging debates over how to properly frame science fiction criticism.[13] A defense of Clute by Brian Stableford quickly appeared in the IAFA *Newsletter*, followed by a response from Latham, and both Andrew Butler and Latham himself revisited the controversy in a 2006 *festschrift* in honor of Clute and his wife Judith entitled *Polder*, edited by Farah Mendlesohn, in which Latham—in his own appreciative essay—expresses regret over his youthful "superior, chastising tone" and "pious postmodernism."[14] Clute himself quoted the review at some length in the opening essay of his very next collection, *Look at the Evidence*, which appeared in 1995. And, in fact, everything quoted above from Latham's review was quoted by Clute himself, in what can only be described as a cheerfully gustatory tone; the overall review, he says, was "hilariously devastating."[15] Although *Strokes* and *Look at the Evidence* each received a fair number of far more enthusiastic reviews, some from academic journals (perhaps the longest and most thoughtful review anywhere of *Look at the Evidence* is one by Istvan Csiscery-Ronay in the March 1997 *Science-Fiction Studies*), it's interesting that this one should have captured Clute's attention so clearly, and it captured it, I believe, not because it was especially damaging, but because it was *interesting*: It raised the issue of what Clute seemed to think he was doing, of what the reviewer thought Clute *ought* to be doing, and of the distance separating the two. In particular, Latham's demand that the contemporary science fiction critic must have a "fairly comprehensive command of recent (postmodern) theory" seemed to be laying out a claim of ownership over the critical discourse about the genre—a claim radically at odds with claims from Budrys and others that academic theorists, for the most part, didn't know what they were talking about. We can use this controversy to investigate what sort of ground Clute inhabits in this complex universe of discourse about popular literature and science fiction, a universe that by now involves not only the communities of fans, scholars, and writers discussed earlier, but ranges from the bloggish grandstanding of self-appointed web-jockey fan "critics" (although in fairness a reasonable number of well-crafted reviews have begun to appear on individual websites, and Clute himself reviews online) to the categorical dismissals of the field in much of the mainstream press (such as *New York Times* reviewer Sven Birkerts' flat assertion, in a 1993 review, that "science fiction will never be Literature with a capital 'L'") to those relatively few academics who still fervently believe the genre ought to calm down and let itself be packed away into the gray suitcase of Theory. Clearly Clute is none of these, but clearly he is *something*, and that something is linked intimately to his long career as a reviewer and as a central figure in the British science fiction community, during which he honed his critical and theoretical approach to the field.

Clute's third collection of essays and reviews, *Scores*, appeared in 2003, and this question of inhabitable space immediately arises again in its introduction, "What I Did on My Summer Vacation." Here he tells the story of an academic acquaintance who, after having amassed a respectable number of academic books and articles, turns to an extensive career as a book reviewer and eventually is challenged by an academic colleague with the question, "but when do you plan to do some *real* work again?"[16] This leads to a quiet rumination on Clute's own career as a "stone extramural" occupying "a niche some light years beyond the pale of the Groves."[17] The issue comes up still again, less overtly, in the two addresses that Clute delivered, to largely academic audiences, on the occasion of receiving the SFRA and IAFA awards. At the Science Fiction Research Association meeting in 1994, where he received the Pilgrim Award, Clute began by thanking the audience for "letting me in here" and went on to describe himself in self-consciously oxymoronic terms, as "a non-academic who does bibliography with violent intensity," "a man of mature years who spends a great deal of his time writing with great passion book reviews for ephemeral journals," and a "solitary unsalaried freelance."[18] Receiving the Distinguished Scholarship Award from the International Association for the Fantastic in the Arts five years later, he identified himself as "a writer of reviews and essays" and "an encyclopedia writer—as opposed, perhaps, to a literary critic" and proceeded to comment on "the cloaking difference between my work and normal criticism" —which difference lies, he said, in the different sorts of truths being sought: the "normal" critic dealing with individual texts, the encyclopedist with sets of texts.[19]

There is, of course, no such creature as a "normal" critic, but there are plenty of conventional critics, and (at least within the fabled Groves) the majority of them are neither reviewers nor encyclopedists. In short, an unstated middle ground lies in Clute's working formulation of his dual career as short-term reviewer and long-term encyclopedist, a middle ground largely occupied by professors for whom "real work" is neither the immediacy of book reviews nor the normative judgments of encyclopedia-making, but rather the research-and-publication cycle of formally vetted essays and monographs. Even in the academic world, though, science fiction and fantasy scholarship occupies something of the same oblique relationship to mainstream academia that genre literature does to mainstream literature; few universities offer degrees specializing in science fiction or fantasy studies, and few seek to hire faculty with particular expertise in these areas. Many of even the most prominent academic scholars have been obliged to treat science fiction or fantasy as a sideline to their primary areas of expertise, many entered the field after earning degrees in more traditional areas (medieval literature, genre theory, even history), and many consequently have faced uphill battles in ensuring that their work on the fantastic is "counted" in the often tradition-bound measures against which tenure and promotion are assessed. It's not surprising that such scholars may feel isolated—regarded as interlopers or carpetbaggers by vocal segments of the fan and professional communities and as renegades and panderers by some of their professorial colleagues. Nor is it surprising that such scholars should be attracted to forming their own professional associations, such as the Science Fiction Research Association or the International Association for the Fantastic in the Arts. Largely through the work of these associations, an increasing number of academics have come to realize that academic scholarship of the fantastic differs from more traditional literary scholarship in at least two significant ways: Few other kinds of critics can interact so freely with, and even join the communities of active writers and readers as in science fiction and fantasy; and few critical traditions draw so heavily on the earlier work of nonacademic (or more accurately, extramural) scholars and critics, from James Blish and Damon Knight to Sam Moskowitz and Everett Bleiler—or to John Clute, who has more convincingly bridged these worlds than anyone else since Delany.

It's worth pausing here to discuss some of the variant meanings that have accrued to such terms as "reviewer," "critic," "scholar," and "academic," even though I hope such a discussion might appear simplistic to the readers of this volume. For a great many practicing writers, "critic" is virtually commensurate with "reviewer," especially when used in the plural (as in the mantra "I never read the critics"). This is related to the commonly held stereotype of reviewers as embittered failed novelists or worse, barely restrained serial murderers masquerading as doctors. But in academia, the distinction can be crucial. Critics may include theorists, savants, essayists, commentators, dissertation-writers, and even historians, but almost never reviewers, who, working under those "journalistic" constraints Latham mentioned, lack the magisterial distancing from the text putatively required by the demands of scholarly synthesis. (To continue the earlier metaphor past the breaking point, reviewers in this formulation are not doctors at all, homicidal or not, but mere paramedics.) Even at that, "criticism" is still a much vaguer term than "scholarship," which by tenure-committee convention is taken to mean the uncovering of new or newly combined knowledge by means of formally described and peer-reviewed processes, the eventual reward for which may be a degree, a job, or promotion and tenure. One might argue that the reviewer is in the business of uncovering new knowledge on an almost weekly basis, but that would be to misunderstand the rules: Knowledge can't really be un*covered* until it has been well buried, and hence a young scholar might well find a more promising career path in examining the popular fiction of the 1840s than that of the 1990s for a variety of reasons. The situation isn't quite as dire as it once was, perhaps, but there is still some cause for the long-held suspicion of many writers that literary academia harbors a terrible Gothic secret: namely, that some professors merely want authors to *die*, or at least to shut up. (In my graduate school days, I met a doctoral student who claimed in exasperation that he was thinking of plotting to murder the novelist Philip Roth, the topic of his dissertation, because each time a draft of the dissertation was complete, Roth published another novel that forced a rethinking of all that had gone before, thus generating another year or so of rewrites. I can even recall the Roth book that spawned the murderous impulse: it was *The Great American Novel*, which appeared just as my acquaintance was completing a full dissertation-revision occasioned by *The Breast*, which had appeared the previous year.)

Partly because of situations like this, the term "academic," sometimes used as a noun, has also taken on a pejorative meaning in the communities of writers and fans—almost, but not quite, as a synonym for "bonehead." But this too conflates a number of meanings: In the broadest sense, it may simply refer to someone who has an advanced degree or holds a university teaching post, while in practice it often becomes a code word for the kind of stilted, theory-laden writing that Budrys complained about, or for the journals that publish these articles, or for those professional associations such as the IAFA or SFRA that also serve as affinity groups and whose conferences may be mightily confusing to fans who show up seeking autographs or to authors expecting the more adulatory atmosphere of a fan convention. In fairness, a great many authors and some fans recognize the value inherent in the methodological discipline imposed by formal peer-reviewed academic work, and the struggles some academics have faced in incorporating these literatures into school and college curricula, and into the broader discourse of literary scholarship. As with "reviewer" or "critic," the meaning of the term depends heavily on one's perspective.

One might think, given these multiple perspectives, that an encyclopedist such as Clute is the epitome of both the academic and the scholar, heir to the grand tradition of Bacon or Diderot—but this, by current practice, would be misinformed as well: The encyclopedist, in the conventional formulation of the modern academy, is the mere synthesizer of received scholarship, a *secondary* scholar, and not the on-site excavator of the ruins. An encyclopedia is not meant to show us ideas that are newly minted or to show us things in radically new lights, but only to describe for us things that would be painstakingly difficult to unearth on our own: It aims for authoritative convenience rather than insight. (Never mind, for the moment, that Clute cavalierly assaults this rule throughout *The Encyclopedia of Fantasy*, a mined harbor of theoretical depth charges and primary arguments; we'll get to that shortly.)

This in turn, leads us to another factor crucial to locating Clute—and by extension a good many of the pioneer scholars of the field—in this universe of discourse; namely, that the particular district he has chosen to inhabit is one that often has been badly served by the traditional machineries of scholarship. One need only speculate what the *Encyclopedia of Science Fiction* or *Encyclopedia of Fantasy* might look like if they had been compiled like some of those hastily produced reference works of the 1970s and 1980s, in which the entries were solicited from an almost random assortment of unvetted academic contributors whose main qualification was that they held university positions: inexplicable lacunae, odd distortions of proportion, inconsistencies of approach, unexamined dogmas and canons, replications of past errors, and general purpose mad-dog howlers. (Refraining from citing the actual sources, I have before me a critical study in which Ray Bradbury's short story collection *Dark Carnival* is described as his "first novel" and a library reference work in which Frank Herbert's novel *Dragon in the Sea* is mysteriously transformed into *Oregon in the Sea*, and Harry Harrison's *Deathworld* becomes *Death Word*, Robert Silverberg is credited as author of *Voyage of the Space Beagle*, and John Brunner as the author of *Timescape*. And that's only the beginning.) Clute and his collaborator Peter Nicholls long ago realized that an encyclopedia of SF would need to be essentially *sui generis*, drawing not only on the received scholarship of the field, but on the *ex cathedra* research of fan critics, collectors, and bibliographers, and on a great deal of entirely original work by the contributors, all carefully reviewed and fact-checked by editors whose own knowledge of the material was daunting. Each successive encyclopedia since the 1979 *Encyclopedia of Science Fiction*—the 1993 revision of that volume and the 1997 *Ency-*

clopedia of Fantasy—has been increasingly *sui generis* in this sense, drawing less on conventional scholarship and theory and more on the work of contributors (among which Clute was easily among the most prolific in each). An entry on "Critical and Historical Works" ran to more than three full pages in *The Encyclopedia of Science Fiction*, but in *The Encyclopedia of Fantasy* there is no such entry, although various individual critics and scholars earn their own entries. In place of the synthesis of critical and theoretical views in *The Encyclopedia of Science Fiction* is what Clute has described as a "secret book" within the *Encyclopedia of Fantasy*, a book that outlines in various entries an emerging theory of fantasy very much of Clute's own making, and almost hypertextual in presentation. Here is part of what I wrote in reviewing the book in 1997:

No one, I suspect, is likely to open the book seeking information about such things as "polder," "thinning," "wainscot," "wrongness," "cross-hatch," "water margins," "instauration fantasy," or (my favorite) "read the small print" for the simple reason that most of these terms (and there are *many* others) do not exist outside the *Encyclopedia*, or exist only in a few scattered essays and reviews. Yet all of them are generously cross-referenced from other entries, most of them are irresistible (how can you not skip over to "polder" once you see it highlighted in small caps?), and together they constitute the core of the theory of fantasy that undergirds the whole project, even as it lurks subversively among the 4,000-odd more "normal" reference entries that make up the bulk of the text. There was some of this language-making going on in the earlier *Encyclopedia of Science Fiction*, but most of it was self-explanatory ("conceptual breakthrough" or "fix-up," for instance), and for the most part that book confined itself to a critical and conceptual vocabulary that had evolved over decades in the SF community.[20]

With the publication of *Scores*, including most of Clute's reviews from the 1990s, we can watch some of these ideas germinate in the reviews that Clute was writing while developing this theory, ideas that evolved into entries such as "instauration fantasy," "Face of Glory," and "polder." "Instauration fantasy," for example, shows up in a 1993 *Interzone* review of Robert Holdstock's *The Hollowing*, in which it is defined it as "a late twentieth century tale in which the contemporary world is transfigured and or/restored [*sic*] through the metamorphic intersection of normal reality and some reality or conjoined realities out of deep fantasy"; in *The Encyclopedia of Fantasy* this becomes, much more broadly, "fantasies in which the real world is transformed; they are fantasies about the MATTER of the world"[21] The reviewer's need for contextualization of the work at hand (i.e., "a late twentieth century tale") gives way to the encyclopedist's need for taxonomy ("fantasies about the MATTER of the world"), and what might have been a passing insight provoked by an intriguing novel is transformed into a broadly theoretical statement (which goes on for more than 1,700 words) about a central function of fantasy in general. As far as I know, no critical essay formally proposes the term, no conference presentation argues its merits (although Clute did test-drive some of his notions in a 1995 interview in *Locus* magazine), no one appeals to the precedent of earlier scholars (unless one counts Sir Francis Bacon, who almost certainly did not have John Crowley in mind when he first used the term in the sense that inspired Clute).[22]

This transformation of a reviewer's insight into a broader principle isn't entirely new, of course, but when it has been done in the past, at least in genre fiction, it has been done fairly waggishly: Terms such as "idiot plot" and "kitchen-sink story," for example, showed up often enough in Damon Knight's reviews to become common shorthand among readers and writers, but such terms were never meant to be part of a consistent argument, let alone a theory. But Clute's reviews reveal a cauldron of intense self-debate, as notions are tested, modified, discarded, and gradually codified into a kind of hermetic and hermeneutic glossary. That same review of *The Hollowing* comments that "Holdstock is a Knot writer," and that capital "K" signals us that yet another weather balloon is aloft, although, as Clute notes in an interpolated comment in *Scores*, the term never quite made it into the *Encyclopedia of Fantasy*, eventually giving way to the entry on "Recognition." (Another example is "Dictates of Story," which shows up occasionally in the reviews complete with the initial capital letters of an encyclopedia-entry *manque*, but never makes it into the final book as an entry.) And since the *Encyclopedia* appeared, we can see in his reviews and review-essays the working out of additional concepts likely to show up in future editions, or at least in future essays (since the *Encyclopedia of Fantasy* appeared, Clute has been developing a massive online resource for fantastic literature). There is an entry for "Portals" in the encyclopedia, for example, but not for "Cloaca," horror fiction's answer to the fantasy portal, because "cloaca" hadn't been worked out yet.[23] "Cloaca" is a needed piece of the puzzle, if Clute's emerging and enlarging theory is to account for the dynamics of horror fiction. Much the same might be said of "Hook," horror's mirror to fantasy's "Quest," and "Equipoise," used to describe works "built upon sustained narrative negotiations of uncertainty, without coming to any necessary decision as to what is real."[24] Both terms appear in the *Conjunctions* essay and later in *The Darkening Garden*, and both (like all of Clute's most useful terms) are negotiations with the text before him (in the immediate case of the *Conjunctions* essay, Conrad's *Heart of Darkness*). The development of Clute's vocabulary—his evolving grammar of the fantastic—is thus derived from primary source texts, and not from prior theories against which texts are measured.

It's not my brief here to either validate or contest Clute's usages of such terms, or the theory of fantasy that they collectively begin to describe. Instead, what interests me is the process by which Clute transforms these immediate negotiations with the text (the work of a reviewer) into taxonomic structures (the work of an encyclopedist) without the conventional mediations of traditional critical dialogue. As Clute himself put it in his 1999 IAFA speech, "A true critical act of apprehension is, I tend to think, an invasive reshaping or recuperation of a particular text. A true encyclopedic act of apprehension . . . consists of an invasive reshaping or sorting of a congeries of texts into a set."[25] To move so boldly, as Clute does, from one to the other, might be viewed as an act of irredeemable *hubris*, a gesture of critical risk-taking so bold as to constitute daredevilry, or—as I prefer to believe—a reclamation of authority from the last theorist to the first reader. This is important. Instead of drawing his concepts from a palimpsest of successive generations of interpretations and positionings of source texts, he draws them from his own readerly apprehensions of the texts themselves. The scaffolding of his approach is the read book, not the mastered theory.

Which brings us back to that original review of *Strokes* that faulted Clute for lacking a solid theoretical grounding for his book reviews. In one sense, that reviewer was exactly right: The foundation of Clute's reviews has always been inductive, drawn from his astonishingly thorough grasp of an immense variety of texts and traditions, rather than from the nests of canon and dogma. He is perhaps the first critic to gain a substantial primary reputation *as a reader* of SF, not as a fan or author or academic, and it is his vast and unreplicable lifetime of reading that sustains his critical practice. He is at heart a clinician, and there is a Vesalius-like flavor to the anatomies he has begun constructing from his long career as a reader and reviewer. The effect of this, which should be both salutary and cautionary for all reviewers as well as academic scholars, is to reclaim the authority of the review as the front line of critical discussion; to reclaim the primacy of the reader who encounters the text without guidance, often without preconception, and certainly without agenda. Anyone who has written very many reviews knows the odd feeling of pathlessness that can come from opening a novel, perhaps still in manuscript, guided by absolutely no prior opinions, often not even a publicist's flap copy, and sometimes no notion of who the author is—and then being expected to make a public statement of some assumed authority on what the key features of the novel are, and what their significance is. One can get it wrong (as Clute has sometimes done; as all we reviewers have sometimes done), but one can't get it wrong too often and survive. Yet this kind of reading, this primal encounter with Story, is one of the deepest attractions of criticism, and underlies all the varieties of critical discourse we've been discussing—the review, the academic monograph, the reference work or encyclopedia, even the panel discussion at a conference.

I'm not arguing here for the act of reviewing as the only legitimate precursor to theorizing, or that writing reviews is in any sense a more fundamental act of criticism than the writing of critical essays or books. Most reviews are disposable and are written to be such, and only by doing some creative fudging can most reviewers find ways of commenting on earlier texts by way of historical context. The traditional functions of the critical essay as a mediator between reading and theory are well established and useful—but they can also get out of hand. I once interviewed a candidate for a teaching position whose doctoral dissertation had involved an interesting aspect of contemporary postcolonial literature, and when I asked her if she had maintained her interest in the kind of texts she had written about, she earnestly explained to me that she didn't really have time to read fiction anymore because she was too busy keeping up with theory. (Even more disturbing was the clear impression that she felt this was the answer she was *supposed* to give.) Individual works of fiction were not the generators of theory for her so much as *illustrations* of theory, much as (I suppose) a botanist might master the phylogeny of orchids in order to identify a particular species when she sees one. I've long since discovered that this attitude is far from uncommon, but it is an attitude better designed for ending discussions than for beginning them. The effective reviewer is forced to recognize almost daily that each new text, good or bad, modifies and revises our understanding of all its predecessors, and that the resulting flux causes older texts to shift and shimmer when we return to them: In reviewing, you can never step in the same text twice.

For decades as a reviewer, Clute has immersed himself in these currents, cascades, eddies, maelstroms, and whooshes of a living literature, and from them he precipitates encyclopedias and glossaries. It would be misleading and misreading to claim that all of his hundreds (thousands?) of reviews and essays have rehearsed directly the various polders, water margins, wainscots, and Faces of Glory that have come to make up his idiosyncratic critical terminology; the vast majority have not, and in fact this fascination with emergent theory is a relatively recent development in his long career (prompted largely, I would speculate, on his discovery of the paucity of usable critical terminology when he began working on *The Encyclopedia of Fantasy*; although any number of fantasy critics and theorists have generated useful terms and concepts, remarkably few have become common currency). Only in very recent years, however, has Clute's critical vocabulary begun to work its way into academic discourse in such studies as Farah Mendlesohn's *Rhetorics of Fantasy* (2008). To the extent that this may serve as a bridge between the competing universes of critical discourse, it's an encouraging development.

The key term in Clute's critical vocabulary is not idiosyncratic at all; it's one that we can find him worrying over in even his earliest reviews, and one that in both reviews and encyclopedias most clearly sets him apart from the armchair botanists. This term is "Story," which earns more than a page and a half in *The Encyclopedia of Fantasy* but which in hard kernel is defined as "a narrative discourse which is *told*."[26] The reason this sets him apart from the botanists is that the botanists generally prefer to talk of "narrative," and "narrative"—which is to Story roughly what an automobile transmission is to a road trip—doesn't even get an entry in the *Encyclopedia*. The act of telling is the crucial distinction, I think, because it raises issues of voice and interactivity, and it permits Clute to organicize the concept, which in turn permits him to speak of fantasy as "a story set in a world which is impossible, but which the story believes" or "Stories that mean themselves" (a continued exploration of this notion can be found in the entry on "Recognition"), or worlds that are "storyable."[27] Story, in this sense, is both more and less than narrative, but mostly more, since it implies a kind of ongoing moral dialogue with the world and with the reader, and since it must be engaged at both the tactical level (through reviews) and the strategic level (through theory).

In the end, Story is the thin hard cable that links Clute's daily engagements with the literature to his more summative pronouncements in his encyclopedias, and it is clearly his passion. Clute believes, or shows evidence of believing, that the wounds of the world are addressable by Story, and it's notable how often images of healing recur in his writing, and how much the notion of healing seems bound up in the notion of criticism. "Writing criticism," he says, "is a surgery of the fall," and "any serious critic of the new must betray the new in order to heal it."[28] At the risk of unmasking the deep sentiment that underlies Clute's most consistent positions, the dialogue between Story and critic, critic and world, Story and world, is a dialogue of healing and belief. It's a dialogue that ties literary criticism directly to the actual world of readers, that welcomes the participation of all the multiple communities we have been discussing, that incorporates and preserves the discoveries and inventions of all those earlier pilgrims.[29]

Notes

Chapter 1. Malebolge, or the Ordnance of Genre (pages 3–17)

1. The article is no longer available on *The Spook*'s website, but remains online on the website of horror writer David J. Schow under the title "Symposium on the Nature of Genre and Pleasure in the 21st Century" at http://www.davidjschow.com/essay/essay _symposium.html (accessed January 2, 2009).

2. See, for example, Gordon S. Haight, ed., *Selections from George Eliot's Letters* (New Haven, Conn.: Yale University Press, 1985); or Rohan Maitzen, " 'The Soul of Art': Understanding Victorian Ethical Criticism," *ESC: English Studies in Canada* 31, nos. 2–3 (June/September 2005). Available online at http://ejournals.library.ualberta.ca/index .php/ESC/article/viewFile/1335/894 (accessed January 2, 2009). Harold Bloom's critical anthology *Bloom's Classical Critical Views: Jane Austen* (New York: Chelsea House, 2007) even reprints "The Progress of Fiction as an Art" as being by George Eliot.

3. Quoted in Lilian R. Furst, *Romanticism in Perspective* (New York: Humanities Press, 1970), 332.

4. George MacDonald, "The Fantastic Imagination," in *Gifts of the Child Christ: Fairy Tales and Stories for the Childlike,* ed. Glenn Edward Sadler (1893; reprint, Grand Rapids, Mich.: Eerdmans, 1973); G. K. Chesterton, "The Ethics of Elfland," in *Orthodoxy* (1908; online at http://www.gutenberg.org/files/130/130.txt); E. M. Forster, "Fantasy," in *Aspects of the Novel* (1927; reprint, New York: Harvest, 1956); C. S. Lewis, *An Experiment* in *Criticism* (Cambridge: Cambridge University Press, 1965); J. R. R. Tolkien, "On Fairy-Stories," in *A Tolkien Reader* (New York: Ballantine, 1966); Ursula K. Le Guin, "The Child and the Shadow," in *The Language of the Night: Essays on Fantasy and Science Fiction* (New York: HarperCollins, 1989).

5. Pinchas Noy, "A Revision of the Psychoanalytic Theory of the Primary Process," *International Journal of Psycho-Analysis* 50 (1969): 155–78.

Chapter 2. Evaporating Genres (pages 18–53)

1. Kenneth C. Davis, *Two-Bit Culture: The Paperbacking of America* (Boston: Houghton Mifflin, 1984), 166.

2. Donald A. Wollheim, "The Science-Fiction Novel," *New York Times*, August 28, 1949. Online at http://select.nytimes.com/gst/abstract.html?res=F40615FE3B5D13728D DDA10A94D0405B8988F1D3&scp=34&sq=%22science+fiction&st=p (accessed April 22, 2008).

3. Villiers Gerson, "Spacemen's Realm," *New York Times*, January 13, 1952. Online at http://select.nytimes.com/gst/abstract.html?res=F30613FD395E107A93C1A8178AD85 F68585F9&scp=203&sq=%22science+fiction&st=p (accessed April 22, 2008).

4. The situation in England was somewhat different in a purely literary sense, less so in terms of book markets. To be sure, a substantial tradition existed of post-Wells "scientific romances," ably documented by Brian Stableford in *The Scientific Romance in England, 1890–1950* (London: Fourth Estate, 1985). But as Stableford notes, this tradition never really cohered as a popular market (only a handful of titles made their way into the Penguin line that dominated British paperbacks until the postwar years) and essentially disappeared as a separate tradition when Americanized science fiction began to appear in substantial numbers. Nor were British readers immune to the attractions of the American pulps: British fan societies existed on the model of the Americans, at least one British pulp (*Tales of Wonder*) began publishing in 1937, and more than one British reader from that era remembers the excitement of finding cheap copies of American pulps, which apparently had been imported after being used as ship ballast during the Lend-Lease years.

5. The term "supergenre" was employed by Eric S. Rabkin in *The Fantastic in Literature* (Princeton, N.J.: Princeton University Press, 1976) and, in a somewhat broader sense, by R. D. Mullen in "Books in Review: Supernatural, Pseudonatural, and Sociocultural Fantasy," *Science-Fiction Studies* 16 (1978): 291–98.

6. In the horror field, an argument could be made that similar canon-defining anthologies include Dorothy L. Sayers' three volumes of *Great Short Stories of Detection, Mystery and Horror* (1929–1934; retitled as *The Omnibus of Crime* series in the United States, and with somewhat different contents) and Herbert Wise and Phyllis Fraser's *Great Tales of Terror and the Supernatural* (1944). The Sayers anthologies, with their substantial content of supernatural fiction in the "Mystery and Horror" sections, were almost certainly among the first respectable twentieth-century anthologies in England to identify horror as a distinct literary tradition, while the Wise and Fraser omnibus shared with Healy and McComas's *Adventures in Time and Space* the distinction of being reprinted by Random House's Modern Library, which meant that the books would remain widely available and in print for decades, thus influencing generations of readers.

7. Admittedly, this choice of key figures is supposed to be somewhat provocative, but not entirely arbitrary; although a case could be made for Isaac Asimov in science fiction and Poe in horror fiction, it seems to me that Heinlein and Lovecraft more directly set the terms of ideological debate for the writers who followed in their wake. These choices are in keeping with my view of genres defined more clearly by world-views than by conventionalized narrative tropes.

8. Edmund Wilson, *Classics and Commercials: A Literary Chronicle of the 1940s* (New York: Farrar, Straus, and Giroux, 1950), 288.

9. Bill Sheehan, *At the Foot of the Story Tree: An Inquiry into the Fiction of Peter Straub* (Burton, Mich.: Subterranean Press, 2000), 148.

10. Peter Straub, quoted in Stephen King, *Danse Macabre* (New York: Berkley, 1982), 251.

11. Rabkin, *The Fantastic in Literature*; W. R. Irwin, *The Game of the Impossible: A Rhetoric of Fantasy* (Urbana: University of Illinois Press, 1976; Rosemary Jackson, *Fantasy: The Literature of Subversion* (New York: Methuen, 1981). It has become virtually a critical commonplace in recent decades to describe the difference between science fiction and fantasy as the difference between the possible and the impossible. A more useful recent approach to discussing a taxonomy of fantasy on its own terms is Farah Mendlesohn, *Rhetorics of Fantasy* (Middletown, Conn.: Wesleyan University Press, 2008).

12. Ryman's work consistently has revealed a desire to meld or break genres: *The Unconquered Country: A Life History* (1984) conflates science fiction, fantasy, and historical realism in a radically distorted but easily recognized analogue of the Cambodian war; *The Child Garden: A Low Comedy* (1988) is a complex mix of alternate worlds, dystopia, drug novel, and realism; *253* (1998), originally published as a hypertext novel on the Internet, freely mixes the formalism of the French new novel (253 chapters of 253 words each, depicting the lives of 253 passengers on a London underground train) with closely observed psychological realism and, it is gradually revealed, elements of fantasy and secret history. More recently, he has revisited the issue of Cambodia from the perspective of an historical novel conjoined with a contemporary thriller (*The King's Last Song*, 2006), the ghost story combined with alternate history ("Pol Pot's Beautiful Daughter (Fantasy)," 2006) and the historical fable combined with fantasy ("The Last Ten Years in the Life of Hero Kai," 2005).

13. The World Fantasy Award is selected annually by a panel of judges rather than by popular vote, and has never seemed too constrained about genre boundaries. The best novel award for 1989, for example, went to Peter Straub's *Koko*, which as we have already seen was a nonfantastic mystery thriller, and in 1992 it went to Robert McCammon's *Boy's Life*, an essentially mainstream novel from a writer known for his horror fiction.

14. Daniel Keyes. *Algernon, Charlie and I: A Writer's Journey* (Boca Raton, Fla.: Challcrest Press, 1999), 111.

15. Lessing's forays into science fiction include not only the well-known "Canopus in

Argos" series of philosophical novels (1979–1983), but substantial elements of other novels such as *The Four-Gated City* (1969), *The Fifth Child* (1988)—which is also viewed by some readers as a horror novel—*Memoirs of a Survivor* (1981), and *Mara and Dann* (1999). Piercy's best-known works in the field are *Woman on the Edge of Time* (1976) and *He, She, and It* (1991). Atwood's are *The Handmaid's Tale* (1985) and *Oryx and Crake* (2003). Theroux's most familiar title is *O-Zone* (1986), Updike's is *Toward the End of Time* (1997), James' is *The Children of Men* (1992), Winterson's is *The Stone Gods* (2007), and Roth's is *The Plot against America* (2004).

16. A similar device, considerably more understated, is employed in Neal Stephenson's ambitious historical trilogy "The Baroque Cycle," consisting of *Quicksilver* (2003), *The Confusion* (2004), and *The System of the World* (2004), and connected to Stephenson's earlier novel *Cryptonomicon* (1999). Although the trilogy is set in the seventeenth and eighteenth centuries and *Cryptonomicon* during World War II and in the 1990s, a mysterious and seemingly ageless character named Enoch Root shows up in all the novels, with fairly overt hints that he may be a time traveler and that the various histories he is involved in may be subject to manipulation.

17. Stephen Baxter, *Conqueror* (London: Gollancz, 2007), 55.

18. British novelists also have taken up the challenge of combining science fiction with the contemporary thriller, with comparably mixed results. Paul McAuley's *Whole Wide World* (2001), *White Devils* (2004), and *Mind's Eye* (2005) have explored different aspects of high-body-count thriller writing, while Ken Macleod's *The Execution Channel* and Charles Stross's *Halting State* (both 2007) might be counted as among the most impressive examples of using the combined science fiction/thriller mode to address contemporary political and social concerns. Meanwhile, other writers have chosen to combine the appropriation of the devices of historical fiction with those of the science-fictional thriller. Two of the more interesting recent forays into historical espionage fiction are Dan Simmons's *The Crook Factory* (1999), which concerns Hemingway's amateur spy ring in World War II Cuba, and Tim Powers' *Declare* (2000), which takes place between the Cold War years of 1948 and 1963 and features Kim Philby as a major character. Simmons, who has sought deliberately to bring his readership across genres, has written successful horror, fantasy, science fiction, and mainstream novels; *The Crook Factory*, with no fantastic elements, is his first serious foray into espionage, although he has written a series of hardboiled novels featuring a private eye named Joe Kurtz. Powers, a fantasist specializing in "secret history" narratives, seems a bit more subversive in *Declare*, which clearly draws its inspiration from John Le Carré during its first half, but then transforms itself into a spectacle filled with supernatural occurrences and fallen angels.

19. Charles Fort (1874–1932) was an American journalist who specialized in popular compilations of mysterious or inexplicable phenomena, which he consistently employed to tweak scientists and the scientific world view. The Fortean Society, founded in 1931,

included such luminaries as Ben Hecht, Theodore Dreiser, and Alexander Woollcott, but his most direct influence in fiction is to be found in the stories of Russell and other contributors to *Unknown* and to a lesser extent *Astounding Science Fiction*. Science fiction writer Damon Knight published a biography of Fort in 1970, and a magazine, *The Fortean Times*, continues to be published.

20. One of Dick's earliest novels, *Time Out of Joint* (1959), has been noted by several critics to bear resemblances to the film *The Truman Show*, in that both begin with characters unaware that their entire community is a sham constructed for their benefit, but Dick quickly moved on to more complex and sophisticated versions of alternate reality, including *The Man in the High Castle* (1962), in which a world where the Nazis won is shown to be a sham—but in which the real world is not our own; *The Three Stigmata of Palmer Eldritch* (1965) and *A Scanner Darkly* (1977), both of which explore the alternate realities of hallucinogenic drugs; *Ubik* (1969), which examines the notion of reality as perceived by a consciousness preserved in a machine; and *Do Androids Dream of Electric Sheep?* (1968), in which androids may be indistinguishable from humans even to themselves.

21. John Clute and John Grant, eds., *The Encyclopedia of Fantasy* (New York: St. Martin's Press, 1997), 801–802.

22. Two of the more insightful discussions of science fantasy as a subgenre may be found in Carl D. Malmgren's *Worlds Apart: Narratology of Science Fiction* (Bloomington: Indiana University Press, 1991) and Brian Attebery, *Strategies of Fantasy* (Bloomington: Indiana University Press, 1992).

23. Lethem's first novel, *Gun, with Occasional Music* (1994) freely mixed elements of fantasy, dystopia, surrealism, and the hardboiled detective novel, and his 1995 collection *The Wall of the Sky, the Wall of the Eye* is a veritable sampler of the free appropriation of multigenre materials. Carroll initially gained popularity among horror readers, although his complex first novel *The Land of Laughs* (1980) borrows at least as much from fantasy. More recent novels like *The Marriage of Sticks* (1999) and *The Wooden Sea* add elements of science fiction and the "village" novel. Auster's *New York Trilogy* (*City of Glass* [1985], *Ghosts* [1986], *The Locked Room* [1986]) ingeniously manipulated the conventions of the detective story to create metaphysical puzzles of identity with overtones of supernatural and horror fiction. Di Filippo's *The Steampunk Trilogy* (1995) is a collection of three tales that draw freely on conventions of fantasy, science fiction, and horror ("steampunk" is a term sometimes used to refer to alternate-world SF based on or in nineteenth-century science, but this is only marginally the case with Di Filippo's tales, one of which, for example, imagines a fantasy-world love affair between Walt Whitman and Emily Dickinson). Stepan Chapman's *The Troika* (1998) begins as a surrealistic fable set in an apparent dreamscape, but increasingly invokes genre tropes to destabilize our initial impression by offering hints of both more traditional science fiction and fantasy. Elizabeth Hand began her career with two science fiction novels, but in the loosely

connected narratives of *Waking the Moon* (1995), *Black Light* (1999), and the title story of the collection *Last Summer at Mars Hill* (1998), she draws upon conventions of fantasy, horror, and the more limited subgenre of occult fiction.

24. "The enormous pressure to become a reliable cash cow has resulted in a big portion of bookstore shelf space being taken up by franchise work, reinforcing wish-fulfillment fantasies of people in search of an entertaining escape from reality," wrote Kim Stanley Robinson in a symposium of comments in *Nebula Awards 33: The Year's Best SF and Fantasy Chosen by the Science-fiction and Fantasy Writers of America*, ed. Connie Willis (New York: Harcourt Brace, 1999), 255. The annual Nebula Awards anthologies often included such "symposia" in which various writers and editors comment upon the state of the field, and Robinson's comment expresses succinctly one of the most persistently recurring themes in these annual assessments. See also the rather gloomy prognostications in *Nebula Awards 30*, ed. Pamela Sargent (New York: Harcourt Brace, 1996) and in *Nebula Awards Showcase 2000*, ed. Gregory Benford (New York: Harcourt Brace, 2000).

25. As an example, the science fiction newsmagazine *Locus* compiles an annual list of recommended books in each of several categories—novels, collections, anthologies, and the like. In the category of single-author story collections (not including British or Australian publications), the recommended list for the year 2000 included twenty-three titles, only seven of which—30.4 percent—were published by large commercial publishers. The same list for the year 1990 yielded eighteen titles, eleven—or 61.1 percent—published by commercial presses. By 2007, the list included seventeen titles, only one of which (5.8 percent) came from such a publisher.

Chapter 3. Tales of Stasis and Chaos (pages 54–67)

1. Greg Bear, *Foundation and Chaos* (New York: HarperPrism, 1998), 172.

2. David E. Kaplan and Andrew Marshall, *The Cult at the End of the World* (New York: Crown, 1996), 31.

3. See Charles Elkins, "Isaac Asimov's 'Foundation' Novels: Historical Materialism Distorted into Cyclical Psycho-History," *Science-Fiction Studies* 3 (1976): 23–36.

4. Henry Adams, *The Education of Henry Adams: An Autobiography* (New York: Houghton Mifflin, 1961), 381–82. Privately printed in 1905; originally published in 1918.

5. Note, for example, how frequently fantasy novels employ the motif of differing time-scales between the primary and secondary worlds; although only days or weeks may pass between the protagonist's visits to the fantasy world, centuries may have passed *within* that world. Examples include George MacDonald's *Lilith* (1895), C. S. Lewis's *Chronicles of Narnia* (1950–1956), and Donaldson's *Chronicles of Thomas Covenant the Unbeliever* (1977–1983). Although vast changes may occur in the fantasy worlds during

these interregna, very little can be seen of what we would term social or industrial progress. The first grandmaster of science fiction pulp illustration, Frank R. Paul, was particularly enamored of giant-dynamo shapes. His interior illustration for John W. Campbell, Jr.'s "The Black Star Passes" in the Fall 1930 *Amazing Stories Quarterly* could almost be an exaggerated version of Adams' Hall of Dynamos, and some of his famous futuristic cityscapes, such as the "City of the Future" on the back cover of the April 1942 *Amazing Stories*, literally transform buildings into enormous capacitors and dynamos. The pattern of imagery has persisted into science fiction films; witness the giant Krell machines in the 1954 *Forbidden Planet* or the ancient subterranean Martian artifacts in 1990's *Total Recall.*

6. In a 1978 review in *Science-Fiction Studies,* Mullen argues that the "fantastic romance" is a supergenre that includes science fiction, fantasy, and horror ("Books in Review: Supernatural, Pseudonatural, and Sociocultural Fantasy," *Science-Fiction Studies* 16 [1978]: 291–98). Rabkin, in his earlier study *The Fantastic in Literature* (Princeton, N.J.: Princeton University Press, 1976), suggests that the "overlapping genres" of science fiction, utopian fiction, and satire could be thought of as a "super-genre" (147).

7. The objection could be raised here that the hardboiled tale actually predates the police procedural by some decades, and indeed the term "police procedural" seems to have been coined to refer largely to the submarket for crime fiction that emerged in the late 1940s and 1950s. But this is to take a rather narrow, American-centered view of the supergenre as a whole; by the 1920s, professional investigators acting as agents of society showed up in the work of authors such as Freeman Wills Crofts (whose detectives were Scotland Yard inspectors) or R. Austin Freeman (whose Dr. Thorndyke was a forensic scientist).

8. Raymond Chandler, "The Simple Art of Murder," in *The Art of the Mystery Story,* ed. Howard Haycraft (New York: Grosset and Dunlap, 1946), 237.

9. The story has been reported widely with Chandler himself as the source. It is recounted, among other places, in Pauline Kael's *5001 Nights at the Movies* (New York: Holt, Rinehart, and Winston, 1982), 54.

10. For a more detailed discussion of Patricia Anthony, see the essay "Evaporating Genre" earlier in this volume.

11. The most famous of the "parlor game" collections of alternate history scenarios is probably John Collings Squire's *If, Or History Rewritten* (1931), which included contributions from Winston Churchill, Hilaire Belloc, Andre Maurois, and G. K. Chesterton. In 1961, *Look* magazine commissioned long pieces from MacKinlay Kantor ("If the South Had Won the Civil War") and William L. Shirer ("If Hitler Had Won World War II")—both scenarios that had been treated in earlier works of science fiction. The contrast between the relatively mechanistic projections of the historians and the imaginative leaps of their science fiction counterparts is rather telling.

12. The Tim Powers' novels mentioned are, in order, *The Stress of Her Regard* (1989;

Keats and Shelley), *The Drawing of the Dark* (1979; the Siege of Vienna), and *Last Call* (1992; Bugsy Siegel). Other authors such as Paul Di Filippo and Powers' friend James P. Blaylock have also written elaborate secret histories, which are not quite the same thing as "steampunk" fiction, which tends to imagine alternate versions of nineteenth-century technology. John Clute's term for hidden societies within the interstices of the historical world is "wainscots" (*The Encyclopedia of Fantasy* [New York: St. Martin's, 1994], 991).

13. One of the earliest tales of uploading a personality into a computer, written when few people had any direct experience with computers at all, was Frederik Pohl's "The Schematic Man," published in *Playboy* in 1969. Significantly (and completely irrationally), the narrator finds his memories and skills in the "real" world—that is, historical reality—disappearing as he replicates them in his computer program.

14. In an article, "What Do They Mean, SF?" in *SFWA Bulletin* 75 (1981: 20–25), Wolfe described the setting of his *Book of the New Sun* series as "posthistorical." The term has, of course, become commonplace among postmodern theorists and art critics such as A. C. Danto, and a German-language variation of it, *Nachgeschichte*, provides the basis of some interesting observations by Czech philosopher Vilém Flusser, who argued that multimedia technology such as computers—and literature such as science fiction—represent modes of posthistorical thought.

15. Mircea Eliade, *Myth and Reality*, trans. Willard R. Trask (New York: Harper, 1968), 76.

16. J. G. Ballard, "Cataclysms and Dooms," in *The Visual Encyclopedia of Science Fiction*, ed. Brian Ash (New York: Harmony, 1977), 130. For a further discussion of this tradition, see "The Remaking of Zero" elsewhere in this volume.

17. Adams, *Education of Henry Adams*, 406.

Chapter 4. The Encounter with Fantasy (pages 68–82)

1. S. C. Fredericks, "Problems of Fantasy," *Science-Fiction Studies* 5 (March 1978): 37.

2. W. R. Irwin, *The Game of the Impossible: A Rhetoric of Fantasy* (Urbana: University of Illinois Press, 1976), 4.

3. Eric S. Rabkin, *The Fantastic in Literature* (Princeton, N.J.: Princeton University Press, 1976), 14–15, 227.

4. C. N. Manlove, *Modern Fantasy: Five Studies* (Cambridge: Cambridge University Press, 1975), 3.

5. Roger C. Schlobin, *The Literature of Fantasy: A Comprehensive, Annotated Bibliography of Modern Fantasy Fiction* (New York: Garland, 1979), xxvi.

6. Ray Bradbury, "Introduction," in *The Circus of Dr. Lao and Other Improbable Stories* (New York: Bantam, 1956), vii–viii.

7. C. S. Lewis, *An Experiment in Criticism* (Cambridge: Cambridge University Press, 1965), 50.

8. H. Rider Haggard and Andrew Lang, *The World's Desire* (London: Longmans, Green, and Co., 1890), 2.

9. Samuel R. Delany, *The Jewel-Hinged Jaw: Notes on the Language of Science Fiction* (New York: Berkley, 1977), 32.

10. Joanne Greenberg, (writing under the pseudonym Hannah Greene), *I Never Promised You a Rose Garden* (New York: New American Library, 1964), 11.

11. Fredericks, "Problems of Fantasy," 37.

12. Manlove, *Modern Fantasy*, 3.

13. Darko Suvin, *Metamorphoses of Science Fiction: On the Poetics and History; of a Literary Genre* (New Haven, Conn.: Yale University Press, 1979), 7–9.

14. Gaston Bachelard, *The Poetics of Reverie*, trans. Daniel Russell (New York: Orion Press, 1969), 177.

15. Ibid., 13.

16. Peter L. Berger and Thomas Luckmann, *The Social Construction of Reality* (Garden City, N.Y.: Doubleday Anchor, 1967), 25.

17. Tzvetan Todorov, *The Fantastic: A Structural Approach to a Literary Genre*, trans. Richard Howard (Ithaca, N.Y.: Cornell University Press, 1975), 25.

18. Bachelard, *Poetics of Reverie*, 14.

19. Ernest Schachtel, *Metamorphosis: On the Development of Affect, Perception, Attention, and Memory* (New York: Basic Books, 1959), 171.

20. Roger Zelazny, *Nine Princes in Amber* (New York: Avon, 1972), 11.

21. Manlove, *Modern Fantasy*, 11.

22. George MacDonald, "The Fantastic Imagination," in *Gifts of the Child Christ: Fairy Tales and Stories for the Childlike*, ed. Glenn Edward Sadler (1893; reprint, Grand Rapids, Mich.: Eerdmans, 1973), 22.

23. J. R. R. Tolkien, "On Fairy-Stories," in *The Tolkien Reader* (New York: Ballantine, 1966), 37–38.

24. David Lindsay, *Devil's Tor* (London: G.P. Putnam's Sons, 1932), 145.

25. Ibid.

26. George MacDonald, "The Imagination: Its Functions and Culture," in *The Imagination and Other Essays* (Boston: Lothrop, 1883), 9.

27. C. S. Lewis, *The Allegory of Love* (New York: Oxford University Press, 1958), 45.

28. Brian Attebery, *Strategies of Fantasy* (Bloomington: Indiana University Press, 1992), 14–15.

29. John Clute and John Grant, eds., *The Encyclopedia of Fantasy* (New York: St. Martin's Press, 1997), 338.

30. Ibid., 338–39.

31. Farah Mendlesohn, *Rhetorics of Fantasy* (Middletown, Conn.: Wesleyan University Press, 2008), xviii.

Chapter 5. The Artifact as Icon in Science Fiction (pages 83–98)

1. Henry Glassie, "Artifacts: Folk, Popular, Imaginary, and Real," in *Icons of Popular Culture*, ed. Marshall Fishwick and Ray B. Browne (Bowling Green, Ohio: Bowling Green University Popular Press, 1970), 113.

2. Arthur Machen, *The Three Impostors* (1895; reprint, New York: Ballantine, 1972), 87.

3. Gary K. Wolfe, *The Known and the Unknown: The Iconography of Science Fiction* (Kent, Ohio: Kent State University Press, 1979), 21–22.

4. Kenneth Bulmer, "Technologies and Artefacts," in *The Visual Encyclopedia of Science Fiction*, ed. Brian Ash (New York: Harmony Books, 1977), 154.

5. The most familiar example from Lem is *Solaris* (1961). Dick provides many examples of alternate or unstable realities, but his most famous treatment of the alternate history scenario as such is *The Man in the High Castle* (1962).

6. Algis Budrys, *Rogue Moon* (1960; reprint, New York: Avon, 1978), 106.

7. Ibid., 121–22.

8. Gregory Benford, *Artifact* (New York: Tor, 1985), 522. Numerous other examples of artifacts appear in Benford's fiction, many of which seem to explore self-consciously some of the various meanings discussed in this essay. The short story "Time Shards" (1979), for example, concerns a researcher who seeks to retrieve actual voices from the ancient past through grooves on pottery, which might have functioned inadvertently as recording devices. For further discussion of Benford novels in which artifacts play a major role, see the essays "Evaporating Genres" and "Frontiers in Space" elsewhere in this volume.

9. The Dyson sphere has become such a commonplace icon in science fiction that it has even been mentioned in TV shows such as *Star Trek: The Next Generation* (in an episode called "Relics"). Recent authors who have featured such artifacts include Jack Williamson and Frederik Pohl (*Farthest Star*, 1975; *Wall Around a Star*, 1983); Peter F. Hamilton (*Pandora's Star*, 2004; *Judas Unchained*, 2005); Alastair Reynolds (*House of Suns*, 2008); Neal Asher (*Polity Agent*, 2006); and John Scalzi (*Old Man's War*, 2006).

10. The novel also promptly won the Hugo, Nebula, and Jupiter Awards, and has since entered the canon of science fiction classics familiar even to casual readers. The manifold mysteries of Rama became increasingly less provocative in a series of sequels co-authored with Gentry Lee, however, which included *Rama II* (1989), *The Garden of Rama* (1991), *Rama Revealed* (1993), and two novels by Lee alone, *Bright Messengers* (1995) and *Double Full Moon Night* (1999).

11. Arthur C. Clarke, *Rendezvous with Rama* (New York: Ballantine, 1974), 150.

12. Budrys, *Rogue Moon*, 180.

13. Harlan Ellison, "Grail," in *Stalking the Nightmare* (Huntington Woods, Mich.: Phantasia Press, 1982), 54.

14. John Clute and Peter Nicholls, *The Encyclopedia of Science Fiction* (New York: St. Martin's, 1993), 118–19.

Chapter 6. The Remaking of Zero (pages 99–120)

1. Ray Bradbury, "The Highway," in *The Illustrated Man* (Garden City, N.Y.: Doubleday, 1951), 62.

2. The symbolic burning of artifacts of the old world is related to the Adamic mythology of the frontier that Bradbury explores throughout *The Martian Chronicles*, and thus it is not surprising that a likely source for this scene, in the story "The Million-Year Picnic," is Nathaniel Hawthorne's 1844 story "Earth's Holocaust," about an immense, apocalyptic bonfire meant to cleanse the Earth of "the weight of dead men's thought." Bradbury anthologized the Hawthorne story in his 1956 collection *The Circus of Dr. Lao and Other Improbable Stories.*

3. Mircea Eliade, *Myth and Reality*, trans. Willard R. Trask (New York: Harper, 1968), 76.

4. Ibid., 30.

5. J. G. Ballard, "Cataclysms and Dooms," in *The Visual Encyclopedia of Science Fiction*, ed. Brian Ash (New York: Harmony, 1977), 130.

6. George R. Stewart, *Earth Abides* (1949; reprint, New York: Ace, 1962), 122.

7. In her insightful study *Fantasy and Mimesis: Responses to Reality in Western Literature* (New York: Methuen, 1984), Kathryn Hume suggests that new imaginary worlds may be created through "augmentation" or through "subtraction and erasure." Much of the fiction of catastrophe that I am discussing here generally would meet Hume's notion of a "subtractive" world. Hume writes "Erasure, destruction of normal order through removal of some element which gives logical coherence, produces a profound challenge to our sense of reality" (92).

8. Eliade, *Myth and Reality*, 72.

9. Bruce Gillespie, "The Long Loud Silence," in *Survey of Science Fiction Literature*, vol. 3, ed. Frank Magill (Englewood Cliffs, N.J.: Salem Press, 1979), 1241.

10. M. P. Shiel, *The Purple Cloud* (New York: Paperback Library, 1963), 13.

11. Norman Cohn, *The Pursuit of the Millennium* (New York: Oxford University Press, 1957), 308.

12. John Bowen, *After the Rain* (New York: Ballantine, 1959), 124.

13. Alfred Coppel, *Dark December* (Greenwich, Conn.: Fawcett, 1960), 191.

14. Ibid., 197.

15. Ibid., 196.

16. Bowen, *After the Rain*, 75.

17. Stewart, *Earth Abides*, 82.

18. Ibid., 96.

19. Ibid., 159.

20. Ibid., 242.

21. Ibid., 288.

22. Willis McNelly, "Earth Abides," in *Survey of Science Fiction Literature*, vol. 2, ed. Frank Magill (Englewood Cliffs, N.J.: Salem Press, 1979), 690.

Chapter 7. Frontiers in Space (pages 121–38)

1. Judith Merril, ed., *Shot in the Dark* (New York: Bantam, 1950).

2. John Wyndham and Lucas Parkes, *The Outward Urge* (New York: Ballantine, 1959), cover copy. The Bleiler and Dikty anthology was published by Bantam Books, New York, 1955.

3. See, for example, David Mogen, *Wilderness Visions: Science Fiction Westerns* (San Bernardino, Calif.: Borgo, 1982); Carl Abbott, *Frontiers Past and Future* (Lawrence: University Press of Kansas, 2006); and the essays in *Space and Beyond: The Frontier Theme in Science Fiction*, ed Gary Westfahl (Westport, Conn.: Greenwood, 2000).

4. John Clute and Peter Nicholls, *The Encyclopedia of Science Fiction* (New York: St. Martin's, 1993), 1138.

5. Bernard De Voto, *Harper's Magazine* 179 (September 1939): 446.

6. Clute and Nicholls, *Encyclopedia*, 245. Geier's story, "Outlaw in the Sky," appeared in *Amazing Stories* in 1953.

7. James Gunn, *The Road to Science Fiction: From Gilgamesh to Wells* (New York: New American Library, 1977), 312–13.

8. The pioneering work remains H. Bruce Franklin, *Future Perfect: American Science Fiction of the Nineteenth Century* (New York: Oxford University Press, 1966; revised and expanded edition New Brunswick: Rutgers University Press, 1995).

9. See, for example, my essay "The Frontier Myth in Ray Bradbury," in *Ray Bradbury*, ed. Joseph D. Olander and Martin Harry Greenberg (New York: Taplinger, 1980), 33–54.

10. Ellis's story was reprinted over the next forty years under such variant titles as *Baldy's Boy Partner* and *Young Brainerd's Steam Man*.

11. Everett F. Bleiler, ed. *Eight Dime Novels* (New York: Dover, 1974), xiii.

12. H. Bruce Franklin, *Robert A. Heinlein: America as Science Fiction* (New York: Oxford University Press, 1980), n.p.: "As a boy, Heinlein was an avid reader of the Frank

Reade, Jr., and Tom Swift science fiction dime novels, and there are still copies of them in his library."

13. Bleiler, *Eight Dime Novels*, n.p.

14. Paul A. Carter, *The Creation of Tomorrow: Fifty Years of Magazine Science Fiction* (New York: Columbia University Press, 1977), 62.

15. Edgar Rice Burroughs, *A Princess of Mars* (1912; reprint, New York: Grosset and Dunlap, 1917), 20.

16. Henry Nash Smith, *Virgin Land: The American West as Symbol and Myth* (New York: Vintage, 1950), 97.

17. Donald A. Wollheim, *The Universe Makers: Science Fiction Today* (New York: Harper, 1971), 42–44.

18. Ibid., 42.

19. Patrick Parrinder, "Science Fiction as Truncated Epic," in *Bridges to Science Fiction*, ed. George E. Slusser, George R. Guffey, and Mark Rose (Carbondale: Southern Illinois University Press, 1980), 103.

20. Tom Godwin, "The Cold Equations," in *The Road to Science Fiction #3: From Heinlein to Here*, ed. James Gunn (New York: New American Library, 1979), 246. Originally published in *Astounding Science Fiction* (August 1954).

21. Ibid., 247, 250, 261.

22. This story has become so iconic, and yet is so manifestly flawed, that it has become something of a hobby among science fiction critics to debunk it. See, for example, Michael Underwood, "The Laws of the Space Frontier" online at http://www.strangehorizons.com/2005/20050131/space-frontier-a.shtml (accessed January 7, 2009); Richard Harter, "The Cold Equations: A Critical Study," online at http://home.tiac.net/cri_d/cri/1999/coldeq.html (accessed January 7, 2009); Brian Attebery, *Decoding Gender in Science Fiction* (New York: Routledge, 2002), 180–83; Andy Duncan, "Think Like a Humanist: James Patrick Kelly's 'Think Like a Dinosaur' as Rebuttal to Tom Godwin's 'The Cold Equations,'" *New York Review of Science Fiction* 94 (June 1996): 1, 8–11; Gary Westfahl, *The Cosmic Engineers: A Study of Hard Science Fiction* (Westport, Conn.: Greenwood, 1996), 74–77; John Huntington, "Hard-Core Science Fiction and the Illusion of Science," in *Hard Science Fiction*, ed. George Slusser and Eric S. Rabkin, eds., 45–57 (Carbondale: Southern Illinois University Press, 1986).

23. Godwin, "The Cold Equations," 258.

24. Ibid., 261.

24. For a further discussion of how major science fiction writers such as Heinlein and Asimov dealt with frontier themes, as well as how later satirists such as Frederik Pohl and C. M. Kornbluth viewed them, see Mogen, *Wilderness Visions*.

25. Gregory Benford, *Against Infinity* (New York: Pocket Books, 1983), 169.

26. Ibid., 190; italics in original.

27. Ibid., 213.

28. Ibid., 228.

29. Ibid., 230.

30. Ibid., 248.

31. Ibid., 244–45.

32. Ibid., 249.

Chapter 8. The Lives of Fantasists (pages 141–50)

1. Alfred Bester, "My Affair with Science Fiction," 47; Damon Knight, "Knight Piece," 102; "Magic and Bare Boards," 183–84, all in *Hell's Cartographers*, ed. Brian W. Aldiss and Harry Harrison (London: Orbit, 1976).

2. Jack Williamson, *Wonder's Child: My Life in Science Fiction* (New York: Bluejay, 1984), 46.

3. James Patrick Kelly, "Daemon," online at http://www.jimkelly.net/index.php ?option=com_content&task=view&id=29&Itemid=50.

4. Daniel Keyes, *Algernon, Charlie and I: A Writer's Journey* (Boca Raton, Fla.: Challcrest Press, 1999), 96.

5. A veritable industry of criticism and commentary has evolved on Dick, but the principal source for actual biographical material is Lawrence Sutin, *Divine Invasions: A Life of Philip K. Dick* (New York: Harmony, 1990).

6. Elizabeth Hand, *Bibliomancy* (Harrogate: PS Publishing, 2003), 289.

7. Ford's short fiction is collected in *The Fantasy Writer's Assistant and Other Stories* (Urbana, Ill.: Golden Gryphon Press, 2002); *The Empire of Ice Cream* (Urbana, Ill.: Golden Gryphon Press, 2006); and *The Drowned Life* (New York: Harper Perennial, 2008), the latter of which includes a brief but informative autobiographical essay.

8. Jeffrey Ford makes this claim in an introductory note for "The Honeyed Knot," in *The Year's Best Fantasy and Horror*, ed. Ellen Datlow and Terri Windling (New York: St. Martin's, 2002), 88.

9. Lessing's comments about *Memoirs of a Survivor* are reprinted in Mike Resnick and Joe Siclari, eds., *Worldcon Guest of Honor Speeches* (Deerfield, Ill.: ISFIC Press, 2006), 192.

Chapter 9. Peter Straub and the New Horror (pages 151–63)

1. It's uncertain when this observation first appeared in print, but it indirectly may have been one of us. In the introduction to his anthology *Foundations of Fear*, David Hartwell writes, "Critic Gary Wolfe's observation that 'horror is the only genre named

for its effect on the reader' should suggest that the normal usage of genre is somewhat suspect here" ([New York: Tor, 1992], 10).

2. Terry Heller, *The Delights of Terror: An Aesthetics of the Tale of Terror* (Urbana: University of Illinois Press, 1987), chapter 3. Online at http://www.public.coe.edu/ theller/essays/delights/contents.html (accessed April 22, 2008).

3. Horror Writers Association, "What is Horror Fiction?" Online at http://www .horror.org/horror-is.htm (accessed April 22, 2006).

4. A considerable body of literature has been written on Poe's "unity of effect" theory, further developed in his 1846 "The Philosophy of Composition" and other essays and fragments. A number of scholars have noted Poe's indebtedness to the German critic A. W. Schlegel's *Lectures on Dramatic Art and Literature* (1809–1811). Schlegel, in turn, was involved in discussions on the art of short fiction that included such other German Romantic writers as Ludwig Tieck, and which, by discussing principles of the *Märchen*, or art fairy tale, were among the most important early discussions on the emergent fantasy tradition. That later horror writers in turn were aware of Poe's notion of unity is evidenced in H. P. Lovecraft's *Supernatural Horror in Literature* (1927), which praises such tales as "Ligeia" and "The Fall of the House of Usher" in precisely these terms.

5. See Paula Guran, ed., *The Best New Paranormal Romance* (New York: Juno Books, 2006).

6. John Clute, *The Darkening Garden: A Short Lexicon of Horror* (Cauheegan, Wisc.: Payseur & Schmidt, 2006), 129, 141, 117, 17.

7. Peter Straub, "Horror's House," *Locus: The Magazine of the Science Fiction and Fantasy Field* 50, no. 4 (April 2003): 66.

8. John Clute, "Beyond the Pale," *Conjunctions: 39: The New Wave Fabulists* (2002): 425.

9. Bill Sheehan, *At the Foot of the Story Tree: An Inquiry into the Fiction of Peter Straub* (Burton, Mich.: Subterranean Press, 2000), 262. For a discussion of Straub's novel *Mr. X* and its relation to the horror genre, see the essay "Evaporating Genres" earlier in this book.

10. Peter Straub, "The Buffalo Hunter," in *Houses without Doors* (New York: Dutton, 1990), 163.

11. Sheehan, *At the Foot of the Story Tree*, 225.

12. Straub, "The Buffalo Hunter," 206.

13. Straub, "Author's Note," in *Houses without Doors*, 357.

14. In *Darkening Garden*, John Clute writes that *Heart of Darkness* "incorporates maybe the definitive—and certainly the best known—utterance of the nature of Horror in all literature, an ultimate gape of rage, a final saying of the world at the close" (88). He discusses the story at somewhat further length in his 2002 essay "Beyond the Pale" in *Conjunctions 39: The New Wave Fabulists*.

15. Peter Straub, *Koko* (New York: Dutton, 1988), 143.

16. Peter Straub, "The Juniper Tree," in *Houses without Doors*, 110.

17. Peter Straub, "The Path of Extremity" (interview), *Locus: The Newspaper of the Science Fiction Field* 32, no. 1 (January 1994): 4.

18. China Miéville, "Fabular Logic" (interview), *Locus: The Magazine of the Science Fiction and Fantasy Field* 57, no. 5 (November 2006): 73.

19. Edmund Burke, *A Philosophical Inquiry into the Origin of Our Ideas of the Sublime and Beautiful* (1757; reprint, Harvard Classics, 2001, vol. 24, part 2). Online at http://www.bartleby.com/24/2/ (accessed April 22, 2008).

Chapter 10. Twenty-First-Century Stories (pages 164–85)

1. All of these events and publications are listed on the Interstitial Arts Foundation's website at http://www.interstitialarts.org/wordpress/. The first Interstitial anthology, *Interfictions: An Anthology of Interstitial Writing*, edited by Delia Sherman and Theodora Goss, was published by the Foundation in 2007.

2. Michael Swanwick, "A User's Guide to the Postmoderns," in *Speculations on Speculation: Theories of Science Fiction*, ed. James Gunn and Matthew Candelaria (Lanham, Md.: Scarecrow, 2005), 314. The essay originally appeared in *Isaac Asimov's Science Fiction Magazine* 10, no. 8 (August 1986).

3. Bruce Sterling, "Catscan 5: Slipstream," *SF Eye #5* (July 1989); online at http://w2.eff.org/Misc/Publications/Bruce_Sterling/Catscan_columns/catscan.05; Jeff Prucher, *Brave New Words: The Oxford Dictionary of Science Fiction* (New York: Oxford University Press, 2007), 189.

4. James Patrick Kelly, "Slipstream," in *Speculations on Speculation: Theories of Science Fiction*, ed. James Gunn and Matthew Candelaria. Lanham, Md.: Scarecrow, 2005), 343, 351. Originally published in *Asimov's Science Fiction* (September 2003), online at http://www.asimovs.com/_issue_0312/onthenet.shtml.

5. James Patrick Kelly and John Kessel, eds., *Feeling Very Strange: The Slipstream Anthology* (San Francisco: Tachyon, 2006), xii–xiii.

6. Quoted in John Joseph Adams, "Award-winning authors James Patrick Kelly and John Kessel team up as editors to define a genre that . . . well . . . *isn't*" (interview), *SciFi.com*, June 12, 2006, at http://www.scifi.com/sfw/interviews/sfw12963.html (accessed June 21, 2008).

7. Ibid.

8. Christopher Priest, "*Ice* by Anna Kavan," *Vector* 253 (July–August 2007): 10.

9. Ibid., 11.

10. Interstial Arts Foundation website, http://www.interstitialarts.org/wordpress/.

11. Kelly and Kessel, *Feeling Very Strange*, xii.

12. Donald Barr, "A Talent for Irony," *New York Times*, April 17, 1949. Online at http://

select.nytimes.com/mem/archive/pdf?res=FB0B11F83D5F177B93C5A8178FD85F4D848 5F9 (accessed June 28, 2008).

13. Stephany Aulenback, "Stephany Aulenback interviews Kelly Link," *Maud Newton*, August 17, 2005. Online at http://maudnewton.com/blog/?p=5492 (accessed June 28, 2008).

14. Kelly Link, one of the authors discussed here, published her first collection of stories for young adults, *Pretty Monsters*, in 2008; Elizabeth Hand has completed her first young adult novel (*Wonderwall*), but it was not yet published as of this writing; and both Link and Jeffrey Ford contributed stories to Jonathan Strahan's young adult science fiction anthology *The Starry Rift* (Viking, 2008).

15. M. Rickert, "Map of Dreams," in *Map of Dreams* (Urbana, Ill.: Golden Gryphon, 2006).

16. See "The Lives of Fantasists" earlier in this volume for a brief discussion of autobiographical elements in Ford's fiction.

17. Theodora Goss, *In the Forest of Forgetting* (Holicong, Penn.: Prime Books, 2006), 106.

18. Even though Cheever has become something of a poster child for the sort of quotidian, suburban tale associated with *New Yorker*–style domestic realism in the 1950s, it's worth noting that in his early career he published stories either with overt fantastic elements ("The Enormous Radio," 1947) or stories strongly suggestive of horror ("Torch Song," 1947), which might well be regarded as among the precursors in the modern short story of the sort of fiction we are discussing here.

19. Elizabeth Hand, "Wonderwall," in *Saffron and Brimstone: Strange Stories* (Milwaukie, Ore.: M Press, 2006), 175.

20. Samuel R. Delany, "About 5,750 Words," in *The Jewel-Hinged Jaw: Notes on the Language of Science Fiction* (New York: Berkley, 1977), 31–32.

21. Aulenbeck, "Stephany Aulenback interviews Kelly Link."

22. Kelly Link, *Magic for Beginners* (Northampton, Mass.: Small Beer Press, 2005), 150.

23. Theodora Goss, "The Rose in Twelve Petals," in *In the Forest of Forgetting* (Holicong, Penn.: Prime Books, 2006), 26.

24. M. Rickert, "Journey into the Kingdom," in *The Best Science Fiction and Fantasy of the Year #1*, ed. Jonathan Strahan (San Francisco: Night Shade, 2007), 312.

25. Ibid., 319.

26. M. Rickert, "Cold Fires," in *Map of Dreams* (Urbana, Ill.: Golden Gryphon, 2006), 116.

27. Ibid., 119, 128.

28. Kelly Link, "The Wrong Grave," in *Pretty Monsters* (New York: Viking, 2008), 7.

29. Hand's essay originally appeared as one of her book review columns in *The Magazine of Science Fiction* (October/November 2002), which is still available on her website

http://www.elizabethhand.com/darger.shtml (accessed January 8, 2009). A somewhat expanded version, "Inside Out: On Henry Darger," was included in *The Year's Best Fantasy and Horror: Sixteenth Annual Collection*, ed. Ellen Datlow and Terri Windling, 447–53 (New York: St Martin's, 2003), one of the few essays ever included as a selection in this annual fiction anthology.

30. M. Rickert, "M. Rickert: The Right Shape" (interview), *Locus: The Magazine of the Science Fiction & Fantasy Field* 60, no. 1 (January 2008): 69.

31. Elizabeth Hand, "Elizabeth Hand: Ink-Stained Wretch" (interview), *Locus* 59, no. 6 (December 2007): 68.

32. Kelly Link, "Kelly Link: Making Strange Things Happen" (interview), *Locus* 49, no. 1 (July 2002): 75.

33. Ibid.

34. Link is not the first editor or writer to use the term "SF" in a pointedly ambiguous sense; Judith Merril began her annual "year's best" series in 1956 with a volume titled *SF: The Year's Greatest Science Fiction and Fantasy*, but by the fifth volume in 1960 the subtitle was dropped, and the book was titled simply *The 5th Annual of the Year's Best S-F*. The final volume in 1968 was simply titled *SF12*. In her editorial comments during these years, Merril hinted that the abbreviation might stand for science fiction, science fantasy, or speculative fiction.

35. Sterling, "Catscan 5: Slipstream."

36. In fact, considerable evidence suggests that stories bearing certain resemblances to these "slipstream" tales were fairly common in both the commercial and literary American short fiction markets in the 1940s, and examples can be found in the work not only of Shirley Jackson and John Collier, but of Robert M. Coates, Truman Capote, Jack Finney, and even such stalwarts of *The New Yorker* as E. B. White and John Cheever. Such stories grew increasingly rare in the 1950s, but began to re-emerge in the 1960s in the work of writers such as Donald Barthelme and Robert Coover.

37. China Miéville, "Fabular Logic" (interview), *Locus: The Magazine of the Science Fiction and Fantasy Field* 57, no. 5 (November 2006): 74.

38. Letter to George and Tom Keats, 21 or 27 December 1817, in *Selected Letters*, ed. Robert Gittings, rev. Jon Mee (Oxford: Oxford University Press, 2002), 41–42.

Chapter 11. Pilgrims of the Fall (pages 189–213)

1. Founded in 1959, First Fandom initially restricted its membership to those fans who had been demonstrably active by 1938, and later to anyone who could demonstrate fan activity prior to the first World Science Fiction Convention (Worldcon) in July of 1939 (a category of membership now called "Dinosaurs"). Currently, Associate Member-

ship is available to anyone demonstrating fan activity for at least thirty years. Their website is http://www.firstfandom.org.

2. Ron Ellik and Bill Evans, *The Universes of E. E. Smith* (Chicago: Advent, 1966). Not surprisingly, given the devotion and meticulousness of many fans and collectors, a fair amount of fan scholarship has been devoted to indexes, checklists, and concordances such as this; another example is Anthony R. Lewis, *Concordance to Cordwainer Smith*, third rev. ed. (Framingham, Mass.: NESFA Press, 2000). A concordance of Robert A. Heinlein's work is maintained by the Heinlein Society at http://www.heinleinsociety .org/concordance/index.htm (accessed January 8, 2009), and one of Larry Niven's "Known Space" series can be found at http://www.freewebs.com/knownspace/index .htm (accessed January 8, 2009). Other concordances cover the *Dark Tower* series of Stephen King, as well as authors such as Lois McMaster Bujold, Marion Zimmer Bradley, and Robert Sawyer, and, of course, *Star Trek*.

3. J. R. R. Tolkien, "On Fairy-Stories," in *The Tolkien Reader* (New York: Ballantine, 1966), 26.

4. "The idea of consolatory fantasy makes me want to puke," Miéville rather bluntly asserts. "I think that fantasy is about the *rejection* of consolation, and the high point of fantasy is the Surrealists . . . that is, using the fantastic aesthetic to do the *opposite* of consolation." "China Miéville: Messing with Fantasy," *Locus: The Newspaper of the Science Fiction Field* 48, no. 3 (March 2002): 5.

5. The DeVoto essay was titled "Doom beyond Jupiter" (*Harper's Magazine* 179 [September 1939]: 445–48). A somewhat more sympathetic treatment of the genre by Clemence Dane, "American Fairy Tales" (*North American Review* 242 [September 1936]) generally was overlooked. Hamling's editorial appeared in *Imagination: Stories of Science and Fantasy* 4, no. 4 (May 1953), and was largely an anticommunist diatribe that attempted to argue that, since science fiction was written for entertainment and money, it was somehow proof of the advantages of American freedom and capitalism over the more repressive Soviet system.

6. Kingsley Amis, *New Maps of Hell* (New York: Ballantine, 1960), 102.

7. James Blish [William Atheling, Jr., pseud.], *The Issue at Hand* (Chicago: Advent, 1964), and *More Issues at Hand* (Chicago: Advent, 1970); Damon Knight, *In Search of Wonder* (Chicago: Advent, 1967).

8. Algis Budrys's reviews in *Galaxy* were collected in *Benchmarks: Galaxy Bookshelf*, 1985); the essay "Paradise Charted" appeared in the academic journal *Triquarterly* 49 (Fall 1980): 5–75.

9. Joanna Russ, *The Country You Have Never Seen: Essays and Reviews* (Chicago: University of Chicago Press, 2007).

10. Algis Budrys's critique appeared in his column "Books," in *The Magazine of Fantasy and Science Fiction* 64, no. 1 (January 1983): 19. Budrys was reviewing George

Slusser, Eric S. Rabkin, and Robert Scholes' *Bridges to Fantasy* (Carbondale: Southern Illinois University Press 1982). Rabkin's response to the review appeared in *Fantasy Newsletter* no. 60 (June/July 1953). The earlier attacks on academia include Lloyd Biggle, Jr., "Science Fiction Goes to College: Groves and Morasses of Academe," *Riverside Quarterly* 6 (April 1974); 100–101, and "The Morasses of Academe Revisited," *Analog* 98 (September 1978): 146–63; William Tenn, "Jazz Then, Musicology Now," *The Magazine of Fantasy and Science Fiction* (May 1972): 107–10; Ben Bova, "Teaching Science Fiction," *Analog* 93 June 1974): 5–8; and Lester del Rey, "The Siren Song of' Academe," *Galaxy* (March 1975): 69–80, reprinted in *Antaeus* 25/26 (Spring/Summer 1977).

11. Budrys, "Books," 19.

12. Rob Latham, "Review Essay: Snobbery, Seasoned with Bile, Clute Is," *Journal of the Fantastic in the Arts* 1, no. 2 (1988): 91.

13. Latham's review of Clute and Peter Nicholls's *The Encyclopedia of Science Fiction* appeared in *The Journal of the Fantastic in the Arts* 6, no. 4 (1995), and the same journal published his review of Clute and John Grant's *The Encyclopedia of Fantasy* (9, no. 1, 1998). His later essay on Clute, in Farah Mendlesohn's *Polder: A Festschrift for John Clute and Judith Clute* (2006) was titled " 'The Job of Dissevering Joy from Glop': John Clute's *New Worlds* Criticism."

14. Farah Mendlesohn, ed., *Polder: A Festschrift for John Clute and Judith Clute* (Baltimore: Old Earth Books, 2006), 28.

15. John Clute, *Look at the Evidence: Essays and Reviews* (New York: Serconia Press, 1995), 6.

16. John Clute, "What I Did on My Summer Vacation," in *Scores: Reviews 1993–2003* (Essex: Beccon, 2003), 4.

17. Ibid., 5.

18. Clute, *Look at the Evidence*, 8.

19. John Clute, "Grail, Groundhog, Godgame: Or, Doing Fantasy," *Journal of the Fantastic in the Arts* 10, no. 4 (2000): 330–31.

20. Gary K. Wolfe, "Reviews by Gary K. Wolfe," *Locus: The Newspaper of the Science Fiction Field* 39, no. 2 (August 1997): 13.

21. "Book Reviews," *Interzone* 74 (August 1993): 62; John Clute and John Grant, eds., *The Encyclopedia of Fantasy* (New York: St. Martin's Press, 1997), 501.

22. "John Clute: The Passage of the Knot," *Locus: The Newspaper of the Science Fiction Field* 35, no. 1 (July 1995), 5, 69–70.

23. The term "cloaca" is defined in Clute's essay "Beyond the Pale," which appeared in 2002 in a special issue of the journal *Conjunctions* edited by Peter Straub, and again in *The Darkening Garden: A Short Lexicon of Horror*, published in 2006 and containing thirty short essays on terms largely of Clute's own concoction.

24. Clute and Grant, *Encyclopedia of Fantasy*, 424.

25. Clute, "Grail, Groundhog, Godgame," 331.

26. Clute and Grant, *Encyclopedia of Fantasy*, 899.

27. Clute, *Scores*, 58.

28. Ibid., 7.

29. While this essay offers a particular view of the development of science fiction and fantasy criticism, other useful perspectives can be found in a special issue of *Science Fiction Studies* 26, no. 2 (July 1999), especially in the essays by Gary Westfahl ("The Popular Tradition of Science Fiction Criticism, 1926–1980"), Donald M. Hassler ("The Academic Pioneers of Science Fiction Criticism, 1940–1980"), and Veronica Hollinger ("Contemporary Trends in Science Fiction Criticism, 1980–1999"). The issue is available at http://www.depauw.edu/SFs/covers/cov78.html (accessed January 8, 2009).

Works Cited

Nonfiction

Abbott, Carl. *Frontiers Past and Future*. Lawrence: University Press of Kansas, 2006.

Adams, Henry. *The Education of Henry Adams: An Autobiography*. New York: Houghton Mifflin, 1961. Originally published in 1918, privately printed in 1905.

Adams, John Joseph. "Award-winning authors James Patrick Kelly and John Kessel team up as editors to define a genre that . . . well . . . *isn't*." Interview. *SciFi.com*, June 12, 2006. Online at http://www.scifi.com/sfw/interviews/sfw12963.html (accessed June 21, 2008).

——. *Wastelands: Stories of Life after Apocalypse*. San Francisco: Night Shade Books, 2008.

Aldiss, Brian W. *Billion Year Spree: The True History of Science Fiction*. Garden City, N.Y.: Doubleday, 1973. Expanded and revised edition as *Trillion Year Spree: The History of Science Fiction*, with David Wingrove. New York: Atheneum, 1986.

——. *The Twinkling of an Eye*. New York: St. Martin's, 1998.

Aldiss, Brian W., and Harry Harrison, eds. *Hell's Cartographers*. London: Orbit, 1976.

Amis, Kingsley. *New Maps of Hell*. New York: Ballantine, 1960.

Anonymous. *The Science Fiction Novel: Imagination and Social Criticism*. Introduction by Basil Davenport. Chicago: Advent, 1959.

Anthony, Piers. *Bio of an Ogre*. New York: Ace, 1988.

Asimov, Isaac. *I. Asimov*. Garden City, N.Y.: Doubleday, 1994.

——. *In Joy Still Felt*. Garden City, N.Y.: Doubleday, 1980.

——. *In Memory Yet Green*. Garden City, N.Y.: Doubleday, 1979.

Attebery, Brian. *Decoding Gender in Science Fiction*. New York: Routledge, 2002.

——. *Strategies of Fantasy*. Bloomington: Indiana University Press, 1992.

Aulenback, Stephany. "Stephany Aulenback interviews Kelly Link." *Maud Newton*, August 17, 2005. Online at http://maudnewton.com/blog/?p=5492 (accessed June 28, 2008).

Bachelard, Gaston. *The Poetics of Reverie*. Trans. Daniel Russell. New York: Orion Press, 1969.

Bailey, J. O. *Pilgrims through Space and Time: Trends and Patterns in Scientific and Utopian Fiction.* 1947; reprint, Westport, Conn.: Greenwood Press, 1972.

Ballard, J. G. "Cataclysms and Dooms." In *The Visual Encyclopedia of Science Fiction*, ed. Brian Ash, 130. New York: Harmony, 1977.

Barr, Donald. "A Talent for Irony." *New York Times*, April 17, 1949. Online at http://select.nytimes.com/mem/archive/pdf?res=FB0B11F83D5F177B93C5A8178FD85F4D8 485F9 (accessed June 28, 2008).

Berger, Peter L., and Thomas Luckmann. *The Social Construction of Reality.* Garden City, N.Y.: Doubleday Anchor, 1967.

Birkerts, Sven. "Present at the Re-Creation." Review of Margaret Atwood's *Oryx and Crake. New York Times Book Review*, May 18, 2003.

Blake, William. "A Vision of the Last Judgment," in *The Complete Poetry of William Blake*, ed. David V. Erdman, 554–65. Berkeley: University of California Press, 1982.

Bleiler, Everett F., ed. *The Checklist of Fantastic Literature.* Chicago: Shasta, 1948.

Bleiler, Everett F., and T. E. Dikty. *Frontiers in Space.* New York: Bantam, 1955.

Blish, James [William Atheling, Jr., pseud.]. *The Issue at Hand.* Chicago: Advent, 1964.

——. *More Issues at Hand.* Chicago: Advent, 1970.

Bloch, Robert. *Once around the Bloch.* New York: Tor, 1993.

Bloom, Harold, ed. *Bloom's Classical Critical Views: Jane Austen.* New York: Chelsea House, 2007.

Bradbury, Ray. "Introduction." In *The Circus of Dr. Lao and Other Improbable Stories,* ed. Ray Bradbury. New York: Bantam, 1956.

Bretnor, Reginald, ed. *The Craft of Science Fiction.* New York: Harper & Row, 1976.

——, ed. *Modern Science Fiction: Its Meaning and Its Future.* New York: Coward Mc-Cann, 1953.

——, ed. *Science Fiction: Today and Tomorrow.* New York: Harper & Row, 1974.

Brigg, Peter. *The Span of Mainstream and Science Fiction: A Critical Study of a New Literary Genre.* Jefferson, N.C.: McFarland, 2002.

Broderick, Damien. *Transrealist Fiction: Writing in the Slipstream of Science.* Westport, Conn.: Greenwood, 2000.

Budrys, Algis. *Benchmarks: Galaxy Bookshelf.* (Carbondale: Southern Illinois University Press, 1985.

——. "Books." *The Magazine of Fantasy and Science Fiction* 64, no. 1 (January 1983), 19.

——. "Paradise Charted." *Triquarterly* 49 (Fall 1980): 5–75.

Bulmer, Kenneth. "Technologies and Artefacts." In *The Visual Encyclopedia of Science Fiction*, ed. Brian Ash, 154. New York: Harmony Books, 1977.

Burke, Edmund. *A Philosophical Inquiry into the Origin of Our Ideas of the Sublime and Beautiful.* (1757; reprint, Harvard Classics, vol. 24, part 2. Bartleby.com, 2001. http://www.bartleby.com/24/2/ (accessed April 22, 2008).

Carter, Paul A. *The Creation of Tomorrow: Fifty Years of Magazine Science Fiction.* New York: Columbia University Press, 1977.

Cawelti, John G. *Adventure, Mystery, and Romance: Formula Stories as Art and Popular Culture.* Chicago: University of Chicago Press, 1976.

Chesterton, G. K. "The Ethics of Elfland." In *Orthodoxy.* London: John Lane, 1908. Online at http://www.gutenberg.org/files/130/130.txt.

Chandler, Raymond. "The Simple Art of Murder." In *The Art of the Mystery Story*, ed. Howard Haycraft. New York: Grosset and Dunlap, 1946.

Clute, John. "Beyond the Pale." *Conjunctions: 39: The New Wave Fabulists* (2002): 420–33.

——. *The Darkening Garden: A Short Lexicon of Horror.* Cauheegan, Wisc.: Payseur & Schmidt, 2006.

——. "Fantastika in the World Storm: A Talk." 2007. http://www.johnclute.co.uk/word/.

——. "Grail, Groundhog, Godgame: Or, Doing Fantasy." *Journal of the Fantastic in the Arts* 10, no. 4 (2000): 330–37.

——. "John Clute: The Passage of the Knot." *Locus: The Newspaper of the Science Fiction Field* 35, no. 1 (July 1995): 5, 69–70.

——. *Look at the Evidence: Essays and Reviews.* New York: Serconia Press, 1995.

——. *Scores: Reviews 1993–2003.* Essex: Beccon, 2003.

——. *Strokes: Essays and Reviews, 1966–1986.* New York: Serconia Press, 1988.

Clute, John, and John Grant, eds. *The Encyclopedia of Fantasy.* New York: St. Martin's Press, 1997.

Clute, John, and Peter Nicholls. *The Encyclopedia of Science Fiction.* New York: St. Martin's Press, 1993.

Cohn, Norman. *The Pursuit of the Millennium.* New York: Oxford University Press, 1957.

Coleridge, Samuel Taylor. *Biographia Literaria.* 1817. Project Gutenberg, online at http://www.gutenberg.org/etext/6081 (accessed May 6, 2008).

Conrad, Joseph. "Preface." In *The Nigger of the Narcissus.* London: Heinemann, 1898. Project Gutenberg http://www.gutenberg.org/files/17731/17731-h/17731-h.htm#2H _PREF (accessed May 6, 2008).

Dane, Clemence. "American Fairy Tales." *North American Review* 242 (September 1936): 143–52.

Davenport, Basil. *Inquiry into Science Fiction.* New York: Longmans, Green, 1955.

Davis, Kenneth C. *Two-Bit Culture: The Paperbacking of America.* Boston: Houghton Mifflin, 1984.

de Camp, L. Sprague. *Science Fiction Handbook.* New York: Hermitage House, 1953.

Delany, Samuel R. *The Jewel-Hinged Jaw: Notes on the Language of Science Fiction.* New York: Berkley, 1977.

De Voto, Bernard Augustine. "Doom beyond Jupiter." *Harper's Magazine* 179 (September 1939): 445–48.

Duncan, Andy. "Think Like a Humanist: James Patrick Kelly's 'Think Like a Dinosaur' as Rebuttal to Tom Godwin's 'The Cold Equations.'" *New York Review of Science Fiction* 94 (June 1996): 1, 8–11.

Eliade, Mircea. *Myth and Reality*. Translated by Willard R. Trask. New York: Harper, 1968.

Elkins, Charles. "Isaac Asimov's 'Foundation' Novels: Historical Materialism Distorted into Cyclical Psycho-History." *Science-Fiction Studies* 3 (1976): 23–36.

Ellik, Ron, and Bill Evans. *The Universes of E. E. Smith*. Chicago: Advent, 1966.

Eshbach, Lloyd Arthur, ed. *Of Worlds Beyond: The Science of Science Fiction Writing*. Reading, Penn.: Fantasy Press, 1947; reprint, Chicago: Advent, 1964; London: Dennis Dobson, 1965.

Ford, Jeffrey. "Kelly Link's 'Lull.'" *Fantastic Metropolis*, January 2005. Online at http://www.fantasticmetropolis.com/i/va-link/2 (accessed January 8, 2009).

Forster, E. M. "Fantasy." In *Aspects of the Novel*. 1927; reprint, New York: Harvest, 1956.

Franklin, H. Bruce. *Future Perfect: American Science Fiction of the Nineteenth Century*. New York: Oxford University Press, 1966; revised and expanded edition, New Brunswick: Rutgers University Press, 1995.

———. *Robert A. Heinlein: America as Science Fiction*. New York: Oxford University Press, 1980.

Fredericks, S. C. "Problems of Fantasy." *Science-Fiction Studies* 5 (March 1978): 37.

Freud, Sigmund. *The Interpretation of Dreams*. 1900. Trans. A. A. Brill. New York: Random House, 1994.

Furst, Lilian R. *Romanticism in Perspective*. New York: Humanities Press, 1970.

Gerson, Villiers. "Spacemen's Realm." *New York Times*, January 13, 1952. Online at http://select.nytimes.com/gst/abstract.html?res=F30613FD395E107A93C1A8178AD85F468585F9&scp=203&sq=%22science+fiction&st=p. 22 (accessed April 22, 2008).

Gillespie, Bruce. "The Long Loud Silence." In *Survey of Science Fiction Literature*. Vol. 3, ed. Frank Magill. Englewood Cliffs: Salem, 1979.

Glassie, Henry. "Artifacts: Folk, Popular, Imaginary, and Real." In *Icons of Popular Culture*, ed. Marshall Fishwick and Ray B. Brown. Bowling Green, Ohio: Bowling Green University Popular Press, 1970.

Greenberg, Martin H., ed. *Fantastic Lives: Autobiographical Essays by Notable Science Fiction Writers*. Carbondale: Southern Illinois University Press, 1981.

Haight, Gordon S., ed. *Selections from George Eliot's Letters*. New Haven, Conn.: Yale University Press, 1985.

Hamling, William L. "The Editorial." *Imagination: Stories of Science and Fantasy* 4, no. 4 (May 1953).

Hand, Elizabeth. "Inside Out: On Henry Darger." In *The Year's Best Fantasy and Horror: Sixteenth Annual Collection*, ed. Ellen Datlow and Terri Windling, 447–53. New York: St. Martin's, 2003. Original version published as a book review in *The Magazine of*

Science Fiction (October/November 2002). Available online as "Darger and Tolkien," at http://www.elizabethhand.com/darger.shtml.

——. "Elizabeth Hand: Ink-Stained Wretch" (interview). *Locus* 59, no. 6 (December 2007): 7, 68.

Harter, Richard. "The Cold Equations: A Critical Study." Online at http:home.tiac.net/cri_d/cri/1999/coldeq.html (accessed January 7, 2009).

Heller, Terry. *The Delights of Terror: An Aesthetics of the Tale of Terror.* Urbana: University of Illinois Press, 1987. Online at http://www.public.coe.edu/theller/essays/delights/contents.html (accessed April 22, 2008).

Horror Writers Association. "What is Horror Fiction?" Online at http://www.horror.org/horror-is.htm (accessed April 22, 2006).

Hume, Kathryn. *Fantasy and Mimesis: Responses to Reality in Western Literature.* New York: Methuen, 1984.

Huntington, John. "Hard-Core Science Fiction and the Illusion of Science." In *Hard Science Fiction*, ed. George Slusser and Eric S. Rabkin, 45–57. Carbondale: Southern Illinois University Press, 1986.

Irwin, W. R. *The Game of the Impossible: A Rhetoric of Fantasy.* Urbana: University of Illinois Press, 1976.

Jackson, Rosemary. *Fantasy: The Literature of Subversion.* New York: Methuen, 1981.

Kael, Pauline. *5001 Nights at the Movies.* New York: Holt, Rinehart, and Winston, 1982.

Kaplan, David E., and Andrew Marshall. *The Cult at the End of the World.* New York: Crown, 1996.

Keats, John. Letter to George and Tom Keats, 21 or 27 December 1817, in *Selected Letters*, ed. Robert Gittings, rev. Jon Mee, 41–42. Oxford: Oxford University Press, 2002.

Kelly, James Patrick. "Daemon." Online at http://www.jimkelly.net/index.php?option=com_content&task=view&id=29&Itemid=50 (accessed July 5, 2008).

——. "Slipstream." In *Speculations on Speculation: Theories of Science Fiction*, ed. James Gunn and Matthew Candelaria. Lanham, Md.: Scarecrow, 2005. Originally published in *Asimov's Science Fiction* (September 2003), online at http://www.asimovs.com/_issue_0312/onthenet.shtml.

Keyes, Daniel. *Algernon, Charlie and I: A Writer's Journey.* Boca Raton, Fla.: Challcrest Press, 1999.

King, Stephen. *Danse Macabre.* New York: Berkley, 1982.

Knight, Damon. *In Search of Wonder.* Chicago: Advent, 1967.

Latham, Robert. "Review Essay: Snobbery, Seasoned with Bile, Clute Is." *Journal of the Fantastic in the Arts* 1, no. 2 (1988): 83–94.

——. "Latham Responds." *IAFA Newsletter* (Spring 1989): 25.

Le Guin, Ursula K. "The Child and the Shadow." In *The Language of the Night: Essays on Fantasy and Science Fiction.* New York: HarperCollins, 1989.

Lethem, Jonathan. "The Ecstasy of Influence: A Plagiarism." *Harper's Magazine*, February 2007, 59–71. Online at http://www.harpers.org/archive/2007/02/0081387 (accessed January 8, 2008).

Lewis, Anthony R. *Concordance to Cordwainer Smith*. Third rev. ed. Framingham, Mass.: NESFA Press, 2000.

Lewis, C. S. *The Allegory of Love*. New York: Oxford University Press, 1958.

——. *An Experiment in Criticism*. Cambridge: Cambridge University Press, 1965.

——, ed. *Essays Presented to Charles Williams*. Oxford: Oxford University Press, 1947.

Link, Kelly. "Kelly Link: Making Strange Things Happen" (interview). *Locus* 49, no. 1 (July 2002): 6–7, 72–73.

——. "Kelly Link: The Uses of Boredom" (interview). *Locus* 562 (November 2007): 75–76.

Lovecraft, H. P. *Supernatural Horror in Literature*. 1945; reprint, New York: Dover, 1973.

MacDonald, George. "The Fantastic Imagination." In *Gifts of the Child Christ: Fairy Tales and Stories for the Childlike,* ed. Glenn Edward Sadler. 1893; reprint, Grand Rapids, Mich.: Eerdmans, 1973.

——. "The Imagination: Its Functions and Culture." In *The Imagination and Other Essays*. Boston: Lothrop, 1883.

McNelly, Willis. "Earth Abides." In *Survey of Science Fiction Literature*, vol. 2., ed. Frank Magill. Englewood Cliffs, N.J.: Salem Press, 1979.

Magill, Frank N., ed. *Survey of Science Fiction Literature*. 5 vols. Englewood Cliffs, N.J.: Salem Press, 1979.

——, ed. *Survey of Modern Fantasy Literature*. 5 vols. Englewood Cliffs: Salem Press, 1983.

Maitzen, Rohan. " 'The Soul of Art': Understanding Victorian Ethical Criticism." *ESC: English Studies in Canada* 31, nos. 2–3 (June/September 2005). Available online at http://ejournals.library.ualberta.ca/index.php/ESC/article/viewFile/1335/894 (accessed January 2, 2009).

Malmgren, Carl. *Worlds Apart: Narratology of Science Fiction*. Bloomington: Indiana University Press, 1991.

Manlove, C. N. *Modern Fantasy: Five Studies*. Cambridge: Cambridge University Press, 1975.

Mendlesohn, Farah. *Rhetorics of Fantasy*. Middletown, Conn.: Wesleyan University Press, 2008.

——, ed. *Polder: A Festschrift for John Clute and Judith Clute*. Baltimore: Old Earth Books, 2006.

Miéville, China. "China Miéville: Messing with Fantasy." *Locus: The Newspaper of the Science Fiction Field* 48, no. 3 (March 2002): 5

——. "Fabular Logic" (interview). *Locus: The Magazine of the Science Fiction and Fantasy Field* 57, no. 5 (November 2006): 9, 73–74.

Mogen, David. *Wilderness Visions: Science Fiction Westerns*. San Bernardino, Calif.: Borgo, 1982.

Moskowitz, Sam. *Explorers of the Infinite.* New York: World, 1963.

——. *Seekers of Tomorrow.* New York: World, 1966.

Mullen, R. D. "Books in Review: Supernatural, Pseudonatural, and Sociocultural Fantasy." *Science-Fiction Studies* 16 (1978): 291–98.

Noy, Pinchas. "A Revision of the Psychoanalytic Theory of the Primary Process." *International Journal of Psycho-Analysis* 50 (1969): 155–78.

Parrinder, Patrick. "Science Fiction as Truncated Epic." In *Bridges to Science Fiction,* ed. George E. Slusser, George R. Guffey, and Mark Rose. Carbondale: Southern Illinois University Press, 1980.

Philmus, Robert M. *Into the Unknown: The Evolution of Science Fiction from Francis Godwin to H. G. Wells.* Berkeley: University of California Press, 1970.

Poe, Edgar Allan. "Hawthorne's Twice-Told Tales." Online at http://xroads.virginia.edu/HYPER/poe/hawthorne.html (accessed April 22, 2008).

Pohl, Frederik. *The Way the Future Was.* New York: Ballantine, 1978

Priest, Christopher. "*Ice* by Anna Kavan." *Vector* 253 (July–August 2007): 10–11.

"The Progress of Fiction as an Art." *Westminster Review* 60 o.s. 4 n.s., no. 2 (October 1853): 342–74.

Prucher, Jeff. *Brave New Words: The Oxford Dictionary of Science Fiction.* New York: Oxford University Press, 2007.

Rabkin, Eric S. *The Fantastic in Literature.* Princeton, N.J.: Princeton University Press, 1976.

Resnick, Mike, and Joe Siclari, eds. *Worldcon Guest of Honor Speeches.* Deerfield, Ill.: ISFIC Press, 2006.

Rickert, M. "M. Rickert: The Right Shape" (interview). *Locus: The Magazine of the Science Fiction & Fantasy Field* 60, no. 1 (January 2008): 69–70.

Rucker, Rudy. "Transrealist Manifesto." *Bulletin of the Science Fiction Writers of America* 82 (Winter 1983). Reprinted in Rucker's anthologies *Transreal!* Englewood, Colo.: WCS Books, 1991; and *Seek!* New York: Four Walls Eight Windows, 1999. Online at http://www.mathcs.sjsu.edu/faculty/rucker/transrealistmanifesto.pdf.

Russ, Joanna. *The Country You Have Never Seen: Essays and Reviews.* Liverpool: Liverpool University Press, 2007.

Schachtel, Ernest. *Metamorphosis: On the Development of Affect, Perception, Attention, and Memory.* New York: Basic Books, 1959.

Schlobin, Roger C. *The Literature of Fantasy: A Comprehensive, Annotated Bibliography of Modern Fantasy Fiction.* New York: Garland, 1979.

The Science Fiction Novel: Imagination and Social Criticism. Chicago: Advent, 1959.

Sheehan, Bill. *At the Foot of the Story Tree: An Inquiry into the Fiction of Peter Straub.* Burton, Mich.: Subterranean Press, 2000.

Slusser, George, Eric S. Rabkin, and Robert Scholes. *Bridges to Fantasy.* Carbondale: Southern Illinois University Press, 1982.

Smith, Henry Nash. *Virgin Land: The American West as Symbol and Myth*. New York: Vintage, 1950.

Stableford, Brian. "Pretending to be an Academic?" *IAFA Newsletter* (Spring 1989): 22.

———. *The Scientific Romance in England, 1890–1950*. London: Fourth Estate, 1985.

Sterling, Bruce. "Catscan 5: Slipstream." *SF Eye #5* (July 1989). Online at http://w2.eff.org/ Misc/Publications/Bruce_Sterling/Catscan_columns/catscan.05.

Straub, Emma. "Symposium on the Nature of Genre and Pleasure in the 21st Century." Online at http://www.davidjschow.com/essay/essay_symposium.html (accessed January 2, 2009).

Straub, Peter. "Fearful Places" (interview). *Locus: The Magazine of the Science Fiction and Fantasy Field* 57, no. 1 (July 2006): 7, 78–79.

———. "Horror's House." *Locus: The Magazine of the Science Fiction and Fantasy Field* 50, no. 4 (April 2003): 8, 66.

———. "The Path of Extremity" (interview). *Locus: The Newspaper of the Science Fiction Field* 32, no. 1 (January 1994): 4, 65.

Sutin, Lawrence. *Divine Invasions: A Life of Philip K. Dick*. New York: Harmony, 1990.

Suvin, Darko. *Metamorphoses of Science Fiction: On the Poetics and History of a Literary Genre*. New Haven, Conn.: Yale University Press, 1979.

Swanwick, Michael. "A User's Guide to the Postmoderns." In *Speculations on Speculation: Theories of Science Fiction*, ed. James Gunn and Matthew Candelaria. Lanham, Md.: Scarecrow, 2005.

Tiedemann, Mark W. "Hybrids." *The New York Review of Science Fiction* 12, no. 10 (June 2000): 15–17.

Todorov, Tzvetan. *The Fantastic: A Structural Approach to a Literary Genre,* trans. Richard Howard. Ithaca, N.Y.: Cornell University Press, 1975.

Tolkien, J. R. R. "On Fairy-Stories." In *The Tolkien Reader*. New York: Ballantine, 1966.

Underwood, Michael. "The Laws of the Space Frontier." Online at http://www.strange horizons.com/2005/20050131/space-fronter-aq.shtml (accessed January 7, 2009).

Westfahl, Gary. *This Cosmic Engineers: A Study of Hard Science Fiction*. Westport, Conn.: Greenwood, 1996.

———, ed. *Space and Beyond: The Frontier Theme in Science Fiction*. Westport, Conn.: Greenwood, 2000.

Williams, Linda. "Film Bodies: Gender, Genre, and Excess." In *Film Genre Reader 2*, ed. Barry Keith Grant, 142 (Austin: University of Texas Press, 1995).

Williamson, Jack. *Wonder's Child: My Life in Science Fiction*. New York: Bluejay, 1984.

Wilson, Colin. *The Strength to Dream: Literature and the Imagination*. Boston: Houghton Mifflin, 1962.

Wilson, Edmund. *Classics and Commercials: A Literary Chronicle of the 1940s*. New York: Farrar, Straus, and Giroux, 1950.

———. "Oo, Those Awful Orcs!" *The Nation* 182 (April 4, 1956): 312–14.

Wolfe, Gary K. "The Frontier Myth in Ray Bradbury." In *Ray Bradbury*, ed. Joseph D. Olander and Martin Harry Greenberg, 33–54. New York: Taplinger, 1980.

——. *The Known and the Unknown: The Iconography of Science Fiction*. Kent, Ohio: Kent State University Press, 1979.

——. "Reviews by Gary K. Wolfe." *Locus* 439 (August 1997): 13.

——. *Soundings: Reviews 1992–1996*. Essex: Beccon, 2005.

Wolfe, Gene. "What Do They Mean, sf?" *SFWA Bulletin* 75 (1981): 20–25.

Wollheim, Donald A. *The Pocket Book of Science Fiction*. New York: Pocket Books, 1943.

——. "The Science-Fiction Novel." *New York Times*, August 28, 1949. Online at http://select.nytimes.com/gst/abstract.html?res=F40615FE3B5D13728DDDA10A94D0405B8988F1D3&scp=34&sq=%22science+fiction&st=p (accessed April 22, 2008).

——. *The Universe Makers: Science Fiction Today*. New York: Harper, 1971.

Fiction

Aldiss, Brian W. *Forgotten Life*. New York: Atheneum, 1989.

——. *Remembrance Day*. New York: St. Martin's, 1993.

Anthony, Patricia. *Flanders*. New York: Ace, 1998.

——. *God's Fires*. New York: Ace, 1987.

Ballard, J. G. *Crash*. New York: Farrar, Straus & Giroux, 1973.

——. *Empire of the Sun*. London: Gollancz, 1981.

Baxter, Stephen. *Coalescent*. London: Gollancz, 2003.

——. *Conqueror*. London: Gollancz, 2007.

——. *Emperor*. London: Gollancz, 2006.

——. *Navigator*. London: Gollancz, 2007.

——. *Ring*. New York: HarperCollins, 1993.

——. *Weaver*. London: Gollancz, 2008.

Bear, Greg. *Foundation and Chaos*. New York: HarperPrism, 1998.

Benford, Gregory. *Against Infinity*. New York: Pocket Books, 1983.

——. *Artifact*. New York: Tor, 1985.

—— [Sterling Blake, pseud.]. *Chiller*. New York: Bantam, 1993.

——. *Cosm*. New York: Avon Eos, 1998.

——. *Eater*. New York: Avon Eos, 2000.

——. *In the Ocean of Night*. New York: Dial, 1977.

——. *Timescape*. New York: Simon & Schuster, 1980.

——, ed. *Nebula Awards Showcase 2000*. New York: Harcourt Brace, 2000.

Bleiler, Everett F., ed. *Eight Dime Novels*. New York: Dover, 1974.

Bleiler, Everett F., and T. E. Dikty, eds. *Frontiers in Space*. New York, Bantam, 1955.

Bowen, John. *After the Rain*. New York: Ballantine, 1959.

Bradbury, Ray. *Dandelion Wine*. Garden City, N.Y.: Doubleday, 1957.

———. "The Highway." In *The Illustrated Man*. Garden City, N.Y.: Doubleday, 1951.

———. *The Martian Chronicles*. Garden City, N.Y.: Doubleday, 1950.

Budrys, Algis. *Rogue Moon*. 1960; reprint, New York: Avon, 1978.

Burroughs, Edgar Rice. *A Princess of Mars*. 1912; reprint, New York: Grosset and Dunlap, 1917.

Clarke, Arthur C. *Rendezvous with Rama*. New York: Ballantine, 1974.

Coppel, Alfred. *Dark December*. Greenwich, Conn.: Fawcett, 1960.

Crace, Jim. *The Pesthouse*. New York: Doubleday, 2007.

Crichton, Michael. *Sphere*. New York: Knopf, 1987.

Dick, Philip K. *Valis*. New York: Bantam, 1981.

Eliot, George. *Adam Bede*. 1859. Online at http://www.princeton.edu/batke/eliot/bede (accessed May 8, 2008).

Ellison, Harlan. "A Boy and His Dog." In *The Beast that Shouted Love at the Heart of the World*. New York: New American Library, 1969.

———. "Grail." In *Stalking the Nightmare*. Huntington Woods, Mich.: Phantasia Press, 1982.

Ford, Jeffrey. *The Drowned Life*. New York: Harper Perennial, 2008.

———. *The Empire of Ice Cream*. Urbana, Ill.: Golden Gryphon, 2006.

———. *The Fantasy Writer's Assistant and Other Stories*. Urbana, Ill.: Golden Gryphon Press, 2002.

———. "The Honeyed Knot." 2001. In *The Year's Best Fantasy and Horror*, ed. Ellen Datlow and Terri Windling. New York: St. Martin's, 2002.

———. "Under the Bottom of the Lake." In *Year's Best Fantasy 8*, ed. David G. Hartwell and Kathryn Cramer, 179–86. San Francisco: Tachyon, 2008.

Frank, Pat. *Alas, Babylon*. Philadelphia: Lippincott, 1959.

Godwin, Tom. "The Cold Equations." 1954. In *The Road to Science Fiction #3: From Heinlein to Here*, ed. James Gunn. New York: New American Library, 1979. Originally published in *Astounding Science Fiction*, 1954.

Goss, Theodora. *In the Forest of Forgetting*. Holicong, Penn.: Prime Books, 2006.

———. "Singing of Mount Abora." 2007. In *The Best Science Fiction and Fantasy of the Year, Volume Two*, ed. Jonathan Strahan, 247–59. San Francisco: Night Shade, 2008.

Gunn, James. *The Road to Science Fiction: From Gilgamesh to Wells*. New York: New American Library, 1977.

Guran, Paula, ed. *The Best New Paranormal Romance*. New York: Juno Books, 2006.

Greenberg, Joanne [Hannah Greene, pseud]. *I Never Promised You a Rose Garden*. New York: New American Library, 1964.

Haggard, H. Rider, and Andrew Lang. *The World's Desire*. London: Longmans, Green, and Co., 1890.

Haldeman, Joe. *War Year*. New York: Holt, Rinehart, Winston, 1972.

Hand, Elizabeth. *Bibliomancy*. Harrogate: PS Publishing, 2003.

——. "Cleopatra Brimstone." 2001. In *Saffron and Brimstone: Strange Stories*. Milwaukie, Ore.: M Press, 2006.

——. *Illyria*. London: PS Publishing, 2007.

——. *Saffron and Brimstone: Strange Stories*. Milwaukie, Ore.: M Press, 2006.

Hartwell, David, ed. *Foundations of Fear*. New York: Tor, 1992.

Interstitial Arts Foundation website. http://www.interstitialarts.org/wordpress/.

Kelly, James Patrick, and John Kessel, eds. *Feeling Very Strange: The Slipstream Anthology*. San Francisco: Tachyon, 2006.

King, Stephen. *'Salem's Lot*. Garden City, N.Y.: Doubleday, 1975.

——. *The Tommyknockers*. New York: Putnam, 1987.

King, Stephen, and Peter Straub. *The Talisman*. New York: Viking, 1984.

Levin, Ira. *Rosemary's Baby*. New York: Random House, 1967.

Lindsay, David. *A Voyage to Arcturus*. London: Methuen, 1920.

——. *Devil's Tor*. London: G. P. Putnam's Sons, 1932.

Link, Kelly. *Magic for Beginners*, Northampton, Mass.: Small Beer Press, 2005.

——. *Pretty Monsters*. New York: Viking, 2008.

——. *Stranger Things Happen*. Northampton, Mass.: Small Beer Press, 2001.

Lovecraft, H. P. "The Shadow Out of Time." In *Tales*, ed. Peter Straub, 719–83. New York: The Library of America, 2005.

McCarthy, Cormac. *The Road*. New York: Knopf, 2006.

Machen, Arthur. *The Three Impostors*. 1895; reprint, New York: Ballantine, 1972.

Merril, Judith, ed. *Shot in the Dark*. New York: Bantam, 1950.

Merle, Robert. *Malevil*. New York: Simon & Schuster, 1973.

Noyes, Alfred. *No Other Man*. New York: Stokes, 1940.

Peake, Mervyn. *The Gormenghast Novels*. Woodstock, N.Y.: Overlook Press, 1995. Includes the trilogy originally published in London by Eyre & Spottiswoode: *Titus Groan* (1946); *Gormenghast* (1950); *Titus Alone* (1959).

Rickert, M. "Journey into the Kingdom." In *The Best Science Fiction and Fantasy of the Year #1*, ed. Jonathan Strahan, 299–320. San Francisco: Night Shade, 2007.

——. *Map of Dreams*. Urbana, Ill.: Golden Gryphon, 2006.

Robinson, Kim Stanley. *Blue Mars*. New York: Bantam Spectra, 1996.

——. *Green Mars*. New York: Bantam Spectra, 1994.

——. *Red Mars*. New York: Bantam Spectra, 1993.

Ryman, Geoff. *Was*. New York: HarperCollins, 1992.

Sargent, Pamela, ed. *Nebula Awards 30*. New York: Harcourt Brace, 1996.

Shiel, M. P. *The Purple Cloud*. New York: Paperback Library, 1963.

Stewart, George R. *Earth Abides*. 1949; reprint, New York: Ace, 1962.

Stewart, Sean. *Galveston*. New York: Ace, 2000.

——. *The Night Watch*. New York: Ace, 1997

——. *Nobody's Son*. Toronto: Maxwell Macmillan Canada, 1993.

——. *Resurrection Man*. New York: Ace, 1995.

Straub, Peter. "The Buffalo Hunter." In *Houses without Doors*. New York: Dutton, 1990.

——. "Bunny is Good Bread" (1994) in *Magic Terror: Seven Tales*. New York: Random House, 2000.

——. *Houses without Doors*. New York: Dutton, 1990.

——. *In the Night Room*. New York: Random House, 2004.

——. "The Juniper Tree." 1988. In *Houses without Doors*. New York: Dutton, 1990.

——. *Koko*. New York: Dutton, 1988.

——. *lost boy lost girl*. New York: Random House, 2003.

——. *Magic Terror: Seven Tales*. New York: Random House, 2000.

——. *Mr. X*. New York: Random House, 1999.

——, ed. *Poe's Children: The New Horror*. Garden City, N.Y.: Doubleday, 2008.

Taylor, Robert Lewis. *Adrift in a Boneyard*. Garden City, N.Y.: Doubleday, 1947.

Tepper, Sheri S. *A Plague of Angels*. New York: Bantam Spectra, 1993.

Tucker, Wilson. *The Long Loud Silence*. New York: Rinehart, 1952.

Vonnegut, Kurt, Jr. *The Sirens of Titan*. New York: Dell, 1959.

Wandrei, Donald. *The Web of Easter Island*. Sauk City, Wisc.: Arkham House, 1948.

Wilhelm, Kate. *Where Late the Sweet Birds Sang*. New York: Harpers, 1976.

Willis, Connie, ed. *Nebula Awards 33: The Year's Best SF and Fantasy Chosen by the Science-fiction and Fantasy Writers of America*. New York: Harcourt Brace, 1999.

Wollheim, Donald, ed. *The Pocket Book of Science Fiction*. New York: Pocket Books, 1943.

Wright, S. Fowler. *Deluge: A Romance*. New York: Cosmopolitan, 1928.

Wyndham, John, and Lucas Parkes. *The Outward Urge*. New York: Ballantine, 1959.

Yolen, Jane. *Briar Rose*. New York: Tor, 1992.

Zelazny, Roger. *Nine Princes in Amber*. New York: Avon, 1972.

Index

About the Author

Gary K. Wolfe is professor of humanities and English at Roosevelt University. He is the author of *Bearings: Reviews 1997—2001* (Beccon Press, 2010), *Soundings: Reviews 1992–1996* (Beccon Press, 2005), *Harlan Ellison: The Edge of Forever*, with Ellen Weil (Ohio University Press, 2001), *Critical Terms for Science Fiction and Fantasy* (Greenwood Press, 1986), *The Known and the Unknown: The Iconography of Science Fiction* (Kent State University Press, 1979), as well as hundreds of essays and reviews, mostly for *Locus* magazine since 1991. He has received the Distinguished Scholarship Award from the International Association for the Fantastic in the Arts, the Pilgrim Award from the Science Fiction Research Association, the Eaton Award, the British Science Fiction Association Award for nonfiction, and the World Fantasy Award for criticism.